BAD TIMES

MARK YARWOOD

For my wife and daughter,
with all my love

ACKNOWLEDGEMENTS

BAD TIMES wouldn't have been written without the help of a few important people, who I shall mention now. Number one, my Editor, John Hudspith, who has worked his magic as always. I gleaned some very important information from Inspector Paul Laity as we chatted after we'd picked our kids up from school.

I'd also like to thank all the Plymouth friends I've made over my last sixteen years here, especially the ones I've left behind recently. I shall never forget you. I'm not going anywhere.

And of course, I want to thank my mum, dad, and brother for all their love and support. But most importantly of all, I'd like to thank my wife and daughter for just being there. I love you both so much.

PROLOGUE

The night rain made everything glisten, caught by the streetlamps dotted along the path that snaked from Argyle's football ground down to Central Park Avenue. He waited, sat in the shadows of the graffiti daubed shelter halfway along the path, watching the raindrops fall in front of him, checking his phone every now and again.

He pulled his raincoat around him, checked his gloves were on snug enough, and pulled his baseball cap down further. There were no cameras here, not even with the building work going on a few yards away.

He stood up, braving the rain that blew in, came at him almost horizontally like people had warned him of when he first moved down.

He checked his phone again, feeling the nervous buzz he always got that travelled to every part of him like a horde of fire ants. He was shaking, trembling all over as he lifted his phone and saw he'd had a message. They were on their way.

He took out the small bottle of whiskey he had brought with him, a sip of Dutch courage before the big date. He laughed to himself, at his own little joke as he took a few gulps as he walked through the darkness.

Even through the rain the sound came to him like a familiar melody, that old click clacking of heels on hard ground. The feminine shape, the shapely silhouette came towards him, growing all the time. The wind carried the perfume to him, wrapped around his head and made his chest thump madly. He clenched his fists tighter as the thing, the creature, stepped into the amber light and smiled nervously.

'Hi,' the creature said, their smile spread wide on their red lipstick lips.

He trembled so much then that he thought he might fall over, his heart pumping the blood around him so fast. Then the thing was closer, the heels tip tapping to him, but he was frozen, fear having stuck him to the ground, unable to even lift his fists.

The kiss landed on his cheek, snapping him out of his dream, sending him backwards, his gloved hand touching his face. He looked at his gloved fingers as if he expected his skin to have come away.

He looked up and the lamplight shone down on him, illuminating his face for all to see, for the creature to see.

When his face changed, its face changed, and all the colour poured out as it turned to go, to run. But he was faster, hurling himself on top of it, raising his fists and pounding down until the thing didn't move under him.

His face had been seen, he thought, burning all over, the puke rising in him as his trembling hands gripped the creature's throat and he began to squeeze.

CHAPTER 1

Moone heard the knocking in his sleep, echoed in his dreams, slowly bringing him back to reality. He peeled open his eyes and stared round the long room, trying to work out where he was as he reached for his pack of fags. He sat up, remembering that he was living in a plastic box, or mobile home people called it. He lit a cigarette, took a puff and looked out the grubby windows, out across the tops of the other caravans and towards the sea that spat and raged at the rocks, echoing what was going on in his head and stomach. Seagulls danced over his roof, squawking out their constant complaints as the knocking that had woken him came again.

He got up and opened the door to a stocky, dark-haired woman, late thirties, dressed in a trouser suit. She looked annoyed, so he said, 'Sorry.'

'What're you sorry about?' she asked and

came closer, taking something from her jacket. She held up her warrant card, 'DS Mandy Butler. I've come to pick you up. You are DCI Moone?'

He nodded, rubbed his eyes, took another long drag and flicked the dog end out the caravan as Butler stepped inside.

She looked over the place, her hands dug into her pockets. 'Why would you choose to live in a caravan?'

He spotted a half-drunk bottle of vodka next his bed and tried to hide it behind his feet as he sat back down. 'It's cheap and there's a nice view.'

'It's all right, Moone, I already saw the bottle. No point trying to hide it.' She gave him the onceover. 'You from London, right?'

'Enfield. Born and bred.'

'Never heard of it. Where's that to?'

He stared at her. 'Sorry? Where's what?'

'Where's that to... where's Enfield?'

'Oh, right. North London. The first cashpoint in the world was put there... David Jason comes from there...'

She shrugged, still looking unimpressed.

'Not far from the Spurs' ground?'

She nodded. 'Got it. We're late. I'm meant to be driving you to a crime scene. Best you throw on some clothes, Enfield boy.'

After a quick shower, Moone headed to DS Butler's car. She was out in front, walking fast, not waiting for him. She was tall, at least taller than him, which wasn't a hard act to pull off. By the time he reached her and opened the passenger door, she was looking him over, examining him head to foot.

'Has anyone ever told you that you look like a whippet, or a greyhound, something like that?' she said, blank faced.

'No,' he said and climbed in. 'No one's ever compared me to a dog before. But thanks.'

'No problem.' She started the engine and took them out of the caravan park and towards the A38, heading towards the city of Plymouth.

'Where we going?' Moone asked, staring out at the beach that sat beneath the road they were on that snaked around the endless rocky hill-sides.

'Admirals Hard,' she said. 'A body's been found.'

'Who's hard?' he said and dredged up a smile.

She didn't even look at him. 'It's a place, in Stonehouse. This isn't Carry On be a Policeman. Suppose I should call you boss or something.'

'Moone will do.' He sat back, barely taking in the country lanes they travelled down and the fields beyond. In his mind's eye he kept seeing the concrete block shapes all round him, hearing the London traffic soundtrack that seemed to play on a loop.

'It is a funny name though,' Butler said

and Moone opened an eye and saw a smile that quickly vanished.

Butler drove them down a narrow street lined with houses and newbuild flats and the occasional pub. They passed an army barracks, then stopped at a corner shop, over the road from a rundown pub. Seagulls squawked from the rooftops while three of the giant birds fought over the crammed contents of a bin. A couple of Devon and Cornwall incident cars were parked across the street, blocking off the road further up.

'This way,' Butler said and took him into a narrower side street that led to a dock. It was low tide and Moone stared out towards the uniformed bodies and the SOCOs that had gathered, stood in welly boots as they slipped and slid across the rocks and seaweed that belched out a smell that reminded Moone of a seafood stall his dad used to take him to on Sunday afternoons. Beyond the crime scene, over the low tide of water, were large warehouses and a huge boat yard. Princess Yachts, he read to himself.

'This a common occurrence?' Moone asked and took out a cigarette.

'Fetching bodies from the water?' she asked. 'It happens a fair amount. We have the occasional murder to deal with.'

At that point, one of the uniforms, which

turned out to be a strawberry blonde, full figured female constable, came striding back towards them as she said, 'Don't look like it's a suicide.'

'What makes you say that, PC Carthew?' Butler asked, looking towards the body.

PC Carthew folded her arms. 'Well, I'll tell you... the body has hardly any skin left on it. Someone skinned the victim before they dumped him in the water.'

Moone sighed, looked at his fag packet, then stuffed it back in his jacket as he headed along the dock to get a better look. The only reason he was in Plymouth in the first place was to be with his kids, but he had had very little visitation so far, because his ex-wife had decided to become a pain in the arse about it.

'Be careful!' Butler called out. 'Those rocks can be treacherous!'

He ignored her and stepped down on to the rocky and slippery ground, the stench of stagnant seawater rising up to his nostrils. One of the uniforms took his arm to steady him, so he nodded and smiled and looked down at the body that was lying awkwardly over a thick bed of seaweed. The PC had been correct, the victim had been skinned, and Moone found himself staring down at grey and pink muscle and bone that protruded from the gaps between the cut away flesh. He was glad he hadn't bothered with breakfast, fighting back his desire to vomit and making himself stare at the remains a little longer.

'The victim's male,' a voice said, and Moone looked up to see a chiselled, pale, and stubble-covered face looking at him from a blue SOCO hood. 'If you were wondering.'

'DCI Peter Moone,' he said.

'I know. Dr Lee Parry. Nice to meet you. Welcome to Plymouth.'

'Thanks. Can you tell me anything else?'

'Like how he died? Not right now. But I noticed marks round the neck, so I'm thinking he was strangled at some point. Not very bloated, so I'm thinking they've been in the water no longer than twenty-four hours. Could've been dumped anywhere, washed up here.'

Moone looked around the place, examined all the buildings, both sides of the water. 'Many cameras round here?'

'None really,' one of the uniforms said.

'They were dumped here,' Moone said. 'No cameras. They knew they could bring the body here and dump it without being caught on camera. Must be a local.'

Moone played back his words in his own head and was surprised how much he'd actually sounded like a detective. He hoped he was fooling more than himself.

'So, we're looking for a local man who likes to skin his victims,' DS Butler said, as she walked up behind Moone.

'You know,' the strawberry blonde PC said, 'we get a lot of military and navy types round here. They come with tattoos.'

Moone turned to her. 'You're thinking they skinned their victim to remove any identifying marks like tattoos. I like it, it's good. What's your name?'

'This is PC Faith Carthew,' Butler said, smirking. 'She's full of good ideas... except, aren't the vic's fingers still intact? I mean, if I was trying to stop them being identified I'd cut their fingers or hands off. And maybe cut their heads off too.'

'Lovely,' Dr Parry said. 'But she's right.'

Moone saw the PC blush and turn away and felt sorry for her. He knew what it was like being new to the game and feeling like you weren't being taken seriously. He made a mental note to get the PC involved a bit more, to help her along.

'It could be sexual,' the doctor said, scratching his pen along his pointed nose.

'Why?' Moone asked.

'Well... I did take a look at the underside of the body, and it looks like the killer had a go at removing their privates.'

'You could've started with that!' Butler said, shook her head and stormed off back along the dock.

'Thanks, doctor,' Moone said and decided to follow her, and put a foot towards the seaweed covered rocks. Then his foot was sliding out in front of him, his arms flailing to get some kind of balance, but failing miserably. He landed on a patch of seaweed and muddy sand and sat for a moment as the uniforms and the doctors rushed to help him up. When he was back on his feet, he nodded to them all and looked to see Butler up ahead, stood by the car watching. When he reached her, a cigarette in his mouth, she was trying not to laugh.

'Please don't say anything,' he said and opened the passenger door.

'I wasn't going to say a thing. Apart from you can't smoke in my car. And you can't get in covered in all that shit.'

They both turned back towards the dock when they heard their names being shouted. It was the strawberry blonde uniform who was jogging towards them looking flushed.

'What's wrong, Carthew?' Butler said.

'Bones,' Carthew said, puffing a bit, pointing a thumb back towards the scene. 'We've found small bones, maybe a child's.'

Moone felt his stomach bite. That was all he needed after his last investigation in London, another dead child. He tried to light his cigarette, but his hands trembled so he gave up and put it away again and trudged behind Butler as she moved quickly towards the crime scene. This wasn't the way it was supposed to go, it was meant to be easier, less death and disaster. Who was he trying to kid? He was cursed, doomed to carry death with him wherever he went, or find it there when he arrived. His ex-wife had said as much the last time they talked, and he got a sense that that was why she was creating a distance between him and the kids, like he was infected or something.

Butler moved round their first crime scene, standing a hundred yards away from the first body and looked down at the ground at which PC Carthew pointed.

'Could be an animal,' Moone heard Butler say, but then the doctor, who had been standing with his back to it all, turned and shook his head. His hood was lowered, and his wild shoulder-length hair shook when he said, 'No, definitely human... mostly likely a child's.'

Then it was quiet, and only a slight wind came in and tugged at Moone's hair as they all stood looking down at the bones that protruded from the sand. Moone felt it, like a wave hitting him, forcing him back to a beach, or a calming hand on his chest. He knew it then, felt it in his chest and in his shoulders, that he was where he was meant to be.

CHAPTER 2

It would be several hours before the remains of the child would be delivered to the post mortem room which Moone had been reliably informed was deep beneath Derriford Hospital, which itself was on the way to Dartmoor.

Butler drove them back mostly in silence as Moone, or probably both of them, contemplated what the next few days would bring, and the fact that some parents somewhere might learn the fate of their missing child. Then other, much darker and sinister thoughts came to him and crowded into his brain. He couldn't take them, so he pushed them out and concentrated on what was outside himself. That's what the counsellor had told him to do, try to concentrate on others or life outside his own. So he stared at the shops that went past, the steady stream of pubs and takeaways that morphed into flats and terraced houses before the city formed around them as they swung round a roundabout where the skeletal remains of a church was sitting. Behind it was a monstrosity, a mish mash of designs all stuck together to form an ugly rectangular building. Moone turned his head to stare at it, then Butler said, 'Horrible, isn't it?'

'What is it?'

'Shopping mall. They flattened some of the city centre a while back, much like the Germans did during the war. Most people don't know that percentage wise, more damage was done to Plymouth than London. I like reading up on history.'

'Do you get many people go missing?'

She looked at him, then back at the road as she drove them into a side street, where a large orange brick police station sat proudly on the corner.

'People go missing,' she said, swiping her ID at a gate that led to a large car park behind the police station that was surrounded by a high metal fence. 'Old people, young runaways, people with problems. They usually come back.'

'Kids?'

'Some. Teenage runaways. You'd be surprised how many run off to London, think the streets are lined with gold, take a few selfies, then they go home. There was a case though... a boy went missing, eleven years old. Daniel, Danny Sawyer. Went missing nearly three years ago.'

'Never found?'

'Never found. No trace.' She turned off the

engine and they sat in silence as the dark shadow of the police station loomed over them.

Butler broke the silence with a weary sigh, 'Welcome to Charles Cross police station. By the way, I was told the Chief Superintendent wants to see you when you get here. Not a bad man, politician like all the rest, only really cares about the press side of things, but don't get on the wrong side of him.'

Moone nodded and climbed out, thinking about little Danny Sawyer and the bones that were being pulled gently from the ground.

'Where you going?' Butler called out.

He turned. 'Inside. To see the Chief Super.'

Butler shook her head. 'You'll have to get in a car and trundle along to Crown Hill.'

'What? Where?'

'Crown Hill police station. That's where his office is. Pain in the arse, I know, but there you go. I'll give you directions.'

Moone walked down a narrow clean corridor, passing the occasional set of wooden doors, looking in at the rooms within, reading the noticeboards. It had been a relatively short drive to Crown Hill nick, thanks to Butler's directions. He reached the last door, which had Chief Superintendent printed on it, with the name Andrew Laptew printed underneath. He knocked and waited, then heard a muffled woman's voice tell him to enter.

A narrow room was beyond the door, a small office where a middle-aged, blonde-haired, smartly dressed woman smiled up at him. 'Morning. Do you have an appointment?'

'DCI Peter Moone,' he said and managed to form half a smile.

'Oh good, he's been waiting for you. Go straight in.'

Moone knocked then went in and found a more spacious office done out like a Victorian library and with a large cumbersome desk. There sat a middle-aged man with dark hair peppered with silver strands. He looked in shape, sharp-eyed and had a determined look on his face as Moone approached his desk.

'Acting DCI Moone,' the Chief Superintendent said in a voice void of any accent and shook Moone's hand. 'Have a seat.'

'Sir,' Moone said and sat down.

'All the way from the smoke,' the Chief Super said.

'Yes, sir.'

'You must have seen some pretty tough things.'

'Some. I try to forget about them.'

The Chief Super nodded. 'But that's not always possible, is it? They made you see someone, something to do with one of your last cases in London. Something to do with the death of a child?'

Moone nodded, not able to bring himself to utter a word, not trusting that his eyes wouldn't well with tears.

'This isn't London. This is the South West. Crime has risen in the last few years. Murder is up, violence, but it's usually pretty straight forward. Man murders his wife, or vice versa. Nothing too complicated. We have a certain way of doing things, but you'll pick it up as you go. You were acting DCI in London, now you're back to plain old DI, I'm sorry to say. How do you feel about being here?'

'Fine.'

'You're a man of few words.'

'Sometimes you can't shut me up.' Moone managed a smile.

'They found some bones this morning, alongside a dead body...'

'That's right.'

The Chief Super sat back. 'I'm putting you in charge... you've got the experience, the rank. We haven't got many people with your amount of experience working on major murder investigations. You up to it?'

Moone opened his mouth, ready to opt out, but the bones of the child rose up before his eyes. 'Yes, sir. I'm up for it.'

'Good.' The Chief Super stood up, shook his hand again, smiling. 'Right, get to the bottom of this, you've got a good team. Keep Butler close, she's tough, knows what she's doing. Anyway, back to work. Good to have you here.'

Moone smiled, then went to turn away, but the Chief Super cleared his throat and said, 'Moone... you're new here.'

'Yes, sir.'

'Toe the line. I know rules are sometimes bent... but let's do this by the book. Promise me that much.'

'Scout's honour.'

Back at Charles Cross, Moone found the major incident room by wandering the building, getting to know the lie of the land. He managed to find a drinks machine and bought a stale tasting coffee that he took into the long narrow office space. There were a few single desks by the windows and one long desk by the wall under a huge whiteboard. There was already a team at work, plain-clothed officers and some civilians manning the phones. He spotted Butler at a desk in the corner and headed over, feeling like the new kid at school who had only made one friend so far.

'So, I met the Chief,' he said, rolling his eyes.

'Good for you,' she said blankly and took some sheets of paper over to the long desk by the wall.

'So, we know anything about the body on the beach?'

She turned and looked at him and sighed.

'He's been printed. They're going through the system. Takes time. Might not even have a record. The bones are on the way to the morgue. It's a waiting game. But you know that.'

'I do.'

'I thought you'd want to brief the team,' she said, and went over towards the team lining the windows. 'Hey, you lot. Here's the new boss, same as the old boss. Say hello.'

The hellos flickered over the group, some smiling, others blank, barely looking his way.

'Thanks,' he said. 'I hope we can work well together...'

'Come on, you lot, this is a briefing,' Butler said, clapping her hands together, making them all straighten up and pay a little more attention, even though a couple of them whispered among themselves.

'As I was saying,' Moone continued. 'You might be aware that a body was found near, well...'

'Where the Cremell ferry goes from,' Butler added.

'The Admirals Hard?' someone said and a few of them laughed.

Moone thought it best to nod and smile a bit before he carried on. 'Yeah, the body was found there. A male, small in stature, aged about thirty. The prints are being run through the system. He'd had a lot of skin removed from his body, but alongside that body, only a few yards away, we discovered what we believe may be the bones of a young child.'

The room suddenly went quiet, the rumble of the traffic pouring around the old bomb-damaged church across the street the only sound. He looked them over and was about to continue when the door opened, and a familiar uniform entered the room.

'Sorry, sir,' PC Carthew said, holding a large envelope.

'That's all right,' he said walking over. 'You got something for us?'

She handed him the envelope. 'They found something buried with the bones... a toy.'

Her eyes were full of sadness as he took the envelope and took out a set of photographs the SOCOs had taken of a cuddly toy. It was a fluffy red bear with a blue cowboy hat, the kind a much younger child might own. 'How old do they think the child might've been?'

'The doctor reckons about nine, ten... about that age.'

'A cuddly bear's a bit young for that age, isn't it?'

'Not necessarily,' a man's voice said from behind him. Moone turned to find himself faced with one of the team, a stocky younger detective with a northern accent. 'I know kids who still go to bed with bears and shit like that.'

'Sorry, what's your name?' Moone asked.

'DC Dave Harding,' he said, staring at Moone

through deep set blue eyes. 'Would you like us to wear name tags?'

There was a bit of laughter round the room, until Moone looked at them all in turn. 'No, that's all right. Let's look into this toy. See where it was manufactured. Maybe we'll get lucky and it'll be local. Harding can be in charge of that job.'

Harding stared at him, his eyebrows raised. 'You're fucking kidding me, right? It's probably from fucking China!'

'It might be.' Moone turned away and looked at Butler. 'Let's find any cameras in that area. I know there doesn't seem to be many, but let's check. We need uniforms going door-to-door, maybe someone saw something or heard something.'

'Already got them knocking on doors,' Butler said. 'There's not much we can do until the prints come back.'

Moone hesitated to say what he was about to say, another well of darkness opening up inside him. He took a breath, then said, 'There is something else we can do. We can...'

Butler sighed and shook her head as she rested her backside on the desk. 'Please don't say what I think you're going to say.'

Moone glanced around the room, seeing all eyes on him, including PC Carthew, who looked sympathetic. 'I was going to say... well, we have the toy... we can...'

'Take it to show the parents of Danny Sawyer and say by any chance did your boy own one of these?'

'Something like that.' Moone's gut knotted itself.

'Loads of kids could've owned a toy like that! What if it's not their boy? Chances are they know he's dead, but maybe they've got some hope, just a little bit of it, and you're about to...'

'Let's talk out in the corridor,' Moone said, pointing to the doors.

Butler turned her head, huffed, then straightened herself and headed through the doors. Moone followed. She leaned against the wall, folded her arms across her chest and raised her eyebrows.

'I'm the boss,' he said, facing her.

'Yeah, I get that, but...'

'I don't know this place. I'm from London. I don't know these people?'

She looked away, her cheeks burning red. 'Something like that.'

'What's this got to do with?'

'What do you mean?'

'You seem to have taken a dislike to me. It's usually a few days before people start to dislike me. Have I done something?'

She fixed her dark eyes on him, the annoyance clearly there. 'No, you've done nothing. I just don't want to see those poor people dragged through all this again... that's all.'

'I understand. Neither do I...'

'But you're the boss... sir. So make a decision.'

He nodded, looked around him and saw PC Carthew stood just inside the doors to the incident room, looking at him through the glass. Her mouth was moving. Moone focused on her lips and realised she was mouthing something.

Do... it.

Do it.

He turned to Butler, who was looking the other way, huffing, waiting.

'Let's go and see them.'

CHAPTER 3

The conservative MP for Sutton and Devonport, Carl Mathieson, was sitting in his office, staring down at Exeter Street below, watching his constituents coming and going. He felt tired all over, and deeply desired to be in Westminster, sitting in his club and tucking into a juicy blue steak. But no, he had to be here to meet with some local businessmen, all to do with investing in the local community. He hated the charade, the pretence of helping the locals when all it was really about was lining their own pockets, cutting corners on building projects, but he would smile and shake their hands. After all, Brexit was in full swing, and the City was going to need every bit of investment it could get when the EU's help was withdrawn.

He kept thinking about the steak though, imagining it being served alongside some triple cooked chips, trying to ignore the phone ringing in the next room.

Then the door was opening and Mary, his part-time, middle-aged, not bad to look at, secretary poked her head in.

'You've got a call waiting,' she said, taking off her glasses. 'Wouldn't say who he was, but said it was urgent.'

'Tell whoever they are that I'm busy.'

'They said to mention a name to you,' she said, looking confused.

Mathieson leaned back in his chair, his chest tightening, his heart beginning to pound. 'What name?'

'Furneaux? They said you'd know what it meant.'

'Fine, fine, put them through.' Mathieson managed a smile as she left, then let his face fall back into panic and fear as he stared at the phone and saw the light flashing. He picked up the receiver. 'Carl Mathieson.'

'Carl...' the deep voice said, the same old London accent he'd come to despise. It had been a number of years since he'd heard the voice, but it was just the same, perhaps a little hoarser from all the smoking. But it had the same affect, making him want to vomit.

'I told you never to contact me here.'

'Carl, don't be like that. We need to talk...'

'Are you on a mobile?'

'Don't be stupid. I'm on a pay phone... a pay phone in a pub. I need to talk to you.'

'Make it quick.'

There was a huff, then a deep cough. 'Not on the phone... don't know who's listening. I'm in the pub down the road...'

'You're in Plymouth?'

'You got it. You were always smart. Be here in five minutes.'

'I can't be seen with you in a pub... what if someone...'

There was that deep rattle of a laugh. 'You're such a fuckin' worrier. The fuckin' pubs not even open. I know the landlord. Just get your posh boy arse down here. Five minutes!'

The line went dead. Mathieson slowly hung up the receiver, put his elbows on the desk and his head in his hands. He buried his face and let out a deep groan, knowing he had no choice but to go and see the old bastard, to face his craggy face, and smell the stench of him.

'Everything OK?'

He looked up, startled to see Mary looking at him in sympathy and concern. 'Yes, fine, just a bit stressed. I just need to pop out for a minute.'

He got up and headed out through the door, passing her by, ignoring her questions as he headed out of the office and down the narrow, rickety stairway, past the solicitors and down to the street. He felt a breeze tug at his jacket and looked up to see grey, miserable clouds crowding the sky, then hurried towards the pub on the corner, next to the chippy. He walked fast with his head down, trying to not to make eye contact with the locals.

He reached the door of the pub and pressed the bell by the side of it, then wrapped his knuckles on the glass.

A bolt slid across, then the thick battered door opened to reveal the same old bony, silver stubble covered face. And the stench, the acrid smell of stale booze and sweat and dirt. No amount of soap could've removed that stench. Not even a bath in a vat of Domestos.

'What do you want, Ray?' he asked, looking round the street in case he was spotted.

'I want you to come in and have a drink,' Ray said, then started to cough as he opened the door wider. 'Come on, get the fuck inside.'

Against his better judgement, Mathieson entered the dimly lit room and looked about at the old bar, and the round, scratched tables scattered haphazardly round the place. There was a big middle-aged man behind the bar, but he was minding his own business, just reading a paper and smoking.

'I'm over there,' Ray said, coughed and headed over to a table near the back.

Mathieson joined him at the table as the old man sipped a pint of ale, then wiped his thin, dirty looking mouth.

'Don't look so horrified, Carl,' Ray said. 'You can't be that fuckin' shocked to see me.'

'I never expected to see you again.'

'Frank, get the man a pint!' Ray called out.

'No, thank you. Just tell me what you need to tell me.'

'You should have a drink, you'll need it.'

Suddenly it wasn't just the smell of stale beer and the stench of the old man that was making Mathieson feel sick; it was the look in the old man's eyes, the fact that behind the dark beady eyes were dark truths, things that should've been long forgotten.

'Will I?'

Ray coughed again, the stench of halitosis bursting from his mouth, making Mathieson sit back, grimacing. 'Aren't you well, Ray?'

The old man wiped the spit from his jaw and shook his head. 'Na, I'm not well. I'm dying, that's what the specialist told me a few weeks ago. Cancer. My lungs and liver are peppered with the bastard stuff. No fuckin' treatment, I'm too far gone.'

'That's why you're here?' Mathieson felt a little of the weight lift from his shoulders. Soon the old man would be gone and with him the dark truths. 'To tell me you're dying?'

'That's why I came back, to tie up loose ends. Then I heard something...'

'Heard what?'

The old man started coughing again, then sipped his pint and lit a cigarette.

'I have a meeting to attend this afternoon,' Mathieson said.

'Alright, I'll get to the fuckin' point. They found a body this morning, where the Cremell ferry leaves from...a man. I don't know who he was, but nearby, they found some bones. child's bones.'

Nausea invaded every inch of Mathieson's body, made him feel weak, unsure if he'd have the strength to get up. He kept the panic from his face, as he'd been trained to do in the Army, to keep calm in the face of disaster. 'So? They found some bones... what's that got to do with me?'

'Every fuckin' thing. And you fuckin' know it!' Ray sat back, coughed, then sucked on his cigarette. 'What're you going to do?'

'How do you know all this?'

'I know people. So, what're you going to do?'

Mathieson had to get out, or else he would throw up or collapse. He got to his feet as he loosened his tie. 'Nothing. It's nothing to do with me. Leave me alone.'

'They'll identify him. Sooner or fuckin' later. Then what? I'll be dead, what about you?!'

'Nothing...' Mathieson made his way to the door, pushed out into the dim morning, his heart thudding, knowing that it had all come back to find him at last.

Butler wasn't happy, that was made perfectly clear by her driving, the way she was gripping the wheel, swinging the Peugeot round the corners, speeding through town. Every now and again she'd point something out, telling him what it was in a manner seething with great annoyance.

'Train station,' she barked, and pointed a thumb to a turning on their right as they went under a bridge. Next, she nodded to a huge box of a building that was held up by giant concrete struts. 'That used to be owned by Royal Mail. Prison before that. God knows what it is now.'

Moone looked down at his lap and the file of photographs of the cuddly toy they'd recovered from the ground, still darkened by mud and sand. His stomach sank, thinking of what they were about to do, the pain and hurt they were about to poke at. It was all in Butler's profile, her tight jaw, the way she gripped the wheel, her foot down hard on the accelerator. For some reason she'd come to despise him, or what he represented, because he guessed it was the fact that she was still a sergeant and had been ignored when it came to being promoted. Now here he was, a big boy from London, coming in and heading a major murder inquiry. They'd had a preliminary report from the pathologist, Dr Parry, and he noted that there were signs of strangulation and no water in the dead man's lungs.

Butler drove them along a straight road, past a Tesco's, a fish and chip shop, then more takeaways before Moone found himself looking upon a mix of old narrow houses, possibly council buildings, and rows of grey boxy looking new builds on either side of the road.

'This is North Prospect,' Butler said, turning into a short road on their left full of terraced houses. 'Also known as Swilly. Don't ask me why.'

She parked outside a small house with an untidy garden, thick with weeds and strewn with children's toys. A rusted car sat half dismantled on the short driveway. Butler climbed out, so Moone followed her lead and they headed towards the house and up the couple of steps to the front door. A dog was constantly barking somewhere, a baby crying, and the grind of traffic trawling past on the main road. Moone felt spits of rain on his face as Butler said, 'This used to be a rough place to live, then it got redeveloped. Not so bad now. It's starting to rain. It always rains in Plymouth.'

Moone stopped dead in his tracks as he heard a sound filling the air, a high-pitched noise sounding out somewhere not too far away. A siren was moaning, the kind he remembered from films about nuclear war.

'What the hell is that?' he asked.

Butler looked around. 'Shit! Nuclear siren! It's happening! World War three!'

'What?!'

Butler huffed out a laugh and shook her head. 'It's the dockyard, they test their warning system every Monday at this time. You didn't shit yourself, did you?'

He gave her a sarcastic smile, then turned to the door.

Butler rang the bell, then stood back as a dog yapped inside and scratched at the door.

As the door was starting to open, Butler looked at Moone and said, 'Let me handle the chitter chatter.'

A skinny woman with straggly blonde hair, decked out in a pink t-shirt and jogging bottoms answered the door and stared at them. 'Yeah, what you selling?'

Butler showed her ID, so Moone did the same.

'Fuck,' she said, shaking her head. 'This about him? That fucking rat...'

'Mrs Sawyer,' Butler said, 'this isn't about whoever you're talking about... look, can we come in?'

She stared at them, her face slowly chan-ging, losing colour, perhaps the realisation dawning, Moone suspected. Then she backed up a little, opening the door wider as a child's voice echoed inside calling for their mummy.

The woman turned and bent down towards the little curly blonde-haired toddler and said, 'What is it now, Tally?'

'I want my pens and my crayons,' the little girl said, darting her eyes at Moone and Butler. Moone smiled, then poked out his tongue at the girl, but she looked away as her mother ushered her into the next room, promising to find her some pens and paper.

The little girl was sharply directed to the living room, then to a small chair by the coffee table, where she was given a bag of pens and some paper by her distraught looking mum.

She faced them as they stood in the door-way, her hands on her hips, then folded over her chest, staring at them as if they were about to be told off. 'Go on.'

'We'd like you to take a look at some photos,' Moone said, and held up the envelope.

Butler flashed a look at him, then stepped closer to the woman. 'Mrs Sawyer...'

'Foley,' she said. 'I got my name back when I got him to sling his hook. So... this is about him, yeah? My boy?'

Moone saw the tears well up in her eyes, so he said, 'I'm really sorry, but we found something yesterday. I know this isn't easy...'

'Found something?' She looked from Moone to Butler. 'What's he mean, found?'

'Why don't you sit down and we'll make you a cup of tea.' Butler got the woman to sit on the sofa. 'Make her some tea, for God's sake.'

But the woman sat up, her face ashen, tears appearing over her eyes. 'I don't want any tea, I just want to know what's going on? Have you found him?'

'We found some... remains,' Moone said, his voice breaking, sounding strange.

The woman's head hung down, a sob rattling from deep within her.

'We don't know if it's him,' Butler said, after staring at Moone, burning her hateful eyes at him. 'Please, keep calm, it may not...'

'Mummy,' the little girl said. 'You all right, Mummy?'

She looked up at her little girl, forcing a smile that Moone thought must have burned her, must have made her sick to her stomach.

'I'm good, sweetie,' she said, then wiped her eyes.

They all turned towards the windows when a car engine roared outside, then skidded to a stop across the pavement. Moone watched a young man get out of the bright yellow sporty car, then storm towards the house.

'Oh, for fu...' the mum said, jumping up, her face turning scarlet as she headed to the front door. 'That's all I need.'

Moone followed her as the man rang the bell then pounded at the door. 'Who's that?'

'Chisel,' she said, shaking her head. 'That's what they call him. His name's Brian. His mum lives a couple of doors away, the interfering old bitch. She must've called him.'

The banging continued, so Moone said, 'Is he... was he Danny's father?'

She nodded. 'I'll have to let him in.'

'It's OK, love,' Butler said. 'Let him in, I'm here.'

The woman opened the door and they all

looked out at the short, but muscular man who was covered in tattoos, and decked out in a tight-fitting grey tracksuit, with a matching baseball cap pulled to one side.

'Weren't you going to fucking tell me?' he growled at her, then turned and spat on her doorstep.

'You're disgusting!' she shouted back.

'What the fuck're you lot doing here?' The yob looked at them both. 'You got news or fucking what?'

Butler stepped past the woman and looked down at the yob father. 'Why don't you calm down and come in. We need to talk to the both of you.'

Still seething, the man stepped in, stormed into the living room and slumped down on to the sofa.

'Daddy!' the little girl cried, running to him. He hugged her, smoothed her hair, but he kept a watchful dead eye on Moone and Butler as they entered the room.

'So?' he said, while the mother sat at the other end of the sofa.

'They found something, Brian...some remains...' the mum said, her words breaking up.

Brian stared at her, blank, the little girl still wrapped round him, then up at Moone. 'What the fuck does that mean?'

'We need you to look at some photos,' Butler said, then nodded at Moone. 'They found a cuddly toy buried at the scene. If you could look at these photos, tell us if you recognise the toy.'

Both of them looked towards Moone, frozen as he pulled out the photos. He struggled, the photographs refusing to come out, time slowing down, all eyes on him. 'Sorry, here.'

He passed them each a photograph of the toy, but it was the mum that let out the howl, while the father, Brian just stared at the photograph, then at his wife, a look of confusion etched into his face.

Butler pushed Moone aside, then sat on the arm of the chair and put a comforting hand on the woman's back. 'I'm sorry, but do you recognise it?'

Between sobs, the woman nodded, croaking out a 'Yes.'

'You sure?' Brian said, staring at her, then back at the photo, but her eyes rose with spite and anger. Her skin was prickled with scarlet as she glared at him.

'Of course I'm sure!' she shouted. 'Don't you remember it? He loved that thing! We had to take it everywhere! How could you forget?!'

'He... I don't know, he had a lot of toys...' The dad stared at the photo, then down at the little girl and hugged her closer to him.

'It could be, that this toy is just similar to something your son had. A coincidence,' Moone said, 'Maybe you could take a look for it sometime, just to make sure.'

The mum sniffed, then nodded. 'OK. I've got all his stuff... Mum's got it in her shed... I couldn't... When will you know?'

'We don't know,' Butler said. 'There's a process, DNA tests.'

The mum looked up, wiping her eyes as the little girl let go of her dad and cuddled up to her instead. 'I have a brush I used on him, we let his hair... He liked it quite long. Can you... would that help?'

'Thanks,' Moone said, feeling like he wanted to run out of the door and not look back. 'That would be a great help.'

'We'll send someone for it,' Butler said as the mum started to get up.

'It's in my room,' she said, looking between them. 'It won't take a second.'

Like Moone, Butler must have felt it, the pain and angst thick in the air, stuck to everything, changing the nature of their world for ever. Moone couldn't imagine losing a child, not knowing what happened to them, the blame and guilt that would build and build until it was suffocating. He tried to imagine losing one of his kids, and remembered a time when his boy had disappeared into some bushes and he hadn't been able to see him for a couple of minutes. His heart began to thud as it had done that day, and his stomach turned over and over.

'Here,' the mum said, coming down the stairs, then holding out a clear plastic food bag with the brush inside. Moone took it gently and saw the many fine blonde hairs wrapped round it. 'We'll look after it.'

She nodded, then stifled a sob.

'Let's go,' Butler said, and opened the front door and stormed on towards the car and climbed in. Moone followed her out and stopped to turn and say goodbye but found the door had already closed.

When he climbed in beside Butler, he found her leant over the wheel, her arms folded, her head buried in her arms. When she sat up, her face was red, her angry eyes finding him. 'What was the bloody point of that?'

'I thought the point was trying to identify...'

'I know that. But all we've done is to cause them more misery. We could've waited, waited for the post-mortem...'

'I know you lived this for a while. I appreciate that it can get to you...'

She stared at him. 'This is not about me or you, it's about those poor bastards in there! They deserve to get some peace!'

'But that's what I'm trying to get for them...' Moone wanted to say more, but couldn't find the words as his mobile started to ring in his pocket. Butler started the engine and took them away from the small street as he answered the call.

'DI Moone,' he said, watching the locals flashing past.

'It's Harding,' the DC said, sounding fed up.

'Thought I'd let you know that the pathologist's been in touch. He's working on the DB found in Stonehouse. Got some interesting news for us, apparently.'

'Cheers. We'll head over.'

'Right. Seen Danny Sawyer's parents?'

'Yes, just come from there...'

The line went dead, and Moone took the phone from his ear and stared at it, realising that it didn't matter how he truly felt; he was in the place he was meant to be. And as long as his colleagues resented him, then he'd feel truly at home.

He looked at Butler, who seemed calmer, driving less erratically.

'Want to tell me where we're going?' she asked.

'To see the pathologist.'

She nodded, then took another turning, putting her foot down.

CHAPTER 4

Moone backed himself up to the wall of the large hospital lift as a couple of porters moved a patient on a bed into the corner. Butler squeezed herself close to the door, her hands dug into her pockets, still looking just as pissed off as before. He made a mental note to find out if it was his appearance alone that had brought on her mood or if sullenness was her default mode. Everyone else left the lift before they reached the bowels of the hospital. They headed towards the Anatomical Pathology department, or the mortuary as he knew it to be called. He clenched his fists as the far too familiar smell wafted out of the rooms beyond the large green doors. Butler seemed unaffected by it all, just pushed on through the doors into the office beyond.

After a few minutes they were allowed into the viewing corridor that ran alongside the post mortem room. It was a smaller room than the ones he was used to in London but it was pretty much same, all lime green tiles and stainless steel sinks.

Dr Parry was pulling on a pair of purple latex gloves, dressed in scrubs and an apron. His shoulder-length dark hair was tied back, allowing Moone a view of a small black hawk tattoo on his neck.

Beside Dr Parry was a table, the shape of a body beneath a green plastic sheet, which the pathologist removed to reveal the light grey body of their unidentified first victim.

When Moone stepped closer, a burst of rancid sea smells rose to him, making his stomach roll over.

'Afternoon,' Parry said, smiling, showing his long teeth. 'Hope you've had a good first day.'

'It's been interesting,' Moone said, looking down at the body, getting a good look at where the skin had been removed, and the pink muscle beneath.

'He's made quite an impression,' Butler said, but there was no sign of humour as she stared down at the body.

'Small, isn't he?' the pathologist said, and looked at them both. 'Five-seven to be precise. Slight. By the way, the cause of death was strangulation. The hyoid bone was fractured, meaning a great deal of pressure was applied during the choking. There are hematomas all over the stomach, and shoulder... oh, and notice that the tips of his fingers and toes have been removed.'

'What the bloody hell happened to him?' Butler said, shaking her head. 'What sort of nutter does a thing like this?'

Moone took a good look at the fingers, examining the cuts where the tips had been severed. 'Secateurs?'

'Maybe. Something like that, something very sharp. The tips were removed in one cut.'

'But we could still print the body, so the killer wasn't trying to stop us identifying him?' Moone straightened himself.

'So why cut off the fingertips?' Butler asked. 'What's he trying to hide?'

'And he removed skin from the legs and arms,' Dr Parry said. 'I did find some kind of sludge or something in his eyes...'

Moone swung round towards the doctor, a flicker of something in the back of his head. 'What colour?'

'Black.' Parry looked down at the face.

'Mascara?' Moone said, looking between Butler and the pathologist.

Parry nodded, then pointed at Moone. 'That's not bad. Why the fingertips? Maybe he was wearing glue-on nails or had real painted nails.'

'And he removes the skin from his legs because he doesn't want us knowing that his victim had shaved his body,' Moone said. 'What do we reckon?'

'I reckon you're right,' Butler said, nodding. 'He comes across a transvestite, seeks them out or something, then kills them, but he's ashamed, so he tries to throw us off the scent by removing any of the telltale signs.'

'What if he didn't seek him out?' Parry asked. 'What if he thought our victim was a she? With the right clothes, makeup, I think he would look like the genuine article.'

'It's possible,' Moone said. 'So it could've been a random attack, thinking it was a woman he was hunting… so how do we find him?'

'You're in charge,' Butler said. 'You figure it out.'

Moone looked away from her, and saw Parry flashing him a look of sympathy. 'So, where's the remains… of the child, I mean?'

Parry beckoned Moone and took them to a door with a window in it. 'I keep the children in here. I do so out of respect, so they've got their own space. I suppose that sounds strange…'

'Not at all,' Moone said and looked into the room and saw the metal table at the centre of the narrow space. On the table the remains were laid out as if a person and not a collection of bones was resting there. The remains didn't take up much space at all. They were all silent for a moment, staring into the window, so Moone broke the silence by saying, 'Have you got anything for us?'

Parry looked down. 'I'm afraid so. I discovered several fractures in the bones... arms and legs.'

'Post mortem?' Moone asked.

'No, peri mortem. Some of them had started to heal prior to death...'

Butler put her face in her hands. 'Jesus... so you're saying this child was beaten before they died?'

'Girl or boy?' Moone asked.

'Definitely a boy,' Parry said. 'Same age as Danny Sawyer. It's almost impossible to tell how they died, but there are possible fractures to the skull. By the way, the soil and dirt around the skull has been examined. Some of the soil dug into the skull is different to the external dirt and sand from the beach.'

'So, the bones were dug up from somewhere else?' Butler said. 'Jesus... where do we go from here?'

'Can we get DNA?' Moone asked.

Parry frowned, then raised his shoulders. 'It's possible, if the bones are cleaned, correctly prepared, there might be traces of DNA. The best method would be to use phenol chloroform. It'll take a while, and they'll have to be sent to Oxford most likely. But if you've got DNA from a missing child, we might get a match.'

Butler sighed. 'So, those poor parents have got a long bloody wait to find out if it is their kid? Jesus.'

Moone didn't say anything for a while, not

wanting to add insult to bloody violent injury. Instead, he looked back at the body, the skinned carcass of the possible crossdresser. He had two cases to work on, two difficult situations to contend with, while trying to get his team to like him. Mission fucking impossible, but there was no bloody sign of Tom Cruise – just himself and a female detective who seemed to despise him.

'You know,' Parry said, staring in at the bones. 'This isn't the only kid to go missing in Devon...'

Moone stared around at him. 'What do you mean?'

Butler sighed. 'He's talking about a spate of child murders that happened nearly ten years ago, all around Devon and Cornwall. But the perpetrator's locked up, has been for seven years, in Dartmoor. So, good theory, but no cigar, doctor.'

The doctor shook his head. 'No, I'm not saying I think Grader killed this boy. I'm just saying, these people, they like to form clubs, they stick together.'

'Not Grader,' Butler shook her head. 'He's like a rogue animal. He doesn't like people, he hates adults. I can't believe we're talking about him. He'd love it!'

Moone watched them both and the uncomfortable looks that the memories of the child killer had delivered. 'Grader?'

'Loy Grader!' Butler groaned. 'You must've heard of him. It's the biggest child murder case in the South West.'

There was a distant spark of memory somewhere in the darkest, dustiest part of his brain. 'How many did he kill?'

Butler made a face. 'Seven. Please don't suggest we go and see him.'

Moone didn't know what to say, because he suddenly felt lost. For one thing, this was only his second time in charge and his second time investigating a child murder. The memories of his first were being churned up, brought into the mix. His hands were shaking, knowing they were waiting for his word, when all he wanted was to grab a coffee and sit somewhere and have a fag.

'Maybe we...' Moone said, but the door buzzer sounded down the corridor, breaking the moment. Moone sighed when the door opened and PC Carthew poked her head round.

'Sorry to interrupt,' she said, coming into the room.

'No, it's fine,' Moone said, wanting to hug her, but realising that would be highly inappropriate. 'What's happened?'

'It's just that the prints on...'

Moone saw that her eyes had jumped to the body on the morgue table, so he stepped into her view. 'He won't bite. Go on.'

She smiled awkwardly. 'Sorry, the prints came back. They've got an ID on our first dead body. Jason Mitchum. I've got the address.'

'That's great.' Moone walked back to Butler and Parry and found them chatting about something and waited for them to stop.

'We've got an ID on our first dead body,' Moone said, looking over to the morgue table. 'I thought I'd let PC Carthew drive me over...'

Butler folded her arms, then huffed. 'Right, I see, someone prettier comes along and I'm dumped.'

'No, I just thought she could do with the experience...'

Butler raised her eyebrows. 'Yeah, I bet you did.'

'It's not like that...'

'Relax, Moone. I'm having you on. Go on. I'll meet you there. She's a bit cakey if you ask me, but each to their own.'

Moone was about to walk away, then stopped. 'I'm sorry... cakey?'

'I forgot I've got to interpret everything... means silly, bit too girly. We'll have to get you a Janner dictionary.'

'Janner?'

'Never mind. Just go and have fun.'

Moone sat back in his seat as PC Carthew drove them down a wide tree-lined street that she promised would take them to an area called Mannamead, which she said was one of the more affluent areas in Plymouth. Moone noticed the large grey stone houses that sat back from the road that had long drives. On the way through the hospital, Carthew had bought him an espresso and pasty in the cafe near accident and emergency. Now he sipped the coffee while the pasty sat in a paper bag, making the whole car smell similar to BO. While she drove, Moone filled her in on their theory that Jason Mitchum might have had a secret life as a crossdresser.

'You can eat your pasty,' Carthew said, smiling.

'I didn't think you'd want me to get crumbs in here. It's very clean and tidy.'

'I have one of those mini-Hoovers in the boot. Anyway, best you eat it before it stinks the car out. They stink like BO.'

He sat up and unwrapped his pasty and took a bite. 'I heard that they put the thick pastry round the edge so the miners could eat them without getting dirt on the rest of it.'

'I've heard that too. I had an ulterior motive for coming to find you at the hospital.'

'Really? What?'

'I'll just say it...' Carthew slowed the car, indicated, took them into a narrow, bush-lined road filled with grand looking Victorian houses with long steps up to the front double doors. 'I someday, sooner rather than later, want to become a detective. I want to do what you do.'

Moone laughed as he took another bite. 'Believe me, you don't want to do what I do. I've made cock up after cock up.'

She parked outside one of the end houses that had light blue tiles around a large archway that led to a set of dark double doors. 'You got this far. You must be doing something right.'

'Carthew...'

'Faith.' She smiled as she turned to face him.

'Faith...sometimes you travel places, but you have no memory of how you got there. You just wake up feeling fucking exhausted and dizzy.'

'So teach me how to do that.' She smiled even more.

He laughed. 'I'll do my best. Let's go in there and break the bad news. Lesson one, the job is all about the dirty, horrible jobs like this.'

They climbed out and headed through the large trees that guarded the front then up the flight of stone steps that led to the double doors. As he stared at the large ornate brass knocker, Moone rang the bell, his stomach trying to hide in his shoes. This wasn't visiting the parents of a murdered child, therefore it had to be easier, he told himself.

'I thought we could go for a drink some-time,' PC Carthew said. 'Then we could talk about the job...'

He looked at her, saw her cheeks were a little flushed, and she was looking up to the windows above.

Before he had the chance to say anything,

the door opened and a woman, who looked to be in her seventies, with greying bobbed hair, dressed in a long flowery dress, looked out at them.

'Hello, can I help you?' the woman asked in a well-spoken voice, no sign of a Plymouth accent.

'I'm DI Peter Moone,' he said and produced his ID. 'This is PC Faith Carthew. Is Mrs Mitchum home?'

The woman stared at them for a moment, confusion spreading across her pink, surprisingly wrinkle free face. Then she opened the door a little and turned towards the interior of the house.

'Charlotte!' the woman called. 'Charlotte! The police are here!'

The older woman stepped back, while footsteps came from within, becoming louder until a slender, brunette woman in a red dress stood at the door staring out at them.

'Has something happened?' she asked, her dark eyes jumping between Moone and PC Carthew.

'Can we come in?' Moone asked.

The woman, Mrs Mitchum, started to move backwards, allowing them to enter while the older woman said, 'What's this about?'

'It's about your husband,' Moone said, noting that Mrs Mitchum's face had grown a few shades paler.

'Jason?' she said. 'Has something... he's in

Birmingham... with work.'

Moone kept on following the woman until they went into a large high-ceilinged lounge, with a corner unit full of books, and a piano by the large, blinded windows. The wife stood by the huge fireplace, staring at Moone, her eyes wide, waiting.

'I'm sorry,' he said, but Mrs Mitchum just shook her head. 'Mrs Mitchum...'

'You're not about to tell me he's been in an accident?'

'I'm afraid we found... the body of a male...'

'That's ridiculous...' The older woman joined Mrs Mitchum, putting a calming hand on her arm. 'She said he's in Birmingham with his work...'

Moone looked round to see PC Carthew watching from near the door. 'When was the last time you saw him?'

'Friday, Friday morning. He drove up to Birmingham. This must be a mistake.'

'When did you last hear from him?' Faith asked, coming further into the room.

'Last... Yes, last night...' The wife looked at the older woman as if for confirmation. 'He sent me a text message. Remember, Mum?'

The older woman nodded. 'Yes, he did. This has got to be a mistake.'

Moone ignored the heavy, slow burning feeling of despair filling up his gut and pushed on. 'What did the text say?'

The wife looked about for her phone then found it on the table. 'Just says, "Hi, I'm fine".'

'Was that a reply to a message you sent?'

'Well, yes,' the wife said. 'I asked how he was earlier on. He never replies very quickly. I'm sorry, but why do you think this person you've found is my husband?'

'Your husband was arrested a few years ago, at an anti-war protest?'

Then her face changed, her hand went up to her mouth, and she moved across the room towards the sofa and sat down, her eyes turning towards the windows. 'Yes...I mean, he went to London, he was very anti-war, anti-establishment. Oh my God...'

'I'm sorry,' Moone said. 'Of course we'll need you to identify him. If you feel you can?'

She looked up at him, blinking, but no tears, just the ashen face of shock. At some time it would hit her, later, maybe weeks later, when she's doing something mundane, he decided. The breakdown would come.

'Yes...' she looked down, then towards her mother. 'Yes, I'll do that.'

'I'm sorry, but there's more. Things we have to ask. Can you think of anyone who might want to harm your husband?'

It was the mother that said, 'Harm Jason? Everyone loved Jason. That's a ridiculous notion.'

'I'm sorry, but we have to ask.'

The wife shook her head. 'I can't think of

anyone, sorry, my head, I just can't.'

'I'm sorry, it's hard to take in,' Moone said. 'But there's something else... you said he was in Birmingham, for work?'

'That's right,' the mother said.

'We found your husband's body here in Plymouth. Stonehouse. Have you any idea why that would be?'

The wife looked up, the confusion clear on her face. 'Stonehouse? He was in Birmingham... he had a work conference.'

PC Carthew cleared her throat. 'Did he go away a lot with work?'

Mrs Mitchum's empty eyes found Carthew. 'Yes... well, occasionally.'

'He went away a lot,' the mother said, then looked down to her daughter when she looked up at her reproachfully. 'Well, he did!'

Moone could feel it was time to back off, time to leave them alone with their grief. 'I'm sorry to ask, but could you possibly, at some point make us a list of his friends, his work details, and... we'd like to look at any computers or laptops he might have used.'

The wife spun her head round and stared up at Moone, then got to her feet. 'Why do you want to do that?'

'It's just routine. Just to get a feel for him as a person and build up a timeline. That sort of thing.' To find out if your husband was dressing up as a woman when he said he was going to conferences, Moone thought. He smiled. 'I'm so sorry for your loss. We'll arrange identification as soon as we can.'

As they were about to leave the house and shut the door behind them, the mother came down the hall and pulled the door open and looked at them, her face quite pale. 'I'm sorry, but am I correct in thinking that you don't believe Jason went to Birmingham with work?'

'We're thinking that might be a possibility.'

She nodded. 'I can't say I'm surprised.'

'Really? Why's that?'

The mother looked back towards the interior of the house then lowered her voice. 'Can I talk to you another time? Somewhere more private?'

'Why don't you come to Charles Cross police station tomorrow? Here's my card. Use the mobile number.'

The woman took the card, smiled awkwardly, then shut the door.

CHAPTER 5

He scanned the paper, flipping through the pages of the Evening Herald, his hands trembling, trying to find any mention of what he'd done. But it was too early, far too soon for them to be reporting on it. He looked up furtively across the pub, seeing that the other punters were chatting, drinking, not paying any attention to him. He looked out of the line of windows that allowed him a view of Royal Parade and the people queuing up for the buses. One bus rumbled past, along with the traffic and the people who went dawdling across his view. He picked up his whisky, took a swig, wiped his chin, and kept on spying on the street, half expecting the pigs to turn up en masse and drag him away.

Nothing.

No one was coming for him. He'd done it, got away with it. Then he started to think, to wonder if he'd done something that shouldn't ever be punished. The thing in the park, the fucking pervert, pretending to be a woman. The rage rose through him again, making him tremble as he took another gulp of whisky. He nodded to himself, scratched at his scalp and decided it must be true, it must be God's will that he'd rid the world of something disgusting.

That was why no one had done anything, hadn't even been bothered by the death of the pervert.

Then fate spoke to him again, showing him the way.

It came along the street, the thing, the disgusting thing came tottering down the street under a stupid looking wig. A man, an aging man wearing thick make up and lipstick, trying to walk in heels.

He finished his drink, got up and hurried through the crowd of tables and into the late afternoon air, through the pungent cloud that hung over the smokers on the street.

There, by the Caribbean restaurant that used to be the post office, the creature, the pervert was tottering along. He put his hands into his pockets and started to follow, hearing something, a whisper in his ear, a voice growing louder, telling him to do something to rid the world of such disgusting foul creatures.

He nodded, knowing it must be the voice of God.

Moone was sitting in the waiting area between the assistant's desk and the Chief Superintendent's door. He was nursing an Americano, with an extra shot of espresso, trying not to catch the eye of his assistant, while also trying to kick start his brain. Then the Chief Super's door opened and he came out, smiled and said, 'DI Moone, twice in one day. Come in.'

Moone went through and sat before his desk and watched his new boss take his large leather seat and raise his eyebrows. 'What is it?'

Moone cleared his throat. 'It's about the child murder we're investigating...'

'Yes, always difficult...'

'Well, it's just there are similarities between our case and a case that happened a few years back...'

Before Moone had time to finish speaking, his boss was nodding, and sitting up straight.

'You're talking about Loy Grader,' he said, making a face as if he'd tasted something bad. 'Yes, a very terrible time for the families and our colleagues. You said similarities?'

'Well, a few. I just thought, if it might be possible to talk to Grader. To see if he has any connection to it, or if he might know the person we're after.'

Laptew sat back in his chair, seeming to mull it all over. 'What does Butler think?'

Moone hesitated, so Laptew smiled and said, 'I only ask because she's been here a lot longer than you, she knows the people around here. Also, there's a lot to consider when you're thinking of talking to a person like Loy Grader. Like it or not, we have to think about the press angle. If they get wind that we've gone to have a conversation with a monster like Grader, and what with the discovery of the bones of a child, well, it doesn't bear thinking about, does it? People can get carried away, fingers get pointed. We don't want a panic on our hands.'

'So, you're saying we shouldn't talk to Grader?'

The Chief Super shook his head. 'No, that's not what I'm saying. What I'm saying is, we have to think carefully about the repercussions of such an action. We have to tread very carefully.'

Moone nodded, even though he hadn't a clue whether he'd been given the green light or not.

'But at the end of the day, it's your decision,' Laptew said, sitting back again. 'You're the SIO on this. I'm going to give you the benefit of the doubt.'

'Thanks.'

'Don't thank me, DI Moone, not yet. Remember, tread carefully when it comes to the press. Even down here, we've got some voracious reporters. So be vigilant.'

Moone decided to get up, feeling the conversation had come to an end. He put out his hand, which the Chief Super shook, smiling.

Outside the office, Moone found a bin and dumped his empty coffee cup, thinking over what the Chief Super had said, but mostly considering what he hadn't said. The press seemed his main concern, which meant he was a man who was scared of looking bad, because that would put his job at risk and probably put him on a bad standing in the local lodge.

He had to decide whether to visit Grader in prison or not, to have a conversation with the child killing version of Hannibal Lecter and therefore risk kicking a nest full of hungry, angry press and families.

Moone didn't like himself for it, but he decided to wait, to be patient and see what they could turn up the old-fashioned way.

By the time he reached the incident room, he'd formulated a plan of sorts, which consisted of dragging in the usual suspects, and which meant having interviews with the scum of the earth sex offenders.

As he entered the incident room, Moone found Butler coming towards him, about to leave.

'Oh, there you are,' she said, holding a file against her thigh. 'Did you have a nice date with PC Carthew?'

'Very funny. We went to see Jason Mitchum's wife. I don't think she's got any idea about her husband's secret life.'

'Bollocks. She knows, or at least she knows something's going on.'

'Her mother's got something to say, so she's going to come in tomorrow.'

'Should be interesting.' Butler gestured to the doors. 'Right, we've got a couple of interviews to conduct.'

'I've been thinking,' Moone said, preparing to lay down his plan. 'We need to talk to…'

'Local sex offenders, the ones with a predilection for young boys? That's what I've been organising while you've been gallivanting about.'

'Oh, right. Well done.'

She stared at him. 'I'm a thirty-eight-year-old woman, not a four-year-old girl trying to take her first shit in a potty. Jesus, look, I've also got the last person to lay eyes on Danny Sawyer waiting to talk to us. Why don't we save time and you talk to the paedophile while I talk to the witness?'

'Why do I get the sex offender?'

'Because he'll feel threatened by me, a woman in authority. Let's go.'

As she moved past, Moone said, 'I've got news for you, it's not just paedophiles that you make feel uncomfortable.'

She turned on the spot and faced him. 'Look, I don't like you. I don't know what it is. Your face or something, maybe your clothes, and you don't like me, but here we are. Let's just get on with it.'

'Fine.' Moone hurried on past her, heading for the interview rooms.

'Here,' Butler said, and held out the file she'd been carrying. 'His name's Martin White. I'll see you in a minute.'

Moone stood outside the door to the interview room for a moment, breathing, trying to clear his thoughts. He didn't want anything clouding his judgement, didn't want his own bias to make him act less than professional. Yet, there was that burning sensation inside him, the burn of discomfort and disgust.

He brushed it aside, put his hand on the door handle, ready to enter. He stopped.

His phone was ringing.

He took it out and saw that an unidentified number was calling, so he answered. 'DI Peter Moone.'

'Dad?'

It was his eldest's voice, Alice. His heart began to thud, and he backed himself up against the wall, gripping the phone closer to his ear. 'Alice? You alright?'

'Hi, yeah, yeah, I'm OK,' she said, but it's not what he heard in her voice, that deep sense that all was not well.

'You sure? I didn't recognise the number.'

'Mum bought me a mobile. She's worried

about where I am.'

'Now you're out of London, she's worried?'

Alice gave a short laugh. 'I know, she's nuts.'

'I'm sorry I haven't seen you... your mum, well...'

'I know. She's still pissed off with you. I was wondering if we could meet up?'

'Of course. What about tomorrow? About twelve?'

'Yeah, that sounds great. There's a cafe on Royal Parade. The Gorge. They do a great breakfast.'

'Where's Royal Parade... don't worry, I'll Google it. I'll see you tomorrow. I've got to go.'

'OK, bye, Dad.'

He lowered his phone, his heart slowing, glad nothing was immediately amiss, but still there was a little part of him that was worried about her. There always was, like a constant distant drumming in the back of his skull, making him think about them every few minutes.

He switched it off, grabbed the door handle and went into the small interview and fixed his eyes on the man sitting at the wood desk. There was an audio recorder attached to the desk.

Martin White wore a thick jumper over a check shirt. He was average build, a round face, with thinning red hair. There was something off about his head, as if one little thing had been put of place on his face, but Moone couldn't work out what it was.

'Afternoon,' Moone said, pulled out a chair and sat down.

White looked up from the cup of tea he was holding and towards Moone. But Moone noticed that his eyes drifted above him, as if the man was looking at something just over his head.

'Is this... is this going to take long?' White said and looked at his tea again.

'Just a few questions,' Moone said, and took out a statement form and a pen. 'Where do you live?'

'Stonehouse. Why?' White stared at the form as Moone wrote. 'You know where I live. I'm on the register.'

'That's right. You tried to abduct a young boy.'

White flinched, then rubbed his arm, and scratched his head. 'I know... I... I wasn't well... I was on pills. I think they messed with my head...'

'There were other offences. You flashed yourself at another boy who was on his way to school. Were you on the pills then?'

He shrugged, scratched his head. 'Can't remember. I feel like they're picking on me.'

'Who?'

'Them.'

'Who's them?'

Martin raised his eyes again, fixing them on a point above Moone's head. 'The government. They see me as a bad man, like I'm evil or something. I can't help it. I can't help what goes on in here.'

Moone watched him tap at his temple. 'You heard of Danny Sawyer?'

White's gaze went to the table, while his fingers scratched at his neck, producing a red mark. He said nothing, just kept scratching and staring downwards.

'Martin?' Moone said. 'Are you going to say something?'

'It was in all the papers.'

'It was. But did you know of him before that?'

More scratching. 'See... you're trying to put words in my mouth.'

'I'm just asking a question. Had you heard of Danny Sawyer before you read about him?'

Butler sat down in the interview room after putting down her travel mug of coffee. Don Sanders was sitting opposite her, his arms folded, watching her carefully as if he expected her to pull a rabbit out of her arse. He was tall, bit lanky, messy brown hair, a long face like a horse. He was only thirty, but Butler thought he had something of the elderly about him, as if he'd been born at the wrong time.

'Hello, Don,' she said, and opened her file, then clicked her pen a few times. 'Thanks for popping in.'

'It's all right,' he said and sniffed.

'You know what this is about, don't you?'

'I'd hazard a guess it's to do with that boy again.'

'You know his name.'

He sniffed, nodded, and looked about the room. 'Yes, I know his name. Daniel. Danny. Little Danny.'

'You were one of the last people to see him before he went missing...'

'That's cause I lived opposite. I used to see him playing outside his house. Used to think he shouldn't be out and about by himself. They never looked after him very well. The world's a dangerous place.' He leaned forward. 'Do you know how many kids go missing every day, all round the world?'

'No, but I bet it's a lot, Don.'

'It is. Millions. Some turn up. Some don't. It's a dangerous world.'

'It is. Why so interested in the missing?'

He shrugged. 'I guess, since he went, one minute he was there, playing outside, then I looked out the window and he was gone, just like that. How can that happen? In this day and age? How can people just disappear?'

'It can't have been easy being the last person to see him like that.'

He lowered his head, then nodded. 'It wasn't. Everyone looks at you funny, you know? Like they think you had something to do with it.'

'People are quick to judge.'

Don nodded. 'People are tossers. I don't trust people. Especially your lot, you should've heard how they talked to me, like they wanted me to say I did something to him. Bastards.'

'Sometimes they get themselves worked up. It's hard not to in this job.'

He looked up at her. 'What about now?'

'Now?'

'All this? All over again. What's this mean? Means you found something, doesn't it?'

Butler sat back, a strange feeling snaking up her spine. 'What makes you say that, Don?'

He kept looking into her eyes. 'You lot don't get off your arses if nothing's going on, do you? He turned up? He has, hasn't he?'

'Na, never heard of him before,' White said and picked up his tea and took a sip.

'You have friends, right?' Moone asked.

'I did. Then I got all this put on me, treated like scum. I had all kinds of nasty stuff painted all over the front of my house.'

'You know what they arrested and charged you for?'

White looked above his head. 'It's because under their draconian laws, what I did is seen as wrong. Now, if we lived in a more enlightened society...'

Moone swallowed down his disgust, pushed back down the vomit that wanted to rise up to his mouth. He was shaking again. 'You know people, people that have the same... *interests* as you, don't you?'

White sipped his tea. 'You want me to grass? You want me to dob them in?'

'I just want to find out what happened to Danny Sawyer.'

'So, you're going to try and pin it on me or one of my friends?'

'You have got friends then?' Moone sat back. 'What about Loy Grader?'

Moone spotted the twitch, the little almost undetectable tremor through his face before he clammed up again.

'Heard of him... just like everyone else.'

'Never met him? Never been to a party or some kind of gathering where he turned up?'

'No.'

'I did some reading on Grader. He liked to host parties, liked to sit and take court. Saw himself as a king.'

'I wouldn't know. Never met him.'

'Plymouth isn't that big a place. Not when you've got the same interests. Is it?'

'Wouldn't know. I keep myself to myself.'

Moone couldn't hold back the exasperated laugh. 'But you don't, do you, Martin? You don't keep yourself to yourself? You like to show yourself to young children. What sort of society would treat that as normal?'

'An enlightened one.'

Moone balled his fists under the table. 'Give me a name. Just a name of somebody who might know something about Danny Sawyer.'

'Like I said, I don't have any friends.'

'You seem quite certain he's turned up, Don. Why's that?'

Don leaned back in his chair, folded his arms. 'I don't like the way this is going. You've got that look in your eye, the same look the other lot had.'

Butler leaned forward. 'What look?'

'Like they wanted to fit me up. I suppose it's easy to look at the last person to see him alive and say he must've done it...'

'Thing was, Don, you couldn't account for your movements. You said you saw him playing outside and then he was gone. But then there was a long gap in your whereabouts.'

'I couldn't remember. I forget things. I was on this medication, fried my brain. I still can't remember things and it made me paranoid. But you found out where I was.'

'Yeah, at a friend's, playing computer games. But you can understand how it looked, can't you?'

Don looked away. 'I suppose. Is he dead?'

'I can't discuss that. It's an ongoing investigation.'

'Yeah, he's dead, the poor little sod. Hope

you get them.'

'We will. Did you see someone that day? Anyone hanging around?'

'The street was empty.'

'No cars you didn't recognise?'

'No, nothing. I told you all this before. He was there, then he was gone.' Don leaned forward, his eyes staring deep into hers. 'Believe me, if I could've done something, if I'd seen some bastard scumbag leading him off, then I would've done something.'

Butler huffed. 'But even though you noticed he was gone, you didn't say anything. He was there, then he was gone. But you only mentioned this when they did door to door. Why?'

Don looked away. 'I told you. My head was messed up... still is. Want a note from my doctor?'

'No, you're all right.' Butler stood up. 'Stay here.'

Moone was quite glad when there was a knock at the door, then Butler poked her pissed off face in. He noticed White's look of panic, his cheeks reddening as Butler came in and stood, arms folded by the desk.

'Having any luck?' she asked, staring down at White, while he avoided her glare.

'Martin was just telling me that his social life's a bit lacking,' Moone said and sat back.

'Really?' Butler leant over the desk, rested on her palms. 'So, Martin, do you know anything about Daniel Sawyer?'

'Apart from what was in the papers, no,' he said and folded his arms, looked at the other wall.

'I don't believe you, Martin. People like you are sneaky, you're used to hiding under rocks, sharing your dirty little ways on the dark web. Aren't you?'

He didn't say anything, just faced the wall, Moone saw his fingers tapping away, fidgeting.

'You must've heard something,' Butler said. 'So, what I'm going to do is make sure everyone knows where you live. All the local right wing, skinhead, mob fuckers. How about that?'

White swung his head back round, his face drawn, skin even more red. 'You can't. You can't do that.'

'Oh, but I can, Martin. And I will. I'll make sure the local papers get wind of you... anonymously, maybe I'll put the word out...'

'They'll kill me. They'll murder me.'

Moone saw the tears come to his eyes and he caught himself on the edge of sympathy, then drew back from that particular distasteful cliff. He looked up and saw the look on Butler's face, the hatred and disgust clear in her eyes, and he realised that the dislike she'd shown him was a piss in the whole ocean. He made a mental note not to really piss her off.

'So, what's it going to be?' Butler asked.

'You won't let on where I live?' he asked, looking ready to cry again.

'No, I won't.' She leaned in, showing her teeth, letting him see her eyes. 'But if I ever hear about you doing your nasty little things again, I swear I'll come down on you like the hounds of Hell and their whole fucking family. Got it?'

'OK,' he said, scratching at his neck. 'OK. Malcolm, Malcolm West. He's a nasty one, not gentle, not at all. Please, promise you won't let on about where I live?'

Moone stood up. 'Scout's honour.'

CHAPTER 6

Malcolm West lived in narrow and steep road not far Pennycomequick, which was an area not far from the train station. There was a roundabout, and as they went round it, Moone noticed a small, almost ridiculous statue of a man in a top hat. The funny statue seemed to go with the funny name of the place and conjured almost pornographic images in his head.

'Isambard Kingdom Brunel,' Butler commented.

'Sorry?' Moone said.

'The weird statue on the roundabout. That's who it's meant to be. Thought you might be wondering. He designed the railway bridge next to the Tamar Bridge.'

'Oh right. I see.'

Butler turned into West's street, then up the hill and parked halfway up it and pulled on the handbrake.

'Hilly round here, isn't it?' Moone said, getting out, trying to make conversation and find common ground.

She gave him a funny look as she headed to the red door of an untidy looking house, not as well looked after as the others round it. 'Hilly? I suppose. You're observant, aren't you?'

Moone rang the bell, then flapped the letter box. 'Just making conversation.'

'Why did you come here? Plymouth, I mean?'

'Family. The ex-wife and kids live here now. She's a teacher.'

Butler rang the bell again. 'Doesn't look like he's home, does it?'

The rain started as they stood there, light spits at first, then large hammering drops that machine gunned the pavement. They turned and ran back to the car, and climbed in, watching the house through the soft blur of the rain-spattered windscreen.

'Now what?' Butler asked.

'Now we wait, I suppose,' Moone said. 'Better put the wipers on.'

'Don't be thick,' she groaned. 'That'll give us away. So, this ex-wife business... you do the dirty on her?'

She turned round sharply, caught Moone off guard, his mouth opening but nothing travelling from his frozen brain to his tongue. He looked away again.

'Thought as much,' she said, sounding a little happy with herself. 'You men, can't keep it in your pants for more than two seconds. Now you're stalking her...'

'I'm not stalking her. I want to be near my kids!'

'Right, so this woman you had a thing with... sorry, it was a woman?'

'Yes.'

'She not about anymore?'

Moone watched the rain travelling down the glass like myriad newly released tadpoles. 'No, she's not.'

'Sensible woman. Got out when the going was good.'

Moone stared at Butler, wanting to tell her how wrong she was, how it wasn't a fling, that he loved her... and now she was dead, and it was all his fault.

'What?' Butler asked. 'You got something to say?'

'No, nothing. You're right, I made lots of mistakes.'

She huffed again, sat back then sat up again. 'Who's this?'

Moone looked to the rain-soaked street and saw a man in blue bomber jacket, his round face awash with messy wet hair. He had walked into the garden of the house they were observing, seemed to produce a key and had entered the house.

'That's not West,' Butler said, producing a mugshot of Malcolm West from the file she'd picked up from the floor. 'So who's the creepy looking tosser?'

'We better find out,' Moone said, and battled open his door against the rain. He pulled his collar up and made a dash for the door with Butler not far behind.

'You knock on the front,' Butler called, 'I'll have a nose round the back.'

Moone got in as close as he could to the door, trying to find some shelter from the cold rain as he pressed the bell and flapped the letter box. He leaned into the window by the side of the door but couldn't see anything going on inside.

He stood there for a while, then decided to head round the back to see if Butler was having any better luck. It was when he reached the cobblestone lane that backed onto the terrace houses that he heard the swearing, and Butler's pissed off voice telling someone to stop resisting arrest.

Butler was sat astride the lanky haired suspicious character, pulling his arms behind his back, so Moone assisted her by pulling him to his feet, pushing him against the wall.

'This is harassment,' the creep said.

'Yeah, yeah,' Butler said and pulled out a wallet from his inside pocket, then opened it. 'Well, it's not very nice to meet you, Mr Gareth Metcalfe. So, what the bloody hell're you doing entering the registered home of a sex offender?'

'I've got a fucking key!' Metcalfe moaned.

'Where?' Moone asked.

'Coat pocket,' he said, so Moone carefully fished around and brought out a set of two keys.

'Why're you here?' Moone asked.

'Watering his plants and feeding his fucking goldfish,' Metcalfe said.

Butler pulled him backwards, dragging his heels across the cobbles, then marched him through the back gate and through a short, overgrown garden towards the back door. 'Open up, Moone.'

Moone did as requested and stepped into a narrow, old-fashioned kitchen with worn and torn laminate flooring. He noted there was no washing up in the sink and no signs that anyone had eaten anything in the kitchen lately, so he opened the fridge and smelt the stale plastic smell of an empty compartment.

Butler frogmarched a moaning Metcalfe through a doorway and along a badly seventies-style decorated hallway and into an equally gaudy front room. There was a worn flowery sofa, a coffee table, and a small TV. Moone went over to a unit that ran along the wall and had a small fish tank sitting on it, while Butler took Metcalfe round the sofa and pushed him into it.

Moone bent down towards the tank. It had a small castle at the bottom of it, which he could barely make out through the murky water. The filter coughed and spluttered in one corner.

'Right,' Butler said, her arms folded across her chest. 'Let's get this straight, what are you doing here?'

'I told ya!' Metcalfe said, trying to sit up. 'I'm just sort of house sitting…'

'Feeding his fish?' Moone asked.

'Yes, but sometimes I forget.'

'Sometimes?' Moone said, his eyes fixing on the floating body of a dead goldfish.

Moone turned and caught Butler's unimpressed look, so headed over to Metcalfe and stared down at him as he said, 'Where's Malcolm West?'

'On fucking holiday!' Metcalfe said.

'You friends with West, then?' Moone asked. 'You old buddies?'

Metcalfe shrugged. 'Sort of. I know him.'

'You share some of his pastimes?' Butler asked, coming closer to him.

'I ain't saying nothing,' he said, lowering his head. 'You better arrest me, and I'll get hold of my solicitor.'

Butler nodded, then took out her mobile. 'Yeah, you've been through the system, I'd bet my reputation on it. Let's find out what you've been up to.'

'Fine,' Metcalfe said. 'I'm on the register. They found some stuff on my computer. I don't know how it got there. There were other people living in the same shared house. I was fitted up. I did my time. So why don't you leave me alone?'

'Because,' Moone said, 'you're looking after, and poorly I might add, the home of another sex offender. Now, why don't you tell us where Malcolm West is?'

'Funny thing is,' Butler muttered to herself as she walked out of the room.

Metcalfe's eyes followed her, then he looked up at Moone. 'Your mate's a right bitch, ain't she? Where's she going?'

'Shut up,' Moone said, then went into the hall to find her, but heard her footsteps travelling up the uncarpeted stairs. He followed and found her standing in a bedroom that was either slept in by the most cleanliness obsessed occupant or wasn't used at all.

'There's something bloody funny going on here,' Butler said, and turned to Moone. 'Does this place look like anyone actually lives here?'

'No, it doesn't. What you thinking? They've got some other hideaway?'

She huffed. 'Maybe some dark little corner where they like to share their...'

Butler stopped talking at the sound of a door closing downstairs.

'What the fuck?' Moone said, then bolted towards the stairs and down them with Butler coming down after him.

They reached the living room and saw it was empty, just the whiff of sweat and grime in the air.

'Shit,' Moone said.

Butler stabbed a finger into his chest. 'Are you for fucking real?'

'Me?'

'Yeah, you bloody left him alone!'

'I just...' Moone stared out at the garden, then sighed and buried his face in his hands. 'Right, OK, my fucking bad. Let's just dig around into any other known associates of the Scarlett paedophile.'

Butler rolled her eyes. 'You're so fucking childish. Come on, let's go.'

As they reached the car, Moone said, 'We've still got the killer of a skinned dead man to find.'

Butler opened the car. 'I've had the team going through CCTV footage but there's nothing yet. Still doing door-to-door, but nothing so far. Maybe the mother-in-law can shed some light.'

'What about his work laptop?' Moone climbed in.

'It's being brought in tomorrow.' Butler started the engine.

'You're very efficient.'

She looked at him, blankly. 'One of us has to be.'

It was a grotty looking flat over Mutley, the short strip of takeaways, pubs and supermarkets between North Hill and Hyde Park. He'd drawn the pink flowery curtains and stared down at the pedestrians through a slither of a gap. Nobody looked up, just kept walking by. He could spot the junkies, they were the ones that had hardly any skin on their bones, and a vacant, addled look in their eyes. There was usually two of them, a bloke and a woman, a kind of drug-taking team. More scum, more useless tossers on the streets.

He turned and looked towards the pink sofa, where the thing, the disgusting creature, was lying half on the sofa, half on the beige carpet. He turned away, fighting the urge to be sick at the sight of it.

Disgusting.

Disgusting little pervert.

The pervert moved, groaned, eyes flickering.

He rushed over, drew back his fist and smashed it down into the thing's face. It rolled down, falling face down onto the carpet, so he sat down on the sofa, thinking, looking round the flat. He got up and went to the small kitchen behind him, separated from the living room by a wall with a hatch in it. He started by going through the cupboards and found a bottle of vodka, opened it and took a few swigs. Then he checked the cupboard under the sink and found some household products and put them on the work surface. After that, still swigging from the bottle, he went slowly into the only bedroom, just over the hall from the kitchen. A laugh burst from his mouth when he stood in the doorway and saw the double bed which had a flowery red and black duvet neatly tucked over it. There was a dresser, and an old wooden wardrobe in the corner. The whole place stank of old ladies' perfume.

He put down the bottle of vodka and went to the wardrobe and pulled it open. The same old lady smells poured out at him, gassing him straight in the face. The wardrobe was crammed with dresses and cardigans and skirts. There seemed to be no clothes that a man might own.

He gripped the wardrobe doors, lowered his head, and let out a deep roar, then started kicking the glass mirror that ran up the wardrobe, smashing it. He pulled out the clothes, throwing them everywhere, across the bed, the floor, then spun round and grabbed the dresser and knocked it over.

He stood, panting, looking down at the mess, then slowly fell to his knees. He let his hand reach out, travelling across the bristly carpet and then onto the soft material of a light blue dress. He dragged it back towards himself, pulling it up to his face.

As he held it close to his face, he buried his head into the dress, as a cascade of memories poured over him and he started to cry uncontrollably.

The pervert.

The scumbag pervert.

He jumped to his feet, took another swig of

vodka, then went storming into the lounge and grabbed the pervert by the back of its dress and dragged it along the hallway and towards the back door.

He stepped over the body, then went to the kitchen and put all the household products in a bin bag and carried them through the back door and down a short flight of iron steps to the tiny yard below. The rain had eased off, and he tipped his head back and looked up into the ash-tinged clouds that only allowed him a glimpse of blue sky.

He went back up the steps, looking down on the similar back yards and the cobblestone lane, to make sure no one was paying him any attention. The only thing that looked his way, was a ginger cat that stopped and stared at him for a moment then scrambled up a wall and onto a garage roof.

The pervert was skinny, just smooth skin and bones, but he still struggled to get it down the iron steps and into the yard. He laid the thing out across the damp cobblestones, then poured the contents of the bin bags over it. He stepped back, then saw a small wall behind him and sat down and stared at the perverted little shit.

Dirty, scumbag little pervert.

He decided to fetch the bottle of vodka, then came back to find the creature coming to, blinking up into the air, wondering what was going on, moaning and groaning.

Then it bent its head forwards, fighting to get up, its makeup and lipstick smeared across its face, mixed with dried blood.

'Please,' it said, tears in its eyes. 'Help me.'

'All right,' he said, then walked over as the thing reached out a hand. He slapped the hand away, making the creature flinch back.

But he climbed on top of it, beating away its arms as it tried to protect itself.

'Dirty, filthy…' He slapped its face, making it beg and whimper. 'Dirty little pervert… you filthy fucking freak…'

He slapped away the arms that clawed at him again, then landed a punch on its jaw, snapping the pervert's head against the flagstone floor. He breathed hard, watching the thing as its eyes swirled, confusion and realisation of the bad thing that was about to happen to it.

Punishment. Punishment for wickedness.

'You're evil,' he whispered, but the thing shook its head, so he grasped it round its stringy throat and clenched tight. It struggled, its legs kicking, digging into the ground, the bony hands reaching up, fighting, trying to tear at his face. He turned his face away, still squeezing, listening to the thing as the hole in its face opened and a strange whining, wet noise came out.

Then nothing, and the hands slowly drifted downwards, the legs not moving anymore. The eyes wide but seeing nothing.

He stayed astride the thing, looking down

into the eyes that held him, silently, accusingly. He closed his eyes and looked away, putting his hands on the flagstones, pushing himself up to his full height, feeling dizzy with all the feelings rushing through him. He'd felt powerful as he gripped the thing's neck and felt the life flood out, but now he was empty, dry, lost and lusting after the feeling again. He'd been in control for once, able to decide what would happen, who would be punished and who wouldn't.

He stumbled backwards, found the wall of the house, and looked down at the lifeless thing. He poured the remaining chemicals over the pathetic creature, then found the box of matches, struck one and threw it.

Immediately the flames sprung from the match and ran hungrily all over the thing, eating, hunting for more, sending smoke into the air.

He picked up the bottle of drink and smashed it on the body. The flames coughed and spat, but then kept on raging.

He opened the back gate, and stepped out, knowing there were more creatures out there that needed punishing.

CHAPTER 7

The dawn advertised itself over the water, a shimmer of electric blue that danced over the deeply black water. Everything was dark grey, especially the fortified building Carl Mathieson was staring at from the car park he was parked in. He looked about the darkened interior of the car, only the light from his mobile phone illuminating the small space. He kept checking to see if he had any messages, while his heart kept filling every part of him with its constant thud. He leaned forward, tapped his head on the steering wheel that wasn't even his; he'd borrowed a friend's car, telling them that his was in the garage. He could see the questions in their eyes, but they knew better than to start digging, so handed over the keys with only a few polite words.

He saw movement in the rear-view mirror, but when he looked again he saw only the empty spaces behind him, and the shadowy outline of the restaurant.

When the back door opened, he jumped, put a hand to his chest.

'For fuck's sake,' he said as a wiry, dirty looking man slipped onto the back seat, clutching a canvas satchel.

Even in the darkness of the car, Mathieson thought he looked wrong, as if Mother Nature had decided to assemble him in such a strange way that it would force him to become strange.

'Did I scare you?' the man asked, the same hint of a Midlands accent somewhere in his rough, grating voice.

'Why'd you have to sneak up?'

'I thought we were hiding from prying eyes?' the man, Malcolm West, looked into his satchel as if to check something precious was still there, then looked up. 'Are they onto us?'

'You lot,' Mathieson said. 'Not me. I'm not part of your dirty little club.'

'Are you sure?' West asked, and Mathieson looked in the rearview mirror to see him grinning, showing that he had several missing teeth. A large part of him wanted to climb into the back seat and do exactly what most people might want to do. In fact, he sat there in a daydream for a moment, imagining what it would be like to hammer his fists into the man until he was no longer breathing. But he would be caught, there was little doubt about that, and although the man was one of the kind that the world likes to detest and demonise, the justice system would churn on, and send him away for the rest of his life.

'You can join at any time,' West said. 'You just have to ask.'

'Don't you dare. I'm only here because of the arrangement... if it comes out, then we're all fucked. I'll lose everything.'

There were dull footsteps coming across the car park, and whoever they were did not like to pick up their feet. The scraping sound got louder and louder until the other door opened and another man sat on the backseat. He looked at Mathieson, then West, his eyebrows raised, his hand brushing his thin, quite long hair from his washed-out face.

'What?!' he said, looking between them. 'You two look scared shitless! You ain't just been fingered by the filth! How do you think I feel?'

Mathieson swung round in his seat, bending his head to stare at the greasy-haired man, while his heart and body trembled at the idea of it all. 'The police? The police have been to see you?'

'Calm down, Carl...'

'Don't say my fucking name!' Mathieson showed his teeth, feeling so close to doing it, so near to getting out, opening the boot and seeing if there was a tyre iron inside.

Metcalfe tutted, rolled his eyes and looked

at West. 'He's so dramatic. I got grabbed when I went in your place, Malcolm. They must've been sat outside...'

'The fuckers, the pig bastards,' West grumbled and gripped his satchel tighter to his stomach.

'Why are you not locked up, then?' Mathieson asked, suspicion slithering across his back.

'They left me downstairs while they had a nose about.' Metcalfe chuckled to himself, shook his head. 'Stupid bastards. I could've pissed myself laughing.'

'I can't see anything to laugh at,' the MP said. 'This is my career, my reputation and you lot... you're all just liabilities. They'll come for you again. They won't give up.'

'You should've seen them,' Metcalfe said, leaning forward, poisoning the air with his musty odour. 'It was like watching Laurel and Hardy.'

Mathieson put his face in his hands, shaking his head then turned to face Metcalfe. 'Who were they? Did you get any names?'

'One of them was a bitch I've seen before... called Butler. She's a DS. The other I didn't know. Sounded like a fucking cockney, fresh off the boat if you ask me.'

The sickness rose up through Mathieson, the realisation of what Metcalfe had told him pouring over him, soaking him head to foot. 'He's from London? You think he's just started here?'

'How the fuck do I know?' Metcalfe said, so Mathieson pushed open the door and walked round to the back. He pulled open the door, grabbed Metcalfe by his collar and dragged him out, then shoved him against the car.

'What the fuck!' Metcalfe moaned, his face red, his bony hands adjusting his clothes. 'What the fuck you think you're doing? MP or no MP, you don't get to push me around!'

Mathieson had had enough. The MP grasped Metcalfe by his coat and pulled him towards him, gritting his teeth, letting the pervert see how pissed off he was. 'You stupid, fucking... you're scum...'

'I'm scum!' Metcalfe let out a laugh. 'Listen to him! He's a politician! Do you know how many of your lot like what we like? Most of the fuckers! And let's not get personal, cause then we'd have to start looking closer to home, wouldn't we, Your Highness?!'

Mathieson pulled back his fist, ready to give in to the rage pounding through him.

West got out the car and came rushing round, poking his ugly face between them. 'Oi! Leave it! We've got to sort all this out!'

Mathieson let go of Metcalfe and looked at his hands then made a show of wiping them on his trousers, letting the disgust show on his face. 'You're weak, that's your trouble. You can't control yourselves. Now look at all this...'

West pointed a black painted nail at him.

'Us? This is your mess too!'

The MP walked away, thinking it all over, wondering about the newbie police officer. 'What was his name? This detective?'

Metcalfe scratched at his face, looked towards the sky for a moment. 'Oh, Moone? Yeah, think that's it. Why?'

Mathieson let out an empty, pitiless laugh. 'That's fucking great. That's wonderful, it's all I need.'

'You know him?' Metcalfe asked.

'Mind your own fucking business. I've got contacts. I can try and make this go away.'

West laughed. 'You're having us on, aren't you? Make this go away? What about Ian? And what about his lord and master up there staying at Her Majesty's fucking pleasure? What about him?'

Mathieson rubbed his eyes, noticed the sun was now sending a deep red beam across the water. It was time to go.

'Ian?' Mathieson asked. 'Who the bloody hell is Ian?'

'Ian Macdonald,' West said, then rolled his eyes at Metcalfe. 'Don't he pay attention? Ian Macdonald. He's the one, you know, who grabbed him. He's bound to squeal on us. He's got grass written all over him. Then you can kiss your job goodbye and say hello to Dartmoor!'

'Jesus...' Mathieson turned away, the sight of the bright new day, hardly a cloud in the sky, making him sick to his stomach. There would no more bright days, no more steak dinners in Westminster, no chance of doing any good, if the truth got out. The words formed in his mind, the unedited truth, but he let them gestate for a moment, sickened by what he was about to say.

'You two,' he said, pointing at them both, hardly able to the look them in the eye. 'You've got to take care of it, you need to deal with him.'

'Deal with him?' West pointed a thumb at himself. 'Us? What do you mean?'

'He can't talk, this can't get out. That's what I'm saying. I'm not going to go to prison. I can't. You've got to make sure he doesn't say anything to anyone. Do you understand me?'

This time, Moone drove himself to the crime scene, after sipping a coffee he'd made in the caravan and put in a flask cup, deciding to get to know the lay of the land. Luckily, he had a sat-nav fitted in his second-hand Renault, so a cold sounding woman dictated the way towards the centre of Plymouth. Butler's call had told him to head for Mutley, a short strip of shops and take-aways. It was student central, she informed him coldly, then hung up.

He was getting pretty pissed off with his partner's shortness and started to wonder how he could ingratiate himself with her and the rest of the team. Maybe she might be into football, he thought and wondered if he could get them tickets for a Plymouth Argyle game.

Then he stopped dead, foot down on the brake when the satnav woman informed him he'd arrived at his destination, but he saw no signs of any incident. The road was quiet, not even one pedestrian walking down the street.

He heard it first, then saw in his rear-view mirror the flashing blue lights of an incident response car racing down the main road, so he turned the car around and followed it. Two roads away, in a small close, he found police tape fluttering in the wind, and three Devon and Cornwall police cars parked along the bend of the street while a single fire engine was parked a little way up from them.

Butler was talking to three uniforms, one of which was PC Carthew. Moone parked up, then strolled over, sipping his slightly warm coffee from his flask cup.

By the time he reached Butler, she had her arms folded across her chest and started walking towards the house that seemed to be getting all the attention.

'You took your time,' she said, directing him towards an alleyway alongside the house that led to a cobblestoned back lane. A line of washing could be seen flapping in the wind, stretched high above a garage that backed onto the lane. Butler went through the garden gate and directed Moone into an untidy yard. He entered as a rancid smell raced up and clasped his face. His eyes jumped to the blackened shape near the back wall, sprawled out amongst a patch of singed weeds and grass that had sprouted through the flagstones.

'I got lost,' he said, then walked round the charred human-shaped silhouette.

'Don't you have a map yet?' she asked, pulling on some latex gloves, while a SOCO came past them and began snapping away with a large camera.

'A map? Are we living in the dark ages?' He knelt close to the body, avoiding the evidence markers.

'Neighbours smelt it,' she said.

'I'm not bloody surprised.'

'Burnt human flesh,' a voice said behind them. 'That's not a smell you ever get out of your nostrils.'

Moone turned and saw Dr Lee Parry staring down at the body, done up in his blue hooded outfit. 'Cause of death?'

'Not sure,' he said. 'But I think the fire was started after they were dead. As you can see the fire was contained in this area... it was fuelled by the clothes and fat, then burned itself out.'

'I take it that it wasn't spontaneous human combustion?' Butler asked, a smirk on her face.

'Well, apart from the fact that little phenomenon doesn't exist,' Parry said, 'the fire team found evidence of accelerants, and a box of matches was lying very close to your feet. Also, there's remains of a broken vodka bottle. Looks like it was smashed near the body.'

'They were drinking during the whole thing?' Moone shook his head.

'Shows you the kind of sick mind we're dealing with,' Butler said.

'Male or female?' Moone asked and saw Parry's eyes ignite a little and his gloved finger point in his direction. 'Now that's the interesting question.'

'Why's it so bloody interesting?' Butler asked, as Parry knelt close to the victim.

'See this?' Parry took some charred material in his hand and gently pulled it apart to show them. 'This I believe is the remnants of women's clothing. But anatomically, this used to be a man...'

'Shit,' Moone said, absently reaching for his cigarettes. 'He's done it again, the bastard's actually killed again... already.'

'We don't know that,' Butler said. 'There are such things as coincidence. We don't know for sure that he or she, whatever they liked to be called, didn't set fire to themselves.'

'Jed,' a voice said behind them.

Moone turned along with Butler and Parry to see Carthew stood at the top of the iron staircase, holding something like a wallet in her gloved hand.

'Found an old wallet in a drawer,' Carthew

said. 'His name was Jed Dalton. There's a few recent birthday cards too. I think he or she, sorry,
called herself Jane.'

Moone met Carthew at the bottom of the
iron steps and took the wallet from her, seeing
a quite plain, androgynous looking man staring
out at him.

'Found this photo too,' Carthew said, holding out a snap, which Butler snatched away.

Moone looked over Butler's shoulder and
saw that she was holding a photograph taken in
a pub, Jane all dressed up, makeup on, bobbed
brown wig in place, a female friend on one side, a
bearded man on the other. They all looked happy,
holding drinks in their hands. Jane was wearing
a large badge on her chest with "50" printed on it.

'Shame,' Butler said. 'They look happy.'

'This can't be a coincidence,' Moone said,
heading to the body once more, staring down at
it, trying to engage his brain. An espresso would
help, he thought. 'He skinned his first victim,
trying to remove evidence of what they were...'

'Maybe this is the same thing,' Carthew said,
and reddened when everyone turned to her.

'What do you mean?' Moone asked.

'Well...' Carthew stood next to Moone. 'The
fire, it's destructive, it burns, cleanses...'

'That's brilliant,' Moone said.

'Big bloody deal,' Butler said and huffed.
'He likes to remove evidence of what they were,
doesn't get us any closer to why he did this, or

who he is.'

'If he hates people like Jane...' Moone said, 'then maybe he might've belonged to a hate group... right wing group or something.'

'It's possible.' Butler took out her notebook and wrote something down. 'We can check out local groups. We'll continue looking through similar attacks and murders. If we do have a serial offender on our hands...'

'What?' Moone asked.

She turned and stared at him as she said, 'Looks like you brought the fucking weather with you, doesn't it?'

'We need to find our primary crime scene,' Moone said, then headed up the metal stairs, looking over the lines and rows of terrace houses that converged on the high street. He stepped through to a small kitchen, then a narrow brightly decorated hallway and along to a small lounge. SOCOs were photographing the scene, concentrating on the sofa area, where the cushions were displaced, and spots of blood were spread across one arm.

'A struggle?' Moone asked.

One of the white suits turned towards him, revealing a quite pretty face even though the tight hood forced her cheeks out. 'Marie Gaze. Crime scene manager.'

'DI Peter Moone,' he said, smiling. 'Was there a fight here?'

She let out a heavy breath. 'I don't think a

fight would be the right term. There's signs at the front door of an altercation. I found blood on the door, where I think the victim was forced towards it, probably hitting their head, then probably dragged inside, put here... maybe they came to and the assailant punched them. The blood here would back up my theory... spatter from a powerful blow.'

Moone nodded. 'Maybe we are dealing with some kind of right-wing yob.'

Gaze shrugged. 'Could be. How can anyone do something like this?'

'I don't know. But I'm going to try and find out.' Moone turned when he heard Butler talking, and saw her on her mobile.

She put it away, then came over to him, her eyes scanning the sofa and then back to his face. 'That was DC Harding. He's been looking into similar recent attacks, found one, nearly a year ago. Gay man attacked on his way home.'

Moone looked over the lounge again. 'OK. Let's go and talk to the victim.'

CHAPTER 8

They parked under the shadow of one of the recently built Plymouth University buildings, another monstrous glass and brown-painted steel construction that had appeared over the last few years, Butler informed Moone. She sounded pissed off as she pointed out that Plymouth University and the student facilities that came hand in hand with it all was expanding, creeping outwards, pushing everything else aside. She made it sound like university life in the city was an uncontrollable blob sent from another planet.

As they walked into a set of revolving glass doors and across a large foyer that echoed with the chatter of students, Butler kept on moaning about the city's student life and the high jinks that cost the taxpayer plenty in drunken hospital visits and the like.

'You don't like students then?' Moone asked as they reached the top of a long white and highly polished set of stairs.

'I don't mind students,' she said as they walked past a crowded cafe, 'as long as they're studying or listening to some self-righteous know it all that calls themselves a lecturer. I just don't want them running amok. It's changing the whole face of the city, making it ugly.'

'Where are we going?'

'In here,' Butler said, then pushed through a door and into a large oblong room fitted out with computers, desks, and whiteboards that lined the walls.

At the far end of the room, by the wide expanse of windows, sat a man, early forties with receding dark hair, wearing a dark brown blazer. He was hunched over some paperwork as they approached and showed their identification.

'DS Mandy Butler,' Butler said, then nodded towards Moone. 'This is DI Peter Moone. You're Colin Samson, yes?'

He frowned, sitting up straight and folding his arms across his chest. 'That's right. Have I done something I don't know about?'

'You reported a violent assault about a year ago,' Moone said, leaning on the desk. 'We'd like to talk to you about it.'

Samson sat up even straighter, looking unimpressed. 'Well, I must say you've taken your time about it. Last time I talked to you lot, no one seemed the slightest bit bothered about it.'

'Sorry you feel like that,' Butler said, 'But we

still need to talk to you about the attack on you.'

'No,' Samson said, shaking his head.

'No?' Moone asked.

'Wasn't me who was assaulted,' Samson said, then got up, picked up his paperwork and dropped it into a filing cabinet. 'It was a friend of mine.'

'A friend?' Butler asked, which made Samson stop and stare at her.

'Yes, a friend,' he said, folding his arms again. 'A close friend. You do know I'm gay, yes?'

'Yeah,' Butler said. 'We don't care about that...'

'You don't care?' Samson asked.

Butler shook her head. 'That came out wrong. I mean...'

Moone came closer. 'We're investigating a spate of attacks on crossdressers...'

'If you cross-dress, it doesn't mean you're gay,' Samson said. 'Most crossdressers are heterosexual males, if there is such a thing these days.'

'Well,' Moone said. 'We believe the attacker has it in for anyone that doesn't fit his idea of normal. Your friend, the one who was attacked, he's not gay?'

Samson let out a sigh. 'I don't know. I thought he was, well, I'm pretty sure he is, but he was still very much in the closet then. I don't know about now. After the attack, well, we drifted apart.'

'Sorry to hear that,' Moone said. 'What's

your friend called?'

'Kieran,' he said. 'Kieran Dobson.'

Butler took out her notebook. 'Do you know where we might find him?'

Samson sat back down. 'Well, at the time he was living with his mother, off of Ham Drive. She was pretty much bedridden then, you know... had a lot of health issues. Smoked like a chimney though.'

Moone nodded, rolled his eyes, but the comment only reminded him that he was dying for a cigarette. 'If you could jot down the address, that would be great.'

'Right, OK,' the lecturer said, then grabbed a sheet of paper, neatly folded it and tore off a piece. He wrote down the address and handed it to Moone.

'I hope he's OK these days,' Samson said, looking regretful. 'He always struggled with it all. That happening to him... I worry that it might have driven him back into the closet. I just hope he's OK.'

Butler huffed, folded her arms. 'If you're expecting us to pass on your regards, we don't do that. We're not a dating agency.'

Moone watched Butler turn round and storm out of the room, then turned to the lecturer who was a little open mouthed. 'I'm sorry, it's not you. I seem to have rubbed her up the wrong way. Thanks for everything.'

Moone turned to go, then looked at Samson

again. 'I'll pass on the message.'

Moone looked either side of the road, Ham Drive as he saw it was called, staring towards the woodland that seemed to be hiding a little below the road, and he only saw glimpses of it until it disappeared behind a school then a row of houses. Houses that were quite different to each other lined the other side of the road, some with large grey roofs that overlapped the house in a similar way that a mushroom cap overlaps its stalk.

He smoked as he drove, his window open. It was quite warm, although the clouds cut out most of the blue sky and threatened another deluge of rain.

Butler took her car into the next turning on the right, which was a long road that snaked all the way to the opening of the woods. Moone got out, stubbed out his fag, then headed towards Butler. The road was filled with the kind of box houses that were built after the Second World War, prefab buildings now pebble-dashed and painted to look like regular houses. Over on the other side of the road a young man in a vest and shorts, covered in tattoos, revved a motorbike on his driveway. The rest of the road was empty, and kid's bikes and toys sat abandoned on untidy front gardens, alongside car parts and rusty white goods.

As Moone reached Butler, she stopped and looked at him. 'I've been thinking, we're spread pretty thinly over all this... two investigations, I mean... a child murder and some psycho attacking gay men...'

'What're you trying to say?' He knew exactly what she was trying to say, but he'd be fucked if he was going to make it easier on her.

She looked towards the house they were about to knock at. 'I don't know, just that maybe one of us should be leading one investigation and the other, the other.'

'I'm in charge,' Moone said, feeling anger rise in him for the first time since he'd arrived in Plymouth.

'Yes, you are, but...'

'I'm in charge... so I say we're going to keep going as we are. End of story.'

As Moone pressed the doorbell, Butler said, 'We're no closer to finding out what happened to Danny Sawyer.'

'I know that. We're waiting to see if anything forensically useful comes off the remains.'

'Which is doubtful, because they've been in the ground so long.'

'Yes, I know. Then we keep talking to the usual suspects in the area. One of them must know...'

'They've all been talked to before.' Butler pressed the bell again. 'Is this bloody thing working?'

Moone saw movement out of the corner of his eye and turned towards the lane that ran down the side of the house. A man was stood there, in his late thirties, short brown hair, deep set eyes, a haunted look in them. He wore a shirt with the sleeves rolled up.

'Kieran?' Moone asked as the rain started to hammer down.

'Who're you?' the man asked.

Moone took out his ID and walked towards the man with Butler following. 'DI Peter Moone. Are you Kieran Dobson?'

The man nodded, then came closer to them, pushing his hands into his pockets. 'What's this about? What have I supposed to have done?'

'Nothing,' Butler said, looking up towards the falling rain. 'Can we get in the dry?'

Kieran Dobson let them in through the back door, which was actually positioned on the side of the house, facing the lane. Moone smelt the smell of the elderly as soon as he stepped inside, walking through a narrow kitchen that desperately needed redecoration, and into an oblong cramped lounge. The wallpaper was flowery, the furniture old and worn. The rain was still hammering against the windows, but a little sunlight had managed to break the clouds and beamed through the grimy net curtains.

Moone was the only one who sat down,

deciding to sit on the sofa, while Kieran rested against an old sixties style corner unit, and Butler stood, arms folded in the doorway to the room.

'What's happened?' Kieran asked, his eyes watchful, glancing from him to Butler.

'We wanted to ask you about the assault on you that happened about a year ago,' Moone said, taking out his notebook.

'That?' Kieran folded his arms. 'I'd forgotten all about it... what's that matter now?'

'Someone's been carrying out similar attacks,' Butler said. 'Targeting certain people...'

'Certain people?' Kieran stared at her.

'Two crossdressers...' Butler started to say, but Kieran huffed angrily.

'I'm not a crossdresser!' he said. 'I think you've made a mistake...'

'Gay men,' Butler said. 'We think he might have a thing against gay men... anyone outside his idea of the norm.'

Kieran looked at them both, then shrugged. 'I still don't get it. I'm not... I'm not gay.'

Moone caught Butler's eyes, but she looked away, let out a tired breath and said, 'Colin Samson...we talked to him.'

Kieran Butler let out a laugh and shook his head. 'Oh right. I get it. Yeah, I know him... or knew him... he's gay. He had a thing for me. I think he got a bit obsessed. I tried to be his friend, but then we walked across the park that night...

I suppose the wanker who attacked me must've assumed that we were together, like, you know, he jumped me, kicked the shit out of me.'

'I see.' Moone noted it all down. 'Did you get a good look at him?'

Kieran looked down, shook his head again. 'What? When I was curled up in a ball, having my ribs kicked in? No, I didn't.'

'Did he say anything?' Butler asked.

'Apart from calling me a queer fucker, scum, a shirt lifter? No, nothing. That's all I can remember.'

Moone sat back. 'If you could try and remember something... I know it's hard... after what happened.'

Kieran sighed. 'Sorry, wish I could help.'

Moone nodded and stood up. 'Right then, we won't waste any more of your time.'

This time Kieran took them to the front door, unlocked it and took them through the porch which was piled up with old unopened letters and junk mail.

Moone let Butler head towards her car before he turned back to Kieran Dobson and said, 'I don't know what happened between you and Colin, but he wanted you to know that he hopes you're OK.'

The man looked up the street. 'Thanks. I appreciate that.'

The inside of the station echoed with the beat of the rain and the water cascaded down the windows, while the bodies all around the incident room sat hunched over computers, or phones or both, while others walked the halls or took reports to another part of the building. Moone had a cigarette before heading inside, stood under the smoking shelter near the car park, watching the rain hitting the tarmac and spitting back up into the air, churning everything over in his mind, feeling bad that he had no answers for the parents of little Danny Sawyer. The truth was he didn't know which way to turn, and was tempted to let Butler take the lead. But how would that look to anyone observing, especially the Chief Super?

When Moone reached the desk set up for him in the far corner, he turned round and saw a short, stocky man, probably about fifty, with a shaved head, dressed in a grey well-worn suit. He was leaning against the whiteboard, nursing a mug of coffee, staring at Moone. He had the look of a thug, and Moone found himself looking round the room to see if anyone else had spotted the criminal-looking elephant in the room.

Then an ill-fitting smile appeared on the man's face as he came toward Moone and put his coffee in front of him. 'DSU Michael Stack. Nice to meet you.'

Moone noted he didn't have a West Country accent or one he could place. 'DI Moone. So, you're in charge?'

'Someone's got to be,' he said, putting his hands behind his back. 'So, you're from the big smoke? That's right, isn't it?'

'Yep. It's good to get away really...'

Stack nodded, his eyes jumping round the room before his gaze returned to Moone. 'My job is to police you, you get that?'

Moone sat up a little, realising what the conversation was really about. 'I understand.'

Then the DSU was leaning in, staring into Moone's eyes, his coffee breath swamping his face. 'You may think you were the big man in London, but you're nothing here... nothing. I'm the big man. I've got a question for you. Why the fuck did you go and visit Danny Sawyer's parents?'

'I thought they needed updating...'

'Updating? Updating on fucking what? Oh, unless you had some kind of definitive knowledge that those bones belong to the Sawyer kid? Did you?'

'No...'

'No, what?'

'No, sir.'

Stack straightened up, glaring at him. 'That's right, Moone. I don't know how they do it in London, but here they wait for the DNA results before even thinking about visiting the fucking parents.'

Moone nodded. 'Right, yes...'

'Poor fucking bastards. Haven't they suffered enough? Jesus.' He pointed at Moone. 'You better watch it, because I'm watching you. You better be on your best behaviour and impress me. I might even pat you on the head now and again... but do something like that again or fuck me around, and start acting like a cockwomble and I'll have you, I mean it, I'll fuck you over. And we don't want any fucking extra expenditures. In case you haven't heard, the police forces of this country are fucking broke. Got it?'

'Got it,' Moone said.

The DSU picked up his mug of coffee like nothing had happened, took a sip, nodded and walked off out of the room.

'Haven't you got to interview the mum?' a voice said from across the room.

He turned to see Harding staring at him. 'She's here?' Moone said, standing up.

'Yeah, boss. Waiting for you. Room 2.'

When Moone walked into the interview room, Jason Mitchum's mother-in-law let out a heavy, annoyed breath as she touched up her bob of silver hair. She was sat upright at the desk, a mug of something by her arm, a plate of biscuits too. They never had biscuits in London, he thought. Like Stack had pointed out, the police were generally broke, so how did Devon and Cornwall afford biscuits?

'I've been waiting quite a while,' she said, huffing.

'I know,' he said and sat down. 'I'm sorry. We had to talk to another witness who might've been able to help in the investigation into your son-in-law, Jason's, death.'

'I know my son-in-law's name,' she said. 'Did this witness help?'

He sat back, tried to smile. 'I can't really discuss the case, but we're getting somewhere.'

'Somewhere?' She made an unimpressed sound in her throat, which reminded Moone of his mother when he was about to get a bollocking.

'You had information for us?' he asked, trying to avoid the conversation.

'Yes, well, I think so.' She sat up straighter. 'Can I trust you? This is quite delicate.'

'Scout's honour.'

She huffed again, so he said, 'Don't worry, this is all confidential.'

'Well, one day, when Jason was home from work... working from home, he had his laptop on the kitchen table. I don't usually snoop, but he was away a lot with work, it made me suspicious.'

'You looked at his laptop?'

She cleared her throat. 'I know very little about these new-fangled gadgets, but I've learnt a bit. He had a website thing open on his laptop, but it was hidden, small, do you understand?'

'I think so.'

'I opened it up.' She looked away, shook her head. 'It was... well, some photos, disgusting photographs.'

'Pornography?'

She nodded. 'Women... well, not really women. Oh God, makes me feel sick to think of it.'

'Take your time.' Hurry up!

'Women, but with... I mean, they had...' the mother-in-law made the universal gesture for 'breasts', and Moone had to stop himself bursting into laughter.

'But they also had,' she said and looked down. 'They had... thingies.'

'These women had penises?'

The mother-in-law's face flushed scarlet. 'If you want to be crude, then yes.'

Moone nodded. 'Thanks for telling us.'

'He didn't go away with work, did he?'

'Not all the time. Certainly not before he was found...'

'Was he?' She leaned forward. 'Was he one of... them?'

'Gay?'

She huffed, so Moone said, 'We don't know. This website you saw, with the photos... did you see anything else?'

'Yes, I did. It was a kind of dating thing. I remember it said something about dating, finding your match.' She twisted her face and shuddered.

Moone stood up. 'Thank you. Thanks for coming in. You've been a great help.'

When Moone hurried into the incident room, he found Butler, DC Harding and a couple of others from the team stood around talking in raised voices.

They saw him and stopped, with Butler huffing and folding her arms across her chest, staring at him.

DC Harding swore, then rubbed his face, then stormed off to his desk.

'What's going on?'

Butler looked over to Harding. 'A bit of a balls up.'

'Thanks, that's great,' Harding said, hunched over his desk, his jaw grinding.

'What balls up?' Moone asked

Butler walked up to him and said, 'We've been going through the local offenders, right?'

'You talking about the Danny Sawyer case?'

She nodded. 'Yeah. We've been talking to the local sex offenders, the paedophiles... well, we've just got round to looking into this lovely chap over here...'

Moone went with her to the desk near the whiteboard, where Butler gave him an arrest sheet and showed him a mugshot of a man called Ian MacDonald. He perused it, noting that the offender had been arrested and charged with downloading child porn. 'Right, so we talk to him?'

Butler huffed. 'We would. But we can't find him. Looks like he might've done a runner.'

'Great.'

'There's more...'

'I'm sorry, all right!' Harding said, kicking his chair away as he stood up. 'I didn't get round to him now, cause I was looking for people who'd been charged with that kind of stuff before Danny went missing and he was after.'

Moone scratched his head. 'So, he's not in the frame? Am I missing something?'

'Look at where he was living at the time Danny went missing,' Butler said, so Moone looked down at a photo of a map of Plymouth. He realised that Ian Macdonald had been living barely a mile away from the boy's home. 'Shit.'

CHAPTER 9

He had to hurry out of the station, rushing across the pedestrian crossing opposite Charles Cross, then into the monstrous Drake's Circus shopping mall, which echoed with chatter and kids screaming, all the time following Butler's directions. He ignored all the clothes and shoe shops as he made his way past the shiny glass and along polished, gleaming floors, dodging the painfully slow crowds of shoppers. He came out near Marks and Spencer's, and found himself opposite yet another coffee chain, while a man in his sixties started preaching about God and the upcoming apocalypse. A woman was doing a great job of singing Wonderwall a little way up the street, but Moone ignored it all and headed up towards the main road.

He stopped, puffing, finding his cigarettes, and lighting one, as he looked about himself, seeing a church across the street and more impressive buildings. On his side were lots more shops and pubs, which had skanky looking people outside puffing hungrily on fags.

All the time he walked, he felt the growing pressure, the weight of both investigations pressing down on his narrow shoulders. After his last case in London, he'd sworn to himself that he'd avoid the lead position if possible, but here he was doing the same bloody thing all over again, making the same mistakes. Although the result had been a good one, and he'd come out looking a hero – he even had a Queen's Police Medal that he kept in its box and refused to look at – he didn't feel it was down to his own good detective skills. It was luck, blind bloody luck.

Now he had an almighty fuck up to contend with; it wasn't of his making, but he knew where the blame would ultimately lie.

Now he was late for meeting his daughter, but managed to find the Gorge cafe and hurried through the entrance and towards the tables at the back that seemed to be sat under a cream painted cave roof. It was crowded, a queue of people at the till and most of the tables that climbed up towards the back were filled with customers.

Then he saw a slender pale hand waving over the other customers, and his eyes fell to see the light brown, long straight hair of his daughter, Alice. A smile stretched her pale, oval face. She looked skinny, seemed far skinnier than when he'd last seen her.

He sat down at her table, seeing himself and her reflected in the mirrors that covered the walls.

Alice had a half drunk cup of coffee in front of her.

'Sorry I'm late,' he said, smiling, feeling so happy to see a familiar face.

'It's alright,' she said, smiling again. 'I know your life. The life of a copper.'

He nodded. 'You'll have to tell me what you want for your birthday...'

'Which was two days ago,' she said and laughed.

'What?' Moone pulled out his phone, checking the date and seeing she was right. 'Shit, sorry. How the bloody hell? Alice, I'm sorry...'

'It's alright, Dad. It's just a birthday!'

'You're seventeen!'

'I know. I'll tell you what, you can buy me a fry up. They do a delicious big breakfast here.'

'How the hell you do you stay so skinny?'

'I stick my fingers down my throat,' she said, no sign of a smile.

'What?'

She laughed. 'I'm kidding! Bloody hell, Dad!'

He laughed, even though he felt like being sick suddenly, everything that had happened to him in the last few days all landing heavily in his gut. But his eldest daughter, Alice, was here, smiling up at him. The sickness faded away, replaced by a feeling that maybe, just maybe things might be OK.

He went to the counter and ordered them both a big breakfast, another latte for Alice and an Americano for himself, then sat back down and smiled at her. 'I can't believe I'm sitting opposite you in... Plymouth. How you finding it?'

'Plymouth?' she asked. 'I like it. It's definitely a slower pace of life.'

'You still getting the bus? You'll be able to learn to drive soon.'

'I know. That's one of the differences I've noticed about living here. Everyone climbs on the bus, no problem, no aggro, no one hurling abuse at the driver, or trying to stab him... and what's weirder... everyone thanks the driver when they get off!'

'Yep, the only people who thank the driver in London...'

'Are the crazy people!'

They both laughed, but Moone recalled that she'd wanted to talk about something that seemed to be bothering her. 'Didn't you want to talk about something?'

Alice's smile faded, her eyes heading down to the mug in front of her as she nodded a little. 'Yeah, it's Mum.'

He sighed, sat back. 'I see. What's she done?'

She looked up. 'Got herself a boyfriend.'

'OK, that sounds like it should be a good thing.'

'I know, but, well, he's this slimy, smarmy... wanker ...'

'*Alice...*'

'Well, he is. You should see him. You'd hate him. He's totally up his own arse and he's always all over Mum. She thinks the sun shines out of his backside.'

'And you obviously don't, but maybe, and I hate to say it, but maybe she's happy.'

Alice huffed out a laugh. 'Yeah, maybe. She seems it... well, is Mum ever happy?'

'I don't know. I think I always fell short of your mum's expectations. But there you go...'

She nodded, then sat back as a young waitress came over and placed their overloaded plates of food in front of them, then left.

'I don't like him, Dad.' Alice picked up a fork and stabbed at a mushroom.

'Why?'

She shrugged. 'I don't know. Just... you always taught me to listen to my gut about people and my gut says he's a wrong 'un.'

'A wrong 'un? You've been spending too much time with your Uncle Fred. Look, what is it about him?'

She shrugged again. 'I don't know, he's just slimy. For one thing, he's always wearing a suit.'

'I'm always wearing a suit!' Moone said, forking a piece of sausage into his mouth.

'Yeah, but you always wear a suit, in a scruffy kind of way.' She laughed.

'Scruffy. Nice. What does he do for a living? Solicitor? Don't tell me... estate agent?!'

'Worse. He's a local politician.'

'What? Oh, for fu... she really picks them. An MP?'

'For the local area. Look, Dad, could you, you know, do your thing...'

'My thing?'

'Yeah, check him out. See what he's about?' Alice beamed him a smile, using her greatest weapon that she knew he wouldn't be able to say no to.

He sighed, sipped his coffee, then eyed her, pretended to look pissed off. 'OK, fine, what's his name?'

'Carl Mathieson. So, you'll do it? You promise you'll look into his background?'

'Scout's honour.'

Alice narrowed her eyes. 'Nan told me before she died that you were only in the scouts for about a week before you were kicked out!'

Moone grinned, then winked. 'Eat your lunch.'

Butler sat nursing a mug of tea in the little room outside the Chief Super's office, pretending to be interested in a celeb mag on her lap that she occasionally turned the pages of. She was doing anything to avoid the eyes of his PA and any conversation she might engage her in and looking

at the inflated lips and boobs of blonde and brunette bimbos from mostly reality shows was all
she could think of to do.

'How's your mum?' the PA asked.

'Fine,' Butler said, smiled politely, then
looked down at a photograph that highlighted
the cellulite on the back of a bikini-clad celeb's
legs. They should see her bloody legs, she
thought, it was like someone had dripped cus-
tard down them.

Thankfully she was saved by Laptew opening his door and smiling. 'Come on in, Mandy.
Good to see you.'

She followed him in and sat as he sat,
watching him adjust his black tie and relax in his
chair.

Tosser, she thought. Tosser accountant who
doesn't give a shit about me or the team.

She smiled or at least tried to, she could
feel something uncomfortable happening to her
face, using muscles she rarely used these days.

'How's it all going?' he asked, as if he could
see she was struggling to begin.

'Good,' she said. 'Fine... well, sort of.'

'Sort of?' He sat forward, put his fingers together. 'Is DI Moone settling in OK?'

She sighed. 'That's the thing, Sir. Me and
Moone, with all due respect, he doesn't understand us down here... he's not lived in Plymouth
very long and...'

'No, he hasn't, Mandy. He's spent years

working in London, working on some very diffi-cult cases.'

'I've worked some difficult cases myself...' she could feel her neck and chest redden as it al-ways did when she got pissed off.

He held up a hand. 'I know. I know you have. You're one of my shining stars...'

She balled her fist, wanting to plant it right between his legs.

He looked at her, nodded to himself. 'Is this because I put Moone in charge and not you?'

'No, I haven't made DI yet. I haven't got the rank.'

'But you will. And you will lead a major murder inquiry... in time. I put Moone in charge because I wanted to see if he'd sink or swim, and to see how you two would work together. There's things you don't know about Moone that perhaps you should...'

'Like what, sir?'

'His last two cases, they were particularly tough cases. He proved himself a hero during the last one. He even received the Queen's Police Medal.'

'Bloody hell...'

'Exactly. Before that he lost a colleague dur-ing a hostage situation at his own police station. His psychological report said he blames himself. So, you see, he's been through a lot. But his former CO couldn't recommend him enough.'

Butler nodded, while feeling like a complete

bitch. 'I see. Well, in that case I'll go easy. Give him another chance.'

'Good,' the Chief Superintendent said and stood up and reached out his hand. 'And I promise you, Mandy, when you make DI, you'll get to head a major murder inquiry team.'

She took his hand, felt his tight grip, saw the political smile in his eyes. 'Thanks, Sir. I appreciate that.'

Tosser, she whispered under her breath as she headed out of the office, her head down, trying to avoid the eyes and conversation of his PA.

Moone stood in front of the team, ready to give them the latest rundown, the flavour of coffee and the fry up fresh on his breath, thinking about Alice and what she'd asked him to do.

Butler came through the door, but didn't apologise for being late, just folded her arms across her chest and stared at him, waiting, like all the rest of the team.

DSU Stack was sat across the room, watching, nursing another mug of coffee.

'Gather round,' Moone said. 'Right, as you know we are working two difficult cases. The first, the death of Jason Mitchum, well, it's the one we have more to go on. As you know we found Mitchum with his skin partly removed his body and the tips of his fingers and toes removed. It seems likely that Jason was a crossdresser, his own mother-in-law informed me this morning that she saw a website on his laptop that was to do with dating she-males...'

'Chicks with dicks?' Harding said, laughing, looking round the room but only getting a few smiles back.

'For want of a more PC phrase,' Moone said, 'yes. We're having his laptop checked out now by our IT team.'

'He's called Barry,' a woman's voice said from the corner. Moone turned to see a young woman with dark bobbed hair, a pale face, a few freckles over it.

'I'm sorry?' he asked.

'The IT team,' the woman said. 'He's not a team... he's one guy. Called Barry. But he knows what he's doing.'

'Thanks, Molly,' Butler said. 'Now listen.'

'Thanks.' Moone looked over their faces, breathing in, ready to talk more about the case. 'So far we've been looking at similar cases, involving attacks on crossdressers, transsexuals and gay men. Not much has come back, we're trying to identify a male who attacked a man called Kieran Dobson, but we haven't got much to go on. Now we turn to the discovery of a child's remains adjacent to the body of Jason Mitchum. We're still waiting on DNA which could take some time, but it looks likely it could be the remains of Danny Sawyer, who went missing over two years ago.'

He noticed most of them looked down at their notebooks or desks, perhaps as a mark of respect or even shame at not having been able to bring closure for the parents. 'Any news on the toy we found in the grave?'

It was Molly who sat up and cleared her throat. 'Not much to go on. I've been trawling through kids' websites and online toy shops, but so far I've not been able to find a toy the same. Sorry.'

'Thanks,' Moone said. 'We've yet to locate Ian Macdonald, who we now know was living not far from the spot where Danny went missing.'

There came a deep groan from Harding has he hunched further over. 'My fuck up, everyone... for fuck's sake...'

Moone looked round the room, his mind whirring, thinking back to his days at Edmonton nick. 'It's not your fuck up, Keith. It's our fuck up... we're a team.'

Harding looked up at him, a look of confusion on his face, so Moone said, 'You wouldn't believe the fuck ups I had working in London, major murder inquiries and I'd go and cause some great big balls up. We had a commander who was, well, he was a Cupid stunt, as they say in my neck of the woods.'

Moone smiled as they all laughed and looked at each other as if they knew what he was talking about.

'Tell us one of your balls ups,' someone

called out.

Moone nodded, smiled, even though his many mistakes came rushing towards him, filling him full of regret.

'DI Moone hasn't got time for this,' Butler said, stepping forward.

'It's all right,' Moone said and he cleared his throat. 'I was working on a serial murder case. It was one of my last. We had a nutter going round stealing the identities of innocent men and then killing them. Turns out the killer was hiding in plain sight. He was working close to us. Thing was, I could've stopped him... I had my chance, but I fucked it up, I was too slow on the uptake. So, some of my team were hurt, two of them died, because of me.'

The room was silent for a moment, everyone staring at him, and he felt the burn of embarrassment rushing all over him, not knowing what to say next.

'Come on, come on,' Butler called out, slapping her hands together. 'Let's get out there and find Ian Macdonald, let's talk to his family, his friends, if he's got any, let's find where this toy came from. You've got your actions on the board, go and get to it... let's find Danny Sawyer's killer!'

As they all got noisily up, chatting and making jokes, collecting their stuff together, Moone just stood and watched, the memories he'd tucked away, that had haunted him for so long, all swirling around inside him, playing in front of his eyes, making his heart pound, the adrenaline kicking in. He recalled what the police psychologist had taught him and put it all into little boxes, turned down the volume, took away the colour, and then shrunk them all until they disappeared.

'Nice try,' Butler said behind him, so he turned and saw her stood by the whiteboard, arms folded across her chest.

'Nice try?'

'Using the deaths of your colleagues to ingratiate yourself with your new team,' she said bluntly.

'I wasn't, they asked...'

She waved away his words. 'Let's just get on and try and catch up...'

His mouth opened, but nothing came out as Butler swung round and headed towards the doors. She was stopped in her tracks by PC Carthew who opened the door and said, 'Got Colin Samson downstairs. Says he got something to tell you.'

CHAPTER 10

The lecturer looked worried when they entered the interview room, sat at the desk, a cup of tea in his hands. Some people are terrified by authority, Moone thought and saw panic and fear in the man's eyes. So Moone smiled and sat opposite him, followed by Butler.

'You wanted to tell us something?' Moone said.

He nodded, cleared his throat. 'I'm not sure if it'll help, or if it's even relative, but that day, when Kieran was attacked... I remember something that happened as we went into the park...'

'Go on,' Butler said, sitting back, arms folded as always.

'Well, we'd been to the Brit for something to eat,' Samson said.

'He means the Britannia pub,' Butler said to Moone. 'Carry on.'

'Yes, the Britannia. Then we headed towards

the park, just for a walk. I'd always leave Kieran there and he'd catch a bus home afterwards. Well, as we were heading towards the park, we heard shouting... a man and woman screaming at each other. The woman was pushing a pram, there was a baby in it, poor thing... anyway, they were not happy people, but the man, he was really aggressive, he had that thuggish look about him, if you understand what I mean?'

Moone nodded. 'I know. Go on.'

Samson nodded. 'Well, I guess we must have been staring, because he turned to us, saw us looking and said something. It wasn't very nice.'

'What did he say?' Butler asked.

'He said something like "what are you looking at, you queers" or something like that. But it was the way he said it. That look in his eyes, like he wanted to do something very violent.'

'How did he know you were gay?' Butler asked.

Samson let out a tired breath. 'It wasn't rocket science. I had a Plymouth Pride T-shirt on. We hurried into the park. I didn't see him again, but what if he followed us and caught up with Kieran?'

Moone sat back. 'It's possible. Sounds like a bit of a strange coincidence otherwise. Can you remember anything about him?'

Samson raised his shoulders. 'Not much. He had short dark hair, looked about thirty maybe, quite muscular. Think he might have had a tattoo on him, on his arm.'

'What sort of tattoo?' Butler asked.

He shrugged. 'Can't remember. Probably something patriotic. Maybe a Union Jack involved in it. But I can't be sure. Sorry...'

Moone sat back, feeling a little deflated, knowing there had to be thousands of thuggish looking, tattoo sporting men in Devon alone; but what if he resided in Cornwall, or somewhere else, maybe even up the line somewhere and was just visiting.

But Butler sat forward. 'Colin... what was his accent like?'

'Oh, right,' Samson said, then he looked up towards the ceiling. 'Local, you know, Plymouth...'

'What was he wearing?' she asked.

'I think... I think a football top. A green one, maybe.'

'Argyle?'

'I think so,' Samson said.

Butler smiled. 'Right. Can you do something for me?'

He looked at her with narrowed eyes, suspicious for a moment. 'OK, what?'

'Close your eyes.'

'Close my eyes?'

'Trust me,' Butler said.

'OK...' He looked at Moone, then Butler, then closed his eyes.

'Good,' Butler said. 'Imagine you're leaving

the Britannia. You're feeling quite full from your food... what did you eat?'

'Er... I had steak. Was nice. Think Kieran had a burger.'

'What was the weather like?'

'Sunny. Quite hot... there was cloud though.'

'You cross the road...'

'Yes, I can hear the couple shouting.'

'Can you see him?'

Samson nodded, his eyes tightly shut.

Moone found himself staring at Butler, feeling surprised, smiling a little as if he was seeing her for the first time.

'Yes... he's wearing a green football top, collar pulled up... it's got... it's got a ship on the front.'

'Look at his body, can you see the tattoos?' Butler asked.

'Yes... there's one on his arm. It's a cross with a Union Jack wrapped round it...'

'Open your eyes, Colin,' Butler said. 'Now, here's my notebook and pen. Can you try and draw it?'

As they headed out of the interview room and back along the corridor, Moone looked over at the straight-faced Butler and said, 'That was pretty impressive.'

She huffed. 'Just a technique I picked up on a course. Now I guess we run that tattoo through the database. A yob like him has bound to have been nicked before.'

'You can bet on it.'

'The IT guy, Barry, wants to tell us what he found.'

'OK. Where's his office?' Moone said, then smiled to himself. 'I'm sorry, I meant where's that to?'

She stopped dead before they reached the stairwell a few yards away. 'Think you're bloody funny, don't you?'

'Just trying to break the ice.'

'Yeah, well, pack it in.'

They went down to the next floor and along a corridor that looked as if it had been recently given a lick of paint. In fact the smell of fresh paint sunk into Moone's face as they reached a small office halfway along the corridor. The door was open, and they looked in at a set of three wood desks all pulled together and filled untidily with laptops and PCs. There were large framed movie posters on the walls, and a few text books strewn about the place but nothing much else. There was another doorway to the right, from where a tall, skinny young man appeared and looked at them and nodded. His face was gaunt, covered in stubble, but his eyes were sharp, Moone thought.

'This is Barry,' Butler said. 'Barry, this is DI Peter Moone.'

Barry looked at him, nodded, then mumbled, 'All right?'

'Yep, I'm good,' Moone said, then followed Barry to the desks where he sat and started tapping away at one of the keyboards.

'Did you find that website?' Butler asked.

'Course,' Barry said. 'Chicks with dicks. That's not what it's called...'

'No, you don't say,' Butler said, groaning. 'What is it called?'

'Shemales R US,' he said. 'Not very original, but gets the job done.'

'So, can you find our victim on here?' Moone asked.

'Already done it,' Barry said, reaching for a bottle of energy drink next to his keyboard.

'You've found Jason Mitchum?' Butler asked, sounding surprised.

'Yeah...' Barry tapped away at his keyboard and brought up an image of what looked like a woman from a distance, but when Moone leaned in he could see that the facial features were a little manly.

'Jasmine,' Butler read from the screen. 'Makes sense. Jason becomes Jasmine.'

'He doesn't look like a Jasmine to me,' Moone said, smiling, but he only got a glare from Butler.

'There's other pics on here,' Barry said. 'But they're a bit... you know... anyway, I was able to use facial recognition to find Jason. Been on here for about three years.'

'Three years!' Butler moaned. 'That means we've got a load of fuckers to trawl through.'

'He's not had many messages,' Barry said. 'I mean, he has, but not replied to that many. He was sent lots of photos of... you know...'

'I get the picture,' Butler said. 'I've been on dating sites.'

'Really?' Moone asked, realising he knew nothing at all about her personal life.

'Yeah, now leave it. So was he talking to anyone before he was killed?'

Barry hit his keyboard again and brought up a profile page, where the member's image appeared in the corner. Moone found himself looking at a cartoon image of a woman with a penis.

'SheHeLover69,' Moone said, and gave an empty laugh. 'So, did they arrange a date?'

'Yeah,' Barry said, bringing up a long line of messages. 'They arranged to meet in Central Park, Sunday night.'

Butler stood up, let out a breath. 'This is him. SheHeLover69. He's our killer... he lures Jason to the park and kills him. Bloody sick bastard.'

'How do we find him?' Moone asked Barry.

'I've contacted the site, but that member no longer exists,' Barry said. 'I could try and get his information, get the IP address, if it's not bounced round the place, but he could've joined this site from anywhere. But chances are he's still under there under a different name.'

'Of course, this is his hunting ground,' Moone said. 'Can you try and track him down?'

Barry shrugged. 'OK, but you might be waiting a while. I'll set up a profile, sort of thing he likes and wait.'

'Just do your best.' Moone patted his shoulder, then turned to Butler. 'We could be one step closer to finding Jason's killer.'

'Yeah, right. Do you really think this guy would've just signed up on his own computer, from his own home, if he was planning on killing Jason? I don't think so.'

'What if he wasn't planning it? What if it's something that just happened?'

Butler shrugged. 'Maybe, but if the person we're after is this tattooed thug, then that means he's been trawling dating sites trying to find people like Jason, targeting them. Do you go to all that trouble if you don't mean to really hurt them?'

Moone knew she had a perfectly valid point. 'So, we're looking for someone who's targeting gay people, or crossdressers.'

'People he thinks are scum.'

Moone nodded. 'But they didn't find any computers at Jed's place. Even his phone was basic, wasn't it?'

Butler made a tired sound. 'True. So maybe that was random...'

Moone headed towards the door. 'Then we need to go over Jed's movements, see where he went. We might discover where our killer spotted him. Thanks, Barry.'

Barry didn't bother to look round, just raised a thumb, then carried on typing.

'That'll take forever.' Butler moved past him, quickening her pace. 'Our killer might not even be back on there, not if he's after people on street like Jed. This is going to go and on.'

'This is the job.'

She turned and looked at him, eyebrows raised. 'I know the job. I know what's involved. I've been on this planet for... forget it. Let's just get on with it, get through the rest of this day.'

It was pretty much a derelict building, a metal shell, originally constructed sometime after the war to store important stuff, whatever that meant. It was just a large empty warehouse on the edge of Cattedown, the industrial area of Plymouth. Metcalfe found it eerie, the wind whistling through, bending its old twisted rusty bones, making it squeal in pain. It was a haunted place that no one liked to enter.

There was a team of security guards that patrolled the area at night, protecting the whole of Cattedown from a potential terrorist attack, but they never ventured near the warehouse either. Metcalfe wondered if they believed in ghosts too.

There was no electricity, so they'd built a fire in a corner, which someone said, he couldn't remember who, was a stupid and dangerous thing. It was something to do with gas from some of the nearby plants, but so far nothing bad had happened.

It's where they met, huddled together by the flickering flames that leapt from the garden incinerator he'd bought.

Metcalfe sat on one the camping chairs, his satchel by his feet, the warmth of the fire dancing across his face, his own shadow moving over the wall, while his mind ached with the state of the police-controlled world. He detested how they still had to find places like the one he was sitting in to hide away. Society was so backwards, he decided, but one day, probably not in his lifetime, they'd come out of the strange sexual cave they'd put themselves in and realise that there was nothing wrong with it.

It.

He ground his teeth, then sat up when he heard the large rusty door squeal and scrape the ground until the light from the factories and the streetlights twinkled in his view, and the familiar silhouette of Malcolm West came limping awkwardly in.

The door squealed shut again.

Malcolm took his seat next to Metcalfe, his satchel still over his shoulder, his mouldy scent drifting over to him, poisoning his nostrils.

'Where is he?' Metcalfe asked, staring at the fire, unable to take his eyes away.

'He'll be here, don't worry,' West said, then was quiet for a while, but Metcalfe could hear his next thoughts travel all the way to his mouth.

'Mathieson was a bit uptight, wasn't he?' West said.

'He's got a lot to lose,' Metcalfe said. 'Wouldn't you be uptight?'

'And I haven't got a lot to lose?'

'Your freedom. That's all you've got to lose. Nobody likes you. Nobody.'

'That's not true. You're a heartless bastard.'

'Nobody!'

There was a knocking on the door, the rattled echo of a fist rapping on it. They both turned round, but it was Metcalfe that nodded to the door, so West begrudgingly got up and limped over to the door and unbolted it.

It wasn't Macdonald, much to Metcalfe's disappointment. It was the monstrous, lardy shape of Ralph Norman that stood in the doorway, huffing, trying to catch his breath. Even in the firelight, Metcalfe could see the fat man was a strange, unhealthy colour. He was barely fifty, but he'd eaten his way towards a heart attack for the last few years. It was psychological, Metcalfe knew that, recognised a mindset that could hardly live with what he was, could not embrace his choice of lifestyle, and therefore chose a path of self-destruction instead. Metcalfe gave him five, maybe ten years at best.

'Your leg still bothering you?' Ralph asked in

his irritating voice, a voice that always sounded as if the man was having trouble speaking because of food caught in his throat. Then Metcalfe let out a breath and shook his head as Ralph lifted a piece of fried chicken to his already greasy lips.

'It is,' West said. 'If I ever find the bastards that did that to me... bloody bastards.'

'You'll do nothing,' Metcalfe said, spitting the words out. 'You see them again and they'll do it again... probably worse... they'll kill you.'

'Fuck off!' West barked.

But Metcalfe had heard something outside and waved his hand, showing his annoyance. 'Listen.'

Yes, there it was again, the sound of feet scraping on the floor, hesitating outside. Metcalfe got up and stepped lightly over to the door, bent over and put his eye to the spyhole.

There he was, the constant moving shape of him, hunched over, hands in his pockets. He could hardly see his face, but he recalled his tiny eyes, dug deep into a grey, stubbly face, the acne scars on his cheeks.

Metcalfe opened the door, carefully, making sure no one was waiting to cosh him on the head. No one trusted Macdonald, least of all him; he had that scent about him, that certain odour of betrayal.

But he wouldn't after tonight.

Macdonald stepped towards the doorway, his head turning left and right, his tiny eyes searching the night.

'Hurry up, get in,' Metcalfe growled, and grabbed his arm and pulled him inside.

He was about to shut the door again, when he saw movement, then heard a step on the ground. His heart thudded, half expecting to see a uniform stood there.

He breathed out when he looked up to see the lanky, withered outline of Ray Benton stood there. He looked even more degraded, as if something had been slowly digesting him over the last couple of years.

'Metcalfe,' Ray said, but his voice was a dusty, empty sound, followed by a rattling cough.

'You coming in?' Metcalfe asked.

Ray nodded and stepped inside, his eyes fluttering over the people already there, a slight nod coming from him as he took them all in.

'Nothing changes, does it?' Ray said, and gave a gravelly laugh. 'Still hiding away.'

'It's what we have to do, Ray,' West said. 'Or else we get banged up.'

Ray's eyes jumped to the fire in the corner, his dark eyes lit up with orange and red flames. 'Still trying to kill yourselves and everyone else with that stupid fire.'

'We're still here,' Metcalfe said, feeling sick at the sight of the old man. 'You don't look well, Ray.'

Ray gave another throaty, painful laugh,

then took out a pack of fags and poked one between his lips. 'I'm not well... seeing as you've got that fire going, I might as well have one of these.'

The old man took a drag, then coughed for a minute before he said. 'That... that's the sound of death. I've got months, maybe weeks. Lung cancer.'

No one said anything, just passed looks between themselves, away from the old man who was already dead, looks that said they were glad. Glad because they knew what sort of man he was.

But Metcalfe turned towards Ian Macdonald, who had pulled up a chair close to the fire and seemed to be staring deep into it. Then he looked back at Ray, who nodded, still smoking, giving him the signal.

'You all right, Ian?' Metcalfe said and walked towards him.

'Not really, what do you think?' Macdonald said over his shoulder. 'I've got 'em all looking for me. For fuck's sake. Maybe I should just... just hand myself in.'

'You shouldn't do that,' Metcalfe said, trying to sound supportive. 'They won't look after you... they want to hurt you.'

'Metcalfe,' a voice whispered behind him, so he turned and found Ray holding out a claw hammer to him.

After pouring himself a glass of beer, Moone carried it to the sofa that formed a U shape at the end of the caravan, then turned on the small TV and found the news. It was late, and a thick blanket of darkness had laid itself on everything, while the cold winter air came in, advertising what was to come. Christmas wasn't that far away and he shivered a little at the thought of it, of the mess and awkward moments to come.

He wanted to find the local news, to see what, if anything, was being fed to the media about the double murder. It was being kept quiet by the force, but they all knew there would be a point where they wouldn't be able to hold it back any longer.

Just as Spotlight news, the local news broadcast, came on, his mobile started vibrating across the small table.

He sighed, then picked it up and sighed deeper when he saw it was his ex-wife calling. It was only then, as he contemplated allowing the call to go unanswered, that he remembered his promise to Alice to look into the slimy MP who was dating his ex.

'Hello,' he said, rubbing his eyes and beard. 'What's wrong?'

She talked, and he listened, the same old moaning, the reprimands for things that were not in his control, then the demands for more money.

'It's fine,' he said. 'Whatever you want. I'll deal with it.'

She sounded surprised for a moment, then her voice changed and she suddenly asked him to come for dinner the following night.

'What? Are you kidding? No, no, I'm not saying I don't want to come, I just don't understand. Right, OK, I see. OK, yes, I'll come and meet your new boyfriend. Fine... for the sake of the kids. Goodnight, Angela. Yes, goodnight...'

Just as Moone was hanging up, there was a knock on the door. A terrible thought occurred to him, the possibility that Butler was outside, ready to drag him off to another crime scene, so he went to the door, gently unlocked it and looked out.

He smiled, then let out a relieved breath when he saw PC Faith Carthew stood there, but not in uniform. Her hair was down, her face was made-up, and she was dressed in a red top and jeans.

'Hey,' he said, dumbstruck as he realised he actually fancied her, which automatically put him in awkward mode.

'Hi,' she said, smiling, her cheeks red. 'I thought we could go out somewhere for that drink we talked about.'

'Well, it's quite late...'

'Oh, OK, maybe another time.'

Her smile faded, and she looked awkward,

her cheeks reddening even more, so he said, 'You could always come in for a drink.'

'You inviting me in for coffee?' she said, stepping closer, her face straight, the smile gone. 'What kind of woman do you think I am?'

'Sorry... I just...'

She started stepping up the steps towards him, her lips forming a smile. 'Don't worry, I'm exactly the kind of woman you think I am.'

She kissed him, pulling the door shut behind her.

'Do it,' Ray whispered. 'Do it quick. It's the best way. He's finished, you'll be doing him a favour.'

Metcalfe took the hammer, turned it around in his hand and stared at the back of MacDonald's head, saw the short hairs at the back of his neck, and the bald spots caused by scars. He gripped the hammer tighter, stepping closer to him, hearing that Ray was also moving along with him. When he looked round, he saw the others, all staring, waiting to see what would happen. Their eyes said it all, their intention he should do it to save all their skins.

He got a couple of feet from him, and raised the hammer, focusing on the back of his head. He looked up at the hammer head, saw it trembling in his hand, saw its shadow flickering on the wall, realising what he was about to do.

Someone said something, breaking the

spell, and he looked down to see that MacDonald had turned in his seat, staring up at him, his mouth opening.

He rushed at him, brought the hammer down, but Macdonald moved, tried to get away from his seat. The blow landed on the side of his head, catching his ear, tearing part of it away from his skull. Blood poured down his neck as he stumbled away from the chair, his hand touching the wound.

Macdonald looked up, his skin losing all colour, as he said, 'Why... why did you do that? I wouldn't...'

'He would!' West said, screaming the words. 'Do it! Do it, Metcalfe!'

The hammer came down, and he watched it, as if he were across the room, near the door, maybe ready to run. It wasn't him. It couldn't be him killing his friend.

Macdonald stumbled backwards, blood pouring from a wound between his eyes.

Metcalfe was stunned, hardly realising what had happened until he saw Macdonald crashing his way towards the metal door, pulling it open and heading out awkwardly into the night. He got up and ran past Ray and reached the door in time to see Macdonald running into the road and waving down a security car. The car stopped, the guards got out and rushed to Macdonald as he collapsed.

As he turned back towards the others, who

all stood frozen, waiting for him to say something, he said, 'Fucking run! Get out of here! It's fucked!'

CHAPTER 11

Moone was in the shower when he heard the familiar banging at the flimsy caravan door. He turned off the water, then poked his head out, listening to the voices in the next room, realising that exactly what he wanted to avoid had happened.

He raced to get dry and threw on some trousers and a shirt, then took a deep breath as he stepped into the lounge area to find Butler stood, arms folded, while Faith was sitting on the sofa, holding a mug of coffee. Both had solemn faces, although it was Faith's that burned and he could almost feel the heat across the room.

'So,' Butler said, 'which one of us gets the pleasure of driving you today?'

Moone looked at Faith, but she shrugged and said, 'Well, I'm off work today, so...'

'Right, let's go,' Butler said and burst out of the caravan.

Moone mouthed an apology, then put on his shoes, and hurried out to Butler's car.

'You know you don't have to fetch me every morning,' he said as she was about to climb in.

She straightened up again as she said, 'I know. But we've got an urgent one and I'm probably a better driver than you. Didn't realise you'd be shacked up with Cakey Sue in there.'

'I wasn't...' Moone said. 'It's not like that...'

'Isn't it? Could've fooled me. You know she wants a leg up, not just a bunk up?'

Moone didn't bother to say anything more, just climbed in and let her drive him out of the park and towards the city.

A long stretch of concrete rolled by, the same he'd seen most mornings for the last few days. Then they turned off, heading for the hospital, Derriford hospital, where Ian MacDonald was fighting for his life. Moone couldn't bring himself to feel anything for the man except for contempt. In fact, he even told himself off for referring to him as a 'man'. But it was the job, and he was expected to lock away all the hatred, loathing and anything else that might make him less effective.

But how could he?

Butler managed to find a parking space after a long while, squeezed in among the throng of other cars that had headed towards the over-stretched hospital.

'He was found in Cattedown,' Butler said, as they walked fast towards the entrance to Accident and Emergency.

'What's Cattedown?' Moone asked. 'Some kind of home for unwanted cats?'

Butler flashed him a look as she passed through the automatic doors. 'Oh, yeah, forgot for a moment you're not from round here. It's an industrial estate, not that far from the city centre. Looks like Macdonald was holed up in a disused warehouse... security guards found him. They said they saw some others fleeing the scene, but didn't bother to give chase, just called us in. Wonderful.'

Moone followed her as she headed towards the reception desk and flashed her ID. 'Ian Mac-Donald?'

A junior sister in her late forties, reddish hair, quite tall, stood up and examined Butler's warrant card carefully before removing her glasses and looking up. 'He's not long out of surgery, and now he's in ICU. He's not going to be talking to anyone for a while, I can assure you.'

Butler put away her ID, then leaned over the desk and huffed. 'So, what's the damage?'

The sister looked her up and down. 'The damage is to his brain. He had swelling. Quite severe. We tried to get some information from him about what happened to him, but he was barely conscious. He had a deep laceration to his forehead. He's in a coma now, so you'll have to wait and see what happens.'

'Thanks,' Moone said, smiled but only got a brief one in return as the sister returned to her work. 'So, we're out of luck.'

Butler looked away, folding her arms, staring across the mayhem of the room, all the people waiting, sat on chairs, holding tissues to wounds, some crying, while the staff rushed back and forth. 'Someone tried to shut him up. Which means he knows something.'

'Which means it's likely he is the one that snatched Danny Sawyer.'

'But looks like we won't get to ask him what the fuck he knows. I'll have a guard put on his room.'

Then Butler started storming down the corridor, heading back towards the entrance, so Moone did his best to keep up. He realised she was heading towards a tall, lanky figure dressed in a security uniform, stood near a vending machine sipping a cup of something hot.

'You,' Butler snapped, showing her ID.

The guard straightened up, nearly dropping his drink, and spilling it down his sleeve.

'Shit... fuck,' he said, shaking his arm. 'What have I done?'

'Nothing, that's what you did,' Butler said, staring at him like she was trying to turn him to stone. 'What the bloody hell did you see?'

'Just this bloke stumbling towards the road, blood pouring from his head. I stopped and got out to see if he was all right, then I heard some noise from that warehouse... I saw people running off. But I couldn't go charging after them, I had to get him to hospital, didn't I?'

'You didn't get a good look at any of them?' Moone asked.

'No, mate,' the guard said. 'It was dark. When I drove off, I did see an old bloke hurrying off down the road. I passed him by... he was coughing his guts up... didn't look too healthy, but I kept on going.'

'Old bloke?' Butler asked, a light on somewhere in her skull. 'Skinny?'

'Aren't they all?' the guard said.

'Would you recognise him again?' Butler asked.

The guard shrugged. 'Maybe. Probably.'

Butler nodded, then started to walk off. 'You need to come with us to the station.'

They had seated the guard in an interview room, letting him stew for a while, during which time Moone fetched them all a coffee. Before they went into the room, where the guard, Paul Walker, no relation to the film star, was sitting, they sipped their drinks and leaned against the wall.

'Do you think you know the old fella with the cough?' Moone asked, then blew on his drink.

'Well, sounds like a creepy fucker that used

to live down here... was one of your lot.' Butler sipped her drink, then made an unpleasant face.

'My lot?'

'From London. Right chatty bastard. Evil scumbag.'

'Sorry, chatty?'

'Dirty. Look, if it's the bloke I'm talking about, and the guard saw others running off, then looks like this could be a ring.'

Moone let out a harsh breath as the muscles in his back and shoulders tightened. 'A ring? Shit. So, you're thinking Macdonald grabbed Danny... then, Jesus, makes me want to throw up. How the bloody hell do these people find each other?'

'Sick birds of a feather...' Butler had the mugshot book under her arm, which she looked at then sighed. 'I really bloody hope it's not him.'

She went barging in, so Moone followed and saw the guard flinch and react as if he was the guilty party. Butler had that effect on people, he had to admit.

Moone sat down, watching as Butler laid out the mugshot book in front of him, then opened it up. 'Please be kind enough to take a look through our catalogue and pick out anything you like the look of.'

Walker looked at Moone, so he said, 'Take a look, see if you recognise anyone.'

The guard, looking uncertain, flipped through the pages, stopping occasionally and studying faces. In the meantime, Butler got

Moone to make a hot drink while they waited, and even ordered him to fetch biscuits. Moone almost told the guard he should feel honoured but took one look at Butler's slapped-arse face and changed his mind.

Eventually, Butler got up, sighing, and grabbed the book from the guard and flipped through the pages. 'What about these couple of pages? Anything there?'

'You can't...' Moone started to say, but Butler held up her hand.

'Hang on,' the guard said, tapping his finger on the next page. 'This fella looks familiar, could be him!'

Butler looked down at the mugshot, her face changing, becoming even more pissed off, then she slammed the book shut. 'Thanks, Mr Walker. That'll be all.'

The guard looked between them. 'That's it? Don't you want me to make a statement?'

'No,' Butler said, like a stern teacher. 'Just piss off.'

The guard got to his feet, anger pouring over his face as he stormed to the door and slammed it behind him.

Butler grabbed the mugshot book, stuffed it under her arm and started heading towards the door, but Moone jumped up and grabbed her arm.

'What the bloody hell was that about?' he said.

Butler tore her arm away and stared at him,

thunder clouds crossing her eyes. 'Don't you dare touch me! Not unless you want a sexual harassment claim stuck on you. Arm or tit, I don't mind what I write down!'

Moone let out an exhausted laugh. 'What the fu... I'm meant to be your partner... your boss, actually...'

'You know what you are to me?'

'No, you tell me!'

'A pain in my big fat arse! You're just some fly by night cockney copper come down here to show off... you might have some bloody medal, but they'll give medals to anyone these days... they give medals to dogs and cats!'

'My medal? I didn't even want the stupid fucking medal!'

'Then why didn't you give it back!'

Moone let out an exhausted breath. 'Oh yeah, imagine how that would look. Thanks, Prince Charlie, but I don't want your fucking mum's medal!'

'I've got stuff to do!'

'Who is he?!' Moone bellowed.

Butler had her back to him, but her shoulders were rising with her angry breaths. Then she turned, opening the book, finding the page and showing him the mugshot that had been identified by the guard. 'Here! You want to see?! Here he is!'

'Who is he?' Moone took the book.

'Ray... Ray fucking Benton.' Butler rubbed

her face, sighed and shook her head. 'He was... a paedophile. A scumbag paedophile, as if they're not all evil scumbags. Anyway, he was also an informant.'

'No! You had him as an informant?'

Butler nodded. 'Happened a few years back. We had all this intelligence come in... some from the States... child abuse stuff... including information that a big ring had formed down here. We used Ray to try and get our own intelligence. He fed us a few names, got a few minor characters. Then he scarpered off to London and got himself nicked. We couldn't help him... and we didn't want to. Now it looks like he's back.'

'Jesus...' Moone leant over the desk. 'What if he was involved in Danny Sawyer's abduction?'

'Well done, Sherlock. Yeah, I've already thought of that. I'm pretty sure he was in London then...'

'But you can't be sure?'

Butler stared at him for a moment, then shook her head. 'No, I can't.'

There was a knock on the door and Moone thanked God for it, glad to have the chance to escape the room that seemed to be getting smaller all the time.

'Come in,' he said, and the door opened and Faith Carthew put her head round and looked at them both.

'Sorry to disturb you,' she said. 'But they think they've got a match on that tattoo.'

Butler and Moone headed into the incident room, where Harding was sat at his desk, waving them over. They joined him and looked at his screen where an arrest mugshot of a thuggish looking lad was staring back at them.

'Horrible looking wanker, isn't he?' Harding said, then used his mouse to bring up the photograph of his tattoo. 'How's that for a match?'

Moone looked at the real tattoo, then the sketch and thought they looked pretty similar. 'Close enough. Leroy Sturkey. Let's bring him in.'

'One problem with that, boss,' Harding said, leaning back in his chair, a smug look on his face. 'We don't know where he is. He was living with his bird, but he's not there now. I gave her a ring.'

'What's the address?' Butler said, standing over Harding.

'You want to talk to her, you go ahead,' Harding said and took out his mobile. 'I'll text it to you. She sounds like a pain in the arse to me.'

Butler checked her phone. 'Ask her out did you? Blew you out?'

Harding looked up. 'Oi, I've got a fiancée, I'll have you know!'

Butler stormed off towards the doors. 'Yeah, but I know you men, can't keep it in your pants for five minutes.'

It was Butler who drove them again, heading up North Prospect road as the rain started to hammer down again, people running to bus shelters, or ducking under the cover of shop doorways. Butler took a left turn up another long street, then another left until Moone found they had parked outside a box-like newbuild, matching all the rest it rubbed shoulders with, weird looking grey stains streaked down the exterior of every one.

'Leanne Sykes,' Butler said and climbed out, hurrying to get under cover. 'This little newbuild cube is where she lives. Hasn't got a job, claims all the benefits in the world. Been done for shoplifting.'

'Lovely,' Moone said, and raced after as she ran to the sheltered front door. Then he remembered something from Samson's statement. 'Hasn't she got a kid?'

'Yes, single mum.' Butler knocked on the door, then rang the bell.

From inside, they heard a kid shouting something. Then came the glorious hitch pitch of a woman shouting back. Moone rolled his eyes at Butler, but she turned and pressed the bell again.

The door was flung open, a young-ish woman with thick makeup and straggly blonde glared at them. 'What?!'

Butler showed her ID. 'Police. Need a word with you.'

The woman straightened up, put her arms tightly across her chest, as she scowled at them. 'What do you think I've done?'

Moone could hear screaming from inside the house, a child's demands for attention, so he pointed inside. 'Do you need to sort that out?'

Sykes shot him a look, her small fists tightening. 'That's none of your fucking business! Why don't you push off?!'

'It's not you that we're after,' Butler said, almost sounding a little softer. 'It's your ex, Leroy, that we're after.'

Sykes' face lost some of its fire and redness, and gained a look of curiosity. 'What's the wanker done now?'

'No love lost between you, I take it?' Butler asked.

'No, not the way he carries on,' Sykes said, then let out a tired huff and looked towards the screaming. 'I got to see to that. Might as well come in.'

Moone followed Butler inside as she walked down the narrow hallway of the house, the flight of stairs on their left. A small, white kitchen was at the back, where a young child, a boy, dressed in jeans and a blue hoody, was red-faced, tears streaming down his chubby face. He quietened down when his mum picked him up, but kept staring at Moone and Butler with his large blue eyes.

As Sykes calmed and cuddled the boy, she turned and looked between them both. 'So? What's he done now?'

'We can't really go into that with you,' Moone said. 'But it's not good. We need to know where he is.'

She stared at them both for a moment, then looked down at the boy. 'He's his boy. Can't have him round him... not like he is. He's always angry... angry at the world. One day somebody'll give him what's for and he won't like it. You need to lock him up for good.'

'We will, if we can find the bastard,' Butler said. 'But maybe you can help us with that.'

'I don't know where he is,' she said, looking down.

Butler stepped up to her, lowered her voice. 'We'll make sure he doesn't come near you. I promise you that.'

'You don't know him.' The boy in her arms struggled to get free, then ran off, leaving Sykes to lean on the work surface. 'If he gets wind that I let on where he was... it's not just me... it's my boy.'

'We won't let on,' Moone said. 'We can only put him away if you help us.'

Sykes picked at her nails, then looked up. 'My cousin thought she saw him working along Greenbank Road. That was a couple of days ago. That's all I know. I hardly hear from him, thank goodness.'

Butler nodded. 'Thanks. We'll do our best to make sure he doesn't hurt anyone again.'

As they were about to leave, Sykes said, 'I'd watch yourselves with him. He can be a real nasty bastard.'

CHAPTER 12

It seemed much darker as Butler drove them down a hilly road, shortly after they turned off from Mutley. It was the dark rain clouds that had covered the sky that made everything dull and washed out as the rain continued to fall.

'I heard you met Stack,' Butler said.

'That's right,' Moone said, keeping an eye out for any building work going on.

'Did he give you the don't fuck with me speech?'

'Something like that.'

Butler gave a brief huff of a laugh. 'Don't worry about it. He gives that little speech to everyone. He keeps a low profile most of the time... until you fuck up. Which you'll do.'

'Thanks for the vote of confidence.'

'Everyone fucks up.'

'Apart from you?'

'Apart from me...'

Moone looked out of the car, not really listening to her, more thinking about the kind of man they were after. A violent man. 'I was thinking, if we find him, maybe we should get some uniforms involved.'

He felt Butler's eyes jump to him. 'Uniforms? Bloody hell. He's just a jumped-up thug. Uniforms? Don't tell me you're scared?'

'I've found myself in similar situations, when things didn't go to plan.'

'Well, I'm sure we can handle him, unless you want the whole station knowing we sent for help to pick up a scrote like Leroy Sturkey?'

Moone let out a sigh. 'All right. We'll play it by ear.'

'Hang on,' Butler said, and started indicating, waiting for the traffic to slow so she could pull into a spot on the opposite side of the road. 'I can see a skip and some workmen.'

Moone spotted the house a couple of hundred yards away, where there was a bright yellow skip in the road, packed out with rocks and rubble. Every now and then some men came out and dumped more rubbish in the skip then went back into the three-storey house.

Butler got out and started storming towards the house which sat back from the road, up a steep path. As Moone caught up with her, Butler had her ID out and was showing it to two shaven-headed workmen, one of which had a thick dusty beard.

'We're looking for Leroy Sturkey,' she said, then nodded to the building. 'He inside?'

One of the men, the beardless one, said something in a foreign language, Polish, Moone guessed. The other man said, 'He doesn't speak much English. But the bloke you're after's inside. He's a wanker. Right gob on him.'

'That's him,' Butler said and headed up the path, then stopped when another workman came out towards her, lighting a fag. He was quite a bit shorter than Butler, but stocky, muscular, Moone noticed. He had short dark hair, and a sharp bony face. And dead eyes. Moone had seen those sorts of eyes before in troublemakers, men prone to violence.

'You're Sturkey,' Butler said, putting her hands in her pockets.

Sturkey took a puff of his fag and leaned against the door frame. 'You're filth.'

Butler huffed out an empty laugh. 'You hardly know me, so how could you know that? We need a word with you.'

'What the fuck've I supposed to have done now?' Sturkey nodded and moved out of the way of the workmen coming back in.

'Let's talk about that at the station,' Butler said, while Moone stood back, all the time examining the thug, trying to read him, weighing it all up.

Sturkey straightened himself up, then glanced over to Moone. 'Fine. Can I get my coat?

Seeing as it's pissing down.'

Butler didn't say anything for a moment, just stared at him. 'Go on then. Don't faff.'

The thug flicked his fag into the rain, then disappeared inside, so Butler turned to Moone. 'See, not much bother. And, so you know, this coat has deep pockets, so my Casco baton is handy.'

'Nice to know.'

Butler shook her head and returned to her vigil, looking up at the building. 'Wonder how much a place like this goes for?'

Moone recalled again that he knew little about her or any family she might have. 'You married?'

'Why? You thinking of proposing? Don't think it would work out between us, do you?'

Moone realised it was her way of bringing down the barriers, so decided to quit while he was ahead.

'Taking his time, isn't he?' Butler said, huffing again, and heading fast into the house. 'Fucking little shit.'

Hard on her heels, Moone found her at the bottom of a wide, dusty hallway, facing one of the workmen.

'Where is he?!' Butler shouted, pointing a finger at the workman.

'Who?'

'Sturkey! Leroy Sturkey! Where's he fucked off to?'

The workman shrugged. 'I dunno. Saw him heading out the back way.'

Butler pushed past him, heading towards a narrower, flowery tiled hallway and then towards an open back door that led into a concrete courtyard. Moone followed her out through a brick archway and into a wide-open parking area. There was no sign of Sturkey, and Butler kicked at a low wall, swearing aloud.

'We'll catch up with him,' Moone said, watching her as she paced up and down, taking out her mobile as she glared at him.

'You're probably bloody glad he got away!' she moaned.

'Oh come on, for fuck's sake!' He'd had enough and was way past his pushing point. 'Stop fucking having a go at me! Whatever's wrong with your home life or whatever it is... I didn't cause it...'

'No! But you're making it worse by being here!'

'I came here because I had to! I don't want to be here either!'

Butler stormed towards him, her arm stretching out, her finger pointing, her face red. 'Then why don't you fuck off back to London?!'

'Oi!'

Moone turned round to see one of the workmen, the first they'd spoken to earlier, standing near the back of the house, looking annoyed.

'You two had enough?' he said, shaking his

head and lighting a fag. 'So you want to know where he's gone, or not?'

Moone sat in the passenger seat, upright, his arms across his chest as Butler swept the car round the traffic, heading to where the workman had said that Sturkey had gone off to. He was going home, off to a little flat where he was staying, not far from where the Torpoint ferry leaves from, wherever the hell that was. He didn't really feel like asking Butler, and her thunderous face and white knuckles told him that she wouldn't feel like answering.

'Maybe it's time to call it quits,' she said, her voice not so strained.

'On what?'

'This... us...'

Moone almost laughed but stopped himself. 'You're splitting up with me?'

'Don't worry, it's me, not you.' She took the car down a hill, past rows of rundown shops and takeaways, then right around a long and high wall lined with barbed wire and cameras. Moone managed to read 'MOD' before they raced down towards some grey buildings and the water beyond where a ferry was loading up with cars. The Torpoint ferry, Moone assumed as Butler pulled in and parked in a side street near a block of flats.

'We'll find the bastard here,' Butler said and climbed out and headed towards the block of flats on the corner, while Moone looked around at the place, noticing a paper shop opposite. He was nearly out of cigarettes, he thought to himself, desperate for a smoke. He shook his head and followed Butler towards the side door. It was open, the lock mechanism twisted and broken, so they headed up the concrete stairwell, following the directions the workman had relayed to them. It was lucky he'd been over to Sturkey's flat for a drink and a go on his PlayStation, Moone decided.

Butler knocked on the door, then rang the bell, and then hammered her fist on the door.

It took a few minutes for Sturkey to come to the door, but when he did he was smirking, a fag in his hand.

'You took your time,' he said, taking a puff of his cigarette, and blowing the smoke out at them.

'You did a runner,' Butler said. 'We don't like that.'

'I said I was getting my coat,' Sturkey said. 'My coat was here.'

'You smart arse,' Butler said, and Moone noticed her hand go into her coat pocket. 'You going to let us in then? Make us a nice cup of tea?'

Sturkey laughed, but there was no humour in his eyes that Moone could see, just the same dead eyes watching them, weighing everything up as he opened the door for them.

'Come on then,' he said, then went over to

a black leather sofa that sat in the centre of the open plan lounge and kitchen. He picked up a can of strong lager from the coffee table and swigged from it. Moone watched him, the way he wiped his mouth with the back of his hand, his eyes on Butler, travelling up and down her with utter disdain.

'You'd be worth a fuck if you dressed up a bit,' Sturkey said, after taking another gulp.

Moone felt his gut tighten.

'If you're trying to get a rise from me,' Butler said, 'you're wasting your time. Where were you on Sunday night?'

'Where was I?' He took another drink. 'Fucking his wife.'

Moone looked away, examining the rest of the flat, but looked up again when he saw Sturkey move, stepping towards him.

'She made all the right noises,' Sturkey said, looking him in the eyes, smirking. But Moone could see it, beyond the smirk, could see his fists flinching, his jaw tightening.

'I'm not married,' Moone said.

'But you was, to some bitch,' he said.

'Shut up, Leroy,' Butler said, coming closer. 'Answer the question.'

'She sucked me off.'

Moone huffed out a laugh, looked towards the window for a moment, saw Sturkey's reflection moving.

Slow motion, everything turning, the world

drifting sideways.

Moone fell backwards, falling to the ground, hitting a table as his jaw and face pounded, the blood gushing round him, pounding at his skull. There was a ringing in his head, and he was deaf to everything as his eyes closed into blackness.

He saw the ceiling, blinking, trying to remember where he was. He sat up, struggled to get to his feet as voices rushed back in, the sound of distant traffic.

'Don't be fucking stupid,' Butler said, her voice trembling.

Moone looked up, his hands on the carpet, shaking his head, hearing the blood pounding in his ears. He focused, saw the shape at the opposite end of the room, the overturned coffee table, the spilt beer on the floor. Butler.

Butler was backed up against the wall, her arm caught behind her back, the baton in her hand. He was in front of her, his muscles tight in his back, his neck, as he stretched out his hand, his fingers round her throat. Her eyes were wide, her skin flushed.

'You fucking come after me, bitch,' he growled, 'this is what you fucking get!'

Moone looked down, still trying to get up, still feeling the burning ache in his face, his jaw, his vision still cloudy. When he looked up, he saw Sturkey's other hand, appearing from out of his pocket, bringing out the blade.

'You've got... Leroy... calm down... don't do something...'

'Don't fucking tell me what to do. I'll tell you what to do...' the blade rose, her big white eyes jumping to it.

'Don't! It'll be murder!'

'I know! I fucking know, bitch! You fucking bitch!'

Moone looked around, saw a metal bar on the floor, near the sofa. There was a small weight next to it. It was part of a dumbbell set. He quietly crawled over and reached out his hand, wrapping his palm round it, feeling how cold it was. He gripped it, trying to get to his feet without making a noise, watching Sturkey and his knife hand that kept being drawn backwards.

Her big white, terrified eyes jumped to Moone, saw what he was doing.

'Sturkey!' she said, her voice trying to lose the tremble. 'Look at me! What you're doing... you don't want to go to prison for the rest of your life, do you?'

'You don't know what I fucking want!' he growled. 'Right now, I want to hear you beg for your life before I cut you open! I don't give a fucking shit what they do to me! You first, then your queer mate!'

Moone stopped near Sturkey, his legs shaking, threatening to drop him to the carpet, his guts trying to rush to his mouth, while his hand rose up, trembling, the bar gripped tight in it.

He thudded it down, hammered it as hard as he could on the back of his head. Sturkey shuddered, stumbling to his left, trying to steady himself, and swinging round, his face wild with fury.

His legs looked weak, but he still came towards Moone even though blood started to leak down the side of his head. His mouth was moving, growling, shouting, the knife hand jabbing towards Moone as he backed up.

Butler had sunk to the floor, her neck red from the attempted strangulation, but Moone no longer registered her, only the knife, knowing it would puncture him. How many times? Would an ambulance be in time to help?

Then Sturkey collapsed to the floor, and Butler stood hunched over him, her body shaking all over, the Casco baton brandished in her hand, vibrating as she let out deep breaths and a strange whining sound.

'It's all right,' Moone said, coming towards her. 'It's all right. He's done. We're OK. You OK?'

She looked up at him, nodded. Then after a pause, with tears filling her eyes, she shook her head.

'Let's cuff him and get out of here,' Moone said, taking out his restraints.

When they got to the ground level of the building, and got out onto the pavement, Butler rested her back to the wall, then slipped down to the floor. As soon as she landed, more tears flooded out in deep sobs that made her body shudder. An incident response car was waiting when they got outside, so Moone told the two uniforms to go up and get the suspect some medical attention.

Then he sat down beside her and wrapped an arm around her shoulders. He was almost surprised when she fell against him, her head resting against his shoulder as she fought to control her tears.

'You tell anyone I cried, I'll kill you,' she said, wiping her eyes.

'I won't, scout's honour,' he said, watching spots of rain hitting the road and pavement.

'I'm sorry,' she said.

'For what?'

'For being such a bitch since you got here. It's not your fault. It's my life, I think it's falling apart.'

'Join the club.'

'I'm so thirsty.'

Moone lifted his head, looking across the street, remembering the paper shop he'd spotted earlier, and climbed to his unsteady feet. 'Wait here. I'll get you a drink.'

'Don't be stupid, sit down,' she said, sniffing.

'I'll be right back.' He waited for a couple of cars to pass that seemed to be heading for the ferry, then hurried across to the other side of the street, where the shop was. It was only a small place, and when he went in he saw that it was almost like a tiny supermarket and souvenir shop. One crowded corner was filled with cheap looking tacky souvenirs and postcards. He spotted the drinks fridge and was about to head over, when something caught his eye among the cheap toys and tat.

There it was, the red toy bear with a blue cowboy hat, the exact copy of the one found buried with Danny Sawyer. He picked it up, fetched a bottle of water, then took them to the counter where an overweight, middle-aged woman was serving.

'You sell many of these bears?' he asked setting down the toy and the drink.

She shrugged. 'Don't Know. We sell all kinds of stuff like that. Think we got a load of them in months back, maybe a year ago.'

Moone fished out his warrant card and showed it. 'Where do they come from?'

The woman let out a sigh. 'Don't tell me they're dodgy?'

'No, I just need to know who made them.'

'Think there's a label on it somewhere. Probably from China.'

Moone turned it over, then found a tiny tag at the back that said, 'Good Times Toys, Exeter.'

He put a tenner on the counter, then said, 'Thanks. Keep the change.'

When he reached the other side of the road, he found Butler stood up, looking a lot more

human again, reaching out her hand for the bottle of water. Her eyes fell on the bear.

'You didn't?' she said.

'I did. I found the bloody bear. I think we're
getting closer.'

CHAPTER 13

DSU Stack slammed the door of the conference room and faced them both, his face hard, a little red around the cheeks. Moone stayed where he was, sat facing Butler who was nursing a cup of tea.

'Are you two stupid?' he asked, flashing them both glowering looks.

'No, sir,' Butler said, and let out a huff.

'Then why the fuck did you go and see a violent wanker like Leroy Sturkey without support?' Stack raised his eyebrows. 'Eh? I knew it wouldn't be long before you fucked up, Moone.'

'It wasn't his cockup,' Butler said. 'I convinced him we didn't need support. I was wrong.'

'But he went along with you,' Stack said. 'He's supposed to be in charge, calling the shots. Your judgement leaves a lot to be desired, Moone.'

'Yes, sir,' Moone said, then looked at Butler

again, concerned for her state of mind after what she'd been through. Being shouted at wasn't what she needed right then.

'And you, DS Butler,' Stack said. 'What the bloody hell were you thinking of? You could've got yourselves killed! Now we've got a suspect in intensive care! For all I care he could die, but how's that going to look? For fuck's sake, you two...'

There was a loud knock on the door, the Chief Super looked in at Moone and Butler, his face straight, nothing giving away his mood.

'Sir,' Stack said, stepping back as the Chief Super came into the room and looked down at them both.

'You're both in one piece,' Laptew said, nodding, staring at Butler. 'Close call. But at least we've got him.'

'If he lives,' Stack said.

The Chief Super looked at him. 'Fuck him... pardon my language. But looks like he will. I've talked to the hospital. Nothing too serious. We'll get him fit for questioning. Only problem is it's going to be a bit of a PR nightmare. How are we on the Danny Sawyer investigation, anything there that we can feed the press?'

Moone reached down and placed the toy bear on the desk. 'I found this.'

Stack laughed without humour. 'You stopped in the middle of all this to buy a fucking teddy bear?'

Moone stared at Stack. 'It's the same toy we found buried with Danny Sawyer. It's made locally by a company called Good Times Toys in Exeter.'

The Chief Superintendent picked it up, smiling a little, and nodding. 'Good. There can't be many of these floating around, so maybe you can find the person who bought the one buried with him. Great work, Moone. That's excellent. Anything else on the Danny Sawyer case to report?'

Moone sat up. 'Only the fact that Ian Macdonald, our main suspect in the abduction of the boy, was smashed over the head. We believe someone was trying to shut him up.'

'Have you talked to him?' the Chief Super asked.

'He's in a coma, sir,' Butler said. 'For all we know he could end up a vegetable.'

'Well,' Stack said, his voice gruff, his arms folded across his chest. 'You going to take some time off, Butler?'

'Maybe that would be a good idea,' the Chief Superintendent said, nodding, a smile on his lips that was meant to be kind.

Moone looked at Butler, watched her stony profile as she raised her head, wondering what, like everyone in the room, she would say.

'I appreciate that,' Butler said, clearing her throat. 'But I'd rather carry on working. I don't need to mope about.'

The Chief Superintendent nodded. 'Fine,

OK, but you'll have to see someone from occupational health.'

'Jesus… Fine, sir…' Butler stood up sharply, straightening her clothes. 'Can we go and visit this toy factory place now?'

Moone decided to drive as they reached the station car park, as he could see that Butler was still trembling. Even though she insisted she was fine, he persuaded her to let him drive, and when they did set off, he thought he saw relief in her face.

She was silent most of the journey along the A38 towards Exeter, her gaze turned towards the fields that floated past.

'Wonder what we'll find when we get to this place,' Moone said, his eyes jumping to the toy bear sat on the dashboard.

'Just some big factory that churns out plastic crap,' she said, without looking round. 'You can talk about what happened you know.'

'I wasn't sure if you'd want to,' he said, signalling, getting ready to overtake an estate car that was trundling along.

She looked at him. 'I meant what I said. You tell anyone I cried and I'll rip your balls off.'

'You'll have to pinch them from my ex-wife's purse first.'

She laughed. 'I can believe that.'

'I thought you hated me.'

'I just put on a show of being a hard bitch. I'm soft as shite really. Look, I wanted to thank you, you saved my life.'

'No, no I didn't.'

She moved round, staring at him, and he could feel her eyes digging into his skin. 'Yes, you bloody well did. I won't forget that. I could've, I could've died.'

'So could've I.'

She faced front again, silent, her breaths heavy, her mind probably flashing back to what happened. His mind was jumping back to it, re-playing the moments over and over again, while his heart started to pump adrenaline around his system, making his hands shake over the wheel.

'I think my marriage is over,' she said, so he looked over.

'I didn't realise you were married.'

'Fifteen years. Used to be, we used to like each other.'

'Me and the ex-wife used to like each other. I'm sorry, I know what's it like. Maybe you need to talk.'

'He won't. He's always got something to do, somewhere to be.'

'You think he's, you know...'

'What?!'

'Seeing someone?'

Her eyes widened. 'No, I didn't, but now I bloody well do! Thanks!'

'Sorry.' He turned towards the road, gripping the wheel tighter, feeling the weight of his stupid words crushing down on his shoulders.

Then she laughed.

He turned to her. 'What?'

She laughed, shaking her head. 'I don't give a shit.'

'About what?'

'About... whether it's over or not. It's not like we've got kids! We nearly died today... life's too bloody short to worry, isn't it?'

He shrugged as the Satnav told him to take the next exit. 'I'd love to stop worrying, and right now life's little annoying things seem insignificant compared to what just happened to us. But over the next few days they'll come into focus... for instance, tonight I'm meant to be having dinner with my ex, and meeting her new bloke.'

'Fuck that. I'd rather be stabbed.'

Moone laughed. 'Exactly. I think we're nearly there.'

Beyond the streets of shops, that were crowded in around the cathedral, there was a wide expanse of industrial land where Good Times Toys had its headquarters. It was a large relatively new looking development, a flat roofed giant warehouse and depot where massive trucks were lined up to take deliveries wherever they were going, and the company's logo printed along the top. After flashing his ID at a security gate, Moone was directed towards the offices that seemed to line the easterly end of the building, and the car park just in front.

The young-looking security guy followed and stood before them holding a tablet.

'I don't have a visit from the law down on here,' he said, eyebrows raised, a slight smile on his lips.

Moone looked around the large car park, and the half-developed land between the warehouse and the motorway, while Butler climbed out and joined him.

'The boss around, Keith?' Butler asked, folding her arms, staring at his ID badge. She was back on form, Moone thought, or at least putting on a good show of it.

'Mr Burton?' the security guard asked, then looked back towards the building. 'He'll be busy. You rung ahead?'

'We're the police,' Butler said. 'We don't ring ahead!'

He looked at her, nodding, then started backing up, while two articulated lorries roared and hissed and started to leave the side of the warehouse. 'Come on, then, you'll have to go through reception and security.'

'I thought you were security,' Moone said, following him round a path that led to a large covered glass and steel arched reception.

'Me?' He laughed, pointing a thumb at himself. 'Na, I'm just for show. Don't really need much security. Who's going to break in here? Terrorists? I don't think so.'

Butler huffed, then followed him into the shiny wide open reception area, while Moone held open the door. There was a dark-haired young woman on the reception desk, so they both took turns to show their IDs.

'Oh, OK,' the young woman said, her nose creasing up. 'You'll have to sign in and take a name badge. Who're you here to see?'

'They want to see Mr Burton,' the security guard said.

'He'll be busy,' the young woman said.

'That's what I told them,' the guard said.

'Can we cut all this crap,' Butler said. 'Is nobody bloody listening? We are the bloody police! Go get Mr Burton! Now!'

The young woman stared at her for a moment, then handed over some badges, looking a little resentful, then hurried off towards a door behind, the sound of her heels clicking off, then fading away.

'What's happened?' the guard asked, looking far too interested for Moone's liking.

'Police business,' Butler said. 'We can't discuss it with you.'

The guard stood up straight, folded his arms tightly across his chest. 'Right. Got it. Fine. I'll go and do my job.'

'Good,' Butler said, then Moone watched him storm off out of the reception, where he stopped and lit a cigarette.

'You all right?' Moone asked.

She glared at him. 'You know the answer to that, Moone.'

'You can call me Pete. You do realise that?'

'I know. You call me Mandy and you'll get a slap.' She turned away, but he thought he saw a smile that faded away as the click clacking heels of the young woman came back.

'I'm sorry, Mr Burton is in a very important meeting right now,' she said, then gestured across the reception. 'But we have a delightful waiting area and I can get you coffee...'

Butler walked up to her, then pointed a finger in her face. 'You go and tell your boss, unless he comes down here and talks to us in your bloody delightful waiting area, then we'll come and interrupt his important bloody meeting. Got it?'

The young woman looked at Moone, as if he would be more understanding, so he nodded. 'Go on, let him know. We'll be waiting over there.'

'Oh, two sugars!' Butler called out as the woman hurried off again.

Moone sat down in the large, airy waiting room and picked up a motoring magazine from a pile on a nearby table, while Butler stood, arms folded, staring through the glass towards the reception.

'You can relax now,' he said, flipping through the pages, trying to focus on the images of the cars, and trying not to let the flashes of the violent day rise up into his mind.

'Doesn't feel like I'll ever relax again,' she said. 'I want to be alone with him in a room... just me, him, and my Casco.'

'You talking about Sturkey or your husband?' Moone smiled when she looked at him and was glad to see her give a half-hearted laugh as she said, 'I don't know right now. Either will do.'

Then the heels were coming but stopped. Moone stood up to see a wide, pinstripe-suited man coming fast across the floor, his fists clenched, his short greying hair neat. His face looked tired, and strained as he pulled open the door and came in.

He folded his arms across his chest and stared between them both.

'OK, I'm here,' he said, obviously seething. 'What's all this about? I was in a very important meeting.'

'Well, we're investigating a crime,' Butler said, looking him up and down as if he smelt of dog mess. 'I think that's more important.'

He let out an empty, angry laugh. 'I suppose you would. What crime have I supposed to have committed? Do tell me...'

'Mr Burton...' Moone placed the bear on top of the magazines. 'You make this?'

'No,' Burton said, hardly looking at the toy.

'No?' Moone said. 'It's got your company's

logo on the label.'

'Well, we may have handled it, but we don't make toys.'

'Hang on,' Butler said, the anger building in her voice. 'You don't make toys? What the hell do you do here?'

He stared at her, then let out a breath full of impatience. 'We export toys all over the world. We get them manufactured all over the world too, they come here, then we sell them on.'

'This is a distribution centre?' Moone said, the penny landing like a weight on the top of his head along with the disappointment.

'Yes!' Burton groaned, then gestured across towards the rest of the building. 'That's what we do here! I was just in the middle of a deal that would secure us a nice little contract supplying airports in Saudi Arabia!'

'So we came here for nothing?' Butler said, then stormed out of the room.

But Moone looked at the pissed off suit in front of him and then looked at the bear, and decided he wasn't going to make his day any easier. 'You distribute toys around the South West?'

Burton's face became curious, but still a little angry. 'Yes, all over the world...why? What the bloody hell's going on?'

Moone stepped up to him. 'I'm going to need a list of the shops you supplied these bears to.'

'What? Why? Why should I?'

'Because a toy bear just like this one was

found buried with the remains of a child... and when I say remains, just bones, that's all that was left. That child was murdered.'

Burton lost all his fury as he cleared his throat and looked awkwardly at the toy. 'OK, but what's that got to do with me? That bear could've come from anywhere.'

'I know.' Moone picked up the bear. 'But you're going to get that list together or get one of your people to do it, and we want it now, before we leave, or you'll find this company mentioned in the papers right alongside the murder of a small boy. You understand?'

Burton nodded, a little of his former anger returning as he took out a mobile phone and rang someone and started barking orders as he walked out of the room.

Moone tried to massage the tension out of his shoulders and neck as he walked out too and found Butler stood outside the reception, arms folded, resting against the wall, watching the motorway traffic roaring past.

'I want to believe we'll find his killers,' Butler said, her voice full of tiredness.

'Then believe.'

She looked at him. 'Look at it all. Look at those people flying past down there... do you think they care about any of it? Do you think they care that a little boy died?'

'I don't know...'

'They don't. All they care about is getting

to where they're going, and eating McDonald's or pizza, staring at their phones, maybe keeping their families safe... maybe.'

'I think people care more than you think.'

'Really? What about the cases you worked in London? Did anyone care?'

He walked round her, faced her. 'I cared. I still care. It's why I find it hard to sleep, why I need to drink a bottle of vodka before bed cause it helps me sleep. And why I smoke a pack of fags a day...'

'I haven't seen you smoke today.'

'No...' She was right, he hadn't smoked, hadn't felt like it, but he didn't know what it meant, if anything.

'Excuse me,' a voice said, and they both turned to see the security guard, Keith, puffing away at a cigarette, watching them.

'What do you want?' Butler asked.

'Didn't mean to interrupt,' he said. 'But this... this thing you're here to look into, has it got anything to do with some of the people they've had working here?'

Moone looked at Butler, but she just shrugged, so he said, 'Maybe. Why?'

'It's just that...' He took another drag of his cigarette. 'They had some right fucking scum-bags working here. I don't even think they were on the books. Probably claiming benefits. That what it's all about?'

Moone walked towards him. 'Something

like that. Anyone particular stand out from these scumbags?'

The guard puffed away, raised his shoulders and thought for a minute before he nodded. 'There was this one, scruffy looking bastard, caught him nicking a load of stuff. They gave him the sack on the quiet.'

'Really? Do you know his name?'

'Can't really remember, was a couple of years ago now. They might have record of him. Don't tell them I told you about him though.'

Moone nodded, then turned and headed back into the building where he found Mr Burton still in the reception, half talking to the receptionist, and half talking on his phone. Moone stood right in front of him, arms folded, until, looking irritated, he took the phone from his ear and said, 'What now?'

'I want a list of all the people you've had working here over the last three years. On the books and off. Now.'

CHAPTER 14

The dark was creeping in by the time they left the Good Times Toys building, with Butler at the wheel after she insisted on driving, and Moone wasn't about to argue. She appeared calmer to him, having seemed to have taken out her anger on the staff of the toy company when she'd stood over them while they came up with the list of former employees.

As they arrived back at the station, and hurried back up to the incident room, Moone scanned over the list of official full-time staff and the 'under the radar' employees who were given cash in hand. There weren't many names on the list, and of course he suspected that most of the names would be false. Before they'd left the building, they had promised Burton that they weren't after him for dodging tax, but they also promised more hell and fury from Butler and the press, if they didn't try and find any photographs

or get descriptions of all the off the books em‑
ployees. The security guard was going to be set
up with a sketch and a mugshot book to see if
he could come up with an ID on the thief who
got fired. They would've tried for CCTV, but their
security friend informed them that it was wiped
not long after being taken, unless there was a
particular incident that caused them to inspect
it. When Moone had asked about the incident in‑
volving the stolen toys, the security team had in‑
formed them that the tape was wiped because of
course they didn't want the police involved.

It was getting late when they reached the
incident room, so Butler started grabbing her
stuff together, but Moone sat down at a desk and
kept going over everything in his mind, trying to
piece things together, but not really coming up
with much.

Butler was about to leave when PC Carthew
came into the incident room and said, 'They've
got Sturkey in the cells. He's been cleared by the
hospital.'

Moone stood up, but saw the tiredness wash
over Butler, so said, 'Go home. PC Carthew and
me can handle this.'

Although she didn't show it, Moone saw the
relief deep in her eyes as she said, 'Thanks. I
could do with a good night's sleep. I'll see you
tomorrow.'

'Relax,' Moone said, and Butler rolled her
eyes then went to leave. But she stopped and

looked at him.

'Haven't you got dinner at your ex-wife's place tonight?'

Moone looked up in panic at the clock across the room and saw that it was close to six p.m. 'I've got time to talk to Sturkey before I need to go. Do you mind sitting in with me, Faith?'

'No, not at all,' she said, blushing.

Butler looked over at Carthew, then Moone, her eyes narrowed as she opened the door. 'Have fun. Behave yourselves!'

As they headed to the interview room, Faith said, 'I guess it was pretty obvious what went on the other night?'

Moone laughed. 'Well, yeah, when she turned up and you were having a morning coffee in my caravan...'

Faith frowned. 'She doesn't like me.'

'I'm not sure she likes anyone. Don't take it personally.'

Before Moone could put his hand on the door, Faith said, 'I heard about today... what happened? You OK?'

'I'm fine. It's Sturkey who was in hospital. Let's go in and have a chat.'

Moone went in and stood in the doorway, watching Sturkey, who was dressed in a light blue forensic outfit. The prisoner looked up and glared at him. There was a bandage wrapped around his head, and Moone found himself wanting to laugh at how ridiculous he looked sat there, trying to look mean.

Moone sat down, noticing the female duty solicitor, who seemed to be quite young, bookish looking with round glasses, hair in a neat bun. He smiled as PC Carthew took a seat, then said, 'Glad to see you've recovered, Mr Sturkey.'

'Yeah, like fuck you are,' he said and turned his head away, looking up at the wall. 'I could have brain damage.'

'How would we tell?' Moone smiled as Sturkey spun his head round at him, the flames in his eyes.

'Did you hear that?!' he asked the duty solicitor, but she raised her shoulders and looked down at her notes. 'I don't fucking get it, it's you lot that go round hassling me, knocking me about, and here I am in trouble? Fucking hell...'

Moone sat forward. 'You pulled a knife on my colleague... let's do this properly. I'm going to record this interview.'

He went through the process, reading out the names, the times, then as the machine recorded away, Moone said, 'Mr Sturkey, where were you on Sunday night, after ten?'

'Why the fuck should I tell you?' Sturkey said.

'Because you'll need an alibi,' PC Carthew said.

Sturkey stared at her. 'Alibi? For what?'

'Murder,' Moone said. 'That's what you were arrested for. Remember? Two murders. The murders of Jason Mitchum, and Jed Dalton.'

'Never fucking heard of them!' He sprung up, slapping his hand on the table.

'Where were you Sunday night?' Moone asked again.

'I went out!' Sturkey said.

'Where?'

'A pub!'

'What pub? Where?' Moone checked his phone. Time was getting on, getting closer to dinner time.

'The Dolphin,' Sturkey said, sitting back, folding his arms. 'The only pub I like these days... one that's not filled with fucking kids or queers.'

'Lovely,' Moone said. 'How long were you there for?'

'After hours, there was a lock in. I don't remember getting home. That all right for you?'

Moone sat back, folded his arms. 'What about Monday?'

'When Monday?' A smug grin spread across his face.

'Let's say the whole day.' Moone's stomach tied itself in a knot, a little itch at the back of his neck telling him that Sturkey might not be their killer.

Sturkey sat forward, the smug grin stretching, obviously savouring the moment. 'I was working. Know where you found me? I was working there all day. Ask the other lads if you don't believe me.'

'Was that Greenbank?' PC Carthew asked, sitting forward.

'Yeah, that's right.' Sturkey stared at her.

'Well,' Carthew said. 'That's not far from the crime scene. You could've popped out for lunch or said you were...'

Moone caught her eye and smiled. 'My colleague's right. Wouldn't take you ten minutes to get there.'

The thug's face changed, the smugness turning to anger once again. 'Fuck off. You're trying to stitch me up! I didn't go anywhere. I was there all day! You go and ask them! Go on!'

Moone sat back, a little disappointed that his gut was telling him that Sturkey was probably telling the truth, and that PC Carthew' moment of victory had sunk away.

'Interview terminated,' Moone said, switching off the machine and noticing Faith's look of disappointment.

In the corridor, as they watched Sturkey being taken back to his cell, complaining all the way, Faith said, 'How come you terminated the interview? We had him.'

'No, we didn't. He's got an alibi.' Moone noticed the time and headed back to the incident room to grab his things.

'You don't believe him, do you?'

Moone stopped at the incident room doors and faced her. 'Sometimes you've got to listen to your instincts. We'll check out his alibi, talk to people, check CCTV, but my feeling is that he's telling the truth. He's a thug...'

'Yeah, he's a thug and a lying one at that. He's going to walk right out of here scot-free... what about the other attack?'

'We've got him on that... at least we'll have to see if we've got enough to charge him with it. I know it stinks when you see people getting away with it, but I don't think he murdered our victims. I think there's more to this than just random violence. You did good in there.'

She nodded and sighed. 'Thanks. But I could do with a drink. Fancy one?'

'I'm sorry, I can't. Not tonight.' As he said the words, he could see her face change, disappointment filling her eyes.

'Oh, OK. That wasn't just a one-night thing, was it?'

'No, no, I'm not trying to put you off... I've just got to go and have dinner with my kids.'

'You've got kids?'

'Yeah. I have. Anyway, I need to go and see them... and have a really awkward dinner. I'll talk to you tomorrow. OK?'

She smiled, but he detected a hint of disappointment behind her eyes. 'That's fine. I'll see you tomorrow. Then we can have that date.'

'We can,' he said, then rushed into the incident room.

He didn't have time to change, even though he felt bedraggled in his creased suit that had already been involved in a scuffle, so he headed straight over to Angela's with his stomach doing forward rolls all the way. The house was in Mannamead, a posher part of Plymouth, along a narrow tree lined street. But of course it was, he thought as he parked and headed towards a large red brick house set back from the street with a small garden and large drive. There was one car parked on the drive, a large Land Rover, a hulk of a vehicle with huge wheels that no one really needed to drive in a city.

He rang the bell, tapping his leg, his stomach tightening, agonising over the fact that he was about to come face to face with Angela's hard face.

But the door opened with force and Alice stood there, a smile spread ear to ear. 'Dad! You made it! You actually made it!'

He laughed and ruffled her hair as he stepped inside. 'All right, don't have to sound so surprised.'

The hallway was massively wide, highly polished real wood flooring flowing off into the rest of the house. As he walked further towards the end of the hallway, by a wide wooden and ornate staircase, the sweet scent of the house greeted him, and it reminded him of how their house used to smell.

'Did you do what I asked?' Alice said, grabbing his arm and making him face her.

He tried to hide the fact that it had slipped his mind but failed miserably.

'Dad!' she moaned. 'I gave you one job to do!'

'I do have another job to do! You do know that, yeah? Look, I will look into him. OK?' Moone looked around the house, up towards the bright floors above, then at the archway that seemed to lead to a large kitchen. 'Where's everyone?'

'Mum's been called into work. Some emergency.'

'She's a teacher, isn't she? What sort of emergency? A teaching emergency?'

'I don't know. Think there's been a leak or something. Rick's in the living room playing on the PlayStation.'

'Right, and Gabriel?'

'Asleep.'

'Of course she is.'

'Go on through to the kitchen, I'll get you a beer.'

Moone followed his daughter through the archway and into the large, bright kitchen. There was an island at the centre, and sat there was a suited man with a glass of white wine in his hand, a newspaper in the other.

The man looked up, smiling at Alice, his

eyes darting over to Moone. 'Is this your father, Alice?'

'It is,' she said, resting her back against the worktop. 'Dad... DI Peter Moone, this is Carl Mathieson... Mum's latest fella.'

Mathieson laughed, but Moone saw the flash of annoyance as he put out his hand towards him and said, 'I've heard a lot about you, Moone. Nice to meet you.'

'Same here,' he said, catching Alice's face as she glared at him, then stuck out her tongue. 'I've been told you're a local MP.'

'Don't hold that against me,' he said, smiling. 'I'm glad you could come. I'm afraid Angela's been called into work.'

'So I hear. That's a shame.'

'Fancy some wine? Or a beer?' Mathieson pointed to the giant American style fridge freezer, then pulled it open.

'Er... a beer would be good.' Moone looked at Alice, who was staring at him, and jerking her head, which he interpreted as 'interrogate' him. 'So, how come you ended up in politics?'

Mathieson opened a beer, passed it to him, then picked up his own wine glass. 'Well, that's a long and boring story. I was in the forces for a while. I came out wanting to help people... believe it or not.'

'There's millions who wouldn't,' Alice said, and Moone saw the unimpressed look that flashed over Mathieson's face before his smile appeared again as he said, 'So I got into local politics... then somehow here I am. But what about you? Must be tough seeing the things you've seen.'

'Nothing like you would've seen out on the battlefields.' Moone swigged his beer.

'Well, that was far from here, and a long time ago. Come and see my office.' Mathieson swung round and headed back through the archway, leaving Moone with Alice.

'Go on,' she said, impatiently. 'He's invited you into his private lair. Go on, dig for dirt.'

Moone huffed, then hurried off towards the stairs, where he found Mathieson waiting for him, looking more serious. Wary that he might've heard what Alice said, he reached the MP, who said, 'Let's clear the air a little.'

'OK.'

'I mean, I'm living with your ex-wife...'

'Yes, yes, you are. More importantly, you're living under the same roof as my kids.'

'I am.' Mathieson nodded as if Moone had made a remarkable observation, and he quickly realised this was probably a face and gesture he made when confronted with questions from the general public. 'I want you to know that I have your children's welfare at heart. I would never allow anything to happen to them. I would sooner die than...'

'I get the point.'

The MP nodded again. 'Very well. Come on.'

Mathieson turned and jogged up the stairs and then opened the door to a large office decked out with antique mahogany furniture and long bookshelves filled with books. As Moone reached the cumbersome desk that sat before an arched window, he noticed the framed photograph of soldiers all stood posing and smiling. He leaned in and noticed a young-looking Mathieson at the centre, as he wondered what exactly about the MP had alarmed his daughter so. Alice had never been one to make things up, not that she lacked imagination as a kid. She didn't, but she wasn't taken to flights of fancy either, and was always clear headed, which made him suspect there might be something to it. But she had also been very protective of her mum in the past, even though she understood what a difficult person she could be.

'Here we are,' Mathieson said, and shut the office door. Moone immediately saw his face change again, and political shades come down as he said, 'Actually, I was hoping to ask you about something...'

'You're not about to get me involved in politics, are you?'

Mathieson gave a laugh. 'I'm afraid that you're already involved. Deeply. You're a policeman. Politics is a massive part of it. But you know that.'

'I do. Only too well. So what did you want to discuss?' Moone's stomach had already sunk to his feet in anticipation.

The MP walked past Moone and rested his backside on the desk. 'I hear you're investigating a particularly delicate case at the moment?'

'I'm working on two, actually. Both pretty delicate.'

'Danny Sawyer?' The MP put on his best sympathetic face.

'I guess you heard about that when he went missing.'

Mathieson sighed and nodded. 'Yes, I heard about it, and got a little involved. Not to any great degree, but I tried my best to help those poor people... his parents, I mean. Have you officially identified the remains?'

'Not officially. But it looks like it's him.'

The MP nodded. 'I see. Are you any closer to finding out who did it?'

Moone studied him for a moment, noting he already had a lot of information that he'd probably got off some of the top brass, like his boss, Laptew. He could almost see them at the local lodge, one trouser leg pulled up, decked out in robes, doing the secret handshake. 'You understand I can't discuss an ongoing investigation?'

Mathieson looked surprised, but then nodded. 'No, of course not. I just thought that what with the situation... it's just that I heard someone was in hospital, and it may be related to the case.'

'Where did you hear that?' Moone could feel the irritation knotting the muscles in his back.

'I have my sources. You know how it is.'

'Unfortunately, I do. Well, yes, there is a man in hospital. But he's measuring six on the Glasgow scale at the moment.'

'So he could recover and give you some information?'

'Hopefully.'

Mathieson smiled. 'Yes, hopefully.'

'But that's all I can say. I'm sure the political grapevine will inform you of the rest.'

'Well, I hope we can be friends and I hope I can help you out along the way. I do have quite a bit of influence.'

'I bet you do. But I'm fine thanks. I like to get where I'm going by my own steam.'

'I understand. Very admirable. I hear you've done good work in London. You even earned yourself a medal, didn't you?'

'Where did you hear that? Angela?'

'We talk. I admire you. I just want us to get on.' Mathieson's pocket beeped so he took out his phone and stared at it. 'Oh dear. Doesn't seem like Angela's going to be back anytime soon. She sends her apologies. Still... we can all sit down and have a pleasant meal, can't we?'

'I guess,' Moone said, lying, wanting to head down the stairs at speed and out the front door. But Alice was down there and he needed, wanted, to spend time with her.

'Come on, then,' Mathieson said, patting Moone's shoulder and then heading past him to hold the office door open with a typical politician's smile. If Moone had been a baby right then, or even resembled a human sized one, he feared he would've been kissed.

There was a ringing somewhere. It was coming from Mathieson's pocket, so he tutted and took out the phone and looked at it, staring at it for a few moments. Then he huffed out a laugh as he slipped it back into his pocket. 'Not a number I recognise, so I won't be answering that. Let's eat.'

Moone followed him down the stairs then down the hallway, preparing himself for an awkward dinner, wondering how long it would be before he could slip away. His mind had started to travel to Derriford Hospital where Ian Macdonald was still in a coma, and something was telling him to pop along and take a look at him.

The doorbell rang. Mathieson froze halfway along the corridor, his head turning towards the front door. 'I wonder who that could be.'

'Angela would have a key, I suppose,' Moone said and laughed.

But Mathieson hardly reacted as he turned and stepped towards the door, his face tight, his body tense. The bell rang again, then again, causing Moone to turn to Mathieson and see his reaction. His eyes were fixed on the door, his mouth a little open.

'Do you want me to answer it?' Moone asked.

'No!' Mathieson said, firmly. 'No, it's OK. You go in and help Alice... spend time with your family. I'll see who it is.'

But Moone only stood in the archway as the MP who looked drawn, worried even, headed to the door and opened it a little way. He couldn't see who was at the door, but whoever it was, the conversation was brief. Mathieson shut the door and stood there for a moment, as though he was gathering himself, then turned and came back.

Before he could see that he'd been watching, Moone headed into the kitchen to find Alice already preparing the dinner, cutting up some salad. He smiled at her, but his stomach was in knots, that old suspicious feeling growing inside him.

CHAPTER 15

Mathieson didn't like sneaking out of the house in the early hours, especially when there was always the risk of Angela waking up and asking him where he was going. She might even suspect him of having an affair, although he felt that might be preferable to what he was actually doing. He didn't want to do what he was doing, but he had to, he had little choice, not when he imagined what would come out if he didn't intervene. But he felt sick at the thought of what he was helping cover up and had found himself on a couple of occasions in the bathroom, retching over the toilet bowl. It was getting that he could hardly look at himself in the mirror as he tied his tie.

He carefully went out the bedroom and down to the front door, quietly unlocked it, then slipped out. It was windy, and rain was falling quite hard, being pushed along the street in waves. He didn't have time to grab a coat, so he jogged into the road and headed to the end of the street where the bus shelter was. He saw a figure inside, made into a blur by the rain that drizzled down the glass.

He stepped inside. Malcolm West was sat huddled in a thick, dirty looking coat, only half his face showing because of the hood that was pulled over his head.

'West,' Mathieson said, making West jump a little and seem to wake up.

'Bloody hell,' West said, throwing him looks as he sat up. 'I'm soaked. I've been waiting here all bloody night. Why didn't you talk to me earlier?'

Mathieson leant in towards him, letting him see his eyes, making sure he could see how pissed off he was. 'Because, you moron, I had a bloody policeman in my house!'

West scrambled to his feet, pushing his hood down, staring at Mathieson. 'What? What did he want? Do they know?'

He shook his head. 'Calm down. No, it was... a friend.'

'A friend? A fucking friend?! You've got a friend who's a fucking copper?'

'I'm a fucking politician! I've got all kinds of friends. Listen, he told me something I found very, very disturbing.'

'What?'

'That MacDonald is still alive. He's in a

bloody coma. What happened?'

West looked away, breathing hard, then ran a hand down his dirty, bearded face. 'It ain't easy doing something like that! Have you ever tried to kill someone?!'

Mathieson stared at him, flashes of things he'd tried to long forget playing in his mind.

As if West had seen into his head, he said, 'Sorry, forgot about the army thing... look, he might not come out of it!'

'What if he does? What if the police talk to him?! Then we're fucked, aren't we? I can't go to prison. I can't lose all that I have!'

West stared at him, nodding, then stepped closer. 'Then, well, we have to get into that hospital before he wakes up... and, you know.'

Mathieson stared back, the sickness rising up in him, the wild spread of panic that was making his heart race. He wanted to turn away, to run back through the rain to the safety of his house, to pretend none of it had happened, just like when he and his mates were trapped, kept back by enemy fire, not knowing if an IED was about to go off nearby. He wanted to be anywhere else, imagined that he was home with his mum and dad and sister... tears would be in his eyes. Then he'd swallow it down, push himself forward, raise his weapon.

'We've got to have a plan,' Mathieson said. 'Let me think about it. I'll come up with a way to get us in there so we can get to him. He can't be allowed to wake up.'

Moone had woken up feeling like he'd sunk a few bottles of wine, even though he'd barely drunk a couple of glasses. He'd showered, thinking back over the awkward evening, remembering the strange conversation and incident he'd endured while in Carl Mathieson's company. Alice was right, there was something off about him, or something that he was hiding behind his over friendliness. No one is that welcoming to an ex-husband. And if it was something bad he was hiding, and no one hides good things, then that meant that his family were at risk. But Moone had little to back up his deep suspicions, apart from the person who turned up at the door and the strange, almost frightened way Mathieson had reacted.

Moone was in a dream, staring at the whiteboard, holding his coffee in his hand, when Butler breezed in looking a lot lighter than she'd done the day before. The evening off had done her the world of good, it seemed.

'Did Sturkey give us anything to go on?' she asked as she hung up her coat in the corner.

'A couple of alibis for our murders,' Moone said, then sipped his drink. 'I've got a strange feeling that they'll stand up to scrutiny.'

Butler stood in front of his desk, arms folded. 'In other words, you don't think he killed our victims?'

Moone shook his head.

'Why?'

Moone shrugged. 'He's full of rage, hate. I don't doubt he attacked Salmon's friend, but our murders, I think our killer sought them out... and the skinning, the burning, he was... I don't know. It just doesn't fit with Sturkey, does it?'

Butler unfolded her arms. 'No, it doesn't. He's a tosser, a violent, homophobic, racist tosser, but I don't think he killed them either. For once we agree with each other. What about our Danny Sawyer murder?'

'Well, I've finally had confirmation through that the DNA is a match. It's Danny.'

Moone watched helplessly as Butler pulled up a chair, fell into it and cupped her face in her hands. She breathed deeply for a few moments, then coughed, and sat up, nodding. 'OK. Well... let's get on with it. I've been looking for Ray Benton on the quiet, but so far nothing. No one's talking.'

'The security guy's looking through the mugshots at the moment,' Moone said, 'so maybe he'll come up with something.'

'Let's go and see him,' Butler said, standing up. She wiped her eyes before heading for the door.

Moone watched her for a moment, realising that she wasn't the hard-faced cow she made herself out to be.

He followed her to the interview room where the security guard, Keith Cramp, was sitting, a hot drink in one hand, the mugshot book in the other. A fair-haired PC was sat next to him looking equally bored, sprawled out a little, but sat up straight when Butler approached.

'Anything?' Butler asked, leaning on the desk.

Cramp looked up, shrugged, 'Do I get a fag break?'

'In a minute,' Butler said, then tapped the book. 'Keep looking. We need to identify the people working at that place.'

'I know. I get it,' Cramp said. 'I keep looking at their faces, but they all start to look familiar after a while.'

'Maybe he should have a break,' Moone said, raising his eyebrows at Butler. 'Let him have a fag, clear his mind a bit.'

'Hang on,' Cramp said, tapping the book. 'I think I recognise this one. Yeah, I'm sure he worked at our place a while back.'

Butler and Moone moved round the table to look at the page the guard had stopped at, his finger still tapping the page. Moone found himself staring at the image of a middle-aged man with a long face, hooked nose and strangely thick lips. His eyes stared out a Moone, and in them there seemed to be an unsettling menace. 'Who's that?'

Butler had already sighed and looked away by the time Moone asked the question. But then she turned back to Cramp as she pointed a thumb towards the door. 'Go on, go for your fag break. Show him out please.'

The PC escorted Cramp through the door, then Butler shut it and faced Moone. 'Well, looks like your wish is going to come true after all.'

'My wish?'

Butler leaned over the book and pointed at the same photograph that the security guard had tapped. 'This is Loy Grader. The most evil child abuser and killer you're likely to meet.'

'So... we go talk to him?'

Butler huffed, then nodded. 'Yes, we do. We haven't got much choice. Have we?'

He left it to Butler to make the arrangements, to phone Dartmoor prison and book them in to see the infamous child murderer. Moone sat at his desk waiting for her to get off the phone, not able to make up his mind which of the two things he was more nervous about, coming face to face with a notorious child killer or the legendary Dartmoor prison. Being so close to so many offenders always made him feel a little sick, as he knew what depraved behaviour was sometimes committed behind prison walls.

Butler put down the phone, let out a breath, then came over to Moone, leaning over the desk, eyebrows raised.

'Well,' she said, sounding a little surprised.

'Looks like we won't be visiting Dartmoor today.'

'We won't?' Moone felt the relief wash over him.

'No, seems Loy Grader's on his way to Derriford Hospital getting checked over. Something to do with his heart.'

'So we haven't got far to go.' Moone got up and grabbed his coat, watching Butler follow suit.

They parked a little way from a row of newly built restaurants that sat under a high-rise car park not far from the main body of Derriford Hospital. They hurried towards the main entrance, then through the automatic doors, past the dribble of patients and hospital workers coming outside. They passed the cafe, then followed the signs to the Medical Assessment Unit, where Butler had been told that Grader would be delivered.

When they arrived, there was a uniform and a stocky, black prison guard already waiting, leaning against the reception desk.

Moone and Butler showed their IDs to the prison guard.

'Detectives?' the guard said and straightened up. 'You the two who I was told want a word with Grader?'

'That's us,' Moone said. 'Where's Grader?'

'Not here yet,' the guard said. 'They're

bringing him up now.'

Butler looked over the shoulder of the guard, towards the ward behind. 'Seems a little empty. Usually this quiet round here?'

The guard shook his head. 'Na, they've cleared the place. Made sure any patients and especially children aren't around.'

'Jesus,' Moone said. 'Is he that dangerous?'

The guard shrugged. 'He's just best kept from the public. For everyone's sake, that's what they tell me. Here he comes.'

Moone turned to see another guard, thick set, with shaved, balding hair, coming down the corridor. He was checking the area before he turned and waved and beckoned to someone. Then another guard came round the corner, followed by a short muscular looking man with obviously dyed brown receding hair. Moone recognised his ugly, hook-nosed face, and his dark peering eyes from the mugshot book. The prisoner smirked as he looked around himself, taking in his surroundings.

'Haven't you left me anyone to play with?' Grader said, in a voice much higher than Moone had expected.

'You know the drill,' the guard said as he put a hand on Grader's arm and directed him further along the corridor. 'They've got a cosy cubicle for you. Nice and private.'

'Oh, that is a shame,' Grader said, looking quizzically over his shoulder as Moone and Butler followed. 'Tell me, John, who are these nosy pair behind me?'

'They're from the police,' John said, then directed the prisoner into a cubicle on their left, where a short, blonde-haired nurse was waiting beside a male health worker.

Moone went in, followed by Butler and the medical team to find the prison guard and Loy Grader getting comfortable. Grader sat on the hospital bed and was cuffed to it.

'We'll need you to roll up your sleeve,' the nurse said in a soft, Northern Irish accent.

Grader did as she asked, giving her a creepy grin that she did her best to ignore. 'Anything else you'd like me to take off?' he asked.

'No, thank you,' the nurse said, while the male nurse stood by watching.

'Behave yourself, Mr Grader,' the guard said, shaking his head.

Moone came in further, and stood by Grader, looking down at him, trying not to let in all the disturbed images that hurried to his mind. 'We need to ask you some questions, Grader.'

But the prisoner didn't look at him, didn't take his eyes off the nurse as he said, 'Tricia. That's a nice name. Got any kids, Tricia?'

'Grader!' the guard barked, which made Grader laugh and cough for a moment before he looked up at Moone.

'What did this fuckwit say?' Grader said, his voice thick with ridicule. 'You want a word?'

'That's right, I want a word.' Moone pulled up a chair, while Butler stood in the doorway, arms folded. 'Heard of a company called Good Times Toys?'

'Can't say I have. You got any kids?'

'Grader!' the guard snapped again. 'It's your favourite show on tonight... remember?'

Grader put on a sickeningly sweet smile that made Moone want to retch.

'Sorry, officer,' Grader said. 'What did you want to ask me?'

'About Good Times Toys.'

'Bad Times Toys,' Grader said, the smile fading, his eyes turning to the nurses as they brought in some kind of machine on wheels. 'That's what I call it.'

'Why?'

Grader looked at him. 'Cause they don't treat their staff very nicely.'

Moone laughed. 'Especially not the ones off the books.'

Grader didn't say anything for a moment, but looked Moone over, perusing him with dark eyes before he stuck out a chubby open hand. 'I'm sorry, we haven't been properly introduced. Loy Grader. You are?'

'DI Peter Moone,' he said, tentatively reaching out his hand.

'I wouldn't if I was you,' the guard said, tutting and shaking his head. 'Just think what he's done with that hand.'

Moone's stomach turned over as he put his hand by his side, watching the child killer's face stretch into a grin.

They had to stand back while the staff went about attaching an ECG machine to Grader. The prisoner was asked to remove his top by the nurse, which Moone noticed he took great joy in and started whispering things.

The nurse huffed and stared up at the guard, 'I can't do this! I'll get someone else.'

Moone and Butler moved out of her way as she stormed past, heading to the main nurses' station.

Grader laughed. 'Some people are touchy,' he said.

A stocky, stern-looking female nurse, with tied-back dyed red hair, came in and stood in front of Grader.

'Been upsetting my staff, have we?' the nurse said, arms folded. 'I won't put up with any of your nonsense. Right, let's get on with this.'

'I'm guessing you don't have kids,' Grader said, as the nurse stuck the small pads to his chest.

'I'm not listening,' she said and went about her work, ordering the assistant to start the machine and warm it up.

'What can you tell us about the other people that worked there?' Butler asked Grader.

'I can tell you're the one who wears the strap-on in this relationship,' Grader said, laughing again. 'OK, I could tell you lots about that place, all the dodgy little goings on, the tax avoidance, the little bits of theft that goes on, but why should I?'

'We want to know about Danny Sawyer,' Moone said, making the offender's eyes jump to him, narrowing.

'Not one of mine,' he said, and the words seemed to hang over Moone, coating him in images he didn't want.

'We know,' Butler said. 'You were locked up. But I bet you heard about it. You like to share your little... adventures, don't you? Like to tell late-night prison stories about the things you've done.'

Grader huffed. 'Tell that lot? In there? You must be doolally! I spend most of my days trying not to get shivved. I wouldn't go talking to them lot.'

'We found him,' Moone said, watching Grader's eyes. 'We found Danny Sawyer.'

The prisoner looked up, scrutinising Moone. 'Good, I'm glad some peace will be brought to his family.'

'You lying bastard,' Butler said, the anger brimming in her.

'What do you want me to say?' Grader said, looking between them. 'I don't know what happened to him.'

'Ian Macdonald,' Moone said and raised his eyebrows. 'You know that name?'

'Must be a pretty common name,' Grader said, looking clear of emotion.

'You know him,' Butler said. 'Was he a member of your club?'

'I've never liked clubs,' he said. 'I've always preferred playing on my own. Even as a child.'

'We think he took Danny Sawyer,' Moone said. 'Right outside his house.'

Grader stared at Moone while the machine whirred, the metal arm with the pen scratching at the paper. 'What do I get if I cooperate?'

'What're you after?' Moone asked.

'They cut certain photos out of the papers and magazines I read,' Grader said. 'I'd like that stopped.'

'No, fucking chance,' the prison guard said.

'Then I want to visit my mum,' Grader said.

'Your mother's dead,' the prison guard said, tutting.

Grader looked over his shoulder at the guard. 'I meant her grave. I'd like to visit, lay some flowers by her gravestone, maybe sit on the bench for a little while.'

'That all?' Butler asked, sounding annoyed.

'I want to watch what I want to watch, not what they say I can watch,' Grader said.

'No chance,' the guard said.

'We'll see what we can do.' Moone folded his arms, staring down at the small, creepy man, wondering what exactly he wanted to watch and feeling his skin crawl. 'So... what do you know?'

Grader looked up, smiling a little. 'There's a lot I know... let me think, I've got to save some stuff. What about accommodation?'

Moone frowned. 'Accommodation? Yours...'

'No. Not mine. Ian MacDonald. Malcolm West. Where do they live?'

'You asking?' Butler said.

Grader shook his head, then sighed. 'No, it was a rhetorical question. Look into their living arrangements... that should put the cat among the pigeons. That's the only thing I'll tell you. For now.'

CHAPTER 16

'We could've got more out of him,' Butler said, driving back along Tavistock Road, slowing as the traffic built up in front of them.

Moone was staring out the window towards the drive thru McDonald's, but he wasn't really seeing it. His mind kept flickering, edging into the imagined horrors that Grader might have committed. He kept trying to empty his mind, but the images kept flashing in front of his eyes. 'I doubt it. You saw the way he buttoned up after he said what he had to say. He's playing the long game.'

Butler groaned. 'Long game? Give me fifteen minutes with him and I'd get him to talk.'

'I'm sure you would,' Moone said and looked at her. 'I'm sure there's plenty of parents that would like the same chance. Accommodation, living arrangements? What's he getting at?'

'Pulling our chain. People like him get off on

it. I mean what was all that rubbish about visiting his dead mother's grave?'

'I don't know...' Moone still felt a little sick and could think of only one thing that would disguise the taste; he took out his pack of fags and his lighter.

'You're not smoking in my car,' Butler snapped.

'I thought we were mates now?'

'We might be, sort of, but I'm not having my car stinking of fags and getting cancer from your smoke! Where we going anyway?'

'Why don't we pay another visit to Malcolm West's place?'

'You're putting too much store in what Grader says,' Butler said, but he saw her signalling, getting ready to change lane.

'Maybe. But what if he is feeding us a little something to keep us interested. It's in his interest to keep us on the hook.'

Butler let out an unimpressed noise, but joined another lane, then headed for Pennycomequick and found the road that West was living in. She parked, then sat back, staring towards the terraced house, the grey, grizzled sky beyond it. Moone got comfortable, or as comfortable as he could, trying to think of some interesting conversation. But his mind kept going over what Grader had said to them until one name seemed to float around his brain.

'Ian Macdonald,' he said aloud, making Butler turn to him.

'What about him? Probably going to be a cabbage for the rest of his life.'

'No, he was living near Danny Sawyer. Right?'

'Yes, we know that.'

Moone sat up. 'Where's he been living since? Didn't I see his address somewhere?'

Butler sighed. 'Yeah, hang on, it's in my notebook.' She took out her notebook. 'Right, yeah… a couple roads over from Milehouse Road. So?'

Moone shrugged. 'Grader talked about their living arrangements. Where Macdonald's been living now, maybe… not then.'

Butler turned to him, narrowed her eyes. 'Now you're grasping at straws, but OK, seeing as he's sort of in our custody, we can have a snoop around.'

Butler then drove them out of the street, round the Pennycomequick roundabout and towards Milehouse Road where she took a turning into a narrow road not far from Stoke Village.

It was a close made up of twelve untidy terrace houses with short front gardens. The street was eerily quiet as they pulled up outside number ten, where MacDonald had been living until his stint in hospital.

'Well, here we are,' Butler said, sitting back, sounding even more grumpy. 'But we haven't got a key. We'll have to send for a uniform to fetch it and implement a proper search.'

'He's in our hands, so it's legal. Don't need a magistrate to sign off on it.'

'He's not been arrested, he's not physically capable of being arrested!'

'OK, so we go home?'

She gave one of her loudest huffs then said, 'Fine. I'll send for the key.'

As Butler took out her mobile, Moone climbed out, looking towards the ramshackle house, the overgrown garden and the row of houses beyond it. He started walking, feeling how much colder it had got, seeing a stream of his own breath trailing off. The street was quiet, only the distant sound of traffic reaching him.

Then another sound. A door opening opposite Macdonald's house. He turned, putting his chilled hands into his pockets, staring towards the figure coming backwards out of the house, fiddling with the lock after he shut the door.

Then he turned and stared at Moone, frozen in his steps. He was at least thirty years old, stocky, with a round, shiny face, wisps of a beard and receding brown hair.

The man nodded, snapped out of his frozen state, and started moving again, but Moone kept watching him, his gut starting to tap at his skull, telling him to talk to him. He produced his ID as he headed over the road, speeding up as he said, 'Excuse me...'

The man slowed, looking over his shoulder

at Moone, a strange look in his eye, perhaps a little fear, Moone thought.

'I don't suppose you know the man that lives opposite you?' Moone asked, showing his ID, noting that the man's eyes seemed to widen at the sight of it.

'No, not really,' the man said, trying to smile as he went to turn away.

'Ian Macdonald,' Moone said and watched as the man stopped moving again.

'Sorry, don't know him,' the man said, gave another awkward smile and hurried off.

'Who's that?' Butler said behind him, but Moone hardly took her in or heard her words, as he was now staring towards the house that the man had just left. 'I don't know. Let's take a note of that address though. There's was something about that guy that didn't sit right with me.'

'You're getting paranoid. Uniform will be here soon with the key.'

It took half an hour for a uniform to drive up with a key. Moone had walked down to a nearby shop and got a couple of takeaway coffees in the meantime, and sat on the wall while the uniform let them in. Then he followed Butler into the musty smelling hallway, still nursing his coffee, looking round at the lime green, marked walls, the stained beige carpet, the dark mould in the corners of the ceilings.

'Never stops raining here,' Butler said. 'Nothing dries out.'

Moone nodded, then headed left into a small lounge and only slightly larger dining area separated only by an archway. Most of the small rooms were taken up by untidy piles of newspapers, which surrounded a motheaten and cigarette-burned flowery sofa.

'Looks like this boy's a hoarder,' the uniform said behind Moone, but he'd already noted that there wasn't anything else being hoarded.

'It's only newspapers,' Moone said, turning to see Butler coming into the room, snapping on some blue latex gloves.

'What's that?' she asked, looking over the place. 'He's a chatty sod, isn't he?'

'Chatty?' Moone asked. 'Oh, yeah, dirty. If he's a hoarder, why's he only hoarding newspapers?'

Butler walked over to a stack and started flipping through them. 'Evening Heralds mostly. These go back a few years.'

'What if he was collecting for a reason?' Moone asked.

'Other than causing a fire hazard?' the uniform said.

'Not very bloody funny,' Moone said, stopping himself from smiling as he squatted next to another pile of newspapers and began searching through them. He stopped when he got to the third newspaper that he found had an article neatly cut from it. After a few more searches, he found another few newspapers that had articles cut out from the front and second pages. As Moone got to his feet, he said, 'Get on to the Evening Herald, and find out what these missing stories were about.'

Butler came over, grabbed a couple of the papers that Moone was holding out, then walked off with her mobile to her ear.

'Want me to look through those, boss?' the uniform asked, stepping closer.

'No, let's have a look around first, see what else we can find.' Moone led the way up the threadbare carpeted stairs, towards an equally musty smelling landing. There were more damp and mould marks on the walls, and large cobwebs in the corners of the high ceilings. He was about to enter the master bedroom, when he heard Butler call from downstairs. He bent over the bannister and shouted down, 'What was that?'

Butler looked up at him, the phone still in her hand. 'Those stories, they're all to do with the disappearance of Danny Sawyer.'

Colin Samson's car coughed and spluttered its way down the road and round the bend. He parked quickly and let the engine die in peace, knowing with regret that it had seen better days and he'd have to fork out for a new motor soon.

But his mind jumped from that subject to the one that had gripped his stomach and twisted it into knots. He looked towards the house on the corner of the street, the one that had long since been turned from a post war prefab to a run of the mill house. Rain spat gently at the windscreen as Colin stared towards the house, trying to build up the courage to go inside.

Then his stomach flipped over and his heart raced as he spotted the front door opening and a figure standing in the open doorway. It was Kieran, he was pretty sure, and knew for certain when he opened the car door and stepped out, feeling the cool rain tapping at his skin.

Kieran stepped away from the doorway and headed down the garden path.

'Hello,' Samson said, his voice breaking, his pounding heart making him deaf to any other sound as he walked up and met Kieran at the gate. He'd planned to come out with something else, something profound and meaningful, but all sentient thought left him as he looked into the sad eyes of the man he'd been holding a candle for, for the longest time.

'What do you want?' Kieran said, coldly, making Colin's heart sink.

'I just... I just wanted to make sure you're OK.'

'I'm fine. Now you can go.' Kieran stared at him, hardly anything in his eyes, but Samson thought he could see hurt and fear.

'I'm sorry about your mum,' Colin said.

'Did you send them?'

'Send them? Who?'

'Who? The bloody police! They came round here asking all kinds of questions! What gives you the right...'

Samson held up his hands, realising this had been a bad decision. 'I'm sorry. I'm really sorry, but they wanted to know about the attack. There's someone out there attacking... killing gay men...'

'I'm not... I'm not gay.'

'OK... then I'm sorry. I just came today to make sure you're OK. That's all.'

Kieran's face seemed to change then, seemed to soften a little, Samson thought.

'Thanks,' Kieran said. 'But there's no need to worry. I'm fine. Everything's good.'

'Are you on your own? I mean, since your mum, you know, passed away?'

The coldness seemed to rise in Kieran's eyes again as he said, 'Yes, I'm on my own. I'm fine with that... you?'

'There was somebody, for a while, but it's over now. Look, if you want to talk or go for a drink, you can have my number.'

'I'm fine.'

'OK.' Samson realised he'd better cut his losses and put his phone away. 'Well, I still work at the uni, so you know where to find me.'

Kieran nodded, but said nothing, so Samson

turned away, feeling a few more spits of rain, the greying sky reflecting the state of his heart. He reached his car, opened the door and was about to climb in, when he heard his name. He turned and saw Kieran had come out of the garden and stood on the pavement.

'Colin,' Kieran said. 'If there is, you know, some person out there, attacking people, you take care.'

Samson found himself smiling, and considered asking to come in, but Kieran turned away and headed back into the house.

'And you!' he called out, his voice sounding pathetic and broken.

Moone and Butler left a couple of uniforms going over the house, careful to leave it just as it had been found. But they'd taken a few of the newspapers with them, neatly concealed in an evidence bag, and returned to Charles Cross and the incident room.

It was its usual hive of activity, with the occasional phone chirping out to anyone who might answer. Moone sat down at a desk, then opened his notebook to the address of the mysterious man who he'd talked to in MacDonald's street.

'Let's take a look at that guy who came out of the house opposite MacDonald's,' he said.

Butler hung up her coat. 'Why exactly? Your

cockney gut instinct telling you something? You've been eating too many jellied eels, that's what it's telling you!'

'I can't stand that stuff.' Moone laughed and shook his head. 'I don't know. It was the way he talked to me. He was far too nervous...'

'We're coppers... that's what people are like. Terrified we're going to stitch them up.'

'Yeah, well...' Moone got up and went over to DC Harding, who was talking on the phone.

When Harding put down the phone, he said, 'Yes, boss?'

Moone passed him the address he'd written down. 'Can you check out this residence and tell me if anything dodgy comes up.'

'Meaning criminal activity?' Harding leaned back in his chair.

'Anything. Anything out of the ordinary.'

'I'll get on it, boss.'

Moone nodded and turned back to see Butler at her desk, facing her computer, a troubled expression on her face.

'You all right?' he asked, breaking her out of her stare.

She sighed. 'I've got the photos of Danny Sawyer here, the ones they're going to release to the press when they officially announce...'

'Right, we need to talk to the parents.'

She nodded. 'Yeah. I can do that, if you like.'

Moone was surprised, but relieved. 'Are you sure?'

'I think it would be better coming from me.'

She looked equally as glum as she spoke, so it was near impossible to decipher whether she was only offering as a gesture. 'OK, as long as you don't mind.'

'It's settled.'

Then the phone was ringing on Butler's desk, so she answered it and nodded and made noises that made little sense to Moone.

When she put the phone down, Moone asked, 'What was that?'

She stood up and grabbed her coat. 'They've just nabbed Malcolm West. He was loitering around Derriford Hospital, acting suspiciously. Shall we go and pick him up?'

He'd driven through town, getting snarled up in the afternoon traffic, parents doing the school run, tying up all the streets. He kept having to brake, buses pulling out as he saw the big ugly bulk of the shopping mall on his left. In front of him was the university and he could see students coming and going, just returned from half term. All they did was drink themselves stupid.

He took the next turning and entered the mall car park and then found a space near the back of the top floor. He looked around, made sure no one was about, then picked up the carrier bag that contained the six pack of beer he'd bought that morning. He opened one, feeling thirst grip his dry throat, hearing the metallic click and the fizz. He gulped half the can down, then sat back and belched and wiped his chin.

The images of what he'd done flooded his mind, so he drank more until the can was empty, and then opened another. He drank half of that and felt better about it all, as if the memory of the death was behind a wall of cotton wool and not really part of his reality. His hands were not shaking anymore either, so he climbed out, feeling the dizziness and the buzz from the alcohol, and started to walk across the stretch of concrete floor towards the lifts.

No one ever paid him much attention, except to move away from him. When he stood waiting for the lift, next to the young blonde woman with the toddler in a pushchair, and the old couple, he saw them all give him the once over.

'What you looking at?' he asked them. He was more asking out of curiosity, to find out what exactly they saw when they looked at him. His mind wandered then as he climbed in the lift alone, the other potential passengers having walked away. He thought back to his days living at home, to his father's angry red face as he would stand over him, growling out his words, telling him off again, usually for no reason at all. Other times he knew what he'd done wrong and he'd cry and beg for forgiveness.

The low winter sun appeared through the

craggy grey clouds and shone right into his eyes as he stumbled along, moving around the people waiting to cross the street.

He moved faster when he saw a group of students outside the main path that led towards the university, right opposite the library. They were handing something out, some kind of flyer. One of the girls, pink hair, black clothes and fishnets, held out the pink flyer towards him, a big smile on her face.

'Two for one drinks,' she said, so he looked down at the flyer, seeing that it was a "gay" night at a club called Hero's.

He snatched the flyer away from her, making her jump, anger flooding her face. He screwed it up in front of her face as he said, half growling, 'What, you think I'm one of them! Those disgusting... evil... you think I'm one of them!'

'Go away before I call the police!' another young woman said, her face red, her eyebrows raised, her mobile clenched in her hand.

He looked around, saw people were staring, so he spun around and started walking up North Hill, head down, not wanting to draw any more attention than he already had. Then he looked at the screwed-up flyer in his hand, seeing that the date of the party was tonight. He nodded to himself, threw the flyer in a bin and headed to a bar up the road a little way. He'd get a drink, something to calm him, to make him feel better while he planned exactly how he would teach them all, all the disgusting creatures in the club just how wrong they were.

CHAPTER 17

They saw the incident response car parked a little way from the maternity unit in the crowded car park a few yards from the entrance. When Moone and Butler parked up and approached the incident response car, Moone could see someone in the back, cuffed with his hands behind his back, hunched over. The uniform was stood by his open door, talking on his radio, so Moone went over and showed his ID. 'DI Peter Moone. Where did you find him?'

The muscular, square headed uniform put down his radio and faced them, smirking a little. 'Little greasy bastard was hanging around the ICU. There was kids around. You seen this bastard's record?'

'I don't think that's it,' Moone said, ducking down, looking at the greasy haired mess in the back seat.

'One of his sick little friends is in the ICU,'

Butler said. 'Probably wanted to say hello.'

'What do we do with the scumbag?' the uniform asked.

Moone opened the back door, then slid inside next to Malcolm West, who shot him a look, then sighed and looked down again.

'Hello again, Malcolm,' Moone said.

'This is fucking uncomfortable,' West said, spitting out his words. 'Can't you get them to cuff me in front?'

'No can do,' Moone said. 'Against protocol. You could use the cuffs as a weapon that way. What were you doing hanging round the ICU?'

'Don't take a bloody genius, does it?'

'Ian MacDonald? Your mate?'

West looked at him. 'So what? No crime against visiting a mate, not like I was hanging round the kids' ward or something.'

'No, I guess not. But, you and MacDonald were mates, good friends?'

'Good friends is pushing it. I know him...'

The front passenger door opened and Butler climbed in, then turned to face West. 'Go on. Don't be shy, Malcolm.'

West sighed. 'Like I said, I know him. Hung out a bit.'

'So you were visiting a bloke you hung around with?' Moone asked.

'Yeah, like I said.' West sniffed, shrugged his shoulders.

Moone watched him, thinking. 'Where were

you Tuesday night?'

West looked away from Moone. 'Don't know. Could've been anywhere.'

'Wasn't in Cattedown, hanging around one of the old disused warehouses, were you?' Butler asked.

'Na, wasn't there,' West said. 'Think I was home in bed.'

'Bet you were,' Butler said, and huffed. 'We believe your mate Ian Macdonald abducted Danny Sawyer, and someone then tried to shut him up before we could get our hands on him.'

'Macdonald wouldn't do anything like that,' West said, shaking his head. 'He wouldn't hurt a kid... not Macdonald.'

'Maybe it wasn't him who hurt him,' Moone said, trying to make eye contact. 'Maybe he got hold of Danny for someone else. But that someone else didn't want MacDonald to start talking.'

'I wasn't there,' West said, sitting up a bit, sounding defiant. 'You got anything on me? You going to arrest me?'

Moone looked at Butler, saw her shrug, then said, 'No, not today, Malcolm. But we're keeping an eye on you.'

Moone climbed out, then approached the uniform. 'Take off the cuffs. Let him go.'

'Let him go, boss?' The uniform ran a hand down his face. 'He's a dirty, bloody...'

'I know what he is, we just haven't got anything on him and we need to keep an eye on him.

Just let him walk.'

The uniform sighed, then went round and dragged West from the car. West moaned and complained all the time the uniform pushed him around and undid his restraints.

As he rubbed his wrists, West looked at Moone and said, 'How's he doing?'

'Macdonald?' Moone asked, and an idea came to him. 'He's not too bad. The doctors tell me he'll probably make a full recovery.'

West tried to hide it, but Moone saw the flicker of panic cross his face before he put on a strained smile and said, 'That's good. That's really good.'

'What was that about?' Butler asked as she climbed out the incident car, just as West was sloping off. 'You telling lies now?'

Moone gave an empty laugh. 'Something like that. I just wanted to know how he'd react if he thought Macdonald might wake up and talk.'

'And?'

'He tried to hide it, but he didn't look best pleased.'

'Do we put some surveillance on him?'

Moone started heading back to their car. 'Yep. Think that would be a good idea.'

Butler was following, then stopped when her mobile started ringing. 'Yes, I'm here. What is it?'

Moone watched her as she talked, her face starting to crease up with confusion.

'What?' she said, starting to head towards the car. 'How's that possible? All right. We'll check it out.'

When she'd ended the call, and they'd reached the car, Moone said, 'What was that?'

She opened the driver's door and looked at him. 'That bloke you talked to, the one coming out of the house opposite Macdonald's place, he's on the register too.'

'What?' Moone stopped dead, thinking there must be a mistake. 'Hang on, you mean we've got one convicted child abuser living opposite another?'

'I know. Doesn't sound right, does it?' Butler climbed in and started the engine, while Moone joined her, thinking it all over. Then it landed in his brain with a thump, Loy Grader's words coming back to him. He turned to Butler as she pulled away. 'What did Grader say? About their living arrangements?'

Butler stared at him, frowning. 'That's what he meant? That a couple of paedos are living opposite each other? But how's that got by the system? Who thought that was OK?'

'It's our register, we're supposed to know where they're living. We must've been given false information or it would've come up.'

'That's why West was poking round that house that hardly looked lived in!' Butler put her foot down, racing them back to the station.

It was Butler that got to work on the sex offenders register, while Moone fetched them both a bitter tasting machine coffee. He pulled up a chair at her desk and looked at the names that came up on the screen. Nearly forty-eight thousand names and addresses in all, which made Moone's stomach turn over. But that was UK wide, and comprised all people convicted of a sex offence since 1997.

'Let's narrow this down,' Moone said.

Butler did as was asked and brought up the Devon and Cornwall section. A list of nearly one thousand, five hundred names appeared. They both simultaneously huffed, then looked at each other and laughed.

'We're going to have to cross reference these with their addresses,' Butler said, 'make sure none of them have been placed in the same street.'

'Look up Ian MacDonald's street,' Moone said. 'See if anyone else comes up.'

After a quick search, Butler shook her head.

'Hugo Webb shouldn't be living there,' she said. 'He's registered in one of the halfway houses near the Hoe. What the bloody hell's going on?'

Moone was about to reply when he heard his name being called and turned to see Stack stood in the doorway, arms by his side, looking like he was about to have a fight.

'Sir?' Moone said as he walked over.

Stack pointed a thick thumb over his shoulder. 'Conference room across the hall. You've got a visitor.'

'A visitor?'

'An honorary gentleman who wants to help out. Go and listen to what he has to say.'

Moone looked across the corridor and at the frosted glass wall where he could see the shape of a man. He walked over, knocked, then went straight in.

Mathieson was stood by the wall, reading a noticeboard, but turned round when he heard Moone. He smiled. 'DI... can I call you Pete?'

Moone looked down at the hand he was reaching out, and reluctantly shook it. 'I'm at work. I prefer DI Moone.'

Mathieson nodded. 'Fine. I can understand that. I'm sure you're very busy.'

'I am.'

A flicker of annoyance travelled over the politician's face, before the smile appeared again. 'I want to be of help... that's the bottom line.'

'Help how? Help your constituents?'

'Help with the Danny Sawyer situation. That's what I mean. I never felt like I helped very much back then. I hope I can make up for that.'

'I don't know what you can do unless you go and see them, offer your help to them.'

'I will, but we need to find out what happened to their child. Loy Grader. He knows all the local child abusers, he probably knows who took him.'

'Maybe. They do tend to share their exploits. But Grader won't say much.'

'What if I went to see him? Appealed to him on behalf of Danny's parents?'

Moone didn't know what to say, but he could see the determination in the MP's eyes. But he knew Grader wouldn't offer up any information without some kind of gain for himself. 'That's very noble, but he'll only try to make deals.'

'What does he want?' The MP raised his eyebrows, probably had the same look as when asking one of his constituents if they had any problems in their area.

'He wants to visit his mother's grave. Lay some flowers on it.'

Mathieson's eyebrows rose higher. 'That's all? I can talk to someone about that.'

Moone put his face in his hands, rubbed his tired eyes, wondering what sort of idiot her wife had got involved with now. 'We're talking about a sex offender, a child... look, he's committed horrible crimes... making deals...'

'What about Danny Sawyer's parents? Don't they need to find out who murdered their child? To see them stand trial for it?'

Moone let out a tired laugh. It was all pointless, he realised. 'You're going to go ahead with this anyway, aren't you? You'll go off and whisper in someone's ear, give them the nod or handshake, but in the end you'll do it anyway.'

Mathieson straightened himself, seemed to stand taller, losing his friendliness. 'You're right, DI Moone. I am going to do it, with or without your support. I just wanted to run it by you first. I have your superior's support.'

Moone shrugged but tried not to show his anger. 'Well, there's nothing more to say then. Good luck.'

Mathieson stared at him for a moment, blankly, then put on his politician's smile and stuck out his hand, 'No hard feelings?'

'No, none at all,' Moone said, then watched him leave the room, his own fists balling up. He stormed towards the incident room, and found Butler still at her desk, a phone in her hand, her head nodding.

'Thanks,' she said, before hanging up.

'What was that?' Moone asked.

'Talked to Hugo Webb's brother. He doesn't like his sibling much. Told me where to find him. Coming?'

'Yep, I could do with a laugh, and a bit of fresh air.'

Turned out there wasn't much that was fresh about the air where they were headed. Butler drove them to Mutley, then parked up a side

street before they headed to the grubby looking bookmakers in the middle of the main strip.
Smoking had long since been banned in public,
but Moone found the stale stink of cigarettes
and roll ups had remained somehow, perhaps
brought by the mix of elderly and bedraggled
customers who hid in the dark corners. There
was a withered old man, wrapped up in a thick
army style coat, holding the lead of a small muscular dog. Next to him was a familiar looking
face glowing from one of the TV screens above.
Hugo Webb was poised to write out a betting slip
as Butler strolled over, looking up to see what he
was watching.

'You'll lose, Hugo,' she said, quite loudly in
his ear, making him jump out of his skin.

'Fuck me,' he said, a hand on his chest. Then
his face changed as he turned his tiny eyes on
Moone, and the penny must have dropped. 'What
do you lot want?'

'A word,' Butler said and showed her ID.

'Bout what?' he asked, fiddling with a tiny
blue pen, his cheeks reddening.

'About where you live.'

He looked at Moone, so he nodded. 'We saw
you coming out and locking up. Remember me
talking to you?'

The panicked thoughts were readable in
Webb's eyes as the pen fiddling became even
faster. 'That was my mate's place...'

'Who?' Butler snapped. 'What's his name?'

The silence, apart from the mumbled TV and the coughing and sneezing of the dog, went on for a while. 'John.'

'John?' Butler said. 'John who? You say Smith and I'm going to knee you in the balls.'

'I forget his name,' Webb said, putting a hand over his crotch. 'He's just John.'

'Thing is,' Moone said, coming closer. 'The house over the road, that's where Ian MacDonald lives.'

'Don't know him,' Webb said too quickly.

'He's a paedophile,' Butler said. 'Just like you.'

'I've changed my ways,' Hugo said.

'Leopards and paedophiles don't change their spots. Tell us about MacDonald. Tell us how come you were in the same street and we walk away.'

'I don't know what to say. I was just locking up for a mate.'

'That's rubbish,' Butler said. 'How come you're living there?'

'I… I'm not…' Webb stuttered, sweat appearing on his upper lip.

'We know you are,' Moone said. 'Do you want to go back inside?'

'I haven't done anything!' he said, on the edge of anger.

'That's not what we'll say,' Butler leaned forward and whispered. 'Not that far from a school here, are we, Moone?'

'Just the round the corner.'

Webb looked between them. 'I... you don't understand. I can't, I heard what...'

Moone stepped forward when he saw Webb's mouth clamp shut, his eyes giving away what he'd almost let slip. 'What? What did you hear? I'm guessing you heard about MacDonald being in hospital? That right? Just nod your head.'

Webb nodded. 'He must've let on. That's why you lot are digging round, yeah?'

'That's right,' Butler said. 'Why don't you tell us the rest.'

Hugo Webb looked terrified and exhausted as he backed up further in the corner, his furtive eyes jumping to rest of the betting shop patrons. 'I don't really know how it came about. I just know that it did. It was fine with me.'

Moone looked at Butler and exchanged confused looks with her. 'Go on... the arrangement...'

Hugo lifted his shoulders and scratched at his face. 'Well, I got my place... MacDonald got his... right over the road. We knew then that someone had bent the rules somewhere, but we weren't about to complain.'

'Hang on,' Butler said. 'So someone sorted it so you two could live in the same road.'

'Yeah, I knew it wouldn't be long before someone cottoned on... taken you a while though. Thought it would happen ages ago.'

Moone rubbed his face, the full extent of

what was reaching his ears, now filling his gut with acid. 'How long? How long you been living there?'

'Nearly four years.'

'Four years?!' Butler let out a deep grunt of a sigh. 'Four years you two have been living opposite each other?'

'And the rest,' Webb said, shaking his head.

'The rest?' Moone said.

Webb nodded. 'The others... don't you know about the rest? All the others they let live in that street?'

Butler looked towards Moone, her eyebrows raised before she stepped closer to Webb, leaning over him. 'What others?'

'Sex offenders,' Webb said. 'All done for the same sort of thing as me. There's loads of them living in that street.'

CHAPTER 18

They left the bookies in a state of shock, neither of them uttering a word as they headed back to the car, then drove off. The hollowed-out shape of the bombed-out church came into view, then the red brick block of Charles Cross police station before either of them dared utter a word.

'How does this happen?' Moone asked, turning to look at Butler as she drove them towards the police car park.

'I don't know,' she said, steering through the gate that opened for them. 'Someone arranged it, someone lied to us, covered it up, let a bunch of paedophiles live in the same fucking street!'

The car stopped with a jerk in a corner parking space. Butler turned sharply to face him. 'So, what does all this bloody mean? We've got a bunch of paedophiles living in the same fucking road! And we've got a dead child. What now? We drag them all in?'

Moone covered his face for a moment, trying to calm himself and bring orderly thought. Nothing worked. 'I think first we need to know how this happened, who's behind this. Don't the council deal with this sort of thing?'

'OK, then we go and see Plymouth council. The housing people.'

'Good. Who do we tell about this?'

Butler stared at him. 'What do you mean?'

Moone let out a harsh breath. 'Well, in my experience, if someone on the council has been doing the dirty, then they've got help. How do you fiddle with the books on something like this without the police – us – knowing?'

'We know now!'

'We know now, cause a body's been found. This was an accident.'

Butler made a pissed off noise in her throat, then said, 'So we keep a lid on it for now? Yeah? That's what you're saying?'

'I honestly don't know what I'm saying. I'm making this up as I go along.'

'What about Harding?'

'You need to talk to him, make sure he's on the same page.'

'For fuck's ...' Butler pushed open the car door then dragged herself out and headed fast towards the entrance.

Moone sat there for a moment watching her disappear inside, still trying to fathom what to do next. He felt like he did when he was a kid in his maths class, staring down at numbers and angles, without a clue what they meant. Then he thought back to what he would do back then, which was to look over to the kid on the next desk and copy his work. Moone looked over to the vacant driver's seat. There was no one else to copy from, no one else who had a clue what to do next, so he took out his phone and stared at it. Who could he call to give him the answers? He desperately needed a "phone a friend", but instead he saw he had a missed call and a voicemail message.

He listened to the call briefly, hearing that it was Dr Parry and called him back, hoping for some good news or a breakthrough.

'Hello, Dr Parry,' a quiet, deadpan voice said.

'It's DI Moone,' he said, and sat back.

'Hello, DI Moone.'

'You can call me Pete.'

'Oh, OK, Pete... want the bad news or the terrible news?'

Moone let out a defeated sigh. 'You pick.'

'Well, I lied... there's only terrible news. Nothing forensically useful has come back from Danny Sawyer's remains. Too degraded. I'm sorry.'

Moone nodded and let out a sick filled laugh. 'It's OK. It's what I expected. Thanks though.'

'You heard from PC Carthew?'

'No... why?'

'It's just that sometimes I see her in the gym, the new one in town, but I haven't seen her recently. She's usually there pretty regular.'

'I don't know. Actually, I can't remember the last time I saw her.' Guilt immediately filled up any space he had left between the plethora of disappointment and failure crammed into his body. 'I'll chase her up.'

'Good. She's a nice one.'

'She is. Thanks.' Moone ended the call, feeling a little like he'd been told off by an older brother. Then his brain switched up a gear, wondering what had happened to Faith and if what he'd said to her had anything to do with it.

But he climbed out, clearing away the debris, preparing to head back into work and face the mess that had been thrown up. His mind swirled again as he headed up to the incident room to find Butler sat talking quietly to Harding by his desk. Everyone else was busy on the phones or typing stuff up. Moone sat at a desk, watching what was going on, noting the uncomfortable, almost angry look on his colleague's face.

'What the...' came loudly from Harding's mouth before Butler gave a deep 'hush', then stared round the room. She talked quietly then while Moone settled in to start on the paperwork, writing up what they'd discovered so far. Then later, on the way home he'd swing by PC Carthew's place to see what was what.

The rest of his workday had gone by as he'd figured it would, just staring at a computer screen, filling in reports, collecting everything together that made sense and staring at the other facts that didn't. The truth was they had little to go on, and it seemed it was only the comatose Ian Macdonald who would be able to shine some light on the death of Danny Sawyer, if he ever woke up. Which looked increasingly doubtful. Moone had been in touch with the hospital and found out that only one person, apart from West's creepy little visit, had been to see him; it had been his older brother, who the nurses reported didn't seem very sad about the state his brother had found himself in. 'What he deserved,' one of the nurses heard him mutter.

But Moone couldn't gather any kind of sorrow for him, only for the boy whose remains could not yet be released to his poor parents.

He thought all this over as he drove, guided by his Satnav, towards a part of Plymouth called Plympton, which seemed to be a wide endless Suburban area, filled with quite newly built tidy estates. It was the area where PC Carthew lived, apparently tucked away in one of the red brick new builds, just past a large family pub, he'd been informed. He found the short close she lived in, then parked up and headed for the door of a small, neat red brick house that had a nice little garden out the front. It was quiet around there, and only the sound of birds tweeting filled his ears. He suddenly realised how far away from home he truly was as he rang the doorbell.

It took a few rings of the doorbell before the door slowly, achingly slowly, opened and a washed out, ponytail wearing, Faith Carthew looked out at him. She looked as if sleep had evaded her for sometime, too, and that made her look older.

'What're you doing here?' she asked, her voice hollow, empty.

'I came to see how you are,' he said, putting on a smile. He recognised the telltale signs of depression, he'd been there himself. 'I heard you were on sick leave.'

'I'll be fine again soon. Thanks for coming.' She started to close the door, so he stopped it with his hand. 'Hang on. Least you can do is make me a cup of tea.'

She stared at him, then turned and walked inside, her body almost trailing behind her head.

'Maybe I'll make the tea,' he said as he observed her slump on to a corner sofa that backed onto an archway that led to a narrow modern kitchen.

He found a kettle and filled it up. 'So... I take it this isn't just man flu?'

She huffed out an attempt at a laugh. 'No.'

'Is this? Is this to do with...?'

'You? No. Not completely. I don't know.

Can't you just leave me alone?'

He went back to the kitchen, made her a cup of tea and put it down on the coffee table in front of her. 'There you go.'

Her eyes fell to the mug, but she hardly moved. 'Will that make me feel better?'

'It's a start. Want to talk?'

'Not really.'

He sat on the coffee table, sipping his tea. 'You feel like this a lot?'

She shrugged, but didn't look at him, just started at the TV, which had some holiday programme on, but the sound far too low for anyone but Superman to hear.

He sighed. 'Talk to me. How long you been feeling like this?'

'A while. Couple of years... I think. Don't worry. It'll pass. It usually does.'

'What if it doesn't?'

'Great way to make me feel better.'

'Sorry. I meant, maybe you need to talk to someone about it.'

She looked up at him. 'I'm never going to be a detective.'

'Is that what this is all about?'

She shrugged. 'Part of it. The realisation probably kicked it off. I'm going to spend the rest of my career as a uniform. A faceless drone.'

'There's nothing wrong with being a uniform. They do all the real work. The hard work. You're an excellent police officer.'

'Did you come here because you wanted to fuck me again?'

He sat back, surprised at the words falling from her mouth. 'No. I came here because I was worried about you.'

'You can if you want. It might make me feel something. I'd like to feel something. Anything really.'

He watched her take off her jumper, revealing a dark pink bra that cupped her pale, freckled, full breasts. He ignored the stir of excitement, pushed it back down as he said, 'I'm not here for that.'

'So you don't even fancy me now?'

'You know that's not true. I just want you to come back to work, to help me...' Moone sat back, thinking through everything, trying to find an argument that might bring her round. He could find only the pathetic truth. 'Faith, the truth is, I haven't got a clue what I'm doing, this is all guess work for me... I'm failing.'

There was a flicker of life in her eyes as she looked up at him. Then she put her top back on and reached for her tea. She took a sip and made a face as if she'd French-kissed a poodle. 'You make crap tea. Did you put the milk in first? Bet you didn't.'

'No, who puts the milk in first?'

'I do. It's the way it's done.' She sat back down, folded her arms across her chest. 'How did you get this far then? You must've done something right?'

'Listening to smarter people than me.' He shrugged. 'That's it.'

'The medal?'

'I got lucky. Simple as that.'

She looked him in the eyes, stared at him and he knew she was trying to read him, tell if it was all bollocks, just like any copper half their worth would. 'OK. Where are we at the moment?'

He told her, spilled it all, everything that had happened so far. The only part that seemed to ignite her eyes was the bit about the street full of child molesters.

'Jesus,' she said, shaking her head. 'I don't get how that happened, how does that happen?'

'Someone arranged it. We need to find out who that is.'

'They council properties?' She sat up, more alert now.

'We think so.'

'We need to talk to them. Whoever's in charge.'

'In the morning.' He stood up. 'Get some sleep. Come to the incident room tomorrow.'

She stood up to see him out. 'I will. Thanks for coming. Not many people would.'

He opened the front door, stepped out, then turned to face her. 'Come tomorrow. We'll get you to detective constable. I promise.'

'Don't make promises. Let's just solve these cases first.'

He nodded, then patted her arm and headed to his car and got in. When he started the engine and turned to face her house, she was gone. He felt bad as he reversed, promising her something he had no idea how he was going to achieve, but all he knew was he needed all the bright minds and hard workers on his side. She was clever, depressives usually were, and she was determined most of the time. Tomorrow they would look into the council and find out what was what.

He sat in his car, listening to the light tap of the night rain, parked only a couple of hundred yards from the club. It sat on the corner of a partly residential street that led onto the Hoe. It would have once been a large Victorian house owned by some local dignitary, he thought, but now it housed all manner of sickening filthy acts. He took another swig of his second bottle of vodka, wiped his face, then opened the holdall he'd put on the passenger seat. He put on the black knitted gloves, then took out the largest knife he'd brought from the set he'd purchased with cash. It glimmered in the amber glow of the streetlight as he slipped it inside his jacket, his eyes rising to the sound of laughing. A group of men and women, all dressed provocatively, stumbled, laughing and screaming towards the club. There was a couple of wide-bodied bouncers on the door, so he wouldn't be able to gain access that way.

He put another smaller knife into his coat, then looked at his hands as he held them in front of him, seeing that they were not shaking. A calmness washed over him as he opened the car door, then stepped out. He took out the balaclava from his pocket and slipped it over his head, adjusting the eye holes so he could see better. He didn't approach the front, because that would be ridiculous, and he would be caught. He knew they'd get him eventually, but not yet, not until he'd done what he must, because he realised now that it was his calling. A voice had whispered to him while at home, sat with a drink in his hand, watching the late-night news, seeing how sin-soaked the world had become. He had sinned himself, he couldn't deny that, but he understood he would be forgiven if he carried out the good work. It could only be one voice talking to him. He almost denied it to himself, but then suddenly there was a light, a bright white light and he knew that *He* was looking upon him.

God. God had spoken to him.

There was a balcony and an iron staircase leading to a fire escape on the side of the building. He headed up that way, knowing the door wasn't ever locked properly, allowing the clubbers to congregate on the roof. He went up fast, taking out a knife in case another bouncer was waiting at the top. It was empty, and only the thumping beat of dance music pounded out of the crack in the solid door. He was right, the door was wedged open, and when he pulled the metal bar across it, it opened easily. He went in, seeing bodies writhing on the dance floor, strobe lights flashing, making them all move in a strange robotic way. The bar was already thick with people.

Then he turned when he heard a voice through the music. It was a man, thick set, muscular, wearing a tight-fitting T-shirt.

He was saying something, looking annoyed, or scared, backing off suddenly as he moved towards him. It was the knife in his hand that he was raising, showing the muscular man as he rushed towards him. His hands started to push him away, flail to get away, but the knife plunged into him, into his gut. The man looked down, his face losing colour, looking at the dark liquid that flashed bright red every second as he fell to his knees, panicked words falling from his mouth.

The music was still pounding, he could hear it but only in the distance, as if the volume was turned down low. But it was his heart that pounded louder, filled him full of power, burned his veins that blocked everything else out as he looked up. Only a few of them had realised what was happening, that a reckoning had begun, and scrambled, panicked, running for safety. The rest danced, drank, trapped in their sinful world as he took out the small knife and stormed towards the crowd.

CHAPTER 19

Moone was having a bad dream full of dirt and milk-white children's bodies when the call came. He hastily made a coffee in his flask and drove through the dark country lanes fast, only occasionally seeing the white glare of a car coming the other way. His heart was beginning to race as he headed towards the city, his hands shaking as he held the steering wheel tight.

There'd been a major incident, a tired, gravelly-voiced inspector had told him. Butler had also been called and was on the scene already.

He saw the flashing blue lights before he even reached the road that sat back a couple of streets from the sea front. A large corner building was surrounded by police tape and uniforms. A couple of ambulances and a scattering of marked and unmarked police cars were parked close to it. Moone parked, then climbed out, his eyes scanning the mayhem, watching the uniforms directing shocked looking witnesses whose faces flashed blue as they were taken off to be questioned or treated in one of the ambulances.

He headed for the front of the club, where two uniforms stood guard, one holding the crime scene log that Moone signed. He then went into the narrow, brightly-lit passageway that was littered with empty plastic tumblers and bottles. More uniforms questioned the customers on the stairs that led up to another larger room with a long bar and a dance floor. The lights were on, and the carnage was clear for him to see.

Butler turned away from a body on the floor, a man who was sprawled out, a blanket over his head and chest. 'Moone, this has to be our killer.'

Moone moved closer, looking over towards another body, a woman lying in a far corner, most of her also covered by a red sheet. 'How many?'

'Dead?' She looked about the room. 'Three so far. Five more have been sent to Derriford.'

'Jesus. What happened?'

Butler opened her notebook, flipped through the pages. 'A man wearing a mask, or maybe a balaclava, appeared in the club from nowhere, started stabbing people randomly. The security staff were called, only one tried to intervene, an ex-soldier called Terry Evans. He's in Derriford being treated for a stab wound and several lacerations. Eventually the assailant turned and ran.'

Moone rested against a table. 'Jesus, this has to be him. He's escalating...'

'That's putting it bloody lightly.' Butler huffed, looked around the room.

Moone followed her eyes, noticing the pale hands of the victims that protruded from under the blankets. Both victims had some kind of purple marking on the back of their hands. 'What's that mark on the back of their hands?'

'Just the stamp the club put on their customers. Nothing more.'

Moone stared at her and could see how pale she was. 'You OK?'

'Yeah, fine. Just thinking this could've been my step-daughter here.'

'I didn't know you...'

'Well, there's lots we don't know. Look, we need to catch up with this psycho bastard. We're falling behind. They'll replace us if we're not careful.'

As Moone turned round, hearing more people coming in, he saw a group of white plastic suited and hooded SOCOs bringing in cases of equipment. 'I know. I know. What's going on with him? What's happened to make him like this?'

'You mean apart from being a nutcase?' Butler shook her head.

'Excuse me,' a voice said behind Moone and

he saw a young woman with dark hair, a round face, peering out of a white hood. 'If you could leave now so we can process the scene?'

Moone nodded, then signalled for Butler to follow him as he headed back down to the ground floor where paramedics were dealing with the wounded and shocked. He looked over the angst ridden and shocked faces being questioned and treated as they sat on the floor or chairs grabbed from somewhere. Then he stopped dead as they were about to leave.

'Colin?' he said, stepping back, making Butler turn to where he was staring.

Colin Samson looked up, his face ashen in colour, a plastic cup of water in his hand. A female uniform had been questioning him, but now also looked towards Moone.

'Thanks,' Moone said to the uniform. 'We'll take it from here.'

After the uniform left, Moone rested his back to the wall, bent over, looking at Samson, while Butler stood in front of him. 'How're you doing, Colin?'

The lecturer put down the water and rubbed his face. 'Not so good. But I suppose I should count myself lucky. He killed people, didn't he?'

'He did,' Moone said. 'Did you see him?'

Samson nodded. 'Briefly. I was at the bar... next thing I knew people were battling past, pushing people out of the way. I turned around and saw someone in a mask.'

'Definitely just one attacker?' Butler asked.

He shrugged. 'I only saw one.'

'Did he say anything?' Moone asked.

'Nothing. Nothing that I heard. He was just slashing and stabbing. Oh God... what sort of person does something like that?'

Moone straightened himself, watching the lecturer begin to cry, his whole body trembling. 'We're trying to find that out. I'm sorry you had to go through this. Is there anyone you can stay with tonight?'

He looked up, wiping his eyes. 'I... I can call my sister. I can stay with her.'

'Good. We'll need to take a full statement tomorrow, but for now just go and stay with her.'

Moone signalled for Butler to follow him.

'The killer headed along to the fire door and out to the roof,' Butler said, pointing a thumb upwards.

Moone nodded. 'We'll need all the CCTV.'

'Already being handled. What you thinking?'

Moone shrugged, unsure what he was thinking. 'I'm thinking we've got ourselves a hate crime. I think maybe the first kill wasn't planned, but now he's got a taste for it.'

'What's motivating him? Just hate?'

'Something kicked him off. I was thinking maybe it was the first kill... he arranges to meet Jason, maybe not sure of what he's doing, all mixed up inside, then, when he sees him, he can't take it, he snaps. Now he's got the taste for it.'

'If Jason's killer is the person that arranged for him to be in the park, we still don't know for sure.'

Moone nodded. 'It all points to it. We'll have to talk to Barry. See where he's at with it all. Let's visit the roof.'

Butler followed Moone back up to the next floor, both of them watching the bodies being bagged up and put on gurneys, ready to be taken away before they went towards the fire door. Moone stopped, then bent down and picked up a wooden wedge. 'So, this fire door was wedged open?'

'Yeah, barman told me that the manager did that so the punters could go out onto the roof.'

'So this is where he got in, climbed up, travelled across the roof and stabs his first victim just over there. No CCTV?'

'No, but maybe we'll pick up something from nearby. Thing is, we probably won't. We need a plan, don't we?'

Then Moone's phone was ringing and he took it out to see an unidentified number was calling him.

'DI Peter Moone,' he said, then heard a hard and sharp huff on the other end.

'This is Stack,' the DSU said, sounding incredibly pissed off, which of course he was liable to feel. Moone was feeling it too, all over him, right down to his bones. 'Boss...'

'You two need to get your arses back here,' the DSU said.

'We do?' Moone made a face at Butler. 'Why?'

'This whole gay club mass murder thing,' Stack said. 'It's getting political. Just get your arses back here. Pronto.'

When Butler and Moone arrived back at the station, they found themselves directed by PC Carthew towards the conference room. Moone smiled at her as they walked instep, Butler hovering behind, obviously giving them space.

'I didn't expect to see you this soon,' Moone said. 'Didn't realise I was that motivational.'

'Don't kid yourself,' she said, still sounding trapped in the darkness. 'Got a call from the boss, they're dragging in the extra manpower.'

'What's going on?' Moone asked as they reached the conference room.

Carthew shrugged. 'Don't know. But everyone's in a panic about something. You better go in.'

Moone nodded, knocked then went in when he heard a gruff sounding Stack say, 'Come in, for fuck's sake.'

When Moone, followed by Butler, stepped in, he found Stack with his back to the window, arms folded, chewing, staring at him, while

Laptew was talking to someone on his phone. There was a dark trouser-suited woman in the room, aged about fifty, greying brown hair pulled back into a neat ponytail. She was sat at the conference table at the centre of the room, a tablet device in her hand, hardly looking up.

'Nice of you to join us,' Stack said, seeming to chew his gum even harder. 'Sit down you two.'

Moone pulled out a chair near the suited woman, watching her, trying to see what she was doing, but he found her screen was blacked out.

Butler closed the door, and put her back to it, arms folded.

When Laptew ended his call, he looked at them all, nodding, until his eyes found the woman with the tablet, who seemed to come out of her own world and looked up with a brief, unconvincing smile. 'Everyone, this is Commander Sally Richer.'

Moone looked at her, and she stared back at him, blankly for a moment, before returning her eyes to Laptew.

'I'm not your commander,' she said, her voice well spoken, clear of any detectable accent. 'But you will take notice of what I say.'

'Where are you from then?' Butler asked, and Laptew looked up as if she'd called Richer a bitch.

'Butler...' the Chief Super started to say, but the woman held up a hand and slightly shook her head, and said, 'It's quite all right. It can be annoying to have someone you don't know walk into your territory and start barking orders. I'm from the Anti-Terrorism Unit.'

'Anti-terrorism?' Moone repeated, an empty laugh falling from his mouth.

'I'm sorry,' Richer said, 'Your file didn't say you were deaf. Yes, anti-terrorism. I'm here about the attack this morning.'

'You got here bleeding fast,' Butler said, and Moone cringed as Richer turned to her and gave a laugh that was poisoned by annoyance.

'Yes,' Richer said. 'I've been following your investigation. Since your second attack. Now this attack in the gay club...'

'You're treating it as terrorism?' Moone asked, unable to hold in his exasperation.

'Your people catch on fast, Andrew,' she said, without emotion. 'Yes, we are. We have a way of doing things in this country, we have a culture that we welcome others to join... to respect. We need to protect the rights of everyone, the freedom to walk the streets without being attacked. Those rights have been abused by a masked individual wielding a knife, indiscriminately attacking anyone he comes across. He is terrorising this city.'

'So, you're taking over?' Butler asked.

Richer turned to her. 'Not quite. You'll carry on following your leads, but all information will be fed to us and we will advise you how to proceed. If we feel the need, we will dispatch our special armed unit to resolve the situation.'

'You'll knock him off?' Butler said, huffing.

'He *knocked* off several innocent people last night. I think we need to deal with this threat in a quick manner.'

Laptew stood up. 'I think we all understand one another. We'll carry on doing our job, and let you know of any developments. My people will carry on passing on information to you. Thank you for coming, Commander Richer.'

Richer stood up, shook the Chief Super's hand, looked them all over with a nod, then walked out of the office.

'You get that?' Stack asked, a smirk on his face.

'I'm sure they did,' Laptew said. 'Good work all of you. Carry on.'

They all stood quietly while the Chief Super gathered his stuff together, then hurried off out of the room, probably to some budget meeting, Moone thought.

'Good job?' Stack said, flicking his eyes from Moone to Butler. 'Fucking shambles, if you ask me. You're both a couple of fucking steps away from being replaced by a review team. You understand that, don't you? You're getting no-where fast on both cases. At least one of them should be handed over to a new team. You've got until the end of the fucking week to show me that you know what you're fucking doing. Got it?'

'Sir,' Moone said, then watched Stack's narrowed eyes jump to Butler as he said, 'You understand me, Butler?'

'Yeah, I get it,' Butler said and turned and opened the door. 'Come on, Moone.'

'Yeah, go on, Moone. Buy yourself a skirt, 'cause we all know she wears the trousers.'

Moone knew better than to rise to it, after all it was what Stack was hoping for, so he didn't say anything as he followed Butler from the room and headed back to the incident room.

The whole morning had been horrific for Carl Mathieson, right from the bad dream he'd woke from in a sweat, up until his arrival at Dartmoor prison. The dream stayed with him as he drove down and down, following the winding road that was enshrouded in a thick grey mist. The enormous prison gates appeared out of the mist as flashes of the dream stabbed into his mind.

The ice-cold desert, the sun rising up, bringing with it the scorching heat.

The sound of goats bleating, the bells ringing as the boy appeared over the rocky hill, while he and the others were dug down, their rifles out in front of them, pointing towards the kid, praying they wouldn't be spotted.

The boy was running, past the rocks, then turning, his glistening dark eyes jumping to them all, holding them in his innocent stare.

Mathieson showed his ID to the man and woman on the prison gate, then they let him through, allowing him to drive round to the car park. He sat for a moment looking up at the dark windows, the stone walls, wondering what the hell he was doing there. But he knew what he had to do, the lengths he had to go to, to stop his world crashing down around his ears.

He stepped out of the car as a wind picked up, bringing with it a little rain that spat into his face as he walked towards the main building.

After showing his ID and filling in the paperwork, he was directed down a long corridor, then to an office where he met a guard with a buzz cut of white hair and a neat goatee. Mathieson shook his hand and noticed a naval tattoo on his arm, which meant he was ex-forces like a lot of the guards and police in the South West.

'Doug Warren,' the guard said, looking Mathieson over. 'Don't get many MPs here. Not unless there's journalist scum following them for a photo op.'

'I bet,' Mathieson said, then walked alongside the guard as he directed him down the next corridor on their right. The noise rose upwards, the bellow of men's voices, laughing and shouting. They walked along a pale yellow, boot marked corridor lined with metal cell doors dug deep into the walls.

'Grader is a special prisoner,' the guard said,

stopping and turning to look down on Mathieson. 'I don't mean in the way you tell your kids they're special. I mean we have to keep him away from certain areas, and family rooms and, well, normal people in general.'

'Yes, I know.'

The guard almost turned away then looked at him, staring. 'You've met him before?'

'No, no. I've just heard of his reputation.'

The guard looked at him for a moment, then nodded and pointed to a door down the corridor that had a metal detector outside, framing the metal door within it. 'You got family? Kids?'

He almost said no, thinking of his old life and the fact that the kids in his life weren't technically his own. Then he thought again and nodded. 'Yes. I have a family.'

'Don't talk about them. He'll want to know about them. Just keep all that stuff to yourself. You OK?'

Mathieson nodded, so the guard opened the door and let him enter the large room filled with old desks and plastic school chairs. Light shone into the gloomy interior, showing off the dust as it beamed arched squares of amber across the dirty floor. The door shut behind him, so Mathieson turned to look at it, then towards the sudden metallic sound across the room. A door was being unlocked, then opened, revealing a small, stocky man who Mathieson recognised. He was ugly, not just in looks, but his aura, if there was such a thing, the MP thought to himself as he sat at one of the desks.

Grader arrived at the desk, his dark eyes not taking in his visitor, just jumping around the room for a moment, as if making sure everything was where it should be.

'You can sit down,' Mathieson said, when the guard retreated and sat at a far table and opened a book.

Grader looked at him, no sign of anything on his face, then pulled out a chair and rested gently into it. 'Carl Mathieson, honorary MP, up-standing member of the community, fancy me having a visitor like you.'

Mathieson shuffled his chair closer. 'Listen, I'm here on behalf of the family of Danny Saw-yer.'

Grader stared at Mathieson for a moment, then burst out laughing. He waited for the child abuser to calm himself before saying, 'They need their minds put at rest.'

Grader stopped laughing, his face becoming taut as he said, 'Is this a joke? It must be. I've heard a lot about you, Carl. How you've moved up in the world. I'd say how the mighty have risen, but you were never that, were you? Not even in your military days, helping the yanks invade another poor country in the hopes of claiming more oil...'

Carl leaned forward, lowering his voice to almost a whisper. 'We need to talk.'

'I thought that's what we were doing, Carl. I've been hearing things about you, Carl. I hear things, even in here nothing escapes me. They tell me you're a family man now.'

'Please, listen...'

'Please? You're begging me? Don't make me laugh. Don't forget I know you, Carl. I know all about you. I know your darkest secrets...'

'Don't, just listen. We're in trouble.'

Grader shook his head and let out an empty, tired laugh. 'You mean you're in trouble. Look at where I am. Do you think I care what trouble you're in?'

'MacDonald. MacDonald is in hospital.'

Grader sat back, folding his arms. 'Yes, I've heard. But he's a vegetable.'

'No, I've been told he's going to recover. If he talks, we're all in the shit.'

'What do you expect me to do? You're the one who's desperate to stop his family name being dragged through the mud, so you sort it.'

'How can I? I can't walk into the hospital, how can I do that?'

'You're trained to kill with your bare hands, you've done it before.'

Mathieson lowered his head. 'I can't. But you can. You've got another appointment at the hospital. You could do it.'

Grader sat back, his eyes widening. 'Me? You expect me to somehow shake off my guards then find MacDonald and knock him off? You're fucking crazy!'

'I'll do all I can for you.'

'What can you do? Get me out of here? You know they'll never let me out. I'm fucked. In here for the rest of my life.'

'What do you want?'

Grader smiled, sitting back, tapping the table. 'What I want? First of all, to visit my mother's grave.'

'You hated your mother. Why do you want to visit her grave? Are you planning on trying to escape?'

'How far would I get? Where the hell would I go? Be serious.'

'Then why do you want to visit her grave?'

Grader leaned forward, smiling. 'Hasn't it occurred to you that I might want to piss on it?'

Mathieson tried to detect whether the prisoner was winding him up or not, knowing that he lived for messing with people's heads. But he knew how much he'd detested his alcoholic, sometimes drug-using mother. 'They wouldn't just stand there and let you urinate on her grave.'

'No, they wouldn't. Shame. No, there's something I need. Tell Malcolm West there's something that I need, get him to take it to my mother's grave and bury it, but only shallow.'

'What is it?' Mathieson's skin crawled.

'Just something to help pass the time in here. Nothing for you to worry about. You arrange that, and I'll do your little job for you.'

'I don't know if I can arrange all that…'

Grader sat back, laughing to himself, starting to shake his head. 'You can't afford not to, can you, Carl? Don't forget I know all about you, all the things you've done, all the bad things. But also there's your father to think about, his reputation, your family's reputation. That means so much to you, doesn't it? You'd do anything to protect that, wouldn't you? Think of all the things you've done so far. What's one more thing?'

Mathieson stared back into the eyes that were devoid of feeling, compassion, anything really human. Yes, he'd done some bad things, but they were things he regretted and felt guilty for. That was the difference between them, what really mattered.

But Mathieson also knew Grader was right, that he had no choice but to go along with what he said. 'Your appointment's the day after tomorrow, isn't it?'

'Yes. Eleven in the morning.'

'I'll arrange it so you go to your mother's grave first. OK?'

Grader smiled. 'You'd better. For all our sakes. Especially your family's.'

Mathieson stood up. 'I'll arrange it. Don't worry.'

'I'm not worried,' Grader said. 'Aren't you going to beg me to tell you what happened to little Danny Sawyer? I mean, I know all there is to know.'

Mathieson looked at the sickening smile on the little man's face. He felt the burning rise in him, the almost overwhelming feeling of wanting to grasp the man around the throat and squeeze the life out of him. He buried it down. 'No, I'm not. We both know that that would be a waste of time.'

CHAPTER 20

'What's he called?' Moone asked as Butler drove them towards the city centre, already getting slowed down in the grinding traffic.

'The councillor?' Butler asked, then huffed and hit the car horn. 'Oh come on, for fuck's... Philip Stanley. He was in charge of all the housing in that street in the time period MacDonald has been living there. He would've known what was going on if anyone did.'

Moone picked up his Americano from the cup holder. 'Someone had to... someone let this happen! What sick bastard thinks it's a good idea to stick a load of paedophiles in the same street?!'

'I can't believe they've fucked us over... what am I saying? Course I can. Anti-terrorism? He's not a fucking terrorist! He's just some fucked up... looney, who hates gays. This is probably to do with money. It's all money. Probably ticks a box so they can get more budget.'

'You might be right.'

Butler took them up a side street that delivered them down another passageway lined with official looking buildings. One of them was a large court building, and over the road Moone noticed a shabby, water-stained tower block type building. Civic Centre the sign said, and Butler took them into the car park beside it.

He followed her as she headed towards another grey, water stained building behind the civic centre. Like the civic centre, it seemed to be another piece of strange architecture left over from the rebuilding of Plymouth after the war. The sign over the entrance said: The Plymouth Council House. Moone followed Butler into the wide-open foyer, towards the desks at the back and the lifts next to them.

A middle-aged woman with wiry blonde hair looked up at them with a half-smile, as they approached the desk, then lost all of it as Moone produced his warrant card. 'Philip Stanley about?' he asked. 'We need a word with him.'

'You haven't made an appointment?' the woman asked, looking a little flustered.

'No,' Butler said. 'We're the police. We don't make appointments. Just let him know we're on our way up. Where's his office?'

'Well, it's on the next floor, but perhaps...'

But Butler had already gone round the desk, heading for the stairs. When Moone looked back at the woman, she was red-faced, on the phone, obviously calling her boss.

Butler was already up to the next floor by the time Moone reached her.

'You in a hurry?' Moone asked, catching up with her as she ploughed through the doors.

'Just can't wait to hear what this wanker's got to say about the whole thing.'

They found themselves on a floor that resembled an old-style department store. Moone almost expected to be confronted by the Grace Brothers as they headed down some steps and towards a corridor of offices. They didn't go far before they found an office door marked Councillor Philip Stanley. Butler knocked, then went straight in, showing her ID to the young, overly made-up, dark-haired woman standing in the hallway, a phone in her hand. She looked as red-faced as the woman they'd confronted downstairs and smiled awkwardly at them.

'Hello,' she said, raising her eyebrows. 'Can I help?'

'Yes,' Butler said, sounding grumpier than ever. 'You can get us Philip Stanley. Right now.'

'We don't need his head,' Moone said, smiling at the woman. 'Just him, all in one piece.' He caught Butler's eyes and saw the glare she fixed him with.

'I'm sorry,' the young woman said. 'He's not here at the moment.'

'Don't give us that crap,' Butler said, looking around over her head. 'Where is he? Mr Stanley!?

Philip Stanley! Get out here. This is the police.'

'He's not here!' the woman groaned and looked at Moone as if for compassion, so he said, 'Where is he, then?'

The woman shrugged. 'I don't know, he was here, he got a phone call, then he looked upset. He really didn't look right, panicked.'

'And he left?' Butler said, moving past her, looking into the two offices and the small toilet.

'Have a look around, if you don't believe me!' the PA said.

'She already has,' Moone said, then smiled at the woman. 'Listen, would he have gone home?'

She shrugged again. 'I don't know... maybe.'

'Where's home to?' Butler asked, so the girl said, 'Plympton. Posh part, apparently. All right for some.'

'Please, get us the address, could you?' Moone said.

The road that Philip Stanley resided on was out in the sticks, not that far from Saltram House, down some winding country lanes. Butler took them down a turning then up a long driveway towards a quite large house with lots of grounds.

'Jesus,' Butler said. 'How does he afford this?'

Moone spotted a Land Rover parked on the driveway. 'That car must've cost a few pennies too. This all makes me a little suspicious.'

'A little?' Butler parked up, then climbed out with Moone on her tail. 'Someone's been taking back handers, you can guarantee that!'

It was Butler who rang the doorbell, then rattled the brass knocker. The door was slowly, and very hesitantly opened by an attractive blonde woman in her mid to late thirties. Moone noticed straight away that she looked concerned, even though she tried to force a smile.

'Hello,' she said, still half hiding behind the door.

Butler showed her ID. 'DS Butler. We're looking for Philip Stanley.'

'He's out,' she said, a little too quickly.

Moone moved closer, lowering his voice. 'Is he? You sure he's not inside? All we need is a word with him.'

'About what?' Her eyes snapped onto Moone. 'What's this about?'

'We can't discuss that,' Butler said. 'Just go and get him.'

'I can't. He's not here.'

'But he's been here, hasn't he?' Moone asked, softening his voice.

'No... no, he hasn't. He's at work.'

Butler leaned over her. 'No, he isn't, we've just been there.'

The sound of an engine starting up came from the side of the house, then the roar of it made them all turn their heads to look towards it as the car raced down the muddy path and roared off down the country lane.

Butler jerked her head round to the wife. 'That him?! Was that him?!'

The woman had tears in her eyes. 'What's happened? Is he in trouble?'

'Where's he going?' Moone asked.

'I don't know!' the wife said.

'What's your name?' Moone asked as Butler huffed and walked towards the car.

'Sandra... you need to help him... please.'

'Then I need to know where he's gone, Sandra.'

'I don't know. I really don't know.'

'Can you think of anywhere he likes to go? A favourite place?'

She sniffed, shook her head and wiped a tear away. 'Not really, he likes to go to Jenny Cliff quite often.'

'Jenny Cliff? Where's that? Never mind. I'll find it, please let us know if you hear from him.' Moone started jogging back towards the car, while hearing Butler had already started the engine and was revving it, ready to roar away. As soon as he shut the door, Butler tore off down the narrow lane, Moone fighting to get his seatbelt on.

'Jenny Cliff,' Moone said.

'Jenny Cliff? Why there?' Butler asked, joining the dual carriageway, the cars flashing past.

'His favourite place. He's on the run. He knows we're onto him. He'll go there, thinking he'll be safe there.'

'But he won't be. The stupid bastard. He's right to run...'

'Let's just calm down. We don't know what sort of state he's in... how far is it?'

'About fifteen, twenty minutes.' Butler put her foot down, roaring past the turning to Saltram House, swerving round a few cars that were dawdling along. Moone sat back in his seat, gripping the handle of the door, watching the road roar past, the taillights of cars coming scarily close, his heart beginning to pound as his stomach turned over and over.

Butler eventually slowed down as they reached the top of a winding lane, following a car park sign, where mist and rain came in, swallowing the view. The damp, windswept grass was visible and the hazy outline of a long low rectangular building near the cliff. Butler parked up, and they watched a slender figure huddled in a hooded waterproof coming down towards them out of the mist, fighting the wind, a small furry dog at her heel.

Moone climbed out, heading towards the dog walker, and called out, 'You seen anyone else around?'

The woman's red face looked at him through the gap in her tight hood. 'Not really. Some other dog walkers...'

'Not a man on his own?'

'Oh, yeah, I just passed a man, he had a suit on...'

Moone turned to Butler, who was still in the car, her mobile to her ear, signalled for her to follow him. Then he turned towards the mist and the rain, pulling up his collar as the cold and wetness hit his face, the wind pushing him sideways as he headed up the muddy path, scanning the horizon. He could hardly see anything, just the jagged outline of the cliff, and the building to his right.

Then he stopped, staring further up, seeing a figure making their way quickly towards the cliffs. Moone hurried towards them, being pushed and pulled, his hair wet to his face, his clothes soaked and sticking to his body. When he got nearer, he stepped on something and looked down to see a piece of clothing lying across the path. He picked it up, noting it was a suit jacket, now covered in mud, his heart now rapidly beating as he raced on.

Stood a couple of hundred yards away was the figure of a man, swaying with the wind. His shirt was wet, clinging to his body.

The man started tugging at his tie, pulling it from around his neck as he moved closer to the cliff edge.

'Don't!' Moone shouted, half the sound being eaten up by the wind and rain.

The man turned. He looked at Moone,

blankly for a moment, his eyes hollow, blinking, not really seeing him at all. He turned back to the cliff again, starting to walk, dropping his tie to the ground.

'Please!' Moone shouted as loud as he could, jogging towards him, then holding up his hands, dropping the suit jacket as the man looked at him again. 'Come back from the edge! Please! Let's talk!'

'There's nothing I can say,' the man said. 'There's nothing anyone can do. It's my fault.'

'I'm sure that's not true, listen...'

'It is! I let it happen. I just wanted... I wanted... greed... it was all greed. I can't live with it. I can't live with it...'

Moone stepped closer, looking half over his shoulder and seeing Butler coming out of the mist. 'You can. It's Philip, isn't it? Can I call you Phil?'

Philip Stanley stepped backwards. 'Tell her I'm sorry...'

'You mean your wife? You can tell her yourself, we'll sort this out.'

'I let them all down... what I did is unforgivable.'

'Who told you to do it?' Butler shouted as she got behind Moone.

'That's not important right now,' Moone said, turning back to Stanley. 'What's important is that we can sort this out. And we will.'

'Did they pay you? Bribe you?' Butler moved

towards him, making the councillor back up.

'Butler!' Moone snapped. 'Come back.'

'If he goes, we won't know...'

'I know,' he said under his breath. 'Phil, the people who put you up to this, it's their fault.'

'The poor kids. I can't stop thinking about them... about him. Oh Jesus... oh God... what did I do...'

Moone rushed forwards, watching helplessly as Philip Stanley turned round, then started moving quickly, breaking into a run, the wind and rain swallowing him up as he seemed to sink, swept down into the greyness.

Moone stopped dead as he realised he was close to the edge, then looked down into the misty sea, the torrent of white foamy water that crashed against the rocks, spewing streaks of spit up at the cliffs.

Moone was frozen to his bones, shivering as he sat in one of offices, a blanket wrapped round him, a small box heater at his feet that had one bar glowing and wasn't really doing much. Someone had brought him some clothes, grabbed quickly from the cheapest shop they could find. He was sat in a pair of oversized, baggy grey jogging bottoms and a t-shirt that said "Get Involved" in luminous colours. Someone was taking the piss. But he couldn't think about anything other than what he'd witnessed,

Philip Stanley vanishing in a cloud of mist, like some amazing illusion. But it wasn't. He knew it wasn't, as much as his mind tried to protect him and convince him that somehow the councillor was hiding somewhere or hanging on to the cliff, waiting for the emergency services to leave so he could make his escape, he knew that he was gone. Wiped off this earth, his body...

He shook away the image, his stomach turning over, his heart pounding in rhythm with his thumping headache.

There were voices outside, raised for the moment, then fading away.

It was coming, the bad things, the stress, but right then he was numb to it.

The door opened and he looked up to see the Chief Super come in, looking deadpan, drawn even, pinching the bridge of his nose after he shut the door behind him and rested his back against the wall.

He was about to say something, then stopped, looked Moone up and down. 'You OK? How are you feeling, Moone?'

'I'm... I'm OK, as well as can be... has his wife...'

'Moone,' the Chief Super said, coming round to stand over him. 'What exactly happened? I mean, how did this all, you know what I mean.'

'Butler and I went to interview Philip Stanley...'

'Why? That's what I don't understand. In

connection to what?'

Moone looked down, aware of what was coming, the bollocking on the horizon, perhaps followed by the end of his career. 'The Danny Sawyer case...'

The Chief Super grabbed a chair, sat down and folded his arms. 'Sawyer? His murder?'

'Well, thing is, sir, we went to Ian Mac-Donald's place... and well, we came to realise that not only was MacDonald, a convicted child abuser, living in that street, but there were others, quite a few registered sex offenders in fact.'

The confusion poured down the Chief Super's face. 'No, that's not possible. There must be a mistake.'

'I'm afraid not. We've checked it out. Someone arranged it. Hid it from us. That's why...'

'Why you went to see Philip Stanley? I see.' His boss pinched his nose again. 'You know how this will play, don't you? When the media get hold of it? Police hound witness until he takes his own life. There's a shit storm waiting to happen.'

'We just went to talk to him about...'

'Why didn't you tell me about this, or anyone? This is the first I'm hearing about this.'

Moone lowered his head, trying to think, trying to scramble his way out of the mess.

Then there was a knock on the door, and Butler opened it before anyone could protest. She looked between them both. 'Everything OK?'

The Chief Super looked at her, then shook his head. 'No, Butler, everything's not OK. Did you know about this? This street where all these paedophiles are allegedly living?'

'It's not allegedly, sir. It's true.'

'Then why wasn't I informed? Or DSU Stack, your commanding officer?'

Butler stepped in. 'Stack did know, sir. He gave the go ahead.'

Moone shot her a look, but she was still looking at their boss, avoiding his stare. What the bloody hell was she doing?

'Stack knew?!' the Chief Super said. 'He never said anything to me.'

'He's in the corridor if you want to talk to him about it, sir.' Butler opened the door for him, which he slipped through.

When Moone and Butler were alone, he said, 'What the bloody hell're you playing at? Stack knew? He didn't...'

Butler put a finger to her lips. 'Shh! Listen, it's all sorted.'

'What do you mean it's all sorted?'

Butler came closer, then sat down. 'Stack owes me one.'

'Owes you one? What for?'

'Never mind that. That's for me to know. But let's just say that it's embarrassing enough that he'll go along with what I say. I was saving it, but, well...'

'I would've been fucked.'

'Yeah, probably.'

'So, you're saving me? That's what you're doing?'

She huffed. 'Well, I probably would've gone with you, so what choice would I have had? Anyway, you need saving. You're pretty useless on your own.'

'Thanks.' He smiled at her, or tried, even though he kept seeing Philip Stanley fading into the mist, then picturing him falling. 'I fucked up. I should've...'

She stood up, glaring at him. 'Don't start that. We went to talk to him, we didn't know his state of mind. How were we supposed to know he'd do that? Let's face it, he must've known more than just what he arranged, otherwise... let's just find out who actually murdered Danny Sawyer. Let's do that and then maybe, maybe we can look at ourselves in the mirror again.'

Moone stood up, removing the blanket from his shoulders. 'OK, yes, you're right. Let's get on with it.'

'Sort of, *get involved*,' Butler said. 'That's what the kids are saying these days, isn't it?'

Moone was confused for a moment, then followed her eyes to the T-shirt. 'Very funny. Did you get them to buy this?'

'Who do you think went out for it? I couldn't resist. Thought it'd cheer you up.'

The door opened and the Chief Super poked his head in again. 'OK, Stack verified your story.

We're going to be very careful how the media angle of this plays out. We don't want to look worse than we already do. Let's keep this quiet for now. I'll have to visit his wife. Talk her down. You two keep a low profile. You got it?'

Moone nodded. 'Yes, sir. Understood.'

The Chief Super nodded, looked disapprovingly as he said, 'Oh, and it seems Barry, the IT guy, wants to see you. Got something to tell you.'

CHAPTER 21

Moone had sent out for a shirt and trousers and changed into them by the time Butler met him outside the IT office. She looked over with a little annoyance as she said, 'I can't believe you changed out of the lovely clothes I bought you!'

He let his face show what he thought of her choice of clothes as he said, 'As lovely as they were, I didn't think they were appropriate for work, unless I was planning on going undercover as a prat.'

Butler laughed a little. 'Prat. Haven't heard that for a long time. They still use that in London?'

'We reserve it for special occasions. Let's see what Barry's got for us, shall we?'

'After you.' Butler gestured towards the door, on which Moone knocked, and came face to face with Barry, the tall skinny IT guy, who looked even more dishevelled than he'd done on their previous encounter.

As he let them into the stale-smelling room, where there were empty takeaway cartons and energy drink cans everywhere, Butler said, 'Please tell me you've been home since the last time we talked, Barry?'

Barry looked absently around the room, running his bony hand over his bearded face and untidy hair. 'Er, not sure when I last went home. Did you want to see what I found?'

'Yes, please,' Butler said and Moone watched her lean over Barry as he sat at his laptop and brought up the dating website that he'd been asked to look into.

Barry looked up at her. 'I've spent a lot of time getting to know some of the members of this site. I made a profile of your killer, tried to figure out his likes and dislikes. Then I looked for other members that he might have been attracted to.'

'Wow, well done,' Butler said, looking genuinely surprised. 'Did you find anything?'

'I'm not really sure.'

Butler patted his shoulder. 'What did you find? Please tell me you found something for us?'

'I found several members that are into crossdressing, and ones that are also into the gay, sissy side of crossdressing who've been contacted by a certain member of the site.'

'Who's that?' Moone said, joining them at Barry's desk.

'Call themselves Roman126,' Barry said, opening another can of energy drink. 'They've chatted to quite a few of the members. I noticed that their profile is pretty much the same as She-HeLover69's profile, almost word for word.'

'That's enough of that!' Butler said, snatching the can of drink from him, making Barry's mouth fall open, unable to speak. 'You're going home to sleep when you've finished telling us about this freak.'

'So,' Moone said, looking beyond them at the screen. 'Roman126? Why that name?'

Barry sat up, looking a little pleased with himself. 'I googled that. The only thing that came up was a passage from the New Testament. Romans 126.' He passed Moone a printout.

'For this cause God gave them up unto vile affections,' he started reading. 'For even their women did change the natural use into that which is against nature. And likewise also the men, leaving the natural use of the woman, burned in their lust one toward another; men with men working that which is unseemly, and receiving in themselves that recompense of their error which was meet.'

'Right,' Butler huffed. 'So, we've got a bible bashing mental case on our hands?'

'Looks like it, and he's back on the dating sites,' Moone said, rubbing his face. 'And now we've got anti-terrorism breathing down our necks. They want a briefing on this tomorrow.

They're basically getting ready to take it all over. Barry, can we trace this Roman bloke?'

Barry flickered to life, his nearly closed eyelids snapping open. 'What? Sorry. Dozed off.'

'Can we trace this Roman bloke?' Moone repeated.

'I've contacted the providers to get IP addresses, so now it's a waiting game.'

'So, we've got nothing?' Butler said.

'Well,' Barry said. 'Roman126 did arrange to meet these people or try to and told them to meet him at these specific locations.'

Moone took another sheet of paper from him with a list of places printed on it. 'We need to mark these on a map.'

'Already done,' Barry said and handed him a printout of a map of Plymouth with the locations marked on it.

'Thanks,' Moone said, hardly able to hold in his delight. 'These locations are within a square mile... and all the murders have also been committed in that square mile.'

'So, chances are he lives in that square mile?' Butler said.

Moone nodded. 'Yep. But where? What do we do, start knocking on every door?'

'Can't we contact this Roman whatever he's called?' Butler asked.

Barry's head was lolling, his eyes shutting, so Butler prodded him, making him jump. 'What?'

'Can't we contact him, set a trap?'

'He set up the profile not long after the first murder, but he's not been active much since,' Barry said. 'I'll have to set up a profile, make it look real. But what do I say?'

'Just read what the other lot chat about,' Butler said. 'Don't go trying to meet up with him too fast.'

Barry's eyes opened wider. 'What about photos? They all have photos uploaded.'

'Can't you nick some you find online?' Moone asked.

Barry shrugged. 'I suppose. As long as he doesn't twig.'

Butler rubbed his shoulder. 'It'll be fine. Let us know if you get a bite. What do they call it?'

'Catfishing,' Barry said, sighed and started typing.

'But go home and get some sleep first,' Moone said, then headed out of the office with Butler on his heels.

'Do you think it'll work?' Butler asked as they reached the incident room.

'I don't know. If this Roman126 hasn't been active since the first murder, then it doesn't look good, does it? Worth a shot though.'

Butler pushed through the door to the incident room and headed to her desk. 'That's if this Roman bloke is the weirdo we're after.'

'He is. He's got to be. Now we know his hunting ground...'

The door to the incident room opened, then the sound of high heels click clacking their way across the wood floor filled the room. Moone turned to see Commander Sally Richer coming towards him, followed by two lean looking men in suits. Probably ex-forces, he thought as he watched them stand either side of her, almost to attention.

'DI Peter Moone,' she said, her eyes sweeping the room, then checking her phone, before she really looked at him. 'So, this is where it all happens?'

Moone looked around the room, at his people who were busy or trying to look it. 'Yes, this is it. As you can see we're busy trying to catch two killers.'

'Two?' She raised her perfectly shaped eyebrows. Moone thought he detected slight redness around them where they might have been recently plucked.

'Yes, we're after our crossdresser killer, your terrorist, and a child murderer.'

She nodded. 'I see. Then it's a good job we're here to lighten the load then, isn't it?'

'More like getting under foot,' Butler said, as she sat at her desk, starting to type on her PC.

Richer stared at her for a moment, seeming to chew over what she'd said, then looked back at Moone. 'We're going to need everything you've got on this guy. Everything. By this evening. Is that understood?'

'Yes, it is. You'll have our full cooperation. But he's not a terrorist.'

'He's terrorising the local gay community, isn't he?' She raised her eyebrows again. 'Our job is to uphold this country's freedoms, to protect its people from the threat of terrorism from outside our borders and within...'

There was a cough and a burst of laughter from across the room. Moone turned to see DC Harding still laughing and wiping coffee from his chin.

'Did you say something?' Commander Richer said to him.

'No, no, nothing,' Harding said. 'It's just that all this anti-terrorism legislation... it's funny how so much of it can be twisted and used against working class, normal people or anyone wanting to protest.'

'I haven't got time for this bullshit,' Richer said, her face reddening. 'Where's my office?'

Moone pointed towards the office at the end of the room that sat beyond the frosted glass walls. 'That's yours. Welcome to hell.'

She looked at him for a moment, turning him over, looking as if she wanted to say something, then turned and took herself, and her people into the office and shut the door.

'Stuff them,' Butler said, coming up to Moone. 'We need to get a team together to go through paedophile street, see who's there, and talk to the neighbours.'

Harding laughed again, and Butler spun round and faced him. 'What you laughing at now?'

Harding shrugged, losing his smile. 'Just thought paedophile street sounds like it'd be a fucked-up soap opera. Look though, we can't let these bastards take over, can we? We've got to find this killer before they do. We really going to hand over all we got?'

Moone looked towards the office where Commander Richer was now on the phone, then walked over to Harding and the rest of the team. Butler came over, folding her arms across her chest. Moone looked them all over. 'We'll have to share most of it. But maybe we can keep the new stuff to ourselves, like the dating site stuff. It'll give us a head start. In the meantime, we need to get you lot over to MacDonald's street, ask the neighbours if they saw anything around the time Danny Sawyer went missing. The Sawyer case is one we've got control of, for now. The fact that our main suspects were all living close to each other when he was taken is significant. Someone must know something. Councillor Philip Stanley killed himself over this, before we could question him. He didn't even know what we were going to ask him. This means people conspired in this...'

'I love a good conspiracy theory,' Harding said, and laughed a little.

'But it's not a theory, is it?' Butler said. 'Not some lonely nutter's crazy thoughts all over the internet. A child was taken and murdered. The only witness we've got is in hospital unconscious.'

'No, he's not,' a voice said next to Harding, and they all looked towards the young dark-haired woman sitting at the desk next to him.

'Sorry, I've forgotten your name,' Moone said.

'DC Molly Chambers,' she said, smiling uncomfortably. 'Ian MacDonald's regained consciousness but he's still not in a very good way. A lot of damage done, they reckon.'

Moone nodded, then looked towards Butler. 'We'd better get down there and see if he's able to tell us anything.'

'Doesn't sound hopeful,' she said.

'I know, but we've got to try.'

Mathieson parked along the path just beyond the big iron gates of Weston Mill cemetery, then climbed out, sweeping his eyes over the crooked rows of graves that rolled over the low hills in the distance. He walked down the path, feeling the wind and light rain hitting him, while reading some of the tumbledown, cracked gravestones, then turned left and headed towards the main office of the cemetery. He knew that close to the other gates, just behind the office, in the shade of a tree, sat Grader's mother's grave. Overlooked, untidy, overgrown. He reached it, noting that someone had left flowers at some time, but they lay rotted in the flowery, disintegrated paper that they'd been wrapped in. The grave was just as unloved and underappreciated as Grader's actual mother, and he wondered what she had done to her child for him to turn out the way he was. But he knew it was never as simple as that, never that straight forward.

He glanced around himself, looking down the well-worn pathways that crisscrossed ahead and beside him, noticing that hardly anyone was around.

He crouched down, staring at the words etched into the headstone, which were merely her name, Elsie Grader, and the date of her death. Nothing more, the bare essentials, he decided as he stretched out a hand over the damp earth. Then he reached into it, feeling it grip his skin with its coldness, the very touch of death coating his flesh.

'It's not there,' a voice said somewhere to his right. Mathieson clambered to his feet, brushing the dirt from his hand as Ray Benton stepped out from behind a tree, looking so much more withered and grey than he had a few days ago in the pub.

'What isn't?' Mathieson said, looking back at the grave. 'Just paying my respects.'

There came a dirty, deep and painful laugh from the old paedophile as he moved closer. 'Paying the respects to a fucking evil old bag you didn't even fucking know? Stroll on, Carl. Who do you take me for?'

'Where is it?'

'Safe... or maybe West never buried any-thing here after you told him to. Maybe Grader was winding you up, getting you here...'

'Why?'

Ray moved closer. 'To warn you. To tell you that he knows all the details, all the bad things... he's going to do what you want him to do, but there's a price.'

'He already said. To bring him...'

'No, not that. Not that at all. When he does what you want, he knows he'll have to fucking run. But he also knows that the fuckers will catch him, that's where you come in.'

'I can't hide him!'

Ray shook his head. 'Fuck off. You thick? He doesn't want you to hide him. We can take care of that. He wants you to help get something for him... a sort of farewell gift.'

'What? A gift? What the bloody hell are you talking about?'

Ray smiled. 'You know.'

Carl Mathieson looked into the old, dying pervert's eyes and the realisation of what was being asked, no, demanded, flooded him, almost drowning him in sickness. He shook his head. 'You're fucking mad. Tell Grader he's crazy, I won't, I can't.'

'You haven't got a choice, have you? We all

know how much you cherish your reputation, and your father's... and your new found family, and if it all came out, what would it do to your poor family?'

Mathieson went to turn away, made it look like he was moving, then snapped round and grasped the old pervert by his windpipe, making him cough and gag.

'Go... on... kill me... what do I care?!' the old man said, defiantly, trying to grin.

'You fucking lot! You should all be lined up, lined up and fucking shot. Right in the back of the heads.'

'What about you?! What do you get for the things you've done?!'

'You bastards, you evil scum bastards. I'm nothing like you lot.'

'Who said you were?!'

Mathieson let go of his throat, letting the skeletal man collapse to the ground, huffing, fighting for breath. He turned away, storming off towards his car, then turned, the fury pulsing in his head, and faced the pervert as he clambered to his muddy knees. 'What the bloody hell does he expect me to do?! Grab some... Jesus... he's warped, sick.'

'Not just any child. The Sawyers. He knows they've got another kid.'

Mathieson stood back, shaking his head, his hands balling into fists. 'Tell Grader he's insane. I won't, he's fucking insane.'

'He told me to tell you that he's got evidence against you.'

Mathieson stared at him, feeling the life drain out of himself. But Grader was a liar, a dirty filthy fucking pervert liar. 'Bollocks. Tell him to go fuck himself.'

'Such colourful language for an MP...' Benton laughed, the same rattling, painful and dirty laugh. 'He's got film of you, he said. Must be pretty bad stuff. Something about being in a certain house.'

Mathieson found himself lurching towards the old man, drawing his fist back, ready to smash his face. But he stopped himself, steadied his trembling body, trying to calm his pounding heart.

The house. He knew the house he was referring to, but he'd only been there once, which meant Grader must have had him secretly filmed while he was inside. Or maybe he was bluffing.

Benton had raised his arms to protect himself, then lowered them, a smile emerging on his face, a grin of victory.

'That's got your old noggin thinking, ain't it?' Benton said. 'Trying to decide if Grader's lying or not, but you can't take the chance, can you? So what do I tell him?'

Mathieson turned away, the pike rising in him like an oily blackness filling up his stomach, then his throat. 'Tell him to do what I asked. If he does that, then I'll... do what he wants.'

Benton laughed, nodding to himself. 'I knew you wouldn't let us down. I knew it. I'll tell him. He'll be so pleased.'

Mathieson didn't want to talk anymore, he couldn't talk anymore, so he stormed off, trying to keep on his feet. The strength had left him, and a headache had started to pound at the top of his skull. He headed to his car, took out his keys, ready to unlock it, his mind flashing images at him that he didn't want to see or remember.

The house.

He closed his eyes, leaned on the car, then he bent over, the vomit pouring out of his mouth. He wiped his face, breathing hard, thinking about what Grader expected him to do in payment. He shook his head, but all the time he climbed into his car and drove away from the cemetery, he tried to think of a way out that wouldn't lead to his family's disgrace and a term in prison for himself.

But there wasn't one, not unless he did exactly what Grader wanted him to.

CHAPTER 22

Moone was looking out at the night through a large window in hospital as he stood in a lime green corridor. There was a little rain hitting the glass, blown by the wind that had picked up. He took another sip of the coffee he'd got from a machine up the corridor, and grimaced, but drank some more. He was probably dehydrated, definitely exhausted. He'd not been sleeping well, the same dark, gruesome dreams involving murdered children kept waking him up. And the wind and rain hammering the caravan didn't help.

Butler had gone home, he'd told her to, to go and see her family. He felt bad that he knew little about her, but he consoled himself with the fact that they'd built up a kind of mutual respect over the past few days.

He turned when he heard the sound of police boots hitting the laminate floor of the corridor and saw PC Faith Carthew coming towards him. He did his best to smile as she approached, but it didn't feel like a smile.

'Oh dear,' Carthew said as she reached him. 'Is that the sort of face you make when you see me?'

'Sorry. I'm just exhausted.' He nodded towards the corridor. 'MacDonald?'

She looked over her shoulder. 'Out of his coma, but it's still early days, they said. They don't know the extent of the damage done. What's happening with your ex-wife?'

He was about to head down the corridor, but her last speedily added question reached his ears. 'What?'

'Pardon, you mean?' She raised her eyebrows.

'You know what I mean, why did you ask about my ex-wife?'

'No reason, well, I thought maybe she's the reason, you know, why you've become so distant.'

Moone found the irritation travelling all over his back. 'We're on duty. I don't think this is the time to discuss this.'

'When?'

He shook his head, then turned away and headed to the unit where they had MacDonald under observation. There was an island in the middle of the corridor, a nurses' station all lit up by hazy, glowing strip lights, making the nurses stood there look decidedly sickly. He walked closer, getting ready to pull out his ID, to ask them for a status report on the patient, but then his eyes jumped to some movement down the end of the corridor, where some of the lights were out and a curtain of grey darkness hid most of the rooms and nooks and crannies from his sight. He quickly looked away, then headed behind the nurses' station, towards a drinks machine and a wall that would keep him from being viewed from the dark corridor. He backed himself up, creeping towards the end of the wall, preparing to sneak a look round it.

'What're you doing?!'

Moone spun his head round to see PC Carthew looking at him as if he'd dropped his trousers. He put his finger to his lips, but then the sound of feet scuffling awkwardly away came from around the corner, so Moone ran round into the dimly-lit corridor, where he could make out the thin shape of a man trying to make his escape. As Moone grabbed his withered arm, the man burst into a bone shattering cough that bent him over, coating his face in redness and sweat.

PC Carthew took his other arm as they carefully escorted the coughing old man back into the light. A couple of the nurses also came towards the scene, watching inquisitively as Moone helped him sit in one of the chairs that lined the corridor.

'Get him some water,' he said to Carthew

and she went scurrying off.

Between aching, deathly coughs, the old man said, 'That's kind of you, son.'

'You don't sound well.'

The old man coughed out a laugh. 'That's putting it lightly. Lung cancer... and it's spread. Ain't got long, son.'

One of the nurses, a full-figured young woman with mousey bobbed hair, came over, looking at the old man sympathetically. 'You all right, love? Anything we can help with?'

The old man looked up at her, with what Moone could see was mock kindness and gratitude. 'Oh, bless your heart... aren't you a kind one. No, love, you can't help me. I'm beyond help. I'm already rotting in hell for the terrible, evil things I've done. You want a list of them? I warn you, it'll make you puke.'

The nurse's face changed, and she looked at Moone, so he produced his ID, which she nodded at then went away. When they were alone again, Moone said, 'What's your name?'

'Ray. Ray Benton.'

Moone nodded, recognising the name, which lifted some of the fog from his eyes. 'Ray Benton. Then I'm guessing you're here to visit your friend, Ian MacDonald?'

Benton lifted his head, scratched his chin, raising his eyes towards the ceiling as he said, 'Ian? Ian MacDonald? No, I don't believe I know the name.'

'Well, that's bloody funny, because you were seen not far from a location where MacDonald was found with his brains bashed in.'

At that moment, PC Carthew came back with a plastic cup of water, and held it out. 'Water?'

'I think he'll be drinking that down the station,' Moone said.

PC Carthew helped Ray Benton to a seat in the interview room, just as another coughing fit overtook him. Then she joined Moone as he stood watching the old dying pervert from the open doorway.

'Seems a bit of a shame all this,' PC Carthew said. 'Seeing as he's dying.'

Moone huffed. 'It's what he deserves. You read his file?'

She shook her head. 'No, but I don't think I'd want to.'

'No, you wouldn't.' Moone sat down, folded his arms and Carthew followed and sat next to him. 'So, Ray Benton... I'd say it's a pleasure to meet at last, but it's really not.'

Benton coughed a little, then looked at the handkerchief he held to his mouth. 'Nothing's a pleasure for me anymore... not even food. I used to love my food, now I can hardly keep anything down. The quacks gave me something to help the sickness, but it don't do much.'

'Drink your water,' Carthew said, pushing a mug of water towards him.

Benton looked at it, made a face. 'Water keeps you alive. Why would I want to be alive a second longer, feeling like this? I got a bottle of fucking morphine I carry round with me... that's all I need.'

Moone leaned forward. 'They say a little suffering is good for the soul. I disagree. I think maybe you need to unburden yourself.'

Benton wiped his mouth. 'Unburden myself? Why the fuck should I feel burdened?'

Moone sat back. 'Well, let's start with the fact you were spotted in the vicinity of Ian Mac-Donald's attempted murder.'

Benton laughed. 'Who says? Got proof? I don't think so. When was this? Middle of the night or something? Fuck me. Know what I'm doing in the middle of the fucking night these days? Pissing. That's all I bleeding do, so no, I was nowhere near wherever this terrible event happened. I say terrible, but MacDonald probably got what he deserved.'

'What he deserved?' Moone laughed. 'And what about what you deserve?'

Benton pointed a withered and dirty looking thumb at himself. 'I've paid for what I done, paid for it at Her Majesty's fucking pleasure. I'm right down the line these days.'

'Bollocks. I've met your kind before, Ray, so many times and your kind never change. Never.

You can't help yourselves.'

'It's a disease,' Benton said, nodding earnestly. 'I'll give yer that. But I'm cured now... but now I got all this... this cancer.'

'Then make amends properly. We know Ian MacDonald took Danny Sawyer. We know that all you lot have been living in the same street for a good couple of years.'

Moone stopped talking when he saw the flicker across Benton's face, the ripple of recognition in the corner of his creased-up eyes. 'I saw that, Ray. You didn't know we knew about the living situation of you lot, but we do. Did you have any dealings with Councillor Stanley? You know, the councillor that took his own life?'

Benton narrowed his eyes. 'I... no, I didn't hear, I didn't know him. I don't know what you're talking about.'

Moone shook his head. 'You want us to believe you didn't know a bunch of sex offenders, most of them known to you, were living in the same street?'

Benton shrugged. 'What can I say? Nothin' to do with me.'

'I'm betting you know who else had a hand in this. Come on, Ray, get it all off your chest. You'll feel better. I mean, you must be feeling something, because you visited the hospital where your friend, Ian MacDonald...'

'He's not my friend!'

'But maybe that's not the reason you were

there, sneaking around. Maybe you were there because you were worried he's about to talk...'

Benton gave a burst of painful laughter that made Moone cringe. 'Me? What have I got to worry about?! I'll be gone soon! There's nothing left for me to worry about.'

'Then who're you protecting?'

'No one. I've said all I'm going to bleeding say!'

Benton folded his arms, stiffened his body, and Moone watched, thinking it all through, trying to find a way in. Benton was already dead, just a living corpse, but there was someone he cared about or was loyal to. He'd turned up on the scene right after the remains of Danny Sawyer had been discovered.

A flicker of light came on in Moone's mind, a dull light at the end of a dark corridor. Moone almost smiled, nearly letting Benton see what he'd worked out.

'You've been away a long time,' Moone said, leaning towards him. 'I mean, away from this city, or so they tell me. Why come back now?'

Benton shrugged, and looked away.

Moone nodded. 'You turned up just after we found Danny Sawyer's body... funny that.'

'What can I say? I missed the fucking god-awful place.'

'Or did you turn up after? Maybe it was before.'

Benton looked at him briefly, so Moone continued. 'Yeah, I'm right, aren't I? When they examined the skeletal remains of little Danny Sawyer, you know what they found? I'll tell you. They found that the bones had been moved. They'd been resting somewhere else for some time, which means someone deliberately dug them up and put them where they'd be found. It was you, Ray. You dug them up.'

Benton laughed, shaking his head, but Moone could see it in him, in the little uncomfortable movements of his body, the look in his eyes, he could see that he was right. And he knew it in his gut. He'd never been more sure of something before.

'Yeah, it was you, Ray. Talk to me about Good Times.'

Benton narrowed his eyes. 'Never heard of the place.'

'Place?' Moone laughed and looked at PC Carthew. 'You hear that? Place? Did I say it was a place? I didn't. You worked there.'

'No, I haven't… don't know it. You can't fucking tie me to it either.'

'I'm sure if I showed your mug around to the people who worked there… yes, I'm positive I'd get someone willing to say you'd worked there. Someone buried a toy with Danny, a toy from that place. Which means you were trying to tell us something, point us in the right direction.'

'Fuck off. I don't know nothin'.'

'But even you didn't think he'd be found

that quickly. We got lucky. Some other nutter decided to dump a body nearby.'

Benton turned to face him, coughing a little,
but trying to smile. 'Even if any of that bollocks
was true, you wouldn't be able to prove it. Would
ya?'

'No, you're right about that. You made sure
you weren't spotted. I must say you've got me in-
trigued. Why would someone with your past try
and uncover something like this?'

'He doesn't... I didn't.' Benton sat up. 'Now
what? You going to fucking charge me or what?'

'We can hold you for a little longer.' Moone
stood up. 'We'll send you to a cell. You can think
it over.'

When Benton was gone, but the acrid scent of
dirt and death lingered, PC Carthew turned to
Moone and said, 'Wow, you were bloody brilliant
right then!'

Moone laughed. 'I wasn't too bad, was I?'

'Not too bad?! That whole he put the body
there... how did you know?'

'I didn't. Something just clicked in my mind.
But I'm right, aren't I?'

'I think so. But why did he do it? They've got
away with it until now, now he's blown the whis-
tle. Why? It doesn't make sense.'

'Not to us it doesn't, but to a dying man with
scores to settle it might. Maybe he's grown a con-

science being so close to death, you know, being close to God. Lots of child abusers turn to God.'

Carthew huffed. 'Yes, when they're facing the parole board, so they might look regretful... lying bastards.'

'You might be right. But something's happened. We just need to figure out what or why, or whatever. I don't know.'

'What about the serial killer? Where are we with that?'

'We know the area he lives in,' Moone said, stifling a yawn and rubbing his eyes. 'We need patrols in that area, extra police presence.'

'What about a trap?' Carthew raised her eyebrows.

Moone laughed and headed out of the interview room and towards the incident room where he fetched his coat. Hardly anyone was there, just a skeleton crew now as he wrapped up and prepared to go home. Carthew came into the room, then up to him and said, 'What's wrong with setting a trap?'

'What? Apart from it sounding like something from Scooby Doo? We get someone to dress up in drag and hang about the street corners?'

Carthew followed him along the corridor as he checked his phone and saw he had a missed call from Alice.

'It could work,' Carthew said.

'Maybe. Probably not. To be honest I don't know what the answer is. I'm hoping Barry will get lucky and contact our killer online. But I doubt that's going to happen, cause our killer's smart, and will probably be suspicious of anything like that now.'

'So what're we doing then?'

Moone turned and saw she looked sad again, and more than a little disappointed in him. But he had little to encourage her with. 'We're waiting to get lucky.'

'Which means unlucky for the poor bastard he stabs or beats next.'

Moone sighed. 'Go home. Get some rest. I'll talk to you tomorrow. We've got an early briefing and we'll decide from there.'

Moone turned away again when she didn't say anything, and headed towards the exit. He went down to the car park and started up his car and headed out into the cold night, his tired eyes scanning the street, Carthew's sad eyes and words haunting his brain.

He put on the brakes, his eyes fixing on a shape on the corner of the police station, a soft voice calling to him. He pulled over, watching the slender hooded shape coming towards his car, away from two young women with long blonde hair and thickly made-up faces.

From the hood appeared Alice's face, now adorned in too much makeup for his liking. She smiled, her hands in her hoodie pockets. 'Hi, Dad.'

'Hi yourself,' he said. 'What the bloody

317

hell're you doing hanging around here? It's getting late.'

She laughed. 'It's dark, it's not late. I came to see you. Can you give us a lift?'

'A lift? Just you?'

Alice looked round at her friends, who were whispering and laughing. 'Them too. You wouldn't want to leave two helpless girls on the street, would you?'

'Get in,' he said. 'Oi! Spice Girls! Get in!'

The girls burst into laughter as they hurried to his car and got in, while Alice climbed into the passenger seat and huffed and tutted.

'What?' he said, driving them away.

'You're so embarrassing!' Alice said. 'Spice Girls? Not exactly current, Dad. And I'm pretty sure there's more than two of them.'

'Where am I dropping you?'

'Off Mutley. Corner of Greenbank will do.'

'I take it you're off to a safe location? Church or something?'

'Funny. We're off to Britney's house.'

'Sleepover? Good. Got good parents has she, this Britney?'

'They're not heroin addicts.'

'Good. So how come you hung around the station? Is that all you wanted? A lift?'

She looked at him, her eyes intense, digging into him. 'You ain't done bugger all about Mum's bloke, have you?'

'I talked to him.'

'And?'

'He's not right. There's something up, but I need more than that to go on.'

'He knew that bloke who did himself in.'

Moone stared at her, flashing his eyes back to the road. 'The councillor? That doesn't surprise me... he's an MP, Alice. They're all in each other's pockets.'

'He came to the house not long ago.'

Moone hit Mutley, then took the turning towards Greenbank and parked just up from a corner pub that was lit up and throbbing with music. He turned round in his seat. 'Alright girls, we're here. I need a word with Alice, OK?'

The girls muttered things between laughter as they hurried out of the car and then stood near the pub watching. Moone took his eyes from them and stared at Alice. 'You're not pulling my chain, are you? I know you don't like him. I know it's tough seeing your mum...'

'It's not that, Dad. I promise!'

He looked into her eyes and saw no hint of a lie. 'When did he come to the house?'

'A few days back. He didn't look happy.'

'Didn't look happy? What does that mean?'

She shrugged. 'I don't know. But he needed an urgent word with his Royal Highness.'

Moone blew out a breath, put his hands on the steering wheel and stared out at the street, but only saw the fragments dancing in his mind trying to join together. The parts that did seem to click into place, didn't make for a pretty picture and filled him full of dread. 'OK... leave it with me.'

'What're you going to do?'

'Look into it.'

She looked doubtful. 'What does that mean?! He's up to something, Dad. He's tied up in something dodgy.'

'Maybe. Maybe not. I'll look into it. I promise you, Alice, if he's up to anything, I'll find out about it.'

'What'll you tell Mum?'

'Nothing for now. Go on, have your sleepover. Go on!'

She looked at him, tried to smile, but then climbed out and hurried to her friends. Moone watched them all turn and disappear into the darkness of the street.

He sat there for a while, absorbed by the beat of his heart and brain, hardly hearing the beat of the pub music. He tried to push away her notion, tried to tidy it away as over-protection. But he couldn't, and a feeling began to push through, a conviction that Alice was right on the money. He recalled Mathieson asking him about the Danny Sawyer case, and the sickness filled his gut.

Carl Mathieson was up to his neck in it all, and sooner or later, he'd have to take him in.

CHAPTER 23

All eyes were on Moone that morning as he stepped into the incident room and put his double espresso down on the desk near the whiteboard. He needed something to keep him awake, a little shot of courage and bravery and alertness, as he'd spent the night tossing and turning. He'd sat up and watched the sun rise achingly slowly from his caravan's window. What Alice had told him, and the fact that he'd have to give a briefing the next day, was what had kept him awake most of the night.

Butler, and everyone on the team, and Stack, were present. But so was Commander Sally Richer, who was sat at a desk, waiting, her arms folded.

'You look like shit,' Stack said as he walked past Moone and stood by the whiteboard, next to all the crime scene photos.

Butler joined Moone and stared into his

barely open eyes. 'How's it going?'

'Not good.'

'What's happened now?' Butler asked, looking actually concerned for once.

'You'll find out in a min. Well, most of it, the rest I'll brief you after.'

'What're you going to tell anti-terrorism? What about the geography issue?'

Moone shrugged. 'I can't see how we can keep it to ourselves. We haven't got the manpower to cover it alone.'

She nodded. 'OK. Fine. You better start it then.'

He was about to nod, when Commander Richer stepped over and said, 'So, you going to tell us what's going on or what? Because we all can't wait to gain your wonderful insights into this case.'

Moone didn't say anything directly to her, but turned to the board, looked over the faces of the victims, taken from family snaps and driving licences. 'This man is not a hater... not of gay people or crossdressers. I don't think this is a hate crime.'

'Not a hate crime?' Richer gave a short laugh.

'Can I continue?' Moone asked, and she nodded, still looking at him with contempt. 'We know our killer was on a dating site for transsexuals and crossdressers, which makes it doubtful that he'd be angry when he met Jason and he turned out to be a man dressed up. Of course he wasn't surprised! This is what he wanted...'

'Because he hates them!' Stack said, shaking his head.

'Thing is,' Moone continued. 'Past cases like this would suggest that our killer is himself a crossdresser or even gay. He just doesn't want to be. So, if he hates anyone, he hates himself. But I think it's not his own hate, but one that's been ground into him by someone.'

'Ok, I'll buy that,' Richer said. 'But how does that help us catch our killer?'

'Our IT guy is working to try and lure him in.'

Richer tutted. 'A honey trap?'

'You got any better ideas, love?' Butler said, the anger thick in her voice.

Richer stared at her for a moment. 'He's not going to fall for that. He knows we're on the hunt for him.'

Moone cleared his throat. 'True. But this guy is escalating. Quickly. The thing in the gay club, he took a big risk. I don't think he cares if he's caught. He just wants to take out as many victims as he can. I don't think it'll be long before he kills again.'

Commander Richer nodded. 'You talk a good game, but how do we catch him?'

Moone let out a breath. 'Our IT guy, Barry, has talked to a few members of the same dating site that the killer used, and it turns out our killer tried to get them all to meet over a reasonably small area.'

'So we know the geographical area in which he hunts?' Richer said, nodding, and watching Moone as he took out copies of the Plymouth map on which he'd circled the potential killing ground. He handed them out, then watched Richer peruse it. She looked up. 'So, we know where he hunts. And we know he'll take as many as he can get. Then we post undercover officers in every bar, every club in this area.'

'That's a lot of ground to cover,' Butler said. 'A lot of manpower we don't have.'

'That's not a problem,' Richer said, then turned to Moone. 'We'll be listening to any emergency calls coming in and we'll be able to react quickly, swiftly.'

Moone nodded. 'Yep, something like that. But there's only one gay bar in that area and he's already struck there.'

'But gay people don't just hang out in gay bars, do they? Single and ready to mingle. All we need to be is ready. He'll strike. Like you said, he's escalating. Well done, DI Moone. This is good stuff. We'll take it from here.'

Moone could only watch her walk away, see her approach Stack, probably arranging more manpower for the surveillance operation. Then he turned away and faced his team that were looking at him with disappointment, especially Butler who was shaking her head.

'Don't,' he said.

'So that's it, boss?' Harding said, sounding more than a little pissed off. 'They go off and get to be the fucking heroes?'

'No one's more upset than me about it,' Moone said. 'But that's the way it is. That's life. That's policing. I hope he's caught and stopped. But right now, all I care about is finding Danny Sawyer's killer. We need to do this for his parents. For any other kids that might fall prey to that ring of... fucking paedophiles. I don't know about you lot, but I'm going to go out there and catch the bastard. Who's with me?'

There were nods around the team, and they looked suddenly excited and up for the fight.

'How exactly do we do that?' Butler asked, folding her arms, a huff in her throat, waiting to escape.

'I'll tell you.' Moone looked round the room to make sure everyone else was busy. 'I've got another lead...'

Butler stepped closer, lowering her voice. 'A lead? What bloody lead?'

'I'll tell you when this lot have gone. There's something else, I've had word that MacDonald's not too badly damaged. He's talking, and making sense. We need to increase security over at the hospital as soon as we can.'

The van door creaked as it opened, spraying

white light across Loy Grader as he sat in the far corner, cuffed and chained. The two guards got up, one of them undoing the lock and allowing him to get to his feet and be pushed and pulled all the way to the open doors. He had only a thin, mouldy smelling prison coat wrapped round him and so the cold gripped him as he was helped down onto the pavement outside the hospital. He smiled when a young woman came out of the entrance talking on her phone, her eyes catching his. She looked away, then hurried off and he laughed.

'Grader!' John snapped and pushed him towards the automatic doors.

The other guards went first, making sure there wasn't anything around that would get him excited. He laughed to himself, working out everything in his head, glancing towards the corridors on his right and left, noting where the toilets were, and the bank of lifts.

That's where they were taking him, towards the lifts, already making sure they claimed the next empty one for him, warning all the other lazy bastards to take the next one.

Grader stood waiting for it, scanning the guards, noting John's taser, both guards' batons and extra restraints. They were relaxed as always. They knew he always behaved himself, never gave much trouble, apart from the occasional inappropriate comment to the nurses. Usually, he would back down and stop mid-word when they threatened to take away his privileges, but not today.

The next floor was clear of children, or most other patients to an extent, for he understood it was almost completely impossible to hide everyone from him. A few sallow, tired-looking nurses were stood waiting for him, all stood to a kind of disgusted and horrified attention, pretending they were better than him, as if they didn't have any sexual fetishes. Everyone does, they're just too scared to admit it to themselves or the rest of society.

'Come on, Grader,' John said and pushed him on, directing him towards the cubicle the army of nurses were waiting outside of.

'I wish you wouldn't do that, John,' Grader said, looking over his shoulder at his guard.

John smiled. 'Do what? Talk to you?'

'Push me. I wish you wouldn't push me.'

John looked down at him, then gave a laugh, and nodded. 'Go on, move it. And behave yourself.'

Grader went on, turning back towards the nurses who were still waiting, looking more impatient than ever.

'Please sit down on the bed,' a heavy set, redheaded nurse said, her words coming out in a breathy huff.

He did as he was told, giving her a big smile, noting that she had a wedding ring on. She also had the haggard look that came with having children, perhaps more than the average two. He kept smiling at them all as they worked as a team, hooking him up to machinery, telling him to take off his top, placing pads over his body.

They all tried to avoid his eyes, but he kept finding them, and would lick his lips, and get told off by John for it. All the time he played the fool, his eyes jumped around the room, noting the equipment the nurses had about their person. The big nurse, the redheaded one, had a pair of very shiny long scissors tucked in her top pocket. He smiled to himself as she came towards him, lifting his arm and producing the blood pressure cuff to take a reading.

'How many do you have?' he asked, smiling up at her.

'Sorry?' she said, still not looking at him.

'Kids. How many kids do you have?'

'Grader!' John said, in his same old grumbling voice.

'I'm just being friendly,' Grader said. 'So how many?'

'Don't answer that,' the guard said. 'You don't want to engage him.'

Grader laughed. 'You're a spoilsport, John. Go on, tell me. At least tell me if they're fat like you!'

The nurse jerked upright, her face reddening, unsure what do to, half looking at John for an answer.

Grader took the chance, snapped out his

hand and grasped the scissors, pushing himself up at the same time. He swung round in one deft movement, sweeping his arm round her throat, digging the scissors into her flesh.

John and the other guard had rushed forward, tasers and batons drawn, but stopped dead as he grinned at them over her shoulder. Her hair covered half his face and he sniffed, smelling her fruity shampoo.

'Grader!' John shouted, holding up his hands, showing his empty palms. 'What do you think you're doing?'

'You smell lovely,' he said to the nurse, whispering the words, although she'd begun to sob and beg to be released.

'Grader!' John shouted again. 'Don't be stupid! Put those down and we can forget this happened.'

'No, John,' Grader said, turning his head towards another of the nurses who was stood frozen by the wall, staring at the scene unfolding. 'I'll tell you what's going on. You two, put down the batons and tasers.'

'We can't do that!' John said, shaking his head. 'This is not you, Grader...'

'Oh, this is very me,' he said, pressing the scissors against the woman's throat, making her cry even harder. 'You want me to cut her throat?'

'You won't do that,' John said. 'You're not stupid.'

Grader pulled the scissors sideways, tearing

the blade across the nurse's throat, the blood seeping down her neck as he dropped her to the floor. He spun round, knowing the guards' next move, and grabbed the other nurse. He got his arm round her, digging the tip of the scissors into her neck, smiling again.

One guard saw to the nurse, trying to stem the bleeding as John stood up, shaking his head. It was only a superficial wound he'd inflicted on the nurse, but it was enough to shake them, to realise he meant business.

'OK...' John straightened himself, his skin looking ashen. 'OK, Grader, calm yourself, I don't know what you think...'

'I want your tasers and batons,' Grader said, pressing the scissors into the nurse's neck, but his second victim was too frightened, to paralysed with fear to cry or try and fight back. 'Slide them across the floor.'

'Grader, you know...'

'Do it! Do you want this poor bitch to have a big fucking hole in her neck?!' Then Grader looked at the young woman, smelling the small amount of makeup she'd applied that morning, and the skin cream on her skin. 'Do you have kids?'

The nurse shook her head, so Grader said. 'Shame. A young bitch like you should be pregnant. Don't want to wait too long.'

John had taken out his baton, and retrieved the other guard's equipment, by the time Grader looked back at the scene playing out on the floor.

'Slide them across the floor,' Grader commanded.

'What you going to do, Grader?' John asked, gripping the equipment on the floor, his eyes lifted to Grader.

'That's for me to know, Johnny boy. Now slide them over.'

'Let her go first,' John said. 'She was just doing her job.'

'You don't slide those over, she won't get to do her job anymore.'

'Please, please...' the nurse said, sounding as if tears were coming.

'You heard her, John. She's pleading with you to help her. But first, I want you to take that taser and stick it in your mate.'

The other guard turned his face round, still crouched by the nurse, his hand over her neck wound. 'You're a fucking bastard, you're a...'

'Yeah, yeah,' Grader said. 'Do it, John, or this bitch gets a new breathing hole. Do it!'

John dipped his head, shaking it, lifting the taser, then turned to his friend, who was shaking his head.

'Sorry, mate,' John said, then stuck the taser into his side.

Grader laughed as the other guard writhed on the floor, half rolling on the body of the nurse. John slid the rest of the equipment across the floor towards Grader, then stood up, holding up his hands as if to surrender. 'Now what, Grader? Now what? How far do you think you'll get?'

'Far enough, John, far enough,' Grader laughed, then turned his attention to the snivelling nurse that he was pressed against, pressing himself tighter to her, so he could feel the tremor of fear she was gripped by. 'Now, darling... actually, what's your name, darling?'

There came a few tears before the nurse managed to say, 'Sa... Sarah.'

'All right, Sarah, darling. I want you and me to crouch down and you're going to pick up that taser.'

'Don't do it, Sarah,' John said, his head shaking, obviously knowing what was coming.

'She hasn't got a choice, has she, John? It's either that or I stab these scissors, these very sharp medical scissors, through her neck. Someone didn't do their job properly did they, John? Didn't make sure there wasn't something dangerous and sharp close by. You got too relaxed with me, didn't you, John?'

'Fuck off, Grader.'

Grader laughed. 'Come on, Sarah, let's crouch down at the same time... on three... one... two... three...'

They went down, then he ordered her to grab the taser, which took her three goes with the help of her foot. But she got it and held it in her trembling hand.

'Now, Sarah,' Grader said, unable to hold

back his victorious smile. 'Don't think about turning that on me. It'll get you and me, but not before I stick these scissors through your pretty neck. Got it?'

The nurse nodded.

'Good. Now, John, come and get your medicine...'

John didn't move, just shook his head. 'No way. I don't trust you. What'll you do once I'm down?'

'Come on, John. I know a little about you, like you used to be a copper, which means you wanted to help people at one time. Help this poor nurse now, cause if you don't, she'll die, and the nurse on the floor will die... so what'll it be, John?'

'Fuck You. I've always done right by you, Grader. I treated you with respect!'

'And it's much appreciated, John. It's why I'm going to get her to tase you and then I'm going to run.'

John stared at him, his jaw grinding, his fists clenching and opening. Then he took a couple of steps closer, bringing himself in range.

'Do it!' Grader screamed and watched with delight as the nurse dug the taser into the guard and fired it, sending John jerking and flailing to the floor, a deep growl of pain escaping his lips.

As soon as he hit the deck, Grader, pulled the scissors away, spun the nurse round and punched her in the face. He laughed when her legs buckled, then she collapsed. He stepped over her and grabbed some restraints. He cuffed them all, the nurse positioned on her knees as Grader crouched in front of John, one of the batons in his hand.

John was coming round, his eyes fluttering, and so was the nurse. She was dazed, and her nose was crooked and spewing blood, but she could see.

'Watch this, Sarah,' Grader said. 'You were always good to me, John.'

Grader raised the baton high, fixing his eyes on the nurse as the realisation hit her, and her eyes grew bigger, her skin losing all colour. Any beauty she had, he noticed, was gone, and she was just a shape, a vessel, with holes for a face.

The baton came down, cracking against hard skull, sending a shockwave up Grader's arm. He kept bringing it down, half watching the nurse, who had gripped her eyes shut, shaking, letting out a strange whine among the many tears.

Grader breathed hard as he stopped hitting, looking down at the mess he'd made of John's head, climbing to his feet. He picked up the scissors, saw the cuffed guard was staring up at him, his face full of horror, his head shaking, pleading in his eyes.

Grader laughed, then swung his boot, sending it into the guard's head. When he was dazed, Grader sat astride him, jerking the scissors into the air, and stabbing them into his right eye.

The screams filled the cubicle, so Grader jumped off him, grabbing the baton and marched out of the room and along the corridor. He ignored the nurses rushing towards him, pushing past them, all of them too scared to stop him.

He found the lift and took it down a couple of floors to the ground level, hiding the baton under his clothing. He was breathing hard, the blood pounding in his ears, as the doors opened. Patients and staff were lined up, a hospital bed being pushed towards him. No one gave him a second glance as he zipped past them all, storming on towards some shops on his left, following the signs for the ICU, the clatter and chatting of the cafe fading in the background, being drowned out by the beating of blood in his ears.

The ICU was crowded, hordes of people sitting along the corridor, mostly looking worried, the glare of the lights making them look ill. He went on, past the nurses' station, looking round the place, searching the corridor, looking in the windows.

Then he stopped dead when he saw a uniformed police officer stood outside one of the rooms, his phone to his ear. Grader began moving again, slowly taking the baton out of his clothing, gripping it by his side as he went round the uniform, listening all the time.

'Yes... all OK here,' the uniform said.

Grader swung the baton, catching the pig on the back of his neck, knocking him forward and smashing his forehead against the window. He tried to turn, dazed, grabbing for his equipment, but Grader swung again, smashing the baton into his face and knocking him to the floor.

There was no time to waste, so Grader pushed through the door and into the cramped room that was filled by the large bed that had the slight, pale shape of Ian MacDonald lying on it, multicoloured worms protruding from his face.

He was sleeping, his eyes tight shut.

Grader leaned over him, whispering his name, nudging him a little. 'Ian... Ian Mac-Donald.'

The eyes flicked open, confusion filling them, before the drop of realisation, the spread of fear, of terror.

'That's right, MacDonald,' Grader said, lifting the baton. 'I knew it was you. You're the reason I was banged up! You grassed me up!'

'What do you think you're doing?!'

Grader didn't turn, even when he felt the woman grasping at him. He lifted the baton and brought it down, smacking away MacDonald's feeble attempts to protect himself. He shoved the woman to the floor, then swept the baton at his head, again and again, until he stood, sweating and panting looking at the lifeless, bloody face of the turncoat bastard.

He dropped the baton, ignoring the nurse's cries for help, and kept on storming down the corridor, even when he heard an alarm screaming out. He'd finished it, saved them all, but most of all he'd got sweet, bloody revenge.

CHAPTER 24

The agitation dug its talons into Moone's back as he headed towards the Chief Superintendent's office, his mind whirring, trying to fathom what the short notice meeting was about. What had they fucked up now? No, not them, him; it was his shoulders that the whole investigation rested on, and if someone had to go it would be him. Last in, first out – London boy tries to look cocky and falls flat on his smug face.

He knocked, then got told to go straight in by the Chief Super's secretary.

When Moone opened the office door, his eyes immediately fell on the pinstriped suit sat opposite Laptew's desk. He turned and looked Moone over, revealing a middle-aged, slightly craggy face, but Moone supposed women might find him handsome.

His boss pointed to the empty chair beside the suit. 'Have a seat, DI Moone. This is Edward

Talbot. He's Mr Benton's solicitor.'

Moone's stomach turned over as he sat down. 'I'm not going to like this, am I?'

'Not really,' the solicitor said and stared at Moone. 'You've had my client, Mr Raymond Benton, locked up in your cells for many hours...'

'We're still entitled to hold him...' Moone started to say, but Laptew coughed, and caught his eye.

'Just listen, please, DI Moone,' the Chief Super said.

The solicitor nodded to Laptew, with a brief smile, which caused Moone to wonder if they belonged to the same chapter of the Freemasons. Then he put away his suspicious thoughts as the solicitor said, 'Mr Benton isn't a well man. He's recently been diagnosed with lung and liver cancer. He has only a matter of months left... if that.'

'He was seen in the vicinity of a crime, an attempted murder,' Moone said, but the solicitor held up a hand as he said, 'I'm sure there were plenty of people in that area at the time of the murder, but my client assures me he plans on passing on any information he can in due course.'

'In due course?' Moone looked at his boss, hoping he was hearing the same bollocks as he was.

The Chief Super looked away from Moone. 'The truth of the situation is that Mr Benton is dying. He'd never see the inside of a prison if we did charge him with anything, but as I understand it, we don't have any evidence that he committed any crime in this instance?'

Moone sighed. 'No, we don't.'

The Chief Super sat upright. 'Then your client leaves today. But with the assurance that he will inform us of anything he does know about the abduction and murder of Danny Sawyer.'

The solicitor stood up, straightening his suit, then shook the hand that Laptew held out, while Moone watched to see if there was anything suspicious about their contact. He didn't see anything, so stood up himself, nodded to Laptew and prepared to follow the solicitor out.

'Moone,' the Chief Super said, so he turned round and faced him, not bothering to hide his great disappointment.

'Sir?' he said.

'Don't be too pissed off,' Laptew said, putting on a sympathetic smile. 'You'll get there in the end. I've got faith in you and your team. And I think Benton will be good to his word. Hang in there.'

'Sir,' Moone said, then went to head out of the Chief Super's office, but stopped, an image of a desperate and depressed PC Carthew popping into his mind. 'Sir, could I ask a favour?'

'I suppose. I guess you deserve one. Depending on what it is?'

'Could you get PC Carthew put on our team? Plain clothes, I mean? She's a hard worker.'

Laptew held up a hand. 'PC Carthew? I have had my eye on her... yes, take her as a detective constable on a probational period.'

Moone nodded, smiled, then left his boss' office to find himself confronted with a very pissed off looking DS Butler.

'What now?' Moone asked.

'Prepare to be pissed off, and very disappointed,' she said.

'I've been preparing for that my whole career. Go on.'

'Ian MacDonald... is dead.'

Moone stared at her, the words slapping him across the face. Shit. 'He died? The bastard died on us?'

'No. He had help. From Loy Grader. He was on a hospital visit, escaped and beat MacDonald to death. Come on, figured you'd want to visit the scene.'

Moone watched her calmly turn and head past the secretary, then open the outer door. He followed, feeling hollowed out and lost.

Moone almost didn't register the journey to Derriford Hospital at all, his mind was so wrapped up working through every event of the last week or so. He felt like he was trying to carry a heavy bin bag full of jagged pieces of broken glass, trying not to stab himself. But every now and again, a thought stabbed into him.

Somewhere among his thoughts, he found himself walking along the wide scuffed yellow floor of the hospital, avoiding the flood of sickly bodies coming the opposite way.

Butler directed him through more corridors until they entered the artificially bright ICU department. The room was sealed off with tape, and evidence markers were strewn about, while white suited SOCOs came and went. They were given polythene overshoes to put on, then went into the small room where another SOCO lit up the room with the blue flash from his camera.

'Jesus,' Moone said, approaching the bed, where MacDonald, or what remained of him, lay under the starched sheets. 'I don't think Grader liked him very much.'

'Really?' Butler said, managing to raise a laugh. 'Where do you get that from?'

'Well, look, this is a pretty savage attack. I'm sure there's less violent, and less messy ways he could've killed him. No, this seems personal.'

'You don't think Grader was trying to shut him up? He was about to spill his guts to us.'

Moone nodded. 'More than likely, but there's definitely more to this than just an execution. What happened to the uniform who was on guard?'

'In A and E being stitched up. He'll be all right. Want to see the real blood bath?'

'I guess we should.'

Butler rolled her eyes and then took them

to the lifts, then up to the second floor up, and along a corridor that was swarming with white suited SOCOs. One of the rooms was guarded by a uniform as a gurney came out and was taken by a couple of staff towards Moone and Butler. They stopped and watched as a nurse with a bandaged neck was taken down the hallway.

'The nurses were lucky,' Butler said, showing her ID to the uniform and then heading under the cordon and into the small white room that had a bed against the wall. Moone's eyes fell to the blood on the floor first, the sprays of it, the splashes on the wall, all the castoff. There was still one of the guards lying sprawled out, his face a pulpy mess, while SOCOs took photos and swabs in every corner.

'Remember the guard we met when we first met Grader here? John?' Butler asked. 'That's him.'

'Shit.' Moone stood over him, then looked over at another smaller pool of blood. 'Seemed like a nice guy, what happened there?'

'There was another guard, still alive but blind in one eye.'

'Fuck. Grader's not a violent prisoner, is he?'

Butler shrugged. 'He was violent before he went to prison, then he seemed to calm down. Been a model prisoner really.'

'Been biding his time.'

Butler looked round the room. 'Wonder what set him off.'

'Or who.' Moone had a slow burning thought climb up into his head from his gut, spreading a sick feeling with it.

'Who?'

'Who went to see Grader recently?'

'I don't know. Who went...' Butler stopped talking as a change crossed her face, her eyes narrowing as she stepped towards him. 'You're bloody joking, you think Mathieson, Carl bloody Mathieson, told Grader to do all this? You've lost the plot.'

As Butler went to go, shaking her head, Moone said, 'Our dead councillor went to see him.'

Butler stopped, looked around, then she gestured with her head for him to follow her. He went, following her as she stormed off, her head turning, searching for an empty room. She found it and let him step first into the small room filled with medical supplies in solid locked cabinets. She shut the door, and faced him, arms folded, looking pretty pissed off. 'Go on, what's all this about? Cause it sounds like you've gone all cakey on me.'

'My daughter's been on at me about Mathieson, saying he's not right, he's up to something...'

'You daughter, how does she know him?'

'Mathieson's... he's my ex-wife's... well, you know.'

Butler laughed. 'I see, he's screwing your wife, so you're trying to get back at him.'

'No!' Moone heard his own violent shout echoing back at him. 'Sorry. No. It's not like that. I don't care who she dates, as long as she leaves me alone. But Alice thinks there's something wrong. I went round there one night and someone knocks at the door, but he's really cagey about it all. Really cagey. And same night he starts asking about Danny Sawyer, then Alice tells me he knew the councillor and that same councillor paid a visit to Mathieson and he was pretty stressed about something... I know it sounds all very...'

'Let's drag the bastard in,' Butler said.

When Moone looked up at her, she looked different, no longer full of doubt. There was now a light behind her eyes, maybe even a full-on forest fire. 'But we haven't got much to go on, and he's a fucking MP, probably in the same Masonic club as our boss.'

'So fucking what?'

'Then how do we get him in?'

Butler looked round the room. 'We want to talk to him about Grader, how he seemed when he talked to him. Worth a punt?'

Moone nodded. 'OK. Then what? Did you put Grader up to this?'

'We'll think of something before then. Let's just get the ball rolling.'

Ray Benton smoked a cigarette, leaning against the wall of the police station car park, watching the plump, suited lawyer fiddling with his brief-case, before he took out his keys and unlocked his flash looking Audi. Then he turned, saw Benton and huffed, the impatience clear in his face as he put his briefcase on the floor.

'Time is money, Mr Benton,' the lawyer said, raising his thick eyebrows.

Benton stubbed out his cigarette, then started coughing all the way to the car and climbed in the passenger seat as the lawyer started and revved the engine.

'I would've thought you would have given those up by now,' the lawyer said as he drove them across the car park and towards the gate at the end of the compound.

'Why?'

'Well, a man in your condition...'

'I thought you lawyers were meant to be fucking clever.'

'I'm a solicitor, a lawyer...'

'What's the bloody point me giving up? I'm already fucking dead, so what's the point of me not having one last pleasurable moment. If I can't smoke, I might as well kill myself.'

'Is that the only pleasure you enjoy these days?'

Benton glanced over to him, and caught the solicitor looking at him accusingly. 'I thought you were meant to represent without fucking judgement or something.'

'Something like that. I was just curious,

now that you're dying... you see my point?'

'You can drop me off here.'

The solicitor pulled over into a space meant for buses, round the corner from the Theatre Royal. 'The man that paid for all this would like to remind you the importance of discretion in this matter.'

Benton opened the door, then looked at him, stared at him. 'Keep my bloody mouth shut, you mean? Yeah, I think I got that. Cheers.'

As soon as Benton shut the door, the solicitor roared the car off, slipping into the sparse traffic. The old man took out another ciggy and poked it into his mouth and lit it, while he searched for his cheap pay-as-you-go mobile. He brought up his list of numbers, which were few, and picked out the only one that really meant anything to him and dialled it. It rang for a while, before the voice he was expecting answered, but sounded blank, maybe annoyed.

'It's me,' he said, and took a puff of his cigarette.

'I know. I know who it is. You smoking?'

He looked at the cigarette in his hand, then dropped it. 'No, not anymore. How're you doing?'

'Fine. Look, I'm busy.'

'How is he? How's Finley?'

There was a pause on the other end, then a tired sigh. 'He's good, he's good, look, thing is...'

'I'd like to see you... both, you know...'

'I don't think that would be a good idea.

Look, I've got to go, sorry...'

'Hang on,' Benton said, but the call had been ended, and he was left in the middle of the city centre, the building traffic rattling past, an icy wind pushing him along while rain spat into his face.

What had it all been for? he asked himself. Why had he started all this if not for some kind of forgiveness? He didn't believe in God or all that shit, but he asked whoever or what was in charge to give him a chance at redemption, or at least a chance to enjoy his last days.

He would try calling again tomorrow, perhaps even tell him how ill he truly was, and then maybe he'd listen and agree to meet up. Benton nodded to himself, then headed down the street.

It was a new dream that had arrived in the night and refused to let him go. Carl Mathieson was sat in his office overlooking Exeter Street, staring at the windows that were being hit by the rain, the rumble of busy traffic that was tearing by outside. Usually dreams faded away, and only left you with a sense of the weirdness involved.

Not this time. This time he was left with an image, burnt into his mind. It was a stark, black and white image of a back door that led out into a barren, weed filled courtyard. To his left was another set of steps that led down to a basement door. The door was open, and he could see the shadows within, and whatever was waiting down the set of stairs that led down into the darkness.

He looked down at his feet, then closed his eyes, blocking it all out, trying to bring himself back to the here and now.

Then it all faded with a knock at the door, and he turned in his seat, rubbing his eyes, putting on a smile that threatened to split his face in two.

'Come in,' he said, but let out a harsh breath when he saw Peter Moone's tired, washed-out face appear in the gap, followed by his wiry body. 'What can I do for you?'

Moone gave a brief smile and stood at the centre of the room while his colleague, a dark-haired woman, who was taller than Moone and looked more the biter than the barker, came in and started looking around.

'Afternoon,' Moone said, then pulled up a chair and sat down. 'This is DS Mandy Butler. Hope we aren't disturbing you.'

'No, no, just dealing with some Brexit issues raised by my constituents.' He smiled.

Moone rolled his eyes. 'Don't envy you there.'

'We voted leave, let's just get on with it,' Butler said, shaking her head and poking around his small library of books.

'What did you both want?' he asked, then added with a laugh, 'I'm not in trouble, am I?'

Moone laughed. 'No. Why should you be in trouble? We just wanted to ask you a few questions about... Loy Grader.'

Mathieson sat back, narrowed his eyes, shaking his head. 'I don't know why I'd be any help in his regards.'

Moone tutted. 'Sorry, my mistake. I haven't told you that he escaped from custody this morning. Injured a member of staff at the hospital, killed one guard and maimed another. He also murdered Ian MacDonald.'

'Jesus.' Thank fuck for Loy Grader, he thought. MacDonald gone. He could breathe a sigh of relief. 'That's awful. Are the members of staff OK?'

'They're recovering.'

'You went to see Grader, didn't you?' Butler asked, folding her arms across her chest.

'I did,' Mathieson said, then looked at Moone. 'You know I did. To help find out what happened to Danny Sawyer.'

'And did he help you?' Moone asked.

'No,' Mathieson said, blowing air from his mouth, looking suitably pissed off. 'He was evasive, amused by it all, wanted to know about my life. He's a very sick and twisted individual.'

'We could've told you that,' Butler said.

'Did he mention MacDonald at all?' Moone asked.

'No, why would he?' Mathieson said. 'Like I said, he just talked about weird stuff, then clammed up. That's it. So I left.'

'Did you know the councillor that killed himself?' Moone asked, his tired eyes digging into Mathieson.

'I... yes, I knew of him. We had dealings, that's about it. Why?'

'Just wondered.'

'Why did he kill himself?' Mathieson asked. 'Did you find out?'

'We can't discuss an ongoing investigation,' Moone said.

'Of course. Well, I wish I could be more help.'

Moone sat forward. 'Did you see Councillor Stanley recently?'

'No, no, I don't think so.'

'You're quite sure?'

'I don't think so. I don't really remember the last time I did see him. I'm sorry.'

Moone stood up. 'Well, let us know if you think of anything. On either matter.'

'I will. I definitely will.'

Moone nodded, then they both left, leaving Mathieson to sit forward and grip his face, running his mind through everything that had happened, trying to see if there was any way he could be linked to any of it now MacDonald was out of the picture. He couldn't find a way, unless any of the others let on about his connection to the whole filthy business. No, they wouldn't dare, as they would only tie themselves to it.

They couldn't prove any of it. He sat back,

breathing deeply, calming himself.

But the image rose again, the bleached out dream, the grainy image of the back door, the stone steps that led to the basement.

Except it wasn't just a dream image, but a real place. A place he'd visited, a house he'd never ever forget.

CHAPTER 25

The traffic lights blazed red through his windscreen, making his face glow, burning his skin. His heart bubbled, his blood scorching his veins. The desire to do it again had been growing inside him, bellowing loudly, screaming. They deserved punishment, and he was the one to deal it out. But there was a risk; there seemed to be a greater police presence on the streets of Plymouth, police cars crawling past, uniforms around the town centre. But now it was dark and he drove around and around, scanning the streets, watching the drunken students stumbling past. He was just about to pass the end of Mutley, when something caught his eye – two men crossing the street towards the bar on the corner, hand in hand. They were flaunting their sin for everyone to see, unashamed of their filthy desires. He turned the car around, watching them, careful of the traffic coming towards him. They went into one of the bars along the Mutley strip, so he parked up in one of the side streets, then opened his boot, found his rucksack and took out a medium size kitchen knife and a claw hammer. He slipped them into his coat, feeling the weight of it tugging at his shoulders.

He walked back towards the lights of Mutley, pulling up his hood, the race of traffic pouring along, the chatter and screams of women filling his ears. They were dressed up, fancy dress costumes, ridiculous makeup.

He kept walking, moving round the crowds, past the packed takeaways, looking into each window of every bar to spot the two filthy bastard men. If he passed a shop or a bank, he put up his hand to cover any part of his face that his hood might not hide. In his inside pocket was his mask and gloves. He started to slip them on when he thought he saw the two sinners walking through the next bar, a cramped little pub that used to a perfectly respectable cafe at one time. The burn rose again, the voice in his head telling him what to do as he took the knife and hammer from his coat.

Butler left her car parked a few streets away from Mutley, close to the train station, then hurried through the spittle of rain up towards the high street, following the sound of music, traffic and girls' screaming. She spotted the dark Renault parked at the top of the road beside the church, then went to the passenger side and tapped the window loudly, making the person inside jump out of their skin. She held in her laughter as she opened the door and climbed in. The car was warm and dry, but the face that turned to her was anything but welcoming. Mousey brown wavy hair framed a harsh, pale face. The eyes took her in with a totally fake smile that faded quickly.

'What're you doing here?' former PC Carthew said, then turned her face back to the strip of pubs and takeaways she'd been keeping an eye on.

'Volunteered for surveillance duty,' Butler said, looking Carthew over. 'Didn't really fancy going home, me and him indoors aren't talking at the moment.'

'What a loss for him,' Carthew said, turning her head back to flash a sarcastic smile.

'Yeah, you're right, I've got so many interesting things to say. Like... I've got you pegged.'

Carthew huffed out a laugh, then stared at her. 'Have you? Have you really?'

'Oh yeah.' Butler adjusted the seat, getting herself more leg room. 'Who sat here before? One of the seven dwarfs?'

'You were saying?'

Butler smiled. 'I was, I was saying I know what you're all about. Fucking DI Peter Moone one minute and then bang, as if by bloody magic, here you are, Detective Constable Faith Carthew.'

'For those who wait...'

'Or for those who fuck their way to the top. I've heard rumours about you...'

'You shouldn't listen to rumours.'

'I know. I don't usually, but when they fit in with what my gut's telling me...'

Carthew laughed. 'And what is your chubby little gut telling you?'

Butler ignored the comment, although her urge to slap the bitch made her hand tremble. 'That you're not right. You're a manipulator.'

'Really? Who you going to tell about all this? Hang on, is this a jealousy thing, cause you want to jump on Moone's bones yourself?'

Butler laughed loudly, shaking her head. 'Oh, come on...'

'You should. Give him a go, he's not bad.'

Butler was about to answer when screaming and shouting started outside one of the pubs opposite. Carthew wound down her window, raising the volume of noise, while the wind lashed the rain into their faces.

'Someone's having a crazy night,' Carthew said.

Butler focused in on the bodies pouring out in a hurry, panicked faces, then a young man shouting for help, for someone to call an ambulance. 'Move! Let's go!'

Butler jumped out of the car, heading across the road, holding a hand up to the taxis and cars that beeped at her as she ran and dodged her way towards the young man that stood, pale, with tears in his eyes, staring at nothing.

'What's happened?' she asked, showing her ID, but he barely glanced at it, his eyes trailing off, closing, then opening. Then she looked down at his blue shirt and saw the blossom of blood opening up. She caught him as he collapsed, and helped him to lie down on the pavement, putting her hand over the wound. When she looked up, Carthew was looking down at them both, her mouth open.

'Don't just bloody stand there, check inside,' Butler ordered, then spotted a uniform running towards her. 'You! Here!'

The uniform knelt down, helping her move the wounded man. She got a credit card from her wallet, then pressed it to the wound. 'Hold this here!'

Butler stormed towards the bar, heading inside, finding most people had left, apart from a few bewildered punters that had no idea anything had happened. There was a bar at the back of the place, where the lights were on full blaze, and a dark-suited, ashen-faced bouncer held a young dark-haired man in his arms. Blood covered the man's chest, while dried blood was caked in his hair.

'He's gone,' the bouncer said, looking up at her like a lost child.

'Call an ambulance,' Butler told a young

blonde woman behind the bar, then looked at the bouncer. 'What happened?'

The bouncer shook his head. 'I don't... I don't know... just heard screaming...'

'There was a bloke...' the girl behind the bar said, her voice shaking. 'He had a hammer... he was waving it about.'

'Did you see his face?'

She shook her head. 'He had a hood and mask on.'

'I sent in another officer...'

The girl pointed to a door beside her that was partly open. 'She went through that way... there's some blood...'

Butler didn't wait for anything more, just headed behind the bar, almost knocking the girl over as she raced through the narrow door into a small office, then through to a hallway that led to a back door. She found herself in a dimly lit courtyard filled with large metal bins and green recycling bins. There was a trail of blood leading off towards the back gate, which she went through and found Carthew shining a torch along the cobblestoned back lane.

'Where is he?' Butler asked, lowering her voice.

'He went this way,' Carthew said, shining her torch on more blood, but only light spots of it. 'Look, over there.'

At the gate of another building, just in front of more brown and green bins and black bin bags, there were two weapons lying discarded. One a bloody knife, the other a claw hammer that was also covered in blood.

'Don't touch them!' Butler snapped as Carthew crouched down, her hand reaching out.

'I wasn't going to,' she said, sounding pissed off. Then she turned her light on Butler, half blinding her with the beam. 'Must be so easy...'

'What? Get that light out of my face!'

'...To pick this hammer up and smash someone's skull in.'

The torch light fell, but she caught sight of Carthew's face for a moment, frozen in a look of absolute hate.

Footsteps echoed down the lane, hammering the cobblestones, a shape heading right, disappearing. Butler started running, full pelt, towards the shape that was racing deeper into Mutley, encircling the strip of pubs.

Then the sound of an engine coughing and spluttering nearby as headlights snapped on. The car roared off, skidding round on itself, heading down the street. Butler spotted the registration number and started repeating it as she hurried to write it down.

When Moone walked into the incident room, he found everyone nursing coffees, looking bleary-eyed. He himself had managed to grab an Americano with an extra espresso on the way. Butler had called him and roughly filled him in on the night's events. He should've been feeling pretty depressed, knowing that the killer had struck again and alluded them once more, but he felt like they were getting closer on the Danny Sawyer case, so he had a little hope left.

'Jesus, look at you lot,' Moone said, facing them all, sipping his coffee. 'Butler, you should be in bed...'

'Fuck that,' Butler said as she got up, sipping her mug of coffee. 'Sir. The fucker did it again and got away.'

'But you got the registration number of his car, that's something.'

'Probably nicked. We're running it now.'

'What car was it?' Moone asked.

'A rust bucket,' Butler said. 'A little shit box on wheels.'

'Sure it wasn't your car, Mandy?' Harding said, laughing as he faced his screen.

'Ha ha. And what do you drive, Harding? A Ford Labia?!'

Harding turned around, faced her, looking confused as Moone held in a laugh. 'Labia? Doesn't sound like a Ford, more like one of those shit foreign cars... why're you all laughing?'

'Right,' Moone said, still trying not to laugh. 'Let's get off the crazy person's version of Top Gear and let's get back to the car, and what happened last night.'

'Got it!' Harding said, sitting back, and

punching the air! 'Car was reported stolen.'

'Bloody great!' Butler said, huffing.

'Stolen from outside a house near Ham Woods. It's owned by a Paul Rogers,' Harding said.

'Rogers got any form?' Moone asked.

'Na, nothing,' Harding said.

'Well, well, what a fuck up,' a woman's voice said behind Moone, and he froze when he realised who it belonged to. He turned to see Commander Richer staring at him, eyebrows raised, sheets of paper held at her side. 'You lot let him get away from you last night, then?'

'Well, we've got a registration number,' Harding said, causing her to laugh with pity, then clap her hands together slowly.

'I heard,' she said. 'Well done. Stolen, is it? Great. Well, I've been doing some digging myself... look at this.'

Moone joined her as she leaned over a desk, spreading the sheets of paper out in front of her. He saw that each one was an arrest record for some local ne'er-do-well.

She stood up, folding her arms across her chest, while the rest of the team gathered round the desk. 'See these?'

Moone looked at them, nodded. 'I do.'

'All local men, all living in the area it is likely that our terrorist...' she said.

'Killer. Serial offender.' Moone smiled.

'All living in the area we've marked out,

where he struck again last night and your lot fucked up and let him go! Look at these men, most of which have a record for violence, wounding or racist behaviour. Why weren't they talked to? Tell me that?'

Moone looked down. Why weren't they brought in? He looked up. 'Because they don't fit our profile...'

'What profile's that? Or should I say whose? Yours? Yes? This neat little image you carry round in your head of some fucked up...'

'It's not neat. We're dealing with a very complicated individual who's had some kind of systematic...'

'We're dealing with a hater!' Richer snapped, slapping her palm on one of the sheets. 'See this particular guy? Shane Williams? He's a racist little, pumped up scumbag. He's been done for numerous hate crimes, including beating up gays, and also Muslims. He's belonged to some very suspect right-wing groups and posted a lot of homophobic abuse online. He also lives in the area we have targeted. Now, this car was stolen from where?'

'Near Ham Woods.'

Richer huffed, then brought out her mobile, her eyes briefly jumping to the arrest sheet of Shane Williams. 'Guess what? His nan lives not far from Ham Woods. This is our number one suspect.'

'I don't think so.'

She shook her head, pinched her nose. 'How do you know? Have you talked to him? Interviewed him?'

'No.'

'No. He's our prime suspect! I'm in charge here. This is who we go after. I want him brought in, and I'll be talking to him. Got it?'

'Got it.'

She stared at him for a moment, the redness of her face and neck glowing with her annoyance. Then she looked over his team. 'Get to work. Bring this scumbag in.'

Moone, along with the rest of the team, watched her leave, then all let out a breath of relief.

'What's up her arse?' Butler said and most of them started laughing, except Harding who faced Moone.

'Sorry, boss,' Harding said and sounded like he meant it. 'Shane Williams was on my list, but after the last homophonic arrest we made, you said...'

Moone held up hand. 'Don't worry. He's not our guy.'

'You sure?' Butler asked, raising her eyebrows.

He nodded. No, he wasn't sure, not one hundred percent, but he couldn't show doubt right then. But he did have that feeling that proper coppers talked about, the little something in his gut that told him that he was right and Richer was wrong. 'I'm sure. You and Molly better bring him in though, go through the motions.'

'What's our next step?' Butler asked.

'Let's go see the man whose car was stolen.'

Butler drove them down the road that snaked parallel with the woods, more prefabricated houses built in the fifties lining their route, most now done up to a better standard. As they came closer to the woods, they saw the house they wanted, a more unkempt terrace house with a driveway that was littered with oily black car parts and rubbish bins.

Moone climbed out, followed by Butler, who said, 'You still think Mathieson has something to do with the whole paedophile street business?'

He stopped, a drizzle of rain tapping at his face. 'I'd put money on it. Why?'

'I might know someone who might know a bit about Mathieson.'

'You might? Or you do?'

She looked away. 'I do.'

'Who?'

She gestured to the house. 'Let's do this and then we'll pay him a visit.'

'Right,' Moone said and walked to the door and pressed the doorbell. It took a few rings, but eventually a chubby, rounded man with dark cropped hair, in his thirties came to the door wearing an Arsenal top, showing off his tattoos on his thick pink arms. It was definitely Paul Rogers.

'Mr Rogers?' Moone asked, showing his ID. 'Paul Rogers?'

He looked them up and down, looking suspicious. 'Who wants to know?'

'We do,' Butler said. 'You report your car stolen?'

He squinted at her, frowning. 'Yeah, I did. Don't tell me you've found the fucking thing?'

'Yeah, we found the old rust bucket,' Butler said.

'I'm betting you don't want it back,' Moone said.

'Not really. Going to get something better.'

'Claimed on the insurance, have we?' Butler raised her eyebrows.

'Well, that's what ya fucking do, don't ya?' he said, rolling his eyes and shaking his head.

'Did you leave the keys where they could be found?' Moone asked.

'What?'

'The keys... look, I don't give a shit if you were trying pull a fast one. We really don't care. Your car was used in a very serious crime last night. We're trying to find the person who might've nicked it.'

'Serious crime?' Rogers looked between them.

'The worst you can imagine,' Butler said. 'Did you leave the keys in the ignition?'

Rogers gave them the same sheepish look again, then nodded. 'Not the ignition. Passenger seat. You ain't fucking with me, are you?'

'Bye, Mr Rogers,' Moone said, then turned and headed back to their car, with Butler right behind him.

'So, what does that tell us?' Butler asked.

Moone stopped by the car. 'Tells us he's not a master car thief. Tells us he probably kept an eye on Rogers, saw that he left the keys there.'

Butler climbed in. 'So bugger all really?'

'He knows this area. Spends time here, I reckon. Get uniforms to go door to door asking if they saw anything unusual around the time the car went missing, get an idea of who comes and goes. Bound to be a local snoop around here.'

Butler started the engine, looking him over strangely. 'You're not as stupid as you look, are you?'

'Thanks. Let's go see your friend.'

'Oh, they're not my friend.'

CHAPTER 26

Butler parked the car in car park at the lower end of Plymouth city centre, a large concrete space that was surrounded by furniture shops and rundown looking pet shops, and graffiti daubed walls. Butler climbed out, pointing towards the exit that led towards the indoor market. Moone followed as she stormed on, looking pretty pissed off, her face red as she turned a sharp left and headed towards a narrow pub tightly packed in between takeaways and a small supermarket.

The place had a lick of paint on the exterior, but inside it was dingy, a bar along the right-hand side and tables and booths crowding the rest of the small space. It smelt of stale alcohol, but he also thought he could detect cigarette smoke.

There were a few old-timers sat around playing cards and dominoes, a few slightly younger punters looking sorry for themselves, and an old white-haired man with a ruddy face, dressed in a blazer, sitting at a table in the corner. He was reading a newspaper and nursing a pint of Guinness. Butler made a beeline for him and stood by his table, her arms across her chest, until he looked up from his newspaper. As Moone joined her, he saw the old man looked genuinely surprised to see her, then a smile crept onto his face.

'Well, bugger me,' he said, folding the paper and sipping his drink. 'Mandy, what brings you in here?'

'We won't take long,' she said, sounding sharp.

'Hello,' Moone said, feeling awkward.

The old guy stood up, putting out his hand for Moone to shake. 'Hello to you, son. I'm Alf... Alf Butler.'

Moone stared at Butler, his partner in crime, but she avoided his eyes. 'Butler? As in...'

'I'm her dad,' he said, looking at her, but he looked awkward, sad even, Moone thought.

'We need some information,' Butler said.

'I might've known,' Alf said, sitting down and sipping his pint. 'Well, sit your bums down. What is it you want to know?'

Butler sat down, but folded her arms across her chest again, so Moone pulled out a chair too.

'Do you know anything about Carl Mathieson?' Moone asked.

'Tory MP, Carl Mathieson?' Alf said. 'I should

coco. I was in the same game for years. I was a Labour MP down here for years. I know all about Mathieson's lot.'

'His lot?' Moone asked.

'Yeah. His family. His father was an MP, then a Lord. Dead and gone now, thank God.'

'Why thank God?' Butler asked.

Alf looked at her, his eyes a little sad, and Moone felt there was other stuff on his mind. 'Because he was a bad man, that's what the rumours were anyway.'

'Only rumours?' Moone asked.

'Well, there were stories, some of them that most of us believed.'

'Involving what?' Moone asked.

Alf looked at his pint as if a bad taste had entered his mouth. 'The worst stuff... the stuff that makes you sick to your stomach.'

'Kids?' Butler said.

Alf nodded. 'Thing is, that sort of thing isn't worried about in political circles. You know why?'

'Why?'

Alf leaned forward. 'Because they can use it. Once they know your weakness, the establishment can use it, make you do things you don't agree with.'

'I can believe that. When did Lord Mathieson die?'

'About eight, nine years ago, I think,' Alf said.

'So, we can rule him out of our suspects,' Butler said, looking at Moone.

Moone chewed it all over, then made a decision. 'Do you think Carl Mathieson could be involved in something like that?'

Alf sipped his pint, then shrugged. 'I don't know him that well, but I think they're all capable of it, the kind of people like Mathieson and the others who came from the same private schools, they're promoted because they'll do whatever they're told to do. He'd do anything to protect his family name.'

'Even cover up something like a paedophile ring that might've kidnapped and murdered a young boy?' Moone asked.

Alf shrugged again. 'Maybe. One thing I heard about Mathieson, was when he was first in the army, out in Iraq, something happened. a young local man died when they were on patrol. There was some kind of scandal. Was the young man armed? That sort of thing. That was when Lord Mathieson was alive, he fixed it, made sure his son got off scot-free.'

Moone sat back, looking at the old man as he sipped his drink, then at Butler, wondering what had happened to make her so off with him. It wasn't any of his business, and he decided to let sleeping dogs lie. 'Well, thanks for the information, Mr Butler,' Moone said, getting up.

'Call me Alf, son,' the old man said, raising his glass. 'Any friend of Mandy's.'

Butler got up as she let out one of her biggest huffs yet. 'Yeah, thanks.'

Moone headed towards the exit, thinking it all over, putting the pieces together and only a few of them falling into place.

'What do you reckon?' Butler asked, as they both reached the rainy street.

Moone shrugged. 'I don't know. But I'm starting to feel very tense about having Mathieson under the same roof as my children. But I haven't got anything to pin on him, or even to take to Angela. All I can do is tell Alice to keep an eye on things.'

'I wouldn't like to be in your position. But I don't think Mathieson's a paedophile. He's just trying to protect the family name by the sounds of it.'

Moone rubbed his tired eyes, aching all over, and feeling sick to his stomach. 'I hope you're right. We need to talk to MacDonald's chums again. Let's put the pressure on, see if any of them crack.'

'OK.'

Moone heard his mobile ringing, then shook his head and answered it. 'Now what?'

'Sorry, boss,' Harding said. 'Twat Face has ordered us all back. They've got their suspect.'

'You should know better than that, Harding. It's Commander Twat Face to you.'

Moone hung up and huffed out a heavy breath. 'We've got to go in. I don't know why the hell they need us.'

As they headed in the direction of the car, Moone said, 'Harding's started calling me boss. Is that good, or a piss take or what?'

'In Harding's world that's a mark of respect. I think he actually likes you.'

'Really? Least that's one good thing to come from this bloody mess.'

There was quite a lot of noise and bustle in the custody suite of Charles Cross police station. Most of it was coming from Shane Williams as he was manhandled, his hands cuffed behind his back, as they directed him towards the desk to be booked in. Moone and Butler stood watching from the back entrance. Williams was overweight, short dark hair, bulbous arms and stomach. His arms were covered in tattoos, the useful football stuff. He was wearing an Argyle shirt that looked far too small for him.

'Fuckas!' Williams shouted at anyone around him as the custody sergeant waited to do the honours.

'He's certainly a piece of work,' Butler said.

'Yep, but he's not our killer.' Moone straightened his clothes, as Commander Richer came through the door and marched over to the suspect.

'Who're you trying to convince?' Butler said, then walked round him and headed towards the door to the stairs.

Moone followed. 'He's not. Yes, he's your typical football yob, but he's not the man who did that last night. He doesn't fit the description of our killer, our killer's taller.'

They went to the interview room next door to the one where Richer was planning on interviewing Shane Williams, where a monitor had been set up so they could watch the whole affair.

'It's Richer you've got to convince,' Butler said, just as the action started on the screen. A couple of uniforms brought Williams into the interview room and seated him at the desk.

Then the door opened where Moone and Butler were and Richer walked in, a triumphant look on her face.

'Now the fun begins,' she said, joining them at the screen.

'I don't think this'll be fun,' Butler said, then shared an exhausted look with Moone.

'You're not going to get what you're after,' Moone said.

Richer stared at him. 'I've been doing this job for quite a while, DI Moone. I get a feeling about people, and that wanker in there is as guilty as sin.'

'Yeah, he's probably guilty of all kinds of shit,' Butler said. 'But he's not our killer. Look at him.'

But Richer didn't say anything for a moment, just shook her head, looking between them, then opened the door. 'I feel sorry for you both, I really do. I didn't mean to come here and put your noses out of joint.'

'Oh, you didn't mean to...' Butler started to say, but Moone shook his head.

'No, I didn't mean to. But I guess I did. Now, watch and see a professional at work.'

After she'd left the room, Butler turned to Moone, her face frozen between anger and hilarity. 'Did you just hear that? Did I imagine that? She's a... twat.'

Moone nodded and turned to the screen. 'But the question is, is she that much of a twat that she would stitch someone up.'

Commander Richer seated herself, a mug of coffee in her hand, smiling a little. 'Afternoon, Mr Williams. I'm Commander Sally Richer. I'll be conducting this interview.'

'I ain't done nothin',' Williams said, sitting forwards, his face red with slow burning anger. 'I don't know what the fuck this is about!'

Richer ignored him, then started the tape and spoke into the machine to give the formal details. Then she sipped her coffee and smiled politely. 'You are Shane Williams of Burrington Way?'

'Yeah, but I ain't done nothin'... what they said downstairs... I don't know nothin' bout all that!'

Richer sat back, arms folded. 'Where were you last night, Mr Williams?'

He looked round the room, then back at Richer. 'Last night? Out for a bit, down the pub... no, the snooker club, then home. Why?'

'Snooker club? Where is this snooker club?'

'Mutley.'

'Mutley. Good. What time did you leave there?'

'I don't know, about nine.'

'Then you went where?'

Williams sprang forward, his hand slapping the table. 'Home! I went bloody well home! What do you think I've done?!'

'Last night, two people were stabbed. One is recovering in hospital, the other died of their wounds.'

'That's got nothin' to do with me!'

'Did you hear about the attack on the gay club, Hero's?'

Williams sat back, his hands touching the desk, a look of realisation covering his round face. 'No way, you're trying to stitch me up. I'm not a fucking patsy. I don't fuckin' believe this.'

'We need to know where you were on the night of the attack.'

'I want someone here!' Williams hit his fist on the table, spit popping from his mouth. 'I want a lawyer!'

'Calm down, Mr Williams,' Richer said. 'Maybe this will help you remember... Steven...'

The man next to Richer opened his brief-case and produced an evidence bag. Richer took it, placed it on the table. There was a knife inside the bag, a long hunting knife. 'I'm showing Mr Williams a knife that was found on his property. You do recognise the knife, don't you?'

Williams was staring at it, his eyes wide, sitting back slowly.

'We found it wrapped in a towel on your property,' Richer said. 'We also found traces of what looks like blood on the blade.'

'What the hell!' Moone stared at Butler. 'Where the bloody hell did that come from?'

'Jesus, she's a crafty bitch,' Butler said. 'She's stitching him up.'

'But where's that knife come from?! He's not our killer. He can't be.'

'Maybe there's more than one?'

Moone looked at her. 'No, this isn't some gang member, this is a loner, a fucked up in the head loner. Jesus fucking Christ.'

'Now what do we do?'

'Well, it's obvious, isn't it? We've got to find the real killer.'

Butler laughed. 'And we've had such good luck with that so far. What about Danny Sawyer?'

Moone sighed. 'I don't know. I wish I did. But I know Mathieson is up to his neck in all this shit.'

'Plus we've got Loy Grader out there somewhere! So far there's been no sign of him.'

There was a knock at the door, then DC Carthew put her head round it. 'Boss, we've got Malcolm West in interview room three. You want to talk to him?'

Moone stared at her. 'Yes, yes I do. Also, read him his rights. I want this all above board. We need to search anywhere he's been staying. Grader might've also been there.'

'Right,' she said then left.

'I don't like her,' Butler said, but her voice was strangely lower.

'I can tell. I don't know why...'

'She threatened me last night.'

'What?'

Butler let out a breath. 'It sounded like a veiled threat.'

'Go on.'

'It's when we found the weapons, the hammer and the blade. It's what she said, and the way she looked at me.'

Moone could see she'd been obviously shaken by recent events. 'What did she say?'

'Something about smashing someone's skull in.'

'But someone had just had their skull smashed in.'

'I know.'

Moone turned and opened the door, realising he didn't have time for flights of fancy. 'Let's talk about this later. We've got a lot to do. Let's find Grader before he does something terrible.'

Moone seated himself down, sipping from his coffee while looking over the dirty looking, hollowed-out frame of Malcolm West. His shifty eyes glanced round the room, his dirty fingers and nails tapping at the table. He smelt. There was a definite odour or something that washed over Moone and made him feel queasy.

Butler sat down, folded her arms and stared at their suspect. 'Welcome back, Malcolm.'

'Why've I been read my rights?' West asked, his eyes darting back and forth.

Moone leaned forward. 'Because you're under arrest, Malcolm. We think you might be harbouring a criminal.'

'I'm not! Search my house!' West put his hands up.

'Oh, we are, don't you worry,' Butler said. 'Very, very thoroughly. We've got search teams going to every address that we know you've ever been to.'

Moone smiled. 'Plus, we've got your mobile phone. Cheap little thing, but should be able to tell us something.'

But West didn't look particularly fazed by any of it, which told Moone that they hadn't got warm yet, not even slightly. 'That phone. Cheap bit of tat, isn't it?'

'Does the job,' West said. 'Sends texts, that's all I need.'

'Video? Camera?' Moone asked.

'No, not a bit of crap like that,' Butler said, shaking her head. 'You need a good smartphone for something like that. Bet you like to take photos, don't you, Malcolm?'

'What do you mean? I don't...'

Butler leaned forward. 'I mean, you have a habit of taking photos of anything, or anyone who takes your fancy, don't you?'

'I don't do anything like that.' West looked down at the desk. 'Not anymore.'

'You might behave yourself these days,' Moone said. 'But you still believe what you've always believed. Don't you?'

West didn't say anything, just kept looking down.

'Yes, that's a definite yes,' Moone said. 'You believe sex between an adult and a child should be legal. Don't you?'

'I know that's wrong,' West said, his voice barely audible.

'There's certainly no photos on that piece of shit mobile you carry round,' Moone said. 'But I wonder if we'll find anything else at your house.'

There was nothing from West, not even a fidget, or a tremor. They were cold still. Moone kept thinking it all over. 'You know MacDonald's no longer with us, don't you?'

West looked up. 'Yeah, I heard. Big fucking deal.'

'No, I didn't think you'd cry over him. He was a liability, he had to go. You ever met the councillor that topped himself? Councillor Stanley? You ever hang out with him?'

'What the bloody hell would I be doing with the likes of him?'

'I see. So you definitely never met Carl Mathieson MP?'

Moone nearly screamed hallelujah when he saw the tell-tale sign, the flicker of his eyes, the minutest fidget. He was getting warmer now.

'No, never met him,' West said. 'I don't even vote.'

'That doesn't surprise me,' Butler said.

'Aren't you worried?' Moone said, sitting back as he picked up his coffee.

'About what?' West said, then smirked. 'Global fucking warming?'

'No, Loy Grader,' Moone said. 'He's murdered MacDonald. He obviously knew too much. What about the rest of you? I bet you know more than MacDonald.'

'I don't know what you're talking about.'

'Oh, I think you do. An attempt on MacDonald's life, then he's murdered in hospital. Someone, probably all of you, were shitting yourselves that he might spill the beans. We think we know who moved the remains to where they were found, because they wanted them found.'

Moone saw the reaction again, the shudder of interest in West, so he said, 'Yep, I'm pretty sure Ray Benton moved the body, and put that toy with him, the toy from the Good Times toy place. Why would he do that? What do you think?'

West stared at Moone, his jaw beginning to grind. 'I don't know anything about that. You're just fishing. I don't know anything. When do I get out of here?'

Moone sat back. 'OK. I believe you. Millions wouldn't. You're free to go. But I'd watch your back if I were you. Someone's trying keep a lid on things. Do you really think they'd hesitate if they decide you're a problem?'

West stood up, still staring at Moone. 'I want to go!'

Moone stayed in the interview room, staring at the wall opposite, resting his chin on his fists, thinking. He had some of the puzzle, little bits that now fitted, but he seemed no closer to finding out who murdered little Danny Sawyer.

'What now?'

Moone started, brought out of his thoughts as Butler stood in the doorway, eyebrows raised.

Moone stood up. 'I scared the shit out of him, wound him up. Now we see where he runs to. I want a surveillance team on him twenty-four seven.'

It was a plan. Not a very good one, but it was the best he had.

CHAPTER 27

Moone was heading away from the interview rooms with Butler behind him when he spotted the tall, skinny frame of Barry the IT guy coming towards them. He had a bottle of some kind of energy drink in his hand as he stopped in front of them.

'Hello, Barry,' Butler said. 'Got something for us?'

'He bit,' Barry said.

'He bit?' Moone said. 'Who bit?'

'The guy,' Barry said. 'Roman126.'

'You're joking? When?' Moone turned Barry round, directing him back towards his office.

'An hour ago. I've been trying to get hold of you both.'

'Sorry,' Butler said, following. 'We've been a bit busy.'

Moone hurried them both back down to Barry's cramped office where the monitors glowed in the darkness. More takeaway food cartons and empty bottles littered the place.

Barry took his place at the desk, tapped the keyboard and brought up a stream of communication. Moone leaned forward, reading it all, realising they'd hit the jackpot. 'If this is him, then we've got him.'

Butler leaned in too. 'He's very insistent on meeting up, isn't he?'

'Yeah,' Barry said. 'He got to that pretty quick.'

Moone let out an exhausted laugh. 'That's it. He's been too high profile. He's going back to how he started this. Probably going for one more kill. Does he say where he wants to meet?'

'Not yet.' Barry sat back, took a swig from his energy drink. 'I'm waiting for him to tell me. But it'll be tonight by the looks.'

Moone put his face in his hands, the glorious realisation coming over him that they might just beat the anti-terrorism lot to the final pinch. 'That's good, Barry. Call us as soon as he agrees a meeting place. Don't be too eager though.'

'I'll let you know,' Barry said, opening a drawer and taking out a chocolate bar.

'Come on,' Moone said to Butler and they headed back out into the bright light and slightly fresher air of the corridor.

'Do you think it's going to be this easy?' Butler asked as they headed for the incident room. 'He says a place and bam, we're waiting?'

'Does sound a bit too good to be true, doesn't it?'

'Very.'

'But on the other hand, I think there's a part of this guy who wants to be caught. I think he's been punished most of his life for being different. It's like he's got two personalities, one that's punishing, killing others like him, and one, well, that's still hurt and, you know, wants help.'

'I hope you're right. At least we might be able to stick our finger up at...'

Moone waved his hand, then put a finger to his lips as they got to the incident room doors.

Commander Richer was coming out, storming towards them. She stopped, folding her arms across her chest, looking between them. 'So, you didn't stay to see the interview to the end?'

'No, sorry, we got called away,' Moone said.

Richer stared at him, her cheeks scarlet. 'Well, you missed out. I had him on the ropes. After we brought out the knife...'

'Yeah, where the bloody hell did you find that?' Butler asked.

Richer turned to her. 'In a shed in his back garden, actually. Nicely wrapped in an oily rag.'

'That's it?' Moone asked, unable to comprehend what he was hearing. 'Just lying there?'

'It was in a drawer.'

'Did you find the hammer?' Butler asked.

'No, no hammer... yet.' Richer looked pissed off. 'We're still searching.'

'You're not going to find it,' Butler said, laughing with exhaustion and anger. 'Because he didn't do it. The killer dropped his knife and hammer, remember?'

'I'm sure he's got plenty more.' Richer folded her arms, a smug smile on her face.

'Well, he's not going to stuff a knife he killed some people with, in a bloody drawer in his shed. Jesus...'

Richer moved closer, pointing a finger into Butler's face. 'Listen to me. People like Shane Williams aren't smart. They just hate. That's all they know. It's what they're good at. They do it online, out in the open, but thankfully there's new legislation coming to deal with people like him.'

'Oh, I see,' Butler said, looking at Moone. 'You hear that? New legislation. That's what this is all about. You want him... no, you need him to be a home-grown terrorist, it backs up your arguments, gives you more powers. But those powers won't stop with people like Shane Williams, will they? No, it'll be everybody that says anything online, any one word deemed a hate word. Which will be any word that goes against your lot, any slight criticism of the government. George Orwell was right!'

'I haven't got time for your nonsense,' Richer said and barged past.

Butler huffed, then pushed through the doors and into the incident room.

'You certainly pushed her buttons,' Moone

said, heading for his desk.

'Damn bloody right,' Butler said, sitting at her desk, every one of the team turning to watch them. 'They want us all under surveillance! We won't be able to say anything even slightly that goes against the status quo or we'll be locked up!'

'She's right, boss,' Harding said. 'We'll be living in Nazi Germany soon.'

Moone sighed and rubbed his face. 'OK. Enough of all the conspiracy stuff. We need to find out who murdered Danny Sawyer, where Loy Grader is hiding, and who really carried out all these attacks that Richer wants to label as terror attacks. Barry's going to let us know when our killer wants to meet up. I want a team ready to swoop in tonight. Who volunteers?'

Most of the team slowly put their hands up, so Moone said, 'OK. Let's note all that down. We need to get a surveillance team on Malcolm West and Carl Mathieson's house. I want to know where they go, who they talk to.'

Butler picked up a phone. 'I'm already on it.'

Moone sat back, feeling that he was closer, a buzz of adrenaline pulsing round his body. His phone was vibrating in his pocket, so he took it out and saw Alice was calling him. He hurried into the corridor, his heart jumping into his throat. 'Alice? Everything OK?'

'Yeah, just wanted to see if you're all right.'

He let out a deep breath of relief. 'Yep. I'm fine. Look, about what you asked me to do...

about Mum's boyfriend.'

'Yeah?'

'Keep an eye on him. Make sure, if he's there in the house, that you're safe and secure.'

'I've been doing that anyway. What's going on, Dad?'

'I don't know. I think you were right about him. He's up to his neck in something.'

'What do I tell Mum?'

'Nothing. Let me deal with that. Just keep an eye on things. Look, I've got to go. I love you.'

'Love you too, Dad.'

He ended the call, his heart aching, and his gut twisted, then headed into the incident room.

'Surveillance team on their way,' Butler said.

'Good. Then tonight is the night.'

Carl Mathieson walked into the house, his brain aching, the uncertainty, the self-loathing crawling up and down his spine. He'd had a couple of moments at the office where he'd found himself reliving everything like it was yesterday. No, like it was happening all over again. The war. Everything after.

He put down his case, then headed for the kitchen and found a bottle of whisky and poured himself one. He drank it down, feeling it burn his throat. It calmed him a little. He almost didn't hear the soft steps coming across the kitchen floor.

He turned to see Alice in the archway, staring at him. 'Alice... what're you doing?'

'Nothing. You?'

'Having a drink.' Usually he'd put on an act, hide away the darkness that was coming over him, but he couldn't bring himself to this time. 'Where's your mum?'

'Parents' evening. You all right?'

'Yes, fine. Stop asking.'

'Fine. I will.'

She swung round, storming out of the room.

'Alice...' he called, but she was gone.

Then his phone was ringing. He took out his mobile and saw a number he didn't recognise. 'Hello?'

'Mathieson.'

He didn't recognise the voice. There was too much background noise, the line breaking up. 'Who's this?'

'Me. I did what you asked. In the hospital.'

The realisation of who was calling him hit him like a punch in the gut. 'I don't know who this is! Don't call me again.'

'Don't you fucking hang up on me! I could destroy you! Destroy your sweet fucking life.'

Mathieson hovered his thumb over the call end button. 'What do you expect me to do?'

'I need your help getting out of the country. You must know people. Get me a passport!'

He gripped his face in his hand, then looked

up to make sure Alice wasn't still around, listening. 'How the bloody hell am I meant to get you a passport! You're fucking crazy. You shouldn't have called here!'

'You need to help me! If you don't, I'll take you down with me. I'll tell them everything I know about your family. Not only that, I'll make sure that family you're living with, well, you know what I'll do, don't you?'

Mathieson found himself trembling, half with fury, half with sickness and angst. 'Look, I don't know about the passport thing but I know a place where you can stay. What's this phone you're calling on?'

'It's a burner.'

'I'll text the address. It's a safe house. That's all I can do for the moment.'

'I'll need money!'

'Fine. I'll get money to you. I've got to go.'

'Don't fuck me over...'

Mathieson hung up, then slammed down the phone, and leaned over the table, breathing hard. MacDonald was gone, but there were other loose ends that were beginning to raise their heads. He picked up the mobile again and text the address to the number Grader had called him on. It was a house up the line, a place the police wouldn't think of looking for him. It would give him time to think, to come up with a solution to his problems.

They were mobilising the team, getting to their cars, putting coffees, sandwiches and crisps onto the back seats. Moone watched them slip into their vehicles as it finally got dark. It was barely half past six as the big metal gate groaned and slid noisily across the end of the compound to let out the stream of vehicles. It wasn't only his team leaving the station, ready for a tedious night stuck in a cramped, hot car; the surveillance team that were being sent to keep an eye on West and Mathieson were pouring out too, in vans and unmarked cars. They were used to the long hours watching nothing much at all, unlike his team who didn't exactly jump into their cars ready for action.

'You ready or what?' Butler said, holding two cups of takeaway coffee, their work car idling away behind her.

He took a coffee, then climbed in.

'Do we even know where they're supposed to be meeting?' Butler asked, as she climbed in and drove them towards the large gates, then out into the damp streets. She flicked on the windscreen wipers as a smattering of rain hit the glass.

'Not yet. Barry's about to arrange a date.'

'Jesus, let's hope they hurry up, I don't want to be driving round all night.'

'Patience,' Moone said, but Butler spun her

face round to him as she said, 'Patience? You, a bloke, are talking to me about patience. Bloody hell…'

'Patience is a virtue, find it where you can, never in a woman, always in a man,' Moone said and smiled, taking a sip of his coffee.

'That's not bloody right!'

'You sure… no, I think it is right.'

'You're a piss-taking tosser,' Butler said, but he could see her holding back a laugh.

When his phone rang in his pocket, Moone fished it out and saw that Barry was calling. 'Please have good news…'

'Sort of,' Barry said, 'He's said where, but not when. He wants me to stay logged in, so he can say when he'll be there.'

'Where?'

'The park, near the Life Centre…'

'Bloody hell, that's where he arranged to meet our first victim, Jason. He's gone full circle. Any luck tracking where he is?'

'I'm working on it. I'm doing my best, but the service providers are always a bit slow on this sort of thing.'

'Threaten them, get them to bloody well hurry up. Keep in contact, Barry.' Moone hung up. 'Head for Central Park.'

Butler swung the car down a side street, then took the back way towards Argyle's home park, then alongside, passing the Life Centre, then parked right in front of it, facing the pathway that would lead all the way to Pennycome-quick.

'So here we are,' Butler said, turning off the engine.

The engine quietened down, ticking and clicking, while the light rain hit the car's body. Moone got comfortable, sipping the last of his coffee, which was now tepid. It would still do the trick, he told himself and ignored the wave of tiredness that tried to knock him backwards into sleep.

'You can shut your eyes for a bit,' Butler said. 'I don't feel tired at all.'

He looked at her. 'How come you volunteered for this?'

'Didn't fancy another night with him indoors. He's doing my head right in.'

'I know the feeling.'

A car swung in behind them, then round and parked right next door. Harding was at the wheel, DC Faith Carthew in the passenger seat, both dressed casually.

'Want us to take a look, boss?' Harding called across Carthew.

Moone noticed Faith looked like she was dressed to go jogging. 'No, just Faith. Go take a jog around there. Put your hands-free in, let us know if you see anything.'

She opened the door, then climbed out, dressed in a black shiny top and tight dark grey leggings and trainers. She put her phone in her

pocket and attached her earphones, then nodded and started jogging down towards the play-
ground.

'Now I can see why you fancy her,' Butler
said. 'Got all the bumps in the right places.'

'I hadn't noticed.'

'Yeah, right. Shame she's a sociopath. You
know she'll be our boss one day, don't you?'

'Then you better keep on the right side of
her.'

Butler huffed, then leaned back. 'If that ever
happens, I'll resign.'

The rain blew hard at the windows making
Mathieson jump a little, his mind torn back from
the battlefield. Hot sun baking the ground and
his mind. Stuck in caves, sewage pipes, no longer
smelling anything, everything bleached white.
Death. Death was soaked into him. He looked at
his hands, back then and in the present. They
looked no different, both guilty of causing harm.
What had he let happen? What had he helped
cover up? It was too late to go back now.

Where was he? He looked around at his
office. Then he swung his head as he heard footsteps along the hallway. The soft steps of Alice,
sneaking around. She was doing that a lot lately
and he got the feeling she was always watching him. Her dad was a copper, and that had
been making him paranoid. At least he had felt

paranoid until he'd found himself chatting to the very same copper and his bitch of a partner across his desk.

They knew about Stanley. No, they only really knew that he'd killed him, not the reason why.

There was a storm brewing outside, rain lashing the windows, beating the house, making his body tense up. MacDonald was dead, and he should have felt happy about that, but there were the others to deal with, and Grader knew too much.

Why had he come to his office? He looked down. He'd moved most of his stuff from his flat to Angela's place. He opened the bottom drawer and took out the small electronic safe, then pressed the numbers on the keypad. The door buzzed open and he looked down at the dark grey semi-automatic that stared up at him. He stared at it for a moment, then reached in, pulled it out and checked the stock. Made sure it was empty and clean, then stripped it down. It took him longer than it used to. He put it back together, then placed it on the desk. He stared at it for a few moments, thinking, picturing the worthless pieces of shit that he'd been helping to protect.

He put the gun back into the safe box, locked it and put it back into the drawer and locked that too.

The storm was raging by the time he headed downstairs, thinking about having another whisky to calm himself down.

When he hit the bottom step, the doorbell rang out and he froze, staring at the large doors.

The police.

He imagined Moone and some uniforms stood there, ready to take him away. He wouldn't let them take him, he couldn't.

'Who's that?'

Mathieson looked towards the kitchen to see Alice standing there holding a can of Diet Pepsi.

'I'll go see. You go back into the kitchen. Go on.'

She stared at him, looking pissed off, then turned and vanished. He went to the door and pulled it open, the cold and wind rushing in, hammering his face with icy rain. He blinked, focusing as his stomach turned over and hatred filled his veins as he saw Malcolm West huddled in a parka.

'What the fuck are you doing here?!' Mathieson shouted, his eyes jumping round the empty street that was being lashed with rain. 'You can't be here! Go!'

'I need to talk to you,' West said, as he was pushed and pulled by the wind, his hands deep in his coat pockets.

'Not now!' Mathieson went to shut the door, but West lunged forward, blocking it from closing.

'It's urgent! It's about Benton!'

Mathieson held on to the door, staring at the drenched figure in front of him, then at the street, terrified that the police might be watching. Benton? What had he done now?

Mathieson grabbed West and pulled him inside, then shut the door, cutting off the battering rain. He swung round, grabbed the man by the scruff of his coat and dragged him towards the kitchen, swinging his head round to make sure Alice wasn't there. He pushed him back, knocking West against the work top.

'All right!' West snapped. 'You don't have to push me around!'

Mathieson grasped his own face, rubbed it, biting down on the anger that wanted to be set free. 'Just talk! Fucking talk! What about Benton? What's he done?'

'He sold us out!' West unzipped his wet coat as it dripped water on the floor.

'What? What the fuck are you talking about?'

'He's talked to the police. He's told them what he knows.'

Mathieson thought, tried to control the panic racing through him. 'No, that can't be right. If that was true...' He looked towards the door, hearing rain, and the wind eerily whistling through the house. Were they watching him?

'It was him!' West said, slapping away Mathieson's thoughts.

'Him? Him what?'

'He's the one who dug up Danny Sawyer's remains, he's the one who put them where the police found them.'

Mathieson stared at nothing, his mind reeling. 'Why? Why would he?'

'I don't know. He put that toy with him, from the place we worked, he must've done it to lead the police to...'

'Jesus...' Mathieson let out a moan, and heard it echo round the kitchen. 'Oh Jesus, that bastard, how do you know all this?'

'The police dragged me in... they told me.'

His heart raced, hammering at his bones, the blood pounding in his skull. 'You fucking idiot!'

'What?'

'The police? They told you all this, this bollocks, then you come here...'

Mathieson hurried towards the front door, then stopped, listening to the rain and the wind, waiting.

'What?' West said, his voice breaking up, weak sounding, as if he might cry.

'They wound you up and let you go. And you came here, you fucking cretin.'

'No, I just... What was I supposed...'

Mathieson spun round, pointed at him. 'Shut your mouth! Don't say another word! You say another thing and I'll break your neck, understand?'

West stared at him, his mouth opening.

Then he nodded.

'Get out! Get out of here. Go! I suggest you run, far away.' Mathieson took out his wallet and started pulling twenty-pound notes and out and stuffed them into West's grubby fist. 'Here. Now fuck off.'

He marched him to the door, then opened it, the wind and rain pushing it open further, the cold coming in with it. West tried to say something, but he pushed him hard down the steps, then slammed the door shut.

Then he ran, hammering up the stairs, heading for his office. He pulled open the drawer, took out the safe box, opened it, and took out the gun.

CHAPTER 28

The car rocked slightly, the wind roaring across the park, pelting leaves and twigs along with the rain. Moone stared through the windscreen, the wipers spoiling his view of the badly lit park.

'No one's coming here tonight,' Moone said, his words solid with his own disappointment.

'Patience,' Butler said, smirking. 'It's only been an hour.'

Moone reached for his coffee, but it'd been sat there open, going cold for the whole time they had been waiting. Tiredness had started to attack him, along with boredom. At the beginning he'd had hope, and the adrenaline had kept his senses on point. Now it all flooded away, leaving him dejected and washed out. Moone picked up his phone and called DC Carthew.

'Yes, boss?' she answered, her breathing coming fast, along with the wind that seemed to be battering the line.

'Where are you?'

'Running towards the pitch and putt cafe,' she said, the line cutting out.

'Seen anyone?'

'Nothing. Not a soul. Do you think he's coming?'

'I don't know. Stay there. It's rough out there so be careful.' He hung up then stared at his phone in his lap, willing Barry to call him.

'A watched phone...' Butler began, but Moone glared at her.

'You're full of them tonight, aren't you?'

'We gave it a shot,' Butler said, 'That's what we do. And the night's still young, we could all go down the pub, maybe go to Reflex afterwards.'

'Reflex? Don't tell me that's a club.'

'Yeah, but I don't even think it's called that anymore.'

'Nobody's coming. You'd have to be crazy to...' Moone heard his own words, stopped talking and looked at Butler. Then they both started laughing.

Moone heard his phone ringing and looked down to see Barry was calling him. He answered, holding his breath. 'Barry?'

'He's on his way,' Barry said. 'Just messaged me. Be about five minutes.'

'Good. That's great.' Moone ended the call, then looked at an expectant Butler. 'Five minutes, he's on his way. Tell Harding. Get the reinforcements ready. Where's everyone else?'

Butler got her phone out. 'Down by the old Royal Mail building, the Mdec, or whatever they call it.'

'Tell them to get ready. He's on his way.' Moone pushed open his door, the wind trying to slam it back on him, then clambered out, the rain spitting into his face. Leaves flew through the air and he looked up to see the claw like silhouettes of the trees being swiped to the side, the creaking of them filling his ears. He called DC Carthew, got her to hide, but to keep watching the path by the Life Centre.

He pushed his hands into his pockets, his heart pounding, blinking into the rain that now coated his face in its iciness.

Butler came round to him, one hand on her hair that was being pulled and played with by the wind.

'We're all set,' she shouted.

'Good. Now we wait.'

But then his phone was ringing again. He took it out, expecting it to be Barry or Carthew, but it was a number he didn't recognise.

'DI Peter Moone,' he said.

'This is DS Matt Harper from the sur-veillance team camped outside Carl Mathieson's house,' the deep, gravelly voice said on the other end.

'Yep, what's happened?'

'The other subject, Malcolm West, he just left Carl Mathieson's house. He was there for fifteen minutes. What do you want us to do?'

Moone looked around at Butler, saw she was asking him several questions with her eyes. What the hell should he do? He had to make a decision. He closed his eyes. 'Pick him up. West. Pick West up.'

'Gotcha. And Mathieson?'

'Bring him in too.' Moone ended the call.

'What was that?'

Moone tucked away his phone. 'Malcolm West just spent fifteen minutes inside Carl Mathieson's house – my ex's house, and my daughter is in there.'

'Bloody hell. So, he knows West? Jesus, he's up to his neck in all this. You're bringing them both in?'

'Yep. Let's see if we can break Mathieson... or even West.'

'Your phone's going again.'

Moone took it out and saw it was Carthew calling. 'Yes?'

'There's someone walking up the hill towards the park, coming from the direction of the Royal Mail building. Looks like they're wearing heels. Don't think it's a woman though. What shall I do?'

'Stay where you are.' Moone ended the call. 'There's someone coming, wearing heels. Carthew doesn't think it's a woman though.'

'That's got to be him!'

Moone stepped away from the car and Butler, moving to the centre of the path, and staring through the badly lit night. The wind and rain hit him, so he covered his face with a hand, staring, watching for the figure. After a couple of minutes he saw the faint silhouette of someone approaching. They wore a long coat, walked like a woman, and had long hair.

'Who is that?' Moone said, but his voice was carried off by the wind.

'What do we do?!' Butler called out to him, her phone by her ear.

He turned to her. 'Tell them to go! Grab them!'

The figure was approaching the shelter that was halfway along the path, trying to get cover from the rain and wind. It wasn't long before Moone could make out the shapes of officers approaching up the bank, spreading out, trying to cut off any escape. Then he saw DC Carthew crossing the path, jogging towards the shelter.

The woman, or man, whoever they were, spun round to see the figures approaching. They kicked off their heels and started running, any pretence of feminine grace being thrown away, as they made a sprint for it. They were fast, but they didn't know there was no escape. By the time the running man had reached the waiting officers, their coat trailing off like a superhero cloak behind them, his wig had gone.

Harding came from nowhere, flying through the air, wrapping his arms round the running man and sending both of them tumbling into the darkness between the trees, their grunts and moans filling the air. Moone jogged over to see Harding getting to his feet, his trousers and shirt caked in dirt as he grasped the man by the scruff of his coat and dragged him up. He had short hair, covered by a hair net, his face thick with makeup. A burst of strong perfume engulfed Moone's face as he got closer, looking into the crossdresser's eyes. 'Who are you?'

He didn't say anything, just breathed hard, hunched over a little, staring at Moone.

'OK,' Moone said, nodding. 'Then I better caution you. You're under arrest on the suspicion of murder. You do not have to say anything. But, it may harm your defence if you do not mention when questioned something which you later rely on in court. Anything you do say may be given in evidence. Do you understand?'

He kept staring at Moone, then eventually nodded, sharp and with anger.

'Take him to the station,' Moone said, then watched as Harding cuffed him and escorted him towards the car.

He stood in his raincoat, his hood pulled up, the rain pouring off him. He had his back to the fence that surrounded the allotments behind him, a tree obscuring him from anyone on the path. He watched as the police officers raced towards the man dressed as a woman. He grinned as the man kicked off his shoes, then made a run for it. He laughed, a hollow sound that was filled with emptiness, darkness. It was what he deserved, what the bible said he deserved, to be punished for lying with another man, for wearing the clothes of a woman.

He stayed still as they took the man away, marched him to a car and then drove him off. Then he moved when he knew it was safe to and walked back down the bank as the clouds grew darker and sent down a stream of rain that hammered the ground and sent a river of dirty water down the road, filling up the gutters. One day, he thought, the water wouldn't stop, and everything, every little dirty sin and every terrible mighty sin would be washed away, drowned like they deserved to be.

Moone watched as their suspect, now dressed in a light blue forensic outfit, was seated opposite them in the interview room. Moone had his phone on the desk, waiting on word about Mathieson. Butler sat on his left, arms folded while the suspect, complete with smudged makeup, sat opposite them.

'What's your name?' Moone asked, leaning forward.

The man stared back at him, then blew him a kiss. 'Sandra. You can call me Sandy.'

'That your real name?' Butler asked, sounding fed up already.

'You for real?' Sandra looked at Moone and rolled his eyes. 'Is she for real? Come on, sweetheart, keep up.'

'Why don't you just tell us who you really are?' Moone said. 'We'll find out soon enough. We've got your prints.'

'What if I ain't been arrested for anything?' Sandra said, smiling. 'Then you're up the creek, ain't yer, lover?'

'What were you doing in the park?' Butler asked.

'Taking a stroll.' Another smile.

'You looked all dressed up for a nice night out to me,' Butler said.

'You want some fashion tips, love? You could do with them.'

'Sandra,' Moone said. 'Whatever you call yourself, we were in that park tonight because there's a man going round attacking gay men.'

'I've got news for you, darling,' Sandra said. 'I ain't gay.'

'It doesn't matter to our killer,' Moone said. 'Gay, crossdresser, transsexual, he thinks it's all wrong, so we need to know what you were doing there because our killer, he'd say he wasn't gay either.'

Sandra pointed a finger at himself. 'You think I'm a... a killer?'

'We're going to need to know where you

were on certain dates,' Butler said, taking out her notebook.

'Are you bloody serious?' Sandra asked, then stared at Moone. 'Is she having a laugh? Do I look like a murderer?'

'What the bloody hell were you doing there then?' Butler said, losing her cool.

'Meeting someone, if you must know! Is that against the law now?'

'No, it isn't,' Moone said. 'If that's all you were there for. Did someone contact you online? Did they tell you to be there?'

Sandra stared at Moone, then narrowed her eyes. 'Online dating? No, that's not my style. But someone did ask me to meet them there.'

'Who?'

'I don't know.'

Butler huffed out a laugh. 'Come on, darling, it's time for you to get real. Right now, you're our number one suspect.'

Sandra held up her hands. 'All right... all right, keep your wig on. I was meeting someone. I don't know their name. I've talked to them before, onn the phone...'

'You've talked to them?' Moone asked. 'But you don't know their name?'

'I advertise on a local website,' Sandra said. 'For chats, possible meetups. You'd be surprised how many men want to spend time with someone like me.'

Moone sat back. 'OK. So someone contacted

you online. On what site?'

'They've contacted me before, ages ago. I gave them my number, they called, wanted to chat, but they sounded pretty mixed up. I think their sexuality was causing them problems. I offered to talk to them, I thought they might be married.'

'Have you got their number?' Moone asked.

'I tried to call them back once. Was a call box.'

'How did they contact you tonight?' Butler asked.

'By text message.'

Moone turned to Butler, but she was already up and said, 'I'll go check Sandra's phone.'

Moone watched her go, then looked at Sandra. 'You telling us the truth?'

'Why would I lie? I'm dying for a ciggy.'

'You can have one soon.' Moone sat back. 'You said he talked to you before?'

'That's right, darling.'

Moone stood up. 'Come on, let's get you that ciggy.'

Sandra stood up, his perfectly plucked eyebrows rising. 'Seriously?'

'Yep. Come on.' Moone escorted Sandra back down through the building, getting strange looks all the way. He laughed when the crossdresser blew them all kisses in response to their stares.

On the way, Moone managed to nick a

couple of cigarettes and a lighter, and handed them over to Sandra as they stood in the car park compound.

Sandra lit up, took a deep suck on the cigarette and then blew out the smoke, looking Moone up and down. 'Must be quite a life being a copper.'

'Must be quite a life, doing what you do.'

Sandra raised her shoulders. 'It's just who I am. I accepted it a long time ago, even if society still has a problem with it.'

Moone nodded. 'So, this guy you talked to on the phone, what do you make of him?'

'Messed up, like I said. Doesn't know what he wants or what he is. And the whole God-bothering bit...'

'So you think he's religious?'

'I don't know. He quoted the bible, but only when he got angry. He'd be all right one minute, then he'd be like a different person. He'd start calling me weird names, horrible things, that's when I'd hang up. I wanted to help him though. You not having a ciggy?'

'I gave up.'

'That was a silly thing to do. You've got to have vices in this life. What have you got if you haven't got a little something to make you happy?'

'The job.'

Sandra stared at him, half closed her eyes. 'You happy?'

He shrugged. 'I don't know.'

'If you ever need to talk, I'm a good listener.' Sandra smiled as she took another drag of the cigarette.

'Thanks. Do you think this person...'

'Roman.'

'I'm sorry?'

'That's what he called himself. Just came to me.'

Moone's heart kicked into gear again. 'Roman? Good. Do you think he's capable of hurting people?'

Sandra thought for a moment. 'Yes, yes, darling, I do. When he's angry, he's like a different person. Nice and polite one moment, crazed and horrible and nasty the next.'

'Thanks, Sandra,' Moone said, then went to head up back to the incident room.

'Paul!'

'Sorry?'

'My name's Paul.'

Moone nodded. 'Thanks, Paul.'

As he raced back up the stairs, buzzing all over, his heart hammering away, realising that he was close, so close to finding their killer. One of their killers. Disappointment flooded him, knowing that he was still so far from finding out who killed Danny Sawyer.

He pushed on through the incident room doors and found Butler sat at a desk looking not too happy. She looked at him, huffed, and shook her head, filling him full of dread.

'What now?' he said.

'That phone number isn't in service any-more. Was a pay-as-you-go. Must have been switched off, or the SIM taken out.'

'What about the messages from the site? Barry working on tracking them?'

'Yes, but he says it could take a while, so don't hold your breath. That's if it's that straight-forward. The killer could be using someone else's IP or something, or a number of other factors that I didn't understand. Where's Sandra?'

'Having a ciggy,' Moone said.

'You left him down there having a ciggy?' Butler stood up.

'He's not the killer. The killer arranged for us to meet him there. He wanted us there.'

'Playing with us... great. Was probably watching... yes, before you ask, I have people still there in case anyone does turn up.'

'Good,' Moone said as his phone started ringing in his pocket. He took it out, holding up a finger to Butler. 'DI Moone...'

'DS Harper again,' the voice said. 'We went into Mathieson's house. We were let in by a young woman who says she's your daughter...'

'Alice.'

'Yeah. Mathieson's not here. Must've snuck out somehow. I don't know how, we had the back covered.'

'He was in the army, did you pick up Mal-colm West?'

'Yeah, he seems pretty scared.'

'I'm on my way.'

Moone headed up the steps of his ex-wife's house, feeling uncomfortable, icy fingers clawing at his back. Butler was at the station, overseeing things, waiting to see if they got a location for their mysterious bible bashing, gay targeting killer. He wanted to be hopeful, but he couldn't muster any, as hard as he tried. The more the clock ticked away, the more his hope dwindled.

There was a uniform on the door, a thick set constable who he didn't recognise, so he showed his warrant card and went into the house, then on to the kitchen. There was a man stood in the kitchen archway. He was lean, deep trenches dug beneath his blue eyes.

'DI Moone?' the deep voice said as he shook Moone's hand. 'DS Matt Harper. Your daughter's in here.'

'Thanks. Where's West?'

'He's in a van down the street. I figured you'd want to talk to him as soon as.'

Moone nodded, then walked further into the kitchen and saw Alice sat at the kitchen table. 'Alice? You OK?'

She looked at him, her hands wrapped round a steaming mug of something. 'Yeah, I'm fine. Where's he gone, Dad? What's he done?'

'I can't really talk about that, not right now.

As long as you're OK.'

'Mum's home. I talked to her, told her what's been going on.'

'I see. How did that go?'

'Not great. She's upstairs. She's not too happy with you.'

'I bet. Normal service has been resumed. Look, I need to...'

Alice laughed, then nodded. 'Go and do what you've got to do.'

'Alice, did you hear anything they talked about?'

She shrugged. 'Not really. I thought they said, Benton? Or something like that. Sorry.'

He smiled. 'It's fine. Thanks. Tell your mum I'm sorry.'

Alice nodded, but rolled her eyes, so Moone turned and saw DS Harper was waiting to escort him to the van. He followed the detective out of the house and into the night that was still filled with rain. Moone saw there was a police van parked a few yards away, and allowed Harper to get there first and open up the back doors. He followed Harper inside and saw Malcolm West huddled in the back, his arms wrapped round himself like he was freezing. He sat opposite him, and saw West shake his head, then look away.

'You're fucked, Malcolm,' Moone said.

'Don't I bleeding well know it.'

'We know about Ray Benton. We know Ian MacDonald snatched Danny Sawyer. Now we know about Mathieson. I was shocked to see he was involved, but it takes all sorts...'

'You know nothing.'

'Then tell me. Because you're about to go down with the lot of them. Whatever you've done, I can square it away, it's Mathieson and the rest I want.'

'Mathieson's not like that, not into kids.'

'Then why's he involved? What have they got on him? His dad?'

West looked surprised. 'You know about him? Yeah, his dad, he was... he was into kids, so they say.'

'What's Mathieson's involvement with Danny Sawyer then?'

West looked away, raised his shoulders. 'I don't know.'

'Tell me what you do know! Save yourself. MacDonald took him, that's true, isn't it? *Isn't it? Malcolm!*'

West jumped a little, then nodded. 'Yeah, he took him. He'd do anything that lot told him. Didn't have a mind of his own.'

'Where did they hold him?'

'I don't know! This is just what I heard!'

Moone leaned forward, gritted his teeth. 'Who bloody killed him, Malcolm! Tell me!'

West grabbed his face, buried it in his dirty hands, then looked up. 'I don't know! All I know is MacDonald snatched him, and that councillor, the one who topped himself, he found the house...'

'What? Stanley? He was involved?'

'Yeah, you didn't know about him. He liked them young.'

Moone got up, feeling sick to his stomach.

CHAPTER 29

He was a creature of habit, like most people, except he was a sick little creature with the sickest of habits. Mathieson sunk down into his car seat, parked along Exeter Street, not far from his own offices. But his eyes were trained on the pub down the street, the shabby little flea pit that they'd tried desperately to give some class with a lick of paint. It was a facelift on a cancer patient. He laughed to himself, realising the irony, that Benton was dying.

Of course, that had to be the reason why he'd suddenly grown a conscience; it was typical of child abusers to try and do some good, or even find themselves reaching out for God when they knew their days were numbered, and Hell was waiting. But most use God as something to hide behind, to make themselves look respectable.

He didn't give a shit about Benton's reasons for stabbing him in the back, he just knew the dirty, filthy scumbag had stuck the knife in and was about to destroy his family's name.

No, no, that wasn't about to happen. He could stop it all. Mathieson opened the glovebox, and saw the rag he'd wrapped the gun in. He slipped it out, then concealed the weapon in his jacket pocket, noting that it was nearly closing time. Ray Benton would stumble out of the pub, coughing his guts up, then head off towards Cattedown. Mathieson would be waiting, and take his time with him, making sure he knew the cost of his actions.

He watched the pub, intently, his hand reaching for the door handle, waiting for the coughing.

It echoed in the street, the deep, painful rattle of the cough that sounded like it had come up from Hell itself. Benton came out of the pub, stumbled towards the gutter, coughing then spitting. Blood, no doubt.

Mathieson opened the car door, watching Benton stand up straight, but not looking his usual drunken self.

He didn't turn right out of the pub.

Mathieson frowned, watching the old paedophile as he turned left in the direction of the Job Centre, and the Jury's Inn beyond it. Where the hell was the dirty bastard heading?

Mathieson climbed out and crossed the road, avoiding the steady stream of cars coming towards him. Then he kept back, watching the skinny wretch, who kept checking his piece of shit phone and walking towards the hotel.

He turned, went into the glass doors of the entrance, and Mathieson stood watching, wondering where exactly the old bastard was going. He didn't have a room in the hotel. There was no way he'd pay for a room for himself, not even when he was close to death.

Mathieson went in and watched him walk to the marble effect bar and the customers that filled it up, the lifts on the right, just past the long reception desk.

Benton stopped when a young-ish man stood up from one of the tables.

Benton smiled, hardly able to believe he was actually looking at him, after all the years apart. He felt his eyes fill with tears, but he coughed them back down, and took a few more steps towards the table that Gary was stood by.

'Let me buy you a drink,' Benton said, looking to see a pint glass on the table, with only a little bit of beer left in it.

'No, you're all right,' Gary said, his face blank, his eyes shifting round the room, not really looking his way for very long.

'Let's sit down then.'

'I'm going in a minute,' Gary said. 'Got an early start tomorrow.'

'What? What about Beck? Where is he?'

Gary blew out a breath. 'He's not here. I didn't bring him.'

'But you said you would. I haven't seen him. I haven't got long left...'

Gary looked into his eyes. 'I know. You keep telling me. What do you expect me to do? You're the one who... you went and...'

'I've... I've changed, listen...'

'You haven't changed, nobody changes, not people like you.'

'Gary...'

He came closer to Benton, his face twisting with anger, his voice lowering. 'You think I'd bring my boy to meet you?! What sort of dad would I be if I let him near someone like you! Jesus, just stay away from us! That's the best thing you can do for him, for us, just stay away.'

Benton was frozen, his cough and the pain rising through him as he watched Gary turn and storm towards the lift and slam his fist on the call button.

'Gary...'

But he didn't turn round, just stared at the lift doors, waiting.

When Moone pushed through the incident room doors, he found only Butler sat at her desk, staring at the screen, a mug of coffee in her hands.

'Didn't expect to see you back,' Butler said.

'Stanley, the fucking councillor,' Moone

said, spitting out the words, putting his palms on the desk. 'He was involved, he was... he was a paedophile.'

'No wonder he topped himself. How did you find that out?' Butler stood up.

'West. Spilt his guts. Mathieson's done a bunk. He's on the run. We need to find that bastard.'

Butler nodded. 'I'll drag some bodies back. Check out any places he might be.'

'He's a soldier, trained for this sort of thing. Stanley. We need to look into his financial dealings, his online history, everything about him. If we look into him we might find out something of some bloody use.'

Butler stared at him. 'All right, we will. You OK?'

Moone pulled out a chair and sat down, shaking all over, sickness in his stomach, the beat and ache in his chest. 'I don't know, I don't know Mathieson's involvement in all this, but he was close, far too close to my family.'

'But he's not now. And he'll never be again.'

'If we can prove he's involved. We've got West's word, but who's going to listen to a paedophile? People like Mathieson, people like his father, they get away with it because people think how could they be a paedophile?'

Butler came over, stared into his eyes. 'We're going to get him. He's finished.'

Moone nodded.

'After all, he's a Remainer. Can't wait to wipe the smile off his face.'

Moone laughed. 'Right, let's get going. Let's talk to his wife too. Get her in.'

Butler picked up the phone and dialled and stood waiting. Then she looked at Moone, strangely, her eyes narrowing. 'Hang on... how did you vote in the referendum?'

'I'm not telling you. Just get on with the bloody job.'

It was nearly eight the next morning, and Moone was feeling like he could drop by the time they reached the Plymouth Council House to meet Stanley's PA. Butler seemed full of the joys of spring, but Moone was buzzing all over from having too much caffeine in his system. He'd lost count of the number of coffees he'd had that morning while Harding, Molly and the rest of the team went through Stanley's financial dealings with a fine-tooth comb. Nothing. Nothing stood out.

Not even any credit card transactions online that might be linked with child porn. He was either innocent, and West was yanking their chain, or he'd been very careful.

The wife was booked in for ten a.m. for an interview that Moone was not in the least bit looking forward to. How was he going to tell a widow that her husband probably took his own life because he was about to be revealed as a paedophile.

Moone flickered out of his nightmare to hear Butler saying something as they stepped out of the lift. 'Sorry?'

'I asked if you're all right,' she said, looking at him strangely. 'You don't look like you're on this planet.'

'I'm not,' he said, then found the office that had belonged to Councillor Stanley and knocked on the door.

The door was opened by his PA, who was dressed in a grey pinstripe dress, her blonde hair falling round her face in curly locks.

'Hi,' she said, backing up, allowing them to enter the narrow hallway.

Moone smiled. 'Is there somewhere we can sit? I'm sorry, I can't remember your name.'

'Lesley.' She smiled awkwardly, then pointed to a room around the corner with a frosted glass door. 'We could go in there.'

Butler went ahead, entering the small, rect-angular room that had a bright yellow sofa at one end, and a leather armchair at the other. Moone followed and sat on the sofa, while Butler stood, arms folded as usual.

Lesley sat on the edge of the leather arm-chair, looking between them. 'What did you want to know?'

Moone rubbed his face. 'This is between us, but we suspect that your boss was involved in something... criminal.'

She sat up a little, her brow creasing, staring at Moone. 'What sort of thing?'

'We can't talk about that,' Butler said bluntly.

'What can I do?' Lesley said, sounding despairing. 'I'm probably out of a job!'

'We need to know if he had any secrets, if he did anything out of the ordinary. Maybe you might have witnessed him acting strangely.'

Lesley shook her head, raised her shoulders. 'I can't think of anything. He came to work, had meetings. I don't know what else to say.'

'What about property?' Butler asked.

Lesley stared up at her. 'What do you mean?'

'I mean did he have any other property apart from his house?' Butler said, huffing out the words.

'No...' Lesley said, a little too hesitant for Moone's liking, so he sat forward. 'What? You hesitated...'

'I don't know. I just remembered he had me looking for a house to rent a while ago. Said him and his wife were going through a rough patch, but that was ages ago.'

'Three years ago?' Moone asked, his heart starting to beat faster.

She shrugged. 'Could be.'

'So,' Butler said. 'Did you find him something or not?'

'I did, I think, but he stayed with her, so I can

hardly remember myself. It was ages ago, like I said.'

Moone stood up. 'What did you use to search for it? A computer here?'

'My laptop. Why?' Lesley stood up.

'Because maybe we might be able to find out what property you found him.'

Lesley nodded, looking at him, her mouth opening again, a horrified look crossing her eyes. 'What's he done?'

'We can't talk about that,' Moone said, then pointed to the door. 'Please.'

She hurried out of the room and Moone followed, half watching her go into a small office where she started typing on a laptop, half watching Butler walk over to him.

'We're close, aren't we?' Butler said.

'I think so. Feels like it. Just need to find out where Mathieson is.'

Then Moone's phone was ringing, making him sigh and roll his eyes at Butler. He answered. 'Moone.'

'It's Barry.'

'Hi, Barry. Got anything for us?' he said, expecting bad news. It was hard to tell with Barry's deadpan voice whether it was good news or not.

'Well, I've got a location where our Roman120 messaged from. If that's any help?'

Moone looked at Butler. 'Barry's found him. You've got an address, Barry?'

'Yeah. Near Ham Woods. Want me to text

you the address?'

'Yeah, do that. Then get Stack or whoever's there to send armed response to the same address.' Moone ended the call, stared at his phone for a moment. 'We've got an address. That can't be right, can it?'

Butler shrugged. 'I don't know, but I remember some wanker saying he might have a self-destructive side... that he wants to get caught. Who said that?'

'Ha ha. Bloody funny.'

'It's not here!' the PA shouted, sounding distraught.

'What do you mean?' Moone asked, entering the office.

'The search history only goes back so far,' she said, looking at Moone as if for an answer.

He sighed, nodded. 'Of course it does. He probably deleted the history.'

'Which means he was up to no good,' Butler said.

'Right,' Moone said, and rubbed his hands together. He then pointed at Lesley. 'You stay here, please. We'll send someone to look at your laptop. Come on, let's go and arrest our killer... hopefully.'

There was a creeping sensation of unease taking over Moone as they turned down the main road, then round a roundabout, past houses on each side, then a row of shops. Unease that grew stronger when they followed the Satnav and Moone realised they'd been there before, to the same road. He was right. The Ham Woods were at the end of it, down the bottom of the road that snaked around the prefab houses that lined it. Butler pulled up sharply, close to an armed response van that was parked to their right. Two armed officers were getting ready beside it, checking their weapons, chatting and laughing about something. Butler looked at Moone and exchanged the same look of realisation, then reversed and parked.

'Kieran Dobson,' Moone said, then climbed out in a daze.

'We're ready when you are,' one of the armed response team said.

Moone nodded, then started heading towards the house.

'Hey, where the fuck're you going?!' someone called out to Moone, but he just kept walking towards the house, like he was caught in a dream where he couldn't escape, couldn't wake up.

The armed response officers hammered their boots alongside him as he reached the front of the house, their MP5 submachine guns held out in front of them.

'We go fucking first, you wanker,' one of the team growled, but Moone looked away when he heard a door opening.

In front of him, beyond the short garden,

Kieran Dobson stood staring at him, wearing a blue shirt and jeans. He looked calm but quizzical as he stared at Moone. His eyes widened when they jumped to the armed officers approaching the house.

'*Get down!*' one of the armed team commanded. '*Get down on your knees! Put your hands on your head.*'

Kieran stood there for a moment, a little bewildered, so Moone stepped closer and said, 'You better do what they say, Kieran.'

So he did, and started kneeling, his eyes still on the armed response team, as his hands rose to his head.

'Kieran Dobson,' Moone said, his stomach filling with lead. 'I'm arresting you on suspicion of murder...'

CHAPTER 30

'Take a look at this,' Butler said. She was at the bottom of the narrow lane that led to the back of Kieran's house. Moone walked towards her, stepping over the weeds that had sprung from the cracks in the paving and the concrete. Beyond the back of the house was Ham Woods, the barren outline of trees and undergrowth that was punctuated by household waste like battered fridges and muddy old television sets.

Butler was standing beside one of the garages that lined the left-hand side of the lane. She signalled for him to look inside, so he turned, saw what she was gesturing to and let out a tired breath. 'Bloody hell...'

Moone found himself staring at the dark and musty interior of the garage and the car that sat there. The same car that had been stolen and used in the stabbing on Mutley Plain.

'Looks like we've got him,' Butler said.

'Yeah, looks like it. Get the SOCOs here. I want this whole place gone over. The car, the house, and we'll need any computers.'

Butler huffed. 'Already ordered. I do know how to handle a crime scene.'

'I know. Sorry.'

She shook her head, then she glanced beyond Moone. He turned to see what she was looking at and saw Kieran Dobson watching them from the back of the incident response car.

'I've got an anti-terrorist Commander who's going to have a heart attack when she sees what we brought her,' Butler laughed.

The first thing Ray Benton knew was that he was jerking up out of bed, swinging his legs over and coughing, really hacking up, as if his lungs might slip out of his throat. He grabbed a handful of tissues he'd put by the bed and held them over his mouth. The coughing calmed down, so he wiped his mouth and looked at the tissue; it was soaked with dark blood and spittle. He had no energy, tired all over, but the first thoughts that came to him were the things he'd done. The faces, flashes of the stuff he'd either done himself or helped others do.

Then the sickness overtook him, filling every empty part of him, even his bones that he felt must be hollowed out brittle husks. It was what he deserved, he decided for the umpteenth time as he pushed himself from the bed and staggered across the narrow room to the small toilet and bath in the corner. He fell to his knees and gripped the toilet as he started coughing and retching again. He didn't bring up much because he'd hardly eaten anything for the last few days. They told him it would be like that for a while, and gave him something for the sickness, but it didn't help.

He managed to get up and held on to the doorframe to steady himself, his eyes finding the bed, and the tissue covered bedside cabinet. On the lower shelf was the bottle of liquid morphine they'd given him for the pain. He made it to the bed, then poured a cup and necked it.

Soon he'd feel a little better. He turned towards the dirty net curtains and the street outside, the people walking past, the grinding noise of a bus pulling up. Beyond the bus was the parade of Cattedown shops.

He flickered out of his stare when he heard the beep of his phone. He picked it up, wondering who it could be, as not many people had his number.

Gary. *Gary*?

He opened the text and read the message: 'Sorry. I shouldn't have said what I did. I'm still at the hotel. Can you come by and we can talk?'

He read it a couple of times before it sank in and the relief flooded him. This was his chance, a chance to make things right. To see his grandson.

A wave of nausea gripped him, then dizziness, so he sat down and typed back a message: 'It's alright. Yes, I'll be there soon.'

Gary: 'See you soon, Dad.'

He stared at the last message. Dad.

He gripped the phone, held it to his chest, trying to blank out the images, the flashes of faces. He wanted to cry, but he coughed it all away and started to get ready to go out again.

It had become a habit to watch the booking-in process, standing by the doors, watching from the shadows, trying to read the suspect's profile, their reactions.

Moone couldn't make out much from Kieran Dobson's manner; he seemed quite calm, even relaxed as they read out all the legal stuff, then the forensic people took his clothes and bagged them up. More of the SOCOs and a search team were going through his house, the garage and the car.

Something wasn't right. Moone couldn't shake the feeling. Some murderers relax when they're caught, the chase is over and relief kicks in. Was it like that with Kieran Dobson?

Eventually Moone found himself opposite Dobson as he sat across the desk in the interview room, the tape machine rolling, the video camera recording all that was said.

It had been Butler who read out all the legal

Stuff, while Moone just watched and observed Kieran as he sat in his light blue forensic suit, his eyes jumping round the room. He was pale, drawn, but quite calm.

'Kieran,' Moone said, resting his elbows on the desk. 'You said you didn't want a solicitor, are you sure about that?'

'Why would I want a solicitor?' he asked, looking straight at Moone. 'I haven't done anything wrong.'

'You do understand why you're here?' Butler asked.

Kieran looked at her. 'Yeah, they told me downstairs. You think I killed some people, but I didn't. I wouldn't do that to anyone.'

Moone nodded, then opened the folder he'd brought with him, that held some of the crime scene photos that had been taken of Kieran's home. He pushed one across the table – a shot of the garage and the car inside. 'You ever seen this vehicle before?'

Kieran looked down at the photo, then shook his head. 'No, I mean... that's my garage, but no, that's not mine.'

'It was stolen. From a house not that far from yours.' Moone pulled back the photo. 'It was used as a getaway vehicle the night of the Mutley stabbing. We will need to know where you were that night.'

'Home,' Kieran said. 'I'm always home.'

'Alone?' Butler asked.

'Yeah. I live alone.'

'What about last night?' Moone asked. 'Where were you?'

Kieran opened his mouth, then hesitated. 'Last night? I was out...'

'Interesting,' Butler said, raising her eyebrows at Moone.

Moone still had the uncomfortable feeling. 'Do you belong to any online dating sites?'

'No, I mean, I used to belong to Plenty of Fish, but I gave up on that.'

'Where were you last night exactly?' Butler asked, leaning forward.

Dobson looked at her. 'At a friend's. They persuaded me to go for a drink, then I ended up at their place.'

'Who is this friend?' Moone asked, taking out a pen.

'I'd rather not say.'

Moone looked up and noticed Kieran looked quite uncomfortable for the first time. 'Male or female?'

'No comment.'

'I see.' Moone sat back. 'Things are not looking good for you, Kieran. We've got a lot of evidence, some circumstantial, which points at you being our killer. You have to understand that. You need to explain to us what's going on, or we can't help you.'

'I haven't really got anything to say,' Kieran said and raised his shoulders.

Moone let out a sigh and rubbed his eyes. 'Was it the attack on you? Did that affect you?'

'No, it didn't have any effect on me.'

'Nothing?' Butler asked. 'Didn't it make you angry?'

'I suppose...'

Moone huffed out an empty laugh, then shook his head. 'Right, Kieran, I'm going to stop this interview and give you time to think.'

Moone got up, then leaned over the desk. 'You might want to think about legal representation because you're in trouble. Serious trouble. You need to start talking to us. Now.'

'No comment,' Kieran said, so Moone picked up his file and left the room.

'Jesus...' Moone slapped the file down on the desk, making everyone stare at him. The whole team were there, waiting for words of wisdom. 'What is it with him? It's like he doesn't care.'

'Maybe he doesn't care,' Butler said. 'Maybe he's a psychopath. Therefore, he doesn't give a shit.'

'No, that's not it,' Moone said, looking at the crime scene photos on the board. 'He's sick, but someone's twisted his mind, but, I don't feel like Kieran is the person we're hunting, do you?'

Butler blew out her cheeks. 'Honestly? I don't bloody well know anymore. He seems pretty calm. The innocent aren't usually that calm when faced with a murder charge.'

'Exactly. Which makes you think he might be guilty, but who's this person he spent the night with?'

'No idea, but by the way, the SOCOs did a quick sweep of the car, you know all the places a driver touches. Nothing. It's been wiped over. None of Kieran's prints anywhere so far.'

'What about his computer?'

'Barry's got it but he's a bit slow. Talk of the devil...' Butler gestured to the doors, so Moone turned round to see Barry coming towards them with an energy drink in one hand and an evidence bag in the other, which contained a mobile phone.

'Any luck, Barry?' Moone asked.

'Depends on what you're referring to.' He looked at them blankly.

'Why don't you tell us what you've found,' Moone said and rested his backside on his desk.

Barry put down his drink. 'I checked that laptop you gave me, the one that belonged to the PA. Couldn't find anything on there really, but I've just been looking at his phone. He made a few calls to a property agency in Mutley a couple of years back.'

Moone got to his feet. 'That's it! What agency?!'

'Mutley Properties Ltd.'

'Right, Butler,' Moone shouted, pushing through the doors. 'Let's go!'

Gary had text the room number, on the fifth floor of the Jury's Inn, so Ray Benton knew exactly where to go when he arrived at the hotel. By the time he got close, he felt a little better, the morphine having kicked in and the nausea retreated to a manageable level. He still felt tired, exhausted really, but Gary's initial text had rallied him, and he felt excitement at the prospect of actually meeting his grandson.

A flash of an image came to him. A young boy staring up at him from a mattress.

He stopped, let out a deep cough as a wave of pain rushed through him. He leant against the wall of the hotel, people hurrying past, only giving him a slight glance. Nobody asked if he was all right, and he was glad. He didn't deserve anyone's sympathy.

He gained his strength and headed through the glass doors, ignoring the bony image of the ghostly old man that appeared in the glass of the door, then went as quickly as he could towards the bank of lifts.

As he went up, he adjusted his clothes, staring down at them, the only smart ones he possessed. He didn't look up, didn't dare look into his own eyes.

Another flash. The boy lying still in the small, damp room, holding a toy. A toy he got for him.

The doors of the lift opened as he pushed away the image. You did some good, he told himself, and this is your chance to do some more.

The room was at the end of the corridor, along the deep red carpet, the last door. He knocked on the door and waited.

'It's...it's open!' a voice called out, as if in pain.

Benton pushed the door, looking through the gap and seeing the end of a bed, a table with tea making faculties and a small TV. 'Gary?'

'Dad...' the pained voice said again.

Benton walked slowly down the short corridor, a clean, shiny bathroom on his right. He stepped into the room, staring at the bed, blinking, trying to take in and understand what he was seeing.

'No... no, please...' Benton raised his hands together, as if to pray.

Mathieson was kneeling on the bed, astride Gary, who was lying on his side, a pillow pressed against his head. A gun was in Mathieson's hand, pressed hard into the pillow. The MP had gritted teeth, his eyes fixed on Benton, sharp and clear.

CHAPTER 31

They parked up and Moone and Butler hurried along Connaught Avenue and turned right towards the parade of shops opposite the Hyde Park pub, which were mostly made up of solicitors and estate agents. Tucked between two of the bigger premises, was a narrow shop where Moone could see a couple of figures sat at desks near the glass front. He pushed the door open, heading past a small sofa near the window and towards a young man in an ill-fitting suit. He got up, smiling, offering his hand. 'Good afternoon, my name's...'

Moone showed his warrant card. 'Cut the claptrap. We need information.'

At the back of the room Moone observed a full-figured blonde woman on the phone, talking to someone loudly.

'What information?' the young man said, his friendliness fading. 'Is there some kind of problem?'

'Who's in charge round here?' Butler asked, walking past the young man, towards the blonde woman.

The blonde woman made eye contact with Butler, then seemed to take in the situation. 'Sorry, Damon, I've got to go. Looks like the police are here.'

She ended the call then looked up at Butler. 'Is there a problem?'

'Do you know this man?' Butler took out a photo of councillor Stanley.

The woman stared at the photograph but shook her head. 'I don't think so, he looks familiar. Who is he?'

'He killed himself a while back,' Moone said, stepping closer. 'Used to be a councillor.'

'I dealt with him, I think,' the young man said, coming round to get a look at the photo. 'Yeah, I saw him in the Herald. Thought I'd dealt with him. Rented out a place I think...'

Moone moved out of the way as the young man went back to his desk, then sat at his computer, typing, bringing up lists of properties. There seemed so many, but the young man used his mouse to easily go through most of them. 'Yeah, that's it. I remember now. Furneaux Road, he rented a two-bedroom house there. We've sold it since then.'

'What number?' Moone asked, leaning over the desk, his heart pounding, feeling a cold sweat break out under his arms.

'Number twelve...'

Moone was gone, out of the shop and jogging back towards the car before he could even gather his thoughts or wait for Butler. As he approached the car, he turned to see her storming towards him, breaking into a jog to keep up.

'Keep your knickers on, Moone,' Butler said, unlocking the car and opening the door. 'I had you down as a faffer, but maybe I was wrong.'

Moone climbed in, sitting forwards, his hands tapping away at the dashboard, staring out at the street, willing Butler to get a move on. The engine started at last, his heart firing up with it, while his stomach turned over, wondering what they would find at this house, if it was even connected to the abduction and murder of Danny Sawyer.

They drove, but Moone didn't remember the journey, was only aware that Butler parked in a short street with a few cramped houses along it. Number twelve was the middle one. It looked quite newly painted, with a small driveway where a boxy silver car was parking up.

Moone climbed out, pulling his ID from his suit jacket, getting ready to show it to the balding man in the hoody and jeans that seemed to be swaggering to the front door.

'Excuse me,' Moone said, showing his warrant card, sensing Butler at his back. 'This your house?'

The man was raising his keys to the door,

but looked Moone and Butler over, looking weary. 'Yeah, mate, this is my house. Who wants to know?'

'Us, the police,' Butler said. 'How long have you lived here?'

'Just over a year. Why?' As the man answered, his voice full of suspicion, the front door opened and a mousey-haired young woman who looked heavily pregnant stood there.

'What's happened, Steve?' the woman asked, looking terrified.

'Nothing to worry about,' Moone said. 'But we need to take a look around.'

'Take a look around?' Steve said, looking between them, a worried expression growing. 'Why?'

'We think this house might have been involved in a crime a couple of years ago.'

'We didn't live here then!' the woman moaned.

'We know,' Butler said, switching into pissed off mode. 'Look, do we have your permission to look around?'

'For what?' the man asked, now sounding annoyed.

'We're not sure,' Moone said. 'It may be nothing.'

The man looked at the woman, who shrugged. 'All right, but don't go trashing the place. You're just looking round, right?'

'Just looking,' Moone said, then gestured to

the front door. 'May we?'

The woman stood back, rubbing her hand over her prominent belly as she watched them come in, wiping their feet on the mat.

Moone noted it looked clean, quite freshly decorated. New laminate flooring, the kind Angela always said looked cheap and tacky. He went through to the kitchen, the dining room, the adjacent narrow lounge, then up the stairs. Butler was following, poking her nose into rooms.

They met on the landing.

'Nothing,' Moone said. 'They've redecorated. We can't rip this place apart looking for blood... or worse.'

Butler huffed, then pinched her nose. 'Now what? There's still the back garden.'

Moone nodded, then hurried back down the stairs, heading for the back door, past the kitchen where the couple stood, the pregnant wife filling the kettle.

'Would you like tea or coffee?' she said, as if they were workmen there to fix something.

'Not for me,' Moone said, then unlocked the back door and found himself standing on a paved patio, facing a small bit of lawn. The paved patio went round to the right in an L shape. A huge slab of concrete seemed to lie over half the paving. Someone had looked after the grass, but little else appeared to be cared for.

'Anything?' Butler said behind him.

'Nothing.'

He turned when he heard a cat meowing and saw a small ginger tomcat rubbing itself against Butler's legs. He was surprised when Butler crouched down and scooped it up, cradling it to her body.

'Hello little fella,' she said. 'You're a little cutie, aren't you?'

'You're a cat person?' Moone asked, still shocked by her show of affection.

'Yeah, aren't you? Look, he's got a collar. He's called Mr Wonky Socks. That's so cute.'

He made a face, then looked around the garden again. 'Shit! Fuck.'

Butler let out a yelp, then swore as the cat leapt out of her hands and landed on the grass and made a run for it. Moone shook his head, then watched the cat head for the concrete slab, nudging it and sniffing round it.

Moone went back into the kitchen. 'What's this concrete slab out here?'

The man of the house, Steve, followed him out. He shrugged. 'Don't know. Been there since we moved in. Keep meaning to move it and redo the paving or lay more gra...'

'Mind if we move it?' Moone said, crouching down beside it.

'No,' the man said and joined Moone, getting his fingers under the thick slab.

They both strained, letting out groans as they slowly ground the slab sideways towards the fence. Moone felt rain tap at his face as the slab groaned its way towards him.

'Shit,' Steve said. 'I didn't know this was here.'

Moone stepped over the slab and stood next to Steve and Butler as they all looked down into a narrow, perfectly square dark hole in the ground.

Moone took out his phone, turned on the torch app and shone it into the hole. He let out a breath when the light showed him concrete steps going down to a small room.

CHAPTER 32

'No! Please don't!' Mathieson dug the gun further into the pillow, pressing Gary's head into the bed, making him let out a painful, fear filled groan. 'How many fucking times must you have heard that! Eh?! Ray?!'

Benton stared at the man on the bed with the gun, then into the terrified eyes of Gary. He almost didn't recognise him. His head was half covered by the bed covers, the pillow. None of it made sense. He'd backed himself up to the wall, bumping into the TV and table. He shook his head, tried to talk, but his voice broke up.

'Ray!?' Mathieson shouted. 'You hear me! Ray, you fucking child molesting... fucking waste of space! You dare sell me out! Did you think I wouldn't find out! You scumbag, paedophile...'

Ray closed his eyes, lowered his head, the room spinning, watching it all happen slowly as if he was outside himself.

'Please, Carl...'

'Don't you fucking dare plead with me!' Mathieson dug the gun into the pillow. 'You've destroyed me! You've destroyed my family. You've killed my mother!'

'I, I tr...'

'Is this it? Is he the reason you did it?! Him and your fucking grandson, who'll probably grow up to be as useless and sick as his grandfather!'

'Don't talk about...' Benton shouted, moving forward.

'Why the fuck not?!' Mathieson took out a mobile phone from his pocket, started tapping on the screen, fiddling with it. 'Look at him, the poor little bastard, doesn't even realise the cell pool DNA he's got in his veins! Doesn't stand a fucking chance! You've destroyed my family, Ray, how about I destroy yours!'

Benton held up his hands as he watched Mathieson stare down at his son, pushing the gun down, his finger wrapping round the trigger. 'I'm begging you, don't, none of this is his fault.'

'I know, you piece of shit, it's you, you and the others. You and your sick desires. Why did you have to take him?!'

'I didn't. It was MacDonald, and Stanley. Grader egged them on, they dragged me in to sort it out.'

'Yes, you're right, it isn't your son's fault. It's all yours. You choose, Ray. You or him? What's it to be? Come on, old man, you're dying already. You'll be gone soon. What do you say, Gary? Should I blow your brains out or his? Him, your father... your father the fucking paedophile.'

Moone pulled on a pair of latex gloves, then some overshoes, then gingerly stepped down into the hole, his mobile phone pointing into the dark. The torchlight caught dark corners, webs covering everything in the damp, musty smelling room. He stepped down a few steps, then shone the torch light opposite him as he caught something. He swept his arm back and stopped, frozen.

In the corner was a worn, dirty looking mattress pushed up against the wall. Moone slowly sat down on the step, staring at the single mattress, the kind that might be found on a child's bed. He lowered his phone, now falling into half-darkness as he found himself overcome, an enormous wave of sadness and horror washing over him. Then he started crying, feeling the tears leak from his eyes, and wiped them away with the back of his hand.

'You OK?' Butler called down, but when he tried to answer, his voice ran dry. He blinked up into the light, saw an upside down Butler staring down at him and nodded, then dragged himself to his feet.

He held a hand over his eyes, squinting into

the bright winter sun that burned his eyes as he started up the concrete steps. His phone was still on, shining against the wall. Something caught the light, so he shone the beam back and tried to find what he thought he'd seen. There it was, three holes drilled into the corner, as if something had been attached to it, placed in a position where a camera might be fitted. He carried on up into the bright burning light.

'They must've...' his voice broke again, and he held himself, unsure if he could continue without crying again, so he walked away, looking towards the house.

'They held him down there?' Butler asked, so he nodded.

'Those fucking... it makes me sick. You ever witnessed anything like this before?'

Moone looked away and nodded.

'Sorry...'

'There's holes drilled in the wall. I wonder if they had a camera positioned there.'

Butler turned a strange colour, made a face. 'Those bastards.'

He nodded, cleared his throat. 'SOCOs on their way?'

'Yeah. Everyone's on their way. You want to stay?'

He hated himself for it, but he shook his head. He was trembling all over as he pulled off his gloves and stuffed them in his pocket as he walked into the fullness of the now empty house.

Butler drove him back to the station in silence as soon as the SOCOs and some of the team arrived. Back at the station, he sat down at one of the desks, not able to concentrate or see anything but the tiny grey room and the small mattress. He felt numb, but still shaking.

Butler came back in and put a mug of tea down in front of him. It was dark in colour and looked quite disgusting.

He looked up at her, seeing her nod to the drink. 'I don't like tea. I hate the stuff. Have you ever seen me drink tea?'

'No, but that's got loads of sugar in. That's what you're supposed to give people in shock.'

He pushed it away. 'I'm not in shock. If I'm in anything, it's rage. Those evil bastards... they... they put him in that.'

Butler rubbed his shoulder. 'I know, but we've got to rise above it and do the job and get the bastards responsible. You up to it?'

He nodded, choking down the tears that threatened to rise again. 'Yep, of course.'

A phone started ringing across the room where one of the civvy team members was sat. Moone watched a redhaired, slightly overweight woman take the call, still unable to remove the image from his eyes. It burned there, hovered like a negative photo.

'Excuse me, DI Moone, sir,' the civvy woman said, holding out the phone. 'Someone asking for you. Said you'd want to talk to them about the

Danny Sawyer case.'

Moone stared at the phone, then got up slowly, his legs feeling weak, his heart starting to beat a little faster as he approached the woman's desk. He took the phone, cleared his throat. 'DI Peter Moone.'

'Moone…' the strained voice said on the other end. 'Peter. Can I call you Peter?'

'Who is this?'

'Mathieson. Carl Mathieson. I believe you've been looking for me.'

Moone twisted round, his eyes finding Butler's, widening, then he mouthed the name Mathieson. 'Where are you?'

'I can help you. I want to help you.'

'Then tell us where you are.'

'I will. But you come here… just you.'

Moone rubbed his beard, his eyes. 'Why me?'

'Because you entrusted me with your family, they were never in danger. I want you to know that.'

'I don't know that, just tell me where you are!'

'The Jury's Inn. Room 15. Don't call in the cavalry, Peter, please. I need to talk to you first.'

'I don't know if I can do that.'

'I have a gun… it's pointed at my own head. You know I'll do it.'

'Jesus…' Moone made eye contact with Butler, saw her picking up her phone. He shook his head. 'OK, Mathieson. Don't do anything stupid.

Let's talk.'

'Come here...'

The line went dead, so Moone put down the receiver and turned to face Butler.

'That was Mathieson?'

'Yes. He's in a hotel room with a gun pointed at his own head. I think he'll do it. He wants to talk to me.'

'You're not going, Moone?!'

'I have to. I have to find out what I think I know.'

'I'm coming too,' Butler said, watching Moone gather his stuff together.

'OK, but let's hurry and get over there before he gets tired of waiting and pulls the trigger.'

Butler followed him out of the incident room and they headed towards the stairs down to the car park. 'I'm not sure that he shouldn't pull the trigger if he's involved with the murder of Danny Sawyer.'

Moone looked at her. 'I agree. But I need answers first. Let's call for armed response to meet us there.'

Butler drove them to the underground car park beneath the Jury's Inn hotel. She parked in a particularly dark corner, a shadow of a pillar blanketing the interior of the car. They sat there for a moment, hearing the engine quietening, ticking a little.

'You sure about this?' Butler asked. 'I heard about the last time you faced a gunman.'

'That's the thing, I didn't face him. My team did. That's why I can't walk away from this. I don't think Mathieson would shoot me.'

'Let's see what armed response say,' Butler said, looking in the rearview mirror. 'That's who you'll have to convince.'

Moone leaned over and watched the reverse image of the armed response team at their black van, suiting up, checking their sidearms and holstering them.

Moone climbed out, the screech of cars entering and leaving the car park echoing around him. He approached the team, and faced the thickest set of them, a man in his fifties, with greying hair at his temples. Moone showed his ID.

'I know who you are, boy,' the man said, hardly looking at him as he adjusted his armour vest, then checked his sidearm. 'You nearly fucked up our last job.'

'I'm sorry about that,' Moone said, feeling like a school kid facing the headmaster.

'You would've been real sorry with a knife in you,' the officer said, then stared at Moone through his craggy eyes. 'Sergeant Mason. That's me. Who's up there?'

'A man called Mathieson. Carl Mathieson.'

Mason looked at him, his thick eyebrows raised. 'The MP?'

'The very same.'

'Shit. He's seen action. I take it he's armed?'

'We believe so.'

Mason nodded. 'This isn't going to be easy.'

'No.'

Butler appeared, her mobile in her hand. 'Guess what? Just found out that the hotel room has been booked under the name Gary Benton.'

Moone put his hands over his face and breathed out. 'Shit! Gary Benton. So, what're we thinking? He's got a relation of Ray Benton's up there. And he's got it in for Ray... so that means.'

'Means Ray and Gary are probably up there,' Butler added.

Mason huffed out a rattle of a laugh. 'That's fucking great. So we've got an ex-army man and two fucking hostages? So, how we going to play this? You need to get a negotiator down here.'

'I don't think there's any negotiating with a man like Mathieson,' Moone said. 'But maybe we'll have to settle for what we can get.'

'Which is?' Mason asked.

'Gary Benton.' Moone blew out the air from his cheeks. 'Maybe I can get him to let him go.'

'You?' Mason said, the thick eyebrows rising.

'He's asked for me. We sort of know each other.'

'Shit.' Mason rubbed his face, then looked at Moone again. 'Well, this is your show. You going in?'

Moone's stomach sank, and the trembling that had already started got a great deal worse as he nodded. Also, he really wanted to pee. 'Yep. I'll go in.'

'Then you'll need one of these,' Mason said, and went to the back of the van and produced a bullet proof vest with 'POLICE' written across it in big bold letters. 'Put it on. I'm not letting you up there without it.'

'And I'm not going up there without it.'

Moone stood at the urinal, staring at the pale yellow tiles opposite him, flashes of recent days filling his eyes. Then the day his team met their fate arrived and the sickness filled his gut. He managed to pee a little, then zipped himself up and washed his hands, ignoring the men coming in, who stared at his police bullet proof vest.

He walked out and into the lobby where Butler and the armed response team held the lift. He went into the small space, and they all stood, crammed in, as the doors shut. There were three armed team members, Butler and himself. He could smell the oily guns and some aftershave. The floor numbers rose as his stomach sank further and his mouth became drier.

Ding.

The doors slid open, and the armed unit went first, clearing the way, making sure any guests went to their rooms or the lobby. He could hear them commanding people as he headed, with Butler in tow, towards the last door in the corridor.

He stopped short when Mason's gloved hand grabbed his elbow.

'How do you feel?' Butler whispered.

'Like I want to pee again,' Moone said, and felt a little calmer when Butler smiled.

'Thanks,' she said.

'For what?'

'For saving my life.'

'Shut up!'

Mason held up a finger, then nodded, and pointed towards the door as the armed team got in position either side of it.

Moone approached the door, paused, then took a breath and knocked.

CHAPTER 33

'The door's open,' Mathieson's voice called out, so Moone gently pushed the door and watched it slowly open, revealing a plain, neat hotel room. His eyes jumped to Ray Benton, who was in the corner, his face turned towards the rest of the room. He glanced at Moone, but his eyes hardly saw him, and his skin was deadly pale. Dead man walking, Moone thought, but wasn't convinced who he was thinking about.

'Come slowly into the room, your hands raised,' Mathieson ordered with all the authority his army day must have ingrained in him.

Moone raised his hands and stepped slowly into the room, his eyes jumping to Mathieson, and the strange position he was in, sat over a man, probably Gary Benton. A gun was pressed into a pillow, which covered most of Gary's head.

'Peter,' Mathieson said, a weird kind of smile breaking on his drawn, pale face. 'It's good to see you. Good to see a friendly face, if that makes sense.'

'It sort of does,' Moone said, looking around at Ray Benton, then back at the situation.

'That's a ridiculous thing they gave you to wear.'

Moone looked down at the vest. 'Supposed to make me feel better, I think.' Moone saw his hands out in front of him, trembling uncontrollably. His stomach was ready to pour up out of his throat, cold sweat running down his sides. He wondered if this was how his colleagues had felt that day.

'It wouldn't if I was to shoot you in the head.'

'Please don't do that, Carl.' Moone laughed, but it broke up in his throat.

'No hard feelings... about your ex-wife.'

'No, none.' Moone looked at Gary as he made a sound, a pained kind of whimper. 'Why don't you let him go? You've got me now.'

'You? I don't want to kill you, Pete.'

'I'm hoping you don't want to kill anyone.' Moone stepped closer, lowering his hands a little.

'Don't come any closer!' Mathieson snapped. 'You! Ray! You come closer!'

Moone turned to see Ray snap out of his horror stare, then step forward unsteadily.

'You see,' Mathieson said, a sick kind of laugh in his throat. 'Ray here, he destroyed my entire life. He couldn't keep his mouth shut. All he had to do was take our secret to the grave, but no, he had to, he had to interfere.'

Moone nodded. 'He decided to move Danny Sawyer's body. He put the toy with his remains, so we'd find it all.'

Mathieson lifted the gun from the pillow and pointed it across the room at the old dying man. 'Yes, he did that, and destroyed my life... destroyed my family's name.'

'What did they have on you?' Moone asked. 'I mean, they managed to get you involved, so they must've had something on you. Was it your father?'

Mathieson turned his eyes to Moone. 'My father, good old Dad, he was a weak man. He didn't deserve my mother, never did. He lied to her, constantly. She always suspected he had affairs, but later I found out the truth. I thought I'd go mad when Grader told me. He had evidence too. Film... he must have it somewhere. I had to protect my mother from it, so I had no choice but to do what they asked.'

'Who was behind the abduction of Danny Sawyer?' Moone asked, watching the gun lowering a little.

Mathieson looked towards Benton, a snarl poisoning his face, tightening his skin, making the gun rise again. 'Benton knows all about that, don't you, Ray? Ian MacDonald snatched him, right outside his home. Jesus, those evil bastards. MacDonald and Stanley, they cooked it all up between them... they planned to, to film what they did, to show off to Grader, their lord and master. Satan himself.'

'Yes, I've met him.' Moone looked down to see Gary crying, his face red. 'Look, can't we get Gary out of here? He's not the issue here. You need to start trying to do a deal, Carl.'

Mathieson's face changed as he swept the gun over to Gary and dug the barrel deep into the pillow. Gary let out a cry, tears flowing, words of pleading spilling from his mouth.

'Carl...' Benton croaked, seeming to sway a little, no colour left in his face.

'Don't you fucking talk to me!' Mathieson roared, digging the gun into the pillow. 'You want to know suffering! I'll take away what you've got left!'

'Please!' Ray put his hands to together.

'Carl...' Moone said, but no one was listening to him.

'On your knees!' Mathieson snapped.

'Please...' Ray Benton slowly, awkwardly got to his knees, his hands together.

'Carl,' Moone said. 'Carl! Look at me. You need to put that gun down. They'll want to come in here... and they'll shoot you. They can't risk more lives.'

'I know how it works!' Mathieson said. 'I'm not going to hurt anyone else. It's up to Ray here who I hurt, him or Gary.'

'Don't do this, Carl,' Moone said, a strange

calmness washing over him.

'You want answers, don't you?' Mathieson said.

'Yes, but you can tell us at the station.'

'You haven't figured it out? Your daughter thinks you're pretty smart...'

Moone nodded. 'OK, I think I might know some things. I think, I think something went wrong. Maybe Stanley panicked and turned to you, maybe Danny Sawyer died and they thought you could help them out. Dispose of his body.'

Mathieson lowered his head, shook it. When he looked up he had tears in his eyes. 'I wish it was that... you're right, they panicked. Stanley came to me. Asked me to help... got me to the house saying he had a problem. Took me down to the basement. I wasn't... I didn't know... Jesus... that little child lying there, so small, help-less.'

'He was alive?' Moone's stomach turned over, the sickness and trembling starting over.

Mathieson nodded. 'Yes, yes, he was alive, but drugged. I don't know what they'd given him. You have to believe me when I say that I wanted to kill them all. MacDonald, Stanley, and especially Grader... but they had me. They were filming the room, the boy, for their lord and master, Grader. So they had me on film. I was up to my neck.'

'What happened?' Moone sensed it, that something had happened to turn it all from bad to worse.

Mathieson's tears came faster, and he looked up, staring at Moone. 'You know I was in Iraq?'

'I heard.'

Mathieson nodded. 'We were dropped in, to go behind enemy lines... only twelve of us. We didn't have much equipment. We were there to cause chaos. Blow up a few compounds. The second day there we were holed up near some caves. We heard a bell, the kind goats have. It was important that no one saw us, but, Jesus, he saw us, a shepherd boy. He stared at us, frozen. We smiled, tried to win him over, but he started running, calling out...'

'What did you do?' Moone trembled, felt sick.

'No one else wanted to deal with the problem,' Mathieson said, his eyes wet. 'But we all would've died. They would've tortured us then killed us. They wouldn't have shown us mercy. A decision had to be made.'

Moone ran a hand down his face. 'You? You dealt with it?'

Mathieson's tears streamed from his eyes. He nodded. 'I had no choice...'

Moone wanted to throw up, wanted nothing more than to run and hide. The question hovered on his tongue for a moment before he managed to say, 'Danny, Danny Sawyer?'

Mathieson sobbed, the gun wavering in his hand, trembling. 'God forgive me, yes, I dealt with him too. I had to. He woke up, saw me. I think he thought I was there to help him. He looked at me. I can still see him. I went to him, I held him. I think, I think he was comforted before... I just held him after... crying.'

Moone stumbled backwards, finding the wall behind him, the room spinning. He could hardly breathe as he focused on the man with the gun, who he no longer recognised as human. He was a monster. 'Carl Mathieson, I'm arresting you for the murder...'

'Not happening, Peter,' Mathieson said, poking the gun back at the pillow, digging it towards Gary, who had started sobbing. 'Time to choose, Ray. You or your son?'

'Please, please...' Ray held up his hands, clenched together. 'Don't...'

'He probably begged too,' Mathieson said, his voice full of spite. 'Begged not to have all those things done to him. Choose, for fuck's sake, Ray!'

'Don't!' Moone shouted as Mathieson raised the gun and aimed it at the old paedophile.

'Please...' Benton said, now crying and rocking.

'You can't even do that one thing for your son!' Mathieson said, then Moone saw him squeeze the trigger.

The shot pounded into the room, bellowed into Moone's ears as Ray Benton flinched then slumped to the floor. Blood covered half his head and was pooling on the carpet.

The whine rang in Moone's ears, as Mathieson lowered the gun, then slumped back against the head of the bed. He cradled the gun, panting, the tears still streaming down his face as he stared towards the man he'd just killed.

'Come over to me,' Moone said, holding out a hand to Gary, who blinked back his tears. His eyes rolled towards Mathieson who still cradled the gun in his hands.

'Go on, Gary,' Mathieson said, blankly, all washed out. 'Get the fuck out of here.'

Gary started to crawl across the bed, then scrambled off it, and rushed towards Moone.

'Peter,' Mathieson said, quietly. 'There's an address in my pocket. You'll find Grader there.'

'Thanks.'

'Tell Angela I'm sorry.'

'Go, get out,' Moone said and pushed Gary towards the corridor and watched him hurry for the door. It was open already, and Mason, and one of his team, a female armed officer were coming towards Moone.

'There's no more hostages,' Moone said, then turned back to Mathieson and saw he'd now pushed the gun under his chin, dug deep into his flesh.

'Please, don't do...' Moone said, but the shot rang out, deafening Moone again, making his ears whine as the two armed officers swept in, pointing their handguns at the dead man.

Moone felt his heart thudding. His eyes took in Mathieson for the last time, blood and skull spattered up the wall behind him, his body slumped to one side.

CHAPTER 34

Moone felt the trembling fading away at last as he sat at the desk, his coat still on, aware that most of the team's eyes were on him. He'd looked up and made eye contact with Harding, who had given him a thumbs-up. Then he'd smiled, or tried to, but the sensation to throw up was still with him. It had been the smell in the room, the cordite and the iron sting of blood that stayed in his nostrils. Mason, the armed officer, had said something about the smell when he helped Moone off his knees and out of the hotel room.

He'd saved Gary Benton's life, that's what everyone kept telling him, including the concerned face of Butler.

What was he going to say to Angela?

'Here.' Butler put a takeaway coffee down in front of him. 'All the way from that posh coffee place you like. That cost over three quid!'

'Sorry, I'll pay you back.'

'Don't be a wally.' She rested on the desk, looking down at him, her head tilted to the side. 'How you feeling?'

'Like I want to vomit.'

'That's to be expected. You just watched two people die. By the way, I just found something out.'

Moone looked up, his stomach tightening. 'What?'

'Mathieson's mother, she was found this morning, in bed. Someone... well, there was hardly a mark on her.'

'Mathieson. Jesus.'

'At least we've got West. And we know what happened. We can talk to the parents and let them know.'

The vomit rose in Moone, and he closed his eyes. He picked up the coffee, took a sip to try and rid himself of the tastes and smells haunting him, but the drink didn't seem to taste of anything much at all.

Then the door was opening and Chief Superintendent Laptew was coming through the door, all done out in full uniform, his sympathetic eyes jumping to Moone.

'Bloody hell, Moone,' the Chief Super said. 'What are you still doing here?'

'I wanted to talk to Kieran Dobson again,' Moone said.

The Chief Super shook his head and huffed. 'This to do with the gay killings?'

'Yes. Our anti- terrorist friends haven't got the right man. I think Dobson is hiding something. Please, let me talk to him and then I'll go home.'

Laptew looked over at Butler. 'Mandy, do you mind if we have a word alone?'

She straightened up, her cheeks reddening a little. 'No, that's fine.'

The Chief Super watched her go over to her desk, then he closed in on Moone, lowering his voice. 'Moone... Pete, you've got to be careful, you don't want to upset someone like Commander Richer. Someone from her world can make life very difficult for you... for all of us.'

'So, I just walk away from this because she's the big *I am*, and let a man go down for something he didn't do?'

'There have been no more murders since...'

Moone sat up. 'No, there hasn't. I think our killer is lying low. He's not stupid.'

Laptew nodded. 'All I'm trying to say is, you better make sure you're right before you go up against her. I have faith in you, DCI Moone.'

As the Chief Superintendent straightened his tie and uniform, Moone said, 'I'm only a DI, sir.'

'Not anymore. You've proved yourself. We need a good DCI. The paperwork will be put through tomorrow.'

'Sir, what about Butler?'

The Chief Super looked confused, then

BAD TIMES

glanced over at DS Butler. 'What about her?'

'She's my, you know, my partner, and she's a DS.'

Laptew nodded, smiled. 'I see. Well, we could do with an acting DI. We'll see where we go from there? OK?'

Moone nodded, then watched on as the Chief Superintendent faced the rest of the team and gave his congratulations. After he'd gone, Butler came over, and stood, hands on hips.

'Well?' she said.

'We're going to interview Kieran Dobson one more time, acting DI Mandy Butler.'

'What? Really? What did you get?'

'DCI. Come on, let's go talk to Kieran.'

Moone led the way after they called down to have Kieran brought up from the cells. He'd almost reached the interview rooms when he saw DC Carthew coming the opposite way.

'Can I talk to you?' she asked, then looked at Butler behind him. 'In private?'

Butler huffed then walked on towards the interview room.

'Now you've pissed her off,' Moone said.

Carthew came closer to him. 'I don't care. But I do care about you. I heard what happened. That's the second time you've nearly been killed.'

'Mathieson wasn't going to kill me.'

'You didn't know that for sure.'

He shrugged, then something came to mind. 'Butler told me about the night those guys

469

were stabbed in Mutley.'

'What did she tell you?'

'What you said to her.'

Carthew laughed, shaking her head. 'I made a joke. She's too up her own arse that one.'

'I think you frightened her.'

'Then she shouldn't be a police officer. Bloody hell. Let's forget all about that. Let's have a drink later.'

'I don't think so.'

'Too busy?'

'Yes...'

'But you don't really want to anyway? You've gone off me? Fine.'

'Look, I've got to go and interview Kieran Dobson. I think he knows our killer... well, he's hiding something.'

'Fine. You go and do that. Fuck you.'

Moone began to say something, but she pushed past him and stormed down the corridor. Maybe Butler had been right about her after all, he decided and carried on to the interview rooms.

The young man who was delivered to them seemed even more tired, and a little more nervous. That's what a few hours in a cell will do, Moone thought, especially to an innocent person. Kieran looked at them, his hands tapping lightly at the desk, then scratching at his stubble and hair.

'You OK, Kieran?' Moone asked. 'Not nice in those cells, is it?'

'No, it's not,' Kieran said. 'When can I go?'

'When you've talked to us properly,' Butler said, folding her arms and leaning towards him.

Moone cleared his throat. 'Listen, Kieran, you need to talk to us, help us understand what's going on in your mind.'

'What do you mean?'

'Come on,' Moone said. 'We found the car used in the last murders in your garage. We've also examined your laptop and it seems your laptop was used to log into a certain dating site on numerous occasions. You heard of the username Roman120?'

'No!' Kieran said, his brow creasing, looking between them. 'What dating site? I don't...'

'Roman120 is the username used to send messages to some of the victims. We've got you bang to rights now.' Moone sat back, folded his arms. 'Did it start after the attack?'

Kieran looked down, breathing out. 'I didn't do anything, you're making a mistake.'

'That must've made you angry,' Butler said. 'Furious. Really messed with your head.'

Kieran looked away. 'I didn't, how could it...'

'How could it?' Moone asked. 'Because... hang on, the attack? The attack in the park, tell us about it.'

Dobson looked at Moone. 'I was attacked by

an idiot, a thug. End of story. But I didn't...'

'What did he look like this thug?' Moone asked, watching Kieran carefully.

He shrugged. 'Can't remember, it happened a long time ago.'

'Yes, it did. But you don't forget things like that. They haunt you, stay with you, they change you, usually for the worst. But the thing is, I don't think it changed you, because it never happened to you, did it, Kieran? You made the whole thing up.'

'No, I didn't,' Kieran said.

Moone leaned forward. 'You're in so much trouble, Kieran. You need to tell me the truth about the attack. Now!'

Kieran stared across at him for a moment, his hand tapping the desk. 'All right. It happened... just not to me. It was Colin that was attacked. But he said he didn't want the publicity or the uni finding out about his life. So he gave the police my name. I owed him, so I went along with it and soon it all died down and went away.'

'Colin?' Moone said, the rush of realisation tingling up his spine and spreading. 'Colin Samson? He was the one who was attacked in the park?'

Kieran nodded. 'I didn't think it would come out like this.'

'Was he who you were with the other night then?' Butler asked.

'Yeah, we went for a drink, then we ended

up at his, had a couple of drinks there. But I must've fallen asleep.'

Moone looked at Butler, and she raised her eyebrows at him. Moone stood up. 'Kieran. We'll be back in a bit…'

They got out into the corridor, then faced each other, but it was Butler who said, 'What the fuck is going on? Samson was attacked?'

Moone nodded, and ran his hands down his face, feeling the stubble covering his chin, his mind putting it together. 'Yes. Samson was the one who was attacked. Kieran stayed with him the other night. He said he fell asleep. What if he was drugged?'

'Samson drugged him? So he could slip out?'

'Nick his keys, then go to his house, use Kieran's laptop to send the message.'

'But he was in the club the night of the attack. It doesn't make sense.'

Moone tried to bring that night back into his mind, imagining the bodies lying on the ground. He stopped, remembering the dead girl's hand sticking out from under the blanket. He looked at Butler, a cold feeling crossing his back as his heart coughed into a hard and fast beat. 'Where's the crime scene photos taken from that night?'

'In the incident room. Why?'

Moone turned and rushed towards the incident room, pushed through the doors and started looking through the crime scene photos, spreading them out across the desk.

'What're you looking for?' Butler asked, standing behind him.

'Did they take any photos of Colin Samson?'

Butler got more crime scene photos and started going through them. 'They would've done. They take photos of all the witnesses, just in case. Here, here it is.'

Moone snatched the photograph of Colin Samson taken in the club as he sat in the corridor, a plastic cup of water in his hand as he was being treated by a paramedic. Moone reached for one of the photos of the victims. 'Look. Look at this victim's hand.'

'The rainbow stamp?'

'Look at Colin Samson's hands.'

Butler leaned over the desk, staring at the photographs. 'No stamp, which meant he didn't go through the front door, or they didn't stamp him.'

'Or because he climbed up the fire escape and then started attacking the people in the club. Then he changed his clothing in the club or outside and slipped back into the club in all the confusion. Either way, no stamp on his hand.'

Butler straightened up. 'That and the whole attack in the park. We need to find him. Put all this to him.'

'If it is him, then he arranged for that crossdresser to meet us in the park. He was probably watching. Why would he do that? Why introduce us to Sandra?'

'Paul...' Butler said. 'Paul Farmer. That was Sandra's real name. That's what he put when he was booked out.'

'Yes, Paul. That's what he said to me too. What if Paul's his next intended victim? What if the part of Colin that wants to stop did all that in the park, so we'd know who he intended to kill next? Have we got an address for Paul Farmer?'

'Yes, as long as he gave us a real address. I'll go check with the custody sergeant.'

Moone watched her go off, his gut churning, a cold feeling passing over him, knowing that he was right. He was certain of it.

Paul Farmer lived in Whitleigh, which Moone realised was a well-known, quite rough area. The place that Butler drove them to was an estate made up of concrete block housing, flats and more concrete all round. As the car pulled up and Butler pulled on the handbrake, Moone looked towards the row of houses in front of them, which had flats built over the top. Farmer lived there, at number thirteen.

'Come on, let's go and check on him,' Butler said and climbed out as spits of rain started to tap at the windscreen. Moone leant forward, looking at the sky beyond the concrete outline of the buildings, where the charcoal grey clouds moved in quickly, threatening to hammer everything with a sudden downpour. He watched Butler, hands in her coat, head towards the houses, trying to pick out the right one.

Moone jumped out as the rain started with force, hammering the ground. Butler had got under the cover that jutted out over the houses. She pressed the doorbell of number thirteen and put her hands back into her pockets, then looked at him. 'You know this is a wild goose chase, don't you?'

'Maybe. Part of me hopes so.'

The door opened and Paul Farmer, or Sandra as they knew him, stood looking at them, wrapped up in a white dressing gown, a long dark wig on his head, and makeup in place. Sandra stared at them through the half open door, looking them over.

'Paul?' Moone said. 'You OK?'

'Yeah, I'm fine, sweetheart,' he said, but Moone noticed he looked a bit furtive, maybe weary.

'You alone?' Moone asked, trying to look into the house.

'Yeah, all alone. Why, you come to take me up on my offer? Well, I'm a bit busy. Why don't you come back another time?'

'You're busy?' Moone nodded. 'Is there anything you want to tell me?'

'Nothing. Now why don't you two fuck off?'

Moone was about to turn and say something to Butler, but he heard her, through the noisy hammering rain. She said his name. Not Moone, but Pete. He turned slowly, catching her out of the corner of his eyes, just a blur, a dark shape through the rain. But there was another shape too.

He turned fully, focused in and saw a hooded figure, in a large dark coat, their arm round Butler, a knife at her throat. Moone looked at her, saw she had lifted her chin, and was trembling, her eyes burning out to him. Then he focused in on the man in the hood, the stubble covering his now more slender, washed out face which was covered in dark stubble. Even from that distance, Moone thought he could smell stale alcohol emanating from him. Colin Samson looked almost unrecognisable. He thought of Ted Bundy, how the evil killer could change his appearance so dramatically.

'Colin,' Moone said, feeling the rain lashing at his scalp. 'Just let her go. Let's talk.'

'You ever been a sinner?' Samson said, his voice a whisper that Moone could hardly catch. 'Course you are. Bet you've fucked another man's wife or cheated on your own. You a policeman, worshipping a false idol. You're scum, like all the rest of the filthy scum, fucking bastards.'

'Please, Colin, let her go, I'm here...'

'Yes, you are here. Where I wanted you. Like lambs to the slaughter. Paul... *do it!*'

Moone swung round in time to see a bottle being lifted and liquid sprayed towards him. Then the burn, the darkness coming in as he clenched his eyes shut. Tears streamed from his face as he collapsed to his knees, letting out a deep moan of pain. He was done, his mind roared, you're finished. You'll die. Butler will die.

Then a hand on his back, grasping his coat, pulling him along, making him fall to his hands. The blow smashed into his ribs, then another to his face, knocking him to the floor. A boot, kicking into him as he lay on his back, the rain hammering into his face. He was a dead man.

CHAPTER 35

'Get up!' the voice roared from above him, then the cold blade pressed against his neck.

'I can't fucking see!' He tried to turn over, but failed, and got a kick in the back for punishment. He tried again, found the brickwork and pulled himself up.

'Sorry, sorry,' Paul seemed to say from his right shoulder as he was helped into the warmth of the house.

The door slammed behind him.

'Pete...'

Butler's voice in front of him, a trembling in it before it was stifled. He tried to open his eyes, but they stung and everything was blurred and misty.

'Wash his eyes,' Colin said, somewhere to his right. He heard footsteps heading off somewhere, then running water, then a wet cloth on his face.

'I'm sorry, so sorry,' Paul said again, whispering. 'He said he'd kill me.'

'It's OK,' Moone whispered. 'Where is he?'

'Stop talking,' Colin said. 'Try anything and your partner, colleague, whatever you want to call her... she gets her throat cut. Or a hammer to her head.'

Moone lifted his head, turning towards the voice, opening his eyes, blinking, feeling the sting. Now he could make out Butler's familiar shape, and the hooded shape next to her. She was on her knees it looked like. He tried to get up onto his knees, blinking, feeling his tears streaming down his face, doing their job. At least he wasn't blind. He wouldn't be blind when he died.

He focused in, saw that Colin had removed the hood of his coat, that dripped rain onto the carpet. There was the knife in his right hand, poised at Butler's throat, his left hand clenched a claw hammer. Her mouth had a gag, a piece of cloth tied tightly round her face, something else stuffed in her mouth.

'You don't want to do this...' Moone said, jerking his face away from the cloth that Paul tried to wipe his eyes with.

'Don't I? What do you know about me? What do you think you know about me?'

'I think... I think you were treated badly as a child. You were treated badly for being different.'

Colin huffed out an empty pitiless laugh. 'What a piece of shit, that the best you can do?'

'This is not you, Colin. This is the other part of you, the part of you that's ashamed of what you are, that's been abused and beaten and taught to be ashamed...'

Colin showed his teeth, his eyes twisting. 'What the fuck do you think I am?'

'Gay. But I think someone made you ashamed of that when you were younger. Maybe they even beat you... and then you were attacked, in the park...'

'Fuck you!' Colin screamed, his teeth gritted, the hammer rising in his left hand. 'You fucking piece of shit! Let's talk about you! I know about you. You cheated on your wife. You committed a sin. You deserve to die!'

Moone hung his head, trying to gather any coherent thought that hadn't been poisoned by fear. 'You're right. I have sinned. Let these two go and deal with me.'

Colin laughed. 'Let them go? What, that thing next to you! That disgusting filthy thing next to you that pretends to be a woman! Jesus Christ! Look at this world. Look at what we've become, so steeped in sin, this whole planet needs to be wiped out.'

'Is that what you're planning, Colin? To wipe us all out? Person by person? It's not going to happen! You know what I've been dealing with? Child abusers... child murderers! How should they be treated, Colin?'

'They should die. Of course they should die.'

'So you decide who dies and lives? That's how it works?'

'No! God decides!'

Moone wiped his eyes, rubbed them, blinking, feeling cold and damp. 'That's who's telling you what to do? I've got news for you... it's not. It's whoever fucked with your head when you were a kid.'

'Don't talk to me like that!' Colin raised the hammer high above Butler's head, the shadow of it flickering over her, letting her know what was happening. She tilted her head back, shouting garbled words through the gag as she raised her eyes.

'You want me to crush her skull?!' he bellowed. 'I will!'

'Don't! Please!' Moone heard the pathetic pleading his own voice, but relief flooded him as the hammer was lowered without injury.

'Paul, tie him up!' Colin said.

'With what?' Paul asked, getting to his feet.

'Find something. Use the cables from the TV.'

Moone blinked, his eyes still streaming, watching Paul going behind the TV, pulling cables out the back of it. He came back carrying a few and knelt behind Moone.

'Tie him up!' Colin shouted. 'Hurry up!'

Moone's hands were gently put behind his back, and he had no choice but to let them as he saw Colin dig the knife into Butler's skin, making an angry red mark on her neck. As he felt the cables being strapped round his hands, his eyes found Butler's. She stared back at him, and he saw fear, but also determination. But what was she telling him to do? He was dead. She was dead.

The straps round his hands tightened, but not too much. He still had movement. Paul had allowed him to have movement.

'What's your plan for us?' Moone asked. 'How're we to die? I mean, you led us here, so you must have a plan.'

'I have a plan,' Colin said. 'I've been aiming too low, that was my mistake. Going out trying to right wrongs, show society the error of its ways... but I could show everyone all at the same time.'

'How're you planning to do that?'

'Where's your phone, Paul?' Colin asked.

Paul got to his feet, his hand reaching into his pocket to take out a silver smart phone.

'Paul here's going to film your executions live,' Colin said. 'Everyone will see you die.'

'They'll take it off the internet,' Moone said.

'Not before someone's downloaded it and then it'll be seen and seen and shared...'

'Proving what? Where will that get you?!'

'I don't have to answer to you! I can just cut her throat and that'll shut you up!' Colin dug the knife in, drawing a little blood.

'Stop!' Moone shouted. 'Please. Just stop.'

'Paul,' Colin said. 'Get your phone ready. Do this and you'll get to live.'

'He won't let you live,' Moone said, then spun his head towards the door when the doorbell echoed through the house. Moone couldn't quite see into the hallway.

'They'll go away,' Colin said. 'Start filming.'

But the doorbell went again, and again. A voice, a woman's friendly voice said something through the letterbox. Postcode lottery, Moone thought he heard.

'Bloody hell!' Colin growled, his eyes burning towards the door. 'Shit. Paul! Answer it! Get rid of them!'

Paul nodded, getting ready to head towards the door.

'You try anything and she dies,' Colin said.

He stared, then nodded again and carried on into the hallway, until Moone couldn't see him anymore. But he heard the door open, then the woman talking, but not loud enough to hear what she was saying.

Then there was silence. Moone leaned backwards, trying to see what was happening.

'What the fuck's going on?!' Colin snapped at Moone.

'I can't see!'

Colin let out a stream of profanities, then looked from Butler to Moone. He pulled the knife from her throat, then stormed towards Moone. He pointed the knife at him. 'You don't move!'

He stepped into the hallway, where he seemed to stand staring at whatever he'd found.

Moone shuffled backwards on his knees, so he could see what was happening.

'Fuck!' Colin shouted, the knife and hammer held tightly in his hands, shaking with anger as he stared towards an open empty doorway.

A crash of breaking glass came from behind Moone. He spun his head round, searching for where the sound was coming from. He couldn't see anything, just heard the sound of glass being smashed.

Colin heard it too. He turned round, the weapons lifting in his hands. 'Who the fuck're you?!'

Moone fell to his side and rolled over, struggling with his tied hands, feeling the cables loosening a little. He turned his head and saw with horror Faith Carthew appearing around the corner, a baton in one hand, and something in the other. She briefly looked at Moone, but only coldly, before she turned back towards Colin.

'I'd drop those weapons if I were you,' she said, sounding calm, in control.

'Fuck you,' Colin said, raising the weapons, seeming to work himself up, while watching her carefully.

Moone kept twisting his arms, fighting to get free, his heart thudding, terrified of what might happen to her. Colin was obviously mentally ill, worse than he'd imagined. The damage done to him, to his mind, was extensive. The hammer was being raised above his head.

'Faith!' Moone called out. 'Run! Just run!'

But she didn't look at him, just stood her ground, still clenching the baton, getting ready to brandish it.

Colin was making a strange noise, an animalistic growl deep in his throat as he stormed to towards her, wielding the hammer, bringing the knife up. He swung it through the air, but Carthew swerved her body, thrashing the air with the baton, and catching him on the wrist.

He let out a furious howl, but spun round, jabbing the air with the knife, getting closer to her.

She'll get stabbed, Moone thought, hardly able to look as his blood froze over, his heart pounding as he struggled to get free. He glanced over at Butler as she fell from her knees to her side, struggling with her binds, grunting against her gag.

But Faith kept moving, blocking Colin's moves with her baton, using the small space to her advantage. Moone realised she was making him back up, trapping him in the corner, making him run out of space to fight. He lurched towards her, swinging the hammer again, letting out a crazed roar as he swung. She brought the baton down hard, cracking it against his arm. The hammer dropped, thudding to the floor.

Carthew lurched, stabbed the air towards him. For a moment Moone thought she had a knife, but it wasn't that at all he realised as Colin jerked and twisted, then collapsed to the ground, letting out a howl of pain. She'd tasered him.

Faith Carthew stood over him, her chest falling and rising, staring down at him. She dropped the baton to the ground, and the taser. Slowly, she bent down, reaching for the hammer, keeping an eye on Colin.

'Faith!' Moone called, finally getting his hands almost free. 'Faith! What're you doing?! Faith!'

But she wasn't hearing him as she kicked away the knife, then sat astride Colin, knocking away his hands that reached up to struggle against her. The hammer rose in her hand, up above her head. Moone felt the cable fall from his hand, then scrambled to his feet and lunged at her, knocked her to the ground.

He grabbed her arms and pinned her to the ground, but she looked up at him with hate in her eyes, almost snarling.

'Get the fuck off me!' she screamed.

'Stop it! Stop it! Calm down!' Moone stared down at her.

She breathed hard, seeming to calm herself. He got up slowly, then looked at Colin, who was coming to.

'Got some restraints?' Moone asked and looked round to see Butler watching horrified, still on her side on the floor.

Carthew pushed Moone out of the way, then kicked Colin over, making him groan. She got his hands behind his back just as he started to struggle and clamped the restraints on his wrists.

Moone went over to Butler and started to untie her.

He removed her gag, and she sat up, letting out a long breath. Moone sat next to her, and rubbed her back as he said, 'It's OK... you're OK. We survived. Once again we survived...'

She looked at him, tears in her eyes. 'That sounds like something from a film.'

He let out a laugh. 'I think it's a Japanese film, a version of the magnificent seven. Just came to me.'

'You're a sad bastard, Moone.' Her voice trembled.

'I know.'

'You know she's a psycho, don't you? Your girlfriend, Faith, I mean. If you don't watch out she'll be boiling your bunny.'

He nodded, then looked towards the door. 'I'll help her. I'll make sure she deals with her issues. Let's keep this between us. OK?'

Butler let out a sound, a kind of huff that he decided to take as agreement. 'I'd better go make sure she's not smashed his skull in.'

'What about Paul?'

Moone shrugged. 'He was scared, we'll find him.'

Moone went out into the now darkening light, welcoming the rain falling on his face. His eyes still stung, but he was alive. He felt a kind of euphoria beating through him, an explosive feeling of a dark sort of joy that told him to go and grab life by scruff of the neck, and never be scared again.

But he knew from past experience that the feeling would pass and he'd wake up tomorrow with the same old fears and doubts.

But he was alive.

CHAPTER 36

They'd gone pretty much straight home after a short debriefing at the station. It had been a journey in silence, both of them dropped off by a police driver. Moone found himself back in his caravan, staring out at the dark sky, drinking wine in the hope it might still his beating heart and let him sleep. But it took a long time for the harrowing memories of all he'd been through to fade, for the imagined scenarios where he wasn't so lucky, to stop playing over and over.

He found himself in the morning lying on the corner sofa, cradling an empty wine bottle.

He showered and grabbed a coffee and headed into the station. He wasn't expecting what greeted him as he walked into the incident room.

He jumped a little as shouts of his name echoed in the room, and streamers were fired off. There was a big pink party banner hung over the room that said, 'Congratulations, it's a girl!'

He held up his hands, shaking his head. Butler was smiling, her face looking bruised. He hadn't even checked to see the state of his.

'Thanks everyone,' he said. 'We did well as a team! All of us!'

'Speech!' someone shouted; it sounded like Harding.

'The person who got me through all this and is probably the bravest person I've ever met is acting DI Mandy Butler.'

Applause started for Butler, but she waved it all down and pointed at Moone. 'You're aware I dislike you, aren't you?' she said, straight faced. Then broke into a smile and winked at him.

The doors of the incident room burst open. Moone turned to see Commander Richer stood there, one of her suited cohorts at her side.

'I wouldn't get too bloody excited yet,' she said, a smirk building on her face. 'Because Colin Samson will be taken into our custody to help with an ongoing enquiry.'

'What?!' Butler snapped and stormed towards her. 'That was our collar! You can't walk in...'

'Oh, yes I can.' She showed her teeth. 'He's going to prove that he was involved in a conspiracy with others. Soon we'll a have whole home-grown terrorist cell...'

'Which will eventually give the government more powers of arrest?' Moone nodded.

'You fu...' Butler started to say but Moone said, 'Don't bother. Just walk away.'

Butler stared at Richer as she looked everyone over then said, 'Enjoy your little party.'

When Richer had left, Butler stormed over to Moone. 'That's it? All that hard fucking work?'

'We got him. We made the arrest. We have stopped him killing again. I don't know about you, but that's enough for me.' He shrugged.

Butler looked at him, her face softening. 'I got this place I like to go and think, away from all the annoying twats.'

'Right...'

'Want to come?'

Moone felt the hairs stand to attention along his spine. 'Yes, OK, I'd be honoured.'

'Shut up, you wally, just grab some of the cake.'

'Not right now,' he said, sighing.

'Now what?'

'Grader. Remember? I've got his address in my pocket.'

'Where is he?'

'Some cottage in wildest Cornwall. I think I should go alone. If he sees the whole circus outside, he'll be gone.'

She stared at him. 'You're probably right.'

'I am right.'

Moone found himself driving along a steep bit of road that led towards the coast, the raging sea off in the distance where seagulls dived and glided over the cliffs. He turned into a road on his left, heading down to a country lane that had an old, battered gate cutting it off. The words 'private land' had been painted on a board a million years ago and nailed to the gate. Moone climbed out, listening to the wind through the barren trees that overshadowed the lane. The crows squawked at him, perhaps trying to tell him to turn and drive away. He undid the rusty bolt on the gate, trying to avoid a puddle of muddy water. He jumped over, nearly losing his balance, then walked further down the lane that grew wider into a kind of drive. He stopped dead as he came out of the treelined lane and faced a large farmhouse cottage. It looked pretty, homely, even on such a horrible day. Then he thought of the horrible creature secreted inside and tried to keep the taste of bile from his mouth as he headed to the house, knowing Grader would have already spotted him.

He reached the old split door and knocked on it as he felt spits of rain land on his head.

'Grader?!' he called loudly. 'It's the police. Moone. I know you're there. He gave you up before he died.'

There was only the wind for a moment and the squawking of the crows in the trees, still warning him off. But they didn't know what he knew.

'I'm alone!' Moone called out.

Then he heard something inside, like the creak of a floorboard. Then a gruff voice said, 'You aren't alone! You wouldn't come alone.'

'Scout's honour. I'm alone out here. No police cars are coming. I told them I could persuade you to come in.'

'Idiot. Liar. Liar. Your little kids' pants are on fire.'

Moone felt the sickness rise to his throat. 'I told you. I'm alone.'

There was laughter inside, then Grader said, 'You're an honourable man, Peter Moone. Swear on your little pretty kids' lives. Go on, swear on their lives that you're alone.'

'I swear... on their lives, I'm alone out here. No backup on its way.'

There was more laughter inside, then the bolt being drawn across. The door creaked open as footsteps retreated.

Moone opened the door, the hairs standing on the back of his neck, his heart beginning to beat faster as he saw the squat and wide man stood at the end of the hall, staring at him. There was a rat-like grin on his face as he shook his head and tutted.

'You're a stupid, stupid, man, DI Moone,' Grader said.

'DCI Moone, actually. Loy Grader, I'm arresting you on suspicion of murder...' Moone stopped talking when he saw Grader take a small knife from his pocket and hold it at his side.

Grader took a step towards him, still shaking his head, staring at him, the grin still burnt into his face. 'You should've brought your friends with you. I think I'll cut you up, see what your insides look like, then maybe I'll visit your family...'

Moone tightened his hands into fists. 'You do not have to say anything...'

'Yes, your cute little family. I think I'll have fun...'

Grader lurched forward, then spread his arms wide, the knife clattering onto the ground. He dropped to the ground, sprawling over it, his body jerking, deep in spasm.

Moone looked up to see DS Butler stood behind him, the taser still in her hand.

'Whatever she can do, I can do better,' Butler said.

Moone couldn't help but smile at that as she went to Grader and kicked him onto his front.

'You deserved that you sick bastard,' she said, then pulled Grader's arms behind his back and cuffed him.

'You liar!' Grader growled as he struggled, his senses coming back. 'You'll burn in hell and so will your kids!'

Moone huffed out a laugh. 'Let's get him out of here.'

As Butler pulled Grader to his feet, she said, 'That was quicker than I thought. We've got to time to pop to Asdas for a coffee.'

'Asdas?' Moone said, rubbing his face. 'You

mean Asda? The supermarket?'

'I mean Asdas.' Butler pushed Grader past Moone. 'You'll get used to it, Moone. Come on.'

Moone was a little bit chilly, sitting on the terrace of the open-air coffee house, but the view of the Hoe and the Plymouth Sound below them was pretty stunning, as Butler had promised. He looked at Butler, who was sipping from a tall glass of latte, practically lying back in her chair.

He wrapped his hands round his warm Americano and sipped it.

'Feeling chilly, Moone?' she asked, smirking.

'It's freezing here,' he said. 'By the way, what happened to "Pete"? That's what you called me back in that house...'

'That was a one off, don't get used to it. Anyway, what're you going to tell your ex-wife?'

Moone sighed, staring out to sea, and spotted a tiny silhouette of a ship on the horizon, while seagulls squawked and divebombed the water. 'I don't know, but I'm not looking forward to having that conversation.'

'Am I ever going to meet her face to face?'

'No! Definitely not. You're never going to meet her indoors. Or the ex-her indoors, I should say.'

They were quiet again, watching the winter sun glimmer on the water.

'I still can't believe we survived,' Moone said.

Butler sat up. 'Let's not talk about work. We can talk about something else…'

'The weather?'

'They say it's going to get very harsh in the new year, lots of snow.'

'Oh great, that's all I need for my first winter in Plymouth.'

'Shut up, Moone, and drink your coffee.'

GET AN EXCLUSIVE CRIME

THRILLER

I think building a relationship with the readers of my books is something very important, and makes the writing process even more fulfilling. Sign up to my mailing list and you'll recieve a FREE copy of my exclusive thriller, BITER.

Just visit markyarwood.co.uk

or you can find me here:

https://www.bookbub.com/authors/mark-yarwood

facebook.com/MarkYarwoodcrimewriter/

@MarkYarwood72

Printed in Great Britain
by Amazon

38393223R00290